D1325335

DECEPTION

Recent Titles by Claire Lorrimer from Severn House

BENEATH THE SUN
CONNIE'S DAUGHTER
THE FAITHFUL HEART
FOR ALWAYS
NEVER SAY GOODBYE
OVER MY DEAD BODY
AN OPEN DOOR
THE RECKONING
THE RELENTLESS STORM
THE REUNION
THE SEARCH FOR LOVE
SECOND CHANCE
SECRET OF QUARRY HOUSE
THE SHADOW FALLS
A VOICE IN THE DARK
THE WOVEN THREAD

DECEPTION

Claire Lorrimer

severn
House

This first world edition published in Great Britain 2003 by
SEVERN HOUSE PUBLISHERS LTD of
9–15 High Street, Sutton, Surrey SM1 1DF.
This first world edition published in the USA 2004 by
SEVERN HOUSE PUBLISHERS INC of
595 Madison Avenue, New York, N.Y. 10022.

Copyright © 2003 by Claire Lorrimer.

British Library Cataloguing in Publication Data

Lorrimer, Claire, 1921-
    Deception
    1.   England - Social life and customs - 19th century - Fiction
    2.   Love stories
    I.   Title
    823.9'14 [F]

    ISBN 0-7278-6032-1

Except where actual historical events and characters are being
described for the storyline of this novel, all situations in this
publication are fictitious and any resemblance to living persons
is purely coincidental.

Typeset by Palimpsest Book Production Ltd.,
Polmont, Stirlingshire, Scotland.
Printed and bound in Great Britain by
MPG Books Ltd., Bodmin, Cornwall.

Safe and frequented is the path of deceit
under the name of friendship;
but safe and frequented though it be, it has guilt in it.

Ovid
Ars Amatoria Book 1

Prologue

1882

T he oil lamp on the leather-topped desk had been turned down. Half a dozen sealed letters ready for posting were propped up in the letter rack. In the semi-darkness Charlotte could see the figure of her father hunched over the blotter. The silence was palpable, broken suddenly by the bracket clock on the mantelshelf striking twice. Filled with a nameless anxiety, she raised the skirt of her white ballgown and took a step forward.

'Papa! Are you asleep? Are you ill?'

Horatio Wyndham's head rose sharply as his hands shot forward to cover the object in front of him. He turned in horror to look at the unexpected figure of his seventeen-year-old daughter.

'Charlotte! What are you doing here? You should be in bed.' His voice was hoarse, barely audible.

'I have only just returned from the ball, Papa. When Thomas told me you were still up, I came to say goodnight.'

As Charlotte took another step towards him, his hands rose as if to ward her off and now she could see what they had been concealing. Her anxiety intensified as she caught sight of the small, engraved gold-plated pistol her father had bought to protect himself against thieves when he travelled.

'Papa? Has there been an intruder? You're not hurt, are you?'

She hurried across the room to his chair and her eye caught sight of the writing on the envelope propped up in front of him.

1

LAST WILL & TESTAMENT
of
HORATIO DARIUS WYNDHAM

It was a full minute before the significance of the official-looking document filled her with an icy feeling of fear. The lateness of the hour, the darkness of the room, the empty brandy decanter, the letters – and not least the pistol which he had attempted to conceal – left her in little doubt about his intentions.

'Oh, Papa, tell me you were not . . .' She broke off, unable to voice the degree of consternation that was causing her to tremble violently. She tried to disbelieve the evidence of her own eyes but was unable to do so. The father she adored, revered above all others, who was the most important person in the world to her, had been on the point of ending his life.

'No, Papa, no!' she whispered.

With a strangled cry, Horatio Wyndham turned his head and buried his face in his daughter's skirts. To her horror she felt and heard his sobs, tearing from his throat in great, painful gasps. Charlotte felt an urgent longing to question him but instinctively she knew she must let this storm of weeping pass.

Perhaps, she thought, he'd had bad news from the doctor about her mother, who had been a semi-invalid for many years now. Charlotte knew how much her father loved his wife. Were her mother to die, he would be broken-hearted. That could be the only feasible explanation for his behaviour – that his burden of grief had become too much for him and he intended to take his own life. It was the only explanation for his tears.

Her mind working furiously, Charlotte found her own explanation hard to believe. Even had her father been out of his mind with grief, surely he would not have departed this world leaving her mother and herself alone and unprotected? There were few Wyndham relatives surviving and those who did lived in remote parts of the Empire.

2

Although now and again Horatio Wyndham still choked on his tears, he began to recover himself and, pulling a handkerchief from his pocket, he dabbed furiously at his eyes and cheeks.

'Forgive me, my darling. The last thing in the world I wanted was for you . . . for you to know what kind of man I really am. One of my great joys in life has been to bask in your total belief in me as a good and honourable person . . .'

'Which indeed you are – and always will be, Papa!' Charlotte cried, close to tears herself, so shocked was she by her father's emotional outburst.

'No, my darling, I am afraid that's not so.'

The colour flared in Charlotte's cheeks. 'I shall never believe otherwise!' she declared, bending over to hug him.

The man gave a long, shuddering sigh. 'Then I am obliged to disabuse you, my darling child. I had hoped . . . Somehow I had hoped that . . . that you and your mother . . . that if I were to end my life, you and your mother would be spared the disgrace. Charlotte, dear child, even now I cannot bring myself to tell you.'

For a moment Charlotte was totally silenced by the implication of his stuttered sentence. *If I were to end my life.* Horrified by the realization that, but for her timely intervention her father had indeed intended to kill himself, she held him even more tightly in her embrace.

'You *must* tell me what is wrong, Papa. I'm not a child any longer. Whatever has happened, I will help you put it right. You have always taught me that if wrongdoing is freely admitted, then it can be rectified.'

'Oh Charlotte, my darling, I wish that were always true!' he said as he rose wearily from his chair and led her over to the leather-covered sofa by the window. He took her warm hand and held it between his own cold ones as if to draw heat from her. Exhausted as he was, he knew deep in his heart that he should not burden this young girl with his confession. Yet part of him longed to explain to one other human being why he must, for his family's sake, take his own life. He did not want people to think he died a coward. Somehow, he must

3

make Charlotte understand that for him to die was the only way left for him to protect her and her mother.

It had been close to midnight when he had realized that this was the only possible solution to the terrible mess he had made of his life. His butler, Thomas, had brought him his usual brandy nightcap and, due to his feelings of utter helplessness, he had probably overindulged. He had completely forgotten that, far from having retired for the night, his daughter was attending the last of the Season's balls with her friend, Verity, chaperoned by her mother, Madame Duprés. When writing his farewell letters to his wife, his solicitor and other associates, and when taking the pistol from the drawer of his desk, the very last person he'd thought might interrupt him at two in the morning was his beloved only daughter. Owing to his wife's invalidity, he had been both mother and father to Charlotte. He had raised her more as a son than a daughter, as a result of which she was not only gentle, sweet-natured and intelligent, but also courageous, resourceful and unusually self-sufficient. Not only did she resemble him in looks, but they were also as close as any two companions could be. He loved her very dearly and the thought of falling from the pinnacle she had put him on appalled him anew.

'Papa!' Her voice dragged him back from his thoughts. 'I will not believe we are unable to put right what is wrong unless you convince me it is hopeless.'

Again, the man drew a deep sigh. 'Then you have to believe what I tell you, Charlotte. I have stepped a long way down from that pedestal on which you chose to place me. I have committed the error – the total folly – of using the gambling tables in an attempt to regain my former income. It was not insubstantial. My father – your grandfather – had invested nearly all his capital in the railways in the thirties and forties. It kept your mother and me in a very agreeable financial position – one you yourself have enjoyed since birth.'

'Indeed, yes, Papa. I have lacked for nothing!' Charlotte murmured.

'But a year ago, almost overnight, a company I had backed

went into receivership and my shares became worthless. Your mother needed constant medical care; you and your little friend, the Duprés child, were planning your coming out the following year; I had a mountain of minor debts piling up – the new brougham as yet unpaid for, my tailor, repairs made to the roof the previous winter, new carpeting your mother wanted for the stairs . . . Endless bills, Charlotte, which I just could not pay.'

He stood up and began to pace back and forth, his words pouring from his lips as if he could no longer control them, or as if he had forgotten the listener was his young, innocent daughter.

'Sometimes – very rarely – I won at the gaming tables. That gave me hope for the next time I played. But the more I needed to win, the less I did. I became worried lest my friends began to suspect the trouble I was in. Then, three months ago, I persuaded the bank to increase my loan, although that only half solved my financial problems. For hours, days on end, I tried to think of some other way to raise funds. I knew how shocked and horrified your mother would be if she knew of my debts. Finally I decided that we must go abroad – Switzerland, perhaps, or Austria – so I could find cheap lodgings and we could avoid the social disgrace of my bankruptcy which would so distress her. I would go before your season started, arrange to sell the house to pay off as many as possible of the remaining debts, and we would move at the end of your Season.'

'Oh, Papa, surely you knew I would not have had a Season at all had I been aware of your financial troubles?'

He paused to give her a sad smile. 'I don't doubt you would have forgone it, my darling, but I wanted you to have this last chance of fun, dances and outings, for I knew your future abroad would lack all those things.'

'So did you find somewhere for us to go?' Charlotte asked, forgetting for the moment what she had seen on her father's desk.

He shook his head. 'You may recall that in March I was supposed to have gone on a business trip lasting three weeks?

5

And that I returned within one? Like every other mistake I had made, I now compounded my gambling follies. On the train travelling through France to Switzerland, I met a fellow traveller – a charming American who was seated at a table playing patience. We exchanged greetings and, to my subsequent downfall, he enquired if I played any card games – vingt-et-un, bezique – and before long we were, by agreement, playing for quite high stakes. I thought if I could only win . . . but that is the downfall of all gamblers. Before my companion and I reached the frontier, I had lost all that I had with me. I no longer had the means to pay a deposit on whatever lodgings I might have found for us in Austria.' He sat down heavily beside Charlotte and buried his head in his hands. 'You see now how weak your father is, Charlotte. I should have stopped playing, or indeed, have refused to play at all. But I convinced myself my luck would change, instead of which I lost everything. So I offered my new acquaintance a promissory note, which I had no right to do as I had no means of honouring it.'

He now looked directly at Charlotte, hollow-eyed, his face haggard as he continued his confession. 'Quite naturally, my companion asked in the politest fashion for some proof of recognition. I was, after all, a total stranger to him. In my card case I had a number of my own visiting cards and was on the point of withdrawing one when another card slipped out. It was that of a London businessman I had met on the ferry – no one I knew – but he was a genial fellow who advised me he was chairman of a shipping line, and he had given me his card. I don't know what overcame me, Charlotte, but God forgive me – I didn't even hesitate – I handed my American travelling companion this fellow's card. He never doubted it was mine and we continued playing for a further two hours. By that time I had to write him another IOU for a thousand pounds.'

'Oh, Papa!' Charlotte whispered. She was deeply shocked, as much by this confession of her father's weakness of character as by the extent of his debt and his terrible predicament. 'So you came straight home?' she whispered. Her father

6

nodded. 'I had my return ticket, which was as well since I did not even have a sovereign to pay for a meal. It was during the journey home that I realized the enormity of what I had done – I had committed fraud. That is a criminal offence, Charlotte. I could only pray that when presented with my promissory notes, the chairman would not remember to whom he had so recently given his card.'

'Could you not have gone to see him?' Charlotte asked. 'You could have paid him back the money—'

'With what?' her father broke in. 'In any event, the American had already discovered who I was. When we disembarked from the train at Geneva he had noticed the label on my valise and, although his suspicions were aroused, he said nothing to me at the time. A week or two later when the promissory notes were presented to and disclaimed by the chairman he put two and two together and at once wrote to me. A week ago, I received his second letter saying that unless I returned the full amount I owed him, he would hand the matter over to the law.'

He drew a long shuddering breath as he relived the horror of the situation. 'As you know, I could not repay what I owed. I was already hopelessly overdrawn at the bank, who were threatening to bankrupt me. It was the end of the road, Charlotte. All I wanted was for you to complete your Season, as you have done tonight. Yesterday I signed the sale documents for the furniture and furnishings. I have enough money put by for you to pay off the staff and buy passage abroad for you and your mother after I am gone. It's not much, I know, but your mother does have the few bonds her father left her, and some valuable jewellery. I . . .'

'Papa! What are you saying?' Charlotte stood up, the colour flaring in her cheeks. 'You can't really believe Mama and I would go abroad without you?' She broke off, the truth suddenly smiting her like a physical blow. It was true. Her father had been and was *still* intending to kill himself; that was why he had the pistol. But for her unexpected entry to bid him goodnight he might now be lying across his desk, beyond hope. 'I don't believe you really think this mad

7

scheme would solve all your problems, Papa,' she said, not angrily but firmly. 'Do you honestly think it would help us for you to have . . . to have taken such a way out? What would Mama have felt? What would I? The staff? Our friends?'

Once more, Horatio Wyndham drew his daughter back to the sofa and imprisoned her hands. 'You have still not understood, child. It is no longer just the disgrace of my bankruptcy. It is only a matter of time before my criminal action becomes known – if not immediately, then when I am summoned to court for my trial. I will be found guilty and I will be sent to prison. I happen to know that, although in normal circumstances ordinary debtors are not sent to prison these days, my offence is not my indebtedness but the crime of fraud. What do you think that would do to your mother, Charlotte? To you?'

'Anything would be better than you leaving us in such a manner!' Charlotte cried emphatically. 'Mama would say the same. You cannot do this, Papa. I won't allow it. Mama and I will face whatever is to come. If you have to go to prison, I will look after her. I will find work. There must be something I can do to earn money.'

Her father's face was a picture of abject misery. 'My darling, you know little of the world outside your home. You are not trained for work; nor accustomed to hardship, poverty. Don't you see, if I die by my own hand there will have to be a coroner's report, but there would be no case against me for fraud; no reportage since I am neither titled nor famous. A dead man is not answerable for the crime of fraud, and if you and your mother went away immediately after my funeral, it would be thought that you had left as a result of my sudden death.'

Charlotte stood up, her cheeks bright with angry red splotches, her eyes flashing. 'Then you should understand this, Papa. For you to shoot yourself would be the action of a coward – it would be escaping. Even were you imprisoned, don't you think Mama and I would prefer that to being in this world without you? Well, I for one would never revere you again; nor would I believe that you had any faith in me. If you

8

did, you would know that if you were imprisoned, somehow I would find a way to take care of Mama as well as myself. If you went to prison I would visit you there. As for society, if Mama and I left London I think it highly unlikely our friends would feel more than a moment or two's curiosity as to where we had gone. Perhaps the members of your club . . .'

'No, not them. I resigned my membership as soon as I realized I was virtually bankrupt.'

Charlotte nodded. 'Then that leaves only the Duprés family, who might well have searched for me but, as you know, Monsieur and Madame Duprés are leaving for Canada shortly. My dearest friend, Verity, and her fiancé, Guy Conniston, will be going there on honeymoon after their wedding. Even were you to be sent to prison for fraud, Papa, I doubt our small family is of such importance that the daily journals will give much reportage to your trial.'

She paused to place her hands on his shoulders and forced him to look at her before she continued in a low, intense tone of voice. 'Papa, you *must* listen to me. I may only be seventeen but I am in good health and do not lack for confidence or determination. You must promise me upon your solemn oath that you will not carry out such a dreadful deed, for that and that alone would have the power to ruin the rest of my life, if not Mama's, too. If you died in such a fashion, I should never recover from it; if you go to prison, then I shall know that you have not lacked for courage after all.'

Overcome with emotion, Horatio Wyndham sat motionless as he watched his young daughter walk across the room to the desk. Carefully, she picked up the pistol and put it in the empty drawer. Without turning to look at him, she locked it, opened the window and threw the small brass key out into the night where it vanished in the dark shadows of the trees.

9

One

Madame Hortense ran a perfectly manicured finger down the page of her appointments book and smiled at the young girl waiting patiently beside her. 'My next client will not be here until three o'clock, Charlotte, so if you are agreeable, my dear, we will go through to the showroom. I have a small favour to ask of you.'

'Of course, Madame! I am in no hurry!'

Nevertheless, as Charlotte followed her employer from the workshop to the elegant salon that fronted Madame Hortense's exclusive dressmaking premises in Hill Street, Mayfair, she hoped the favour would indeed be a small one and not take up too much of her precious time. At home there was a large pile of sewing that must be completed before the weekend, quite apart from the three gowns she now carried which Madame Hortense wanted within one week 'at the very latest'. One beautiful satin ballgown needed only a hem of pleated flounces lifted, but the circumference of the garment was twelve yards and the material slippery to handle, thus requiring more time than might at first seem necessary.

Not that Charlotte was complaining. She needed the work and considered she had been extremely fortunate to be given regular employment by the woman who had once made gowns for her late mother and for Charlotte herself. When financial misfortune had overtaken her family five years previously, Charlotte had no single qualification which would enable a seventeen-year-old girl of her upbringing to earn a living. Even had she been considered old enough to be a governess she could not have left her mother, who had

10

been a semi-invalid and unable to leave their spartan lodgings. Fortunately for Charlotte, her childhood French governess had taught her to emulate her own talent for exquisite needlework, if little else in the academic line, and now Charlotte was continuing to survive albeit in impecunious circumstances.

For the first two years of her father's imprisonment for fraud, she and her mother had just about managed to exist on her mother's meagre inheritance. The increasing medical bills as her mother's health deteriorated had been met by the sale of her jewellery. Her own limited earnings from taking in sewing paid for little but her cab visits to Pentonville prison to visit her father, and for the gifts of food and tobacco she had determined to take him. Ill though she could afford such tiny luxuries, and limited as they were, she knew it gave him the comforting illusion that his wife and daughter were not entirely penniless.

When he was released and discovered the true extent of their poverty, he tried without success to find work. His wife's health finally failed and when she died, he, too, lost the will to live and succumbed to the influenza epidemic the following winter.

Now alone in the world and without even her mother's legacy, which had ceased on her death, Charlotte moved to even cheaper lodgings in Clerkenwell and managed to obtain more regular work by taking in sewing from the couturier in Hill Street known as the Maison Hortense. It was to this establishment she had just returned with finished garments and to collect some of the work which always awaited her.

As she and Madame Hortense entered the salon, Charlotte's eyes were drawn to a beautiful bronze velvet and silk evening gown spread out over the chaise longue.

'What a lovely dress!' she cried out involuntarily, unable to hide the wistful note of longing in her voice. It was not so very many years since she might have had such a dress made for herself and she knew it would become her wonderfully well with her russet-coloured hair and hazel brown eyes.

Madame Hortense looked pleased by her praise. 'I thought

11

you would like it, my dear!' she said. 'Which brings me to that little favour I asked you to grant me. Would you consider wearing that dress for a short while? That is to say, when my client arrives? I am well aware that it would not normally be your wish to model a gown for . . . well, for a young lady such as you once were, if you understand my meaning. But as it happens, I made this dress for Lady Hermitage using the very best silk velvet, and to this somewhat unusual design that her ladyship professed she wanted. Yesterday she came for a final fitting and, to my dismay, decided that it was a great mistake; that the colour did not suit her and – to put it in a nutshell – she no longer wanted it.' She sniffed disapprovingly.

Charlotte's smooth forehead creased into a frown. 'But that is unethical, surely, Madame? Did she not offer to recompense you, at least for the material?'

The dressmaker drew a deep sigh, her ample bosom lifting and falling beneath her black bombazine dress. 'I regret to say I have had to learn in the course of my life not to take ethical behaviour by aristocrats as a matter of course, my dear. I sometimes wonder if it ever enters the heads of such wealthy people that there are others to whom a few guineas are the difference between survival and penury! No doubt you, poor child, understand only too well what I am talking about. However, let us not dwell on the vagaries of the rich. What I am hoping is that my next client will be persuaded to buy the gown even though it was not designed for her. I think it will suit you to perfection, and seen with life and movement the colour and material will be much enhanced. Would you do this for me, my dear?'

Charlotte let out the breath that she had only just realized she had been holding. To act as a model did not seem too difficult a task, and as for the social implications, she had long since given up any pretence to being a young lady of 'good' family. She was now nothing more than a working girl, no different from any of the other seamstresses Madame Hortense employed.

The last five years had taught her many things, not least that she could no longer hope to have a husband and children

12

and the security of a suitable marriage. No man of good family would consider marrying her, even were she to meet such a person in her present surroundings. The most she could aspire to in the future, she had realized, was to save enough money to open her own dressmaking establishment. To this end she sometimes managed to save a shilling or even two in a week. Madame Hortense was a not ungenerous employer and she, Charlotte, was pleased to have an opportunity to do her this favour costing no more than a few minutes of her time.

Madame was delighted to hear it and beamed at Charlotte as, behind the Chinese screen she helped her to remove her plain grey wool dress and ease the soft bronze velvet gown over her head.

'I have here some amber beads for you to wear,' the dressmaker told Charlotte. 'How well the dress fits you, my dear! You look quite lovely in it!'

For a moment, the older woman felt choked by a variety of unexpected emotions. Born plain Doris Briggs and raised in the east end of London, she had dragged herself out of the slums and, over three decades, had transformed the Cockney girl she had been into a 'French' couturier patronized by the rich and titled. Years ago, Charlotte's mother had ordered clothes from her and had sometimes brought her pretty little dark-haired daughter along to the fittings. These last few years, seeing Charlotte in her drab, patched garments, her fingers pricked by needles and her face thin, white and drawn with fatigue, Doris had more or less forgotten Charlotte's upper class orgins and treated her as the working girl she had perforce become. Now, seeing Charlotte standing there, cool, poised, elegant in the bronze gown, Doris Briggs was filled both with admiration and pity, for was this young woman not the very opposite of herself?

'Stand just there so that the back of the gown can be seen as well as the front,' she said, rearranging the shining pleated chignon and black bow holding back Charlotte's hair. 'It is a pity you are so pale, but never mind! The overall effect is enchanting. There is no need for you to talk, my dear. I will handle the client myself. You can give a half smile, perhaps,

13

as if to indicate that you are happy with the way the dress becomes you!'

'Indeed, I am quite overcome, Madame!' Charlotte said, smiling. 'I have not worn anything so beautiful in a long while. I am sure you—'

She broke off as the jangle of the doorbell interrupted her. A moment later, Madame's maid opened the door of the salon. 'Mrs Conniston, Madame,' she announced, 'for her three o'clock appointment.'

Madame Hortense swept forward, her bulk hiding the new arrival from Charlotte's gaze. 'Dear Mrs Conniston!' she said in her best French accent. '*Enchantée de vous voir.*' She dismissed the maid and took the client's fur-trimmed dolman, hat and gloves. As she put them on the gilt chair beside the door, Charlotte and the newcomer were suddenly brought face to face.

'Charlotte! Can it really be you? Oh, my dearest, *dearest* friend. What a wonderful surprise!'

Wordless, Charlotte stared at the young woman in front of her. Her first thought was that Verity Duprés had hardly changed at all from the golden-haired, violet-eyed, sweet-natured friend of her teenage years. She was exquisitely dressed in a gown of pale blue silk. It had an elaborately pleated and frilled overskirt in a deeper shade of blue. As well as the diamond rings on her fingers, there was a silver filigree locket round her neck. Her hair was dressed fashionably high in a looped pleat.

Impulsively, Verity Conniston stepped forward and flung her arms around Charlotte's waist. 'I'm so very happy to have found you, dearest, after all this time!' she cried, planting moist kisses on Charlotte's cheeks. 'Wherever did you disappear to just before my wedding? Do you realize that was about five years ago? Did you go abroad? My parents went back to Canada – to Quebec – where Guy and I honeymooned. I wrote to you a dozen times when we came back to England, and called at your house but was told it had been sold and the new owners had no idea where you had gone. In fact, none of our mutual friends could give me

14

a forwarding address, and I could do nothing but pray you would write to me. I—'

A discreet cough from Madame Hortense brought her monologue to a halt. She turned to face the dressmaker. 'Madame, I do apologize! You must understand Miss Wyndham is a very dear friend of mine and we haven't seen each other since our last coming out party. Charlotte, we have so much to talk about. As soon as we have finished our fittings, you must come back to tea with me. I'm staying with my godmother . . .' She turned to Madame Hortense. 'You remember Lady Hardcastle, do you not, Madame? You made that lovely figured silk gown for her last autumn. She presented Miss Wyndham and me when we were debutantes. Are you going to buy that dress, Charlotte? It looks quite lovely on you.'

She paused long enough for Charlotte to find her voice. 'No, I shall not be buying it, Verity. I don't think the colour becomes me. But it would look just right on you, don't you agree, Madame Hortense?'

Laughing excitedly, Verity agreed to try on the dress. It did indeed suit her almost as well as it had Charlotte.

'If you are quite certain you don't want it, Charlotte dearest, then I will certainly take it, Madame Hortense!' she said. 'If you will wrap it for me, perhaps your maid would give it to my coachman. Do you have your coach here, Charlotte? You must send your driver home as I am determined not to let you out of my sight.'

Not without curiosity, Madame turned to look at her outworker who had now changed back into her plain, dark grey day dress, brightened only by a stiff white lace collar and cuffs. She looked more like young Mrs Conniston's maid than her friend. Mrs Conniston, however, seemed oblivious to Charlotte's appearance. She radiated excited happiness as, with Madame's assistance, she struggled out of the velvet dress.

'I shall postpone the fitting for my tea gown until tomorrow,' she said. 'Now I cannot wait to have you to myself, Charlotte. We have so much to tell each other.'

And just how much *would* Charlotte tell her old friend? Madame Hortense asked herself as she took the bronze dress out to the workroom to be folded in tissue paper for its new owner. There had been no mention of the cost of the gown, so in the circumstances she might well add a few guineas to the price she had hoped to get from the errant customer who had rejected it. She could thank Charlotte for the happy outcome. Charlotte was a good girl and she, Doris Briggs, would not be the one to give away her secrets.

'I will have these dresses delivered this evening, Miss Wyndham,' she said to Charlotte with a knowing smile. 'You will not want to be bothered with them if you are going to take tea with Mrs Conniston.'

Now wearing her mantle, Verity slipped her arm through Charlotte's. 'I see you've been indulging yourself, too, dearest!' she said, eyeing the bundle of dresses Madame was carrying over her arm. 'My husband is always telling me I spend far too much money on my clothes, but I tell him it is he who is at fault because he demands to see me in pretty dresses! Come along, Charlotte. Why, you look as if I were about to take you to prison. You're coming to tea with me, remember?' Laughing happily, she did not see the quick rush of colour staining Charlotte's cheeks as they walked, still chattering, towards the door. 'Ah, there is Andrews with the coach. Get in, dearest. Goodbye, Madame Hortense! The rust-coloured dress is quite beautiful, and I shall come in again tomorrow for my fitting. Off you go, Andrews, as quick as you can. First stop, Eaton Square!'

Fortunately, Charlotte told herself, Verity never stopped chattering all the way along Park Lane and round Hyde Park Corner. She was miserably conscious that, sooner or later, Verity must notice the darns in her gloves; the rubbed elbows and cuffs of her jacket; the quite unladylike pincushions that were her fingers; the cracks in her patent leather boots. How could she maintain the illusion – even for a few hours – that she was living happily with her family somewhere in the country, or in London, as they had in the days when she and Verity had been such friends? Verity would be bound to

16

ask where she lived now; why she wasn't married; to what address she might write; what had become of their mutual friends.

Whatever she told Verity, it could not be the truth, Charlotte realized. This last hour had reminded her all too clearly how immensely affectionate, generous and outgoing this friend had always been, and clearly still was. Were Verity to know the truth, she would immediately be filled with pity for the misfortunes that had befallen her friend, and insist upon taking her under her wing, regardless of whether her husband and family approved or not. And how could they approve if ever they learned that her father had been sent to prison for fraud? Somehow, she must now devise a story Verity would believe.

'We sail for India tomorrow, so you see why I can't give you even a poste restante address!' she said a short while later as Verity poured the tea in Lady Hardcastle's elegant drawing room. Mercifully, the good lady herself had gone out to tea. Avoiding Verity's anxious gaze, Charlotte continued to lie. 'But I will have an address to give you as soon as Papa has decided where we shall reside.'

'Then you must write to me without fail just as soon as you know where you will be living,' Verity said. 'Promise me, Charlotte. I can't bear to lose you again now I have finally found you. Do you know, I wrote to all my friends after I had returned from my honeymoon and not one single person knew what had become of you. It was as if the man in the moon had come down and scooped you and your parents off the face of the earth! I was quite devastated, most especially after the birth of my little daughter, Kate. I had so wanted you to be her godmother.'

Handing Charlotte another cup of tea, she gave her a loving smile. 'But never mind. You shall be godmother to the new baby.' She dropped her voice and said confidentially: 'I have not told anyone else yet, dearest – not even my darling Guy – but I am almost certainly two months with child. I am so very happy. You see, the doctor had told Guy I might not be able to have any more children after I had two miscarriages following the birth of my second daughter, Lottie. It was

17

so sad, losing those two babies, although I had not carried them long enough for them to seem very real. But this time I intend to take the greatest care of myself – no long walks, no hunting, lots of early nights and afternoon rests. That's why I am in London now – to indulge myself for these few weeks before I begin to lose my figure. My darling Guy thinks I need cheering up after the last miscarriage, so he has told me to buy whatever takes my fancy! He's such a wonderful husband, Charlotte. I'm so happily married. I would think myself the most fortunate woman in the whole world if only I could give Guy the son he wants so badly.'

Relieved to have the conversation centred on Verity's life rather than her own, Charlotte gave her friend's hand a quick squeeze. 'I'm sure that will happen soon!' she said reassuringly. 'I have heard many women have miscarriages yet still have healthy babies afterwards.'

Verity was smiling again. 'I have heard that, too, and I have a premonition that this child I am carrying will be a boy. With my last pregnancies, I felt so nauseous right from the first few weeks, but this time I have no such feelings. In fact, I have never felt so well. Which brings me to your life, Charlotte. Did you really mean what you said about having no wish to be married? That you are more than happy living with your parents? I always thought that, like me, you longed to fall in love. It all sounds so very unlike the Charlotte I used to know. Remember how we shared our dreams about the kind of men we would like to marry and how many children we would have and even what we would call them? Yet now you say you want none of that and prefer to be a companion to your parents. Much as I love Mama and Papa, I simply can't imagine preferring to be always in their company rather than with my darling Guy! We are so happy with one another – so perfectly suited, despite my father-in-law's predictions that Guy will rue the day we were wed.'

'That I find impossible to believe!' Charlotte cried. 'You were the most eligible debutante of us all, as well as being the most beautiful. How could your father-in-law be so . . . so unpardonably rude?'

Verity gave a deep sigh. 'I don't think Guy's father would agree that I was a good choice of wife for his eldest son. You may not have known this, dearest, but he is an immensely rich man who made his fortune out of railway investments. So, although Papa could afford a very generous dowry, the Connistons had no need of it. I is not, therefore, eligible in that respect. As to beauty, my father-in-law is not concerned with looks, only with breeding!'

Charlotte gasped. 'But Verity – you of all people to say such a thing! Why, your father is one of France's premier aristocrats.'

Verity nodded. She was no longer smiling. 'But Guy's father considers that very point to be a disadvantage. Although he has aspired to be – and indeed has become – one of the gentry, he told me after my first miscarriage that he was not surprised since the aristocracy were all inbred and physical weaklings.'

She looked momentarily saddened by the memory. Then she gave a rueful smile. 'I suppose I should not blame him too severely for his rudeness. You see, he had set his heart on Guy marrying the eldest daughter of one of his neighbours. To quote him: "a big, wide-hipped, healthy girl who would make an excellent brood mare"! He can be very coarse at times. It upsets Guy who, according to his father, takes after his aristocratic mother who died at his birth. His father, Sir Bertram, never forgave her for that. I don't think he really likes Guy very much. He gets on better with Matthew, the elder of Guy's two half-brothers. But I'm sure I am boring you with these family portraits. Let's talk about you, Charlotte. I seem to be monopolizing the conversation. You said you were leaving for India tomorrow. Is your mama well enough for such an undertaking? She was never very strong in health, was she? I have heard the climate there is not kind to Europeans.'

Charlotte put down her teacup, afraid lest the trembling of her hands should cause it to rattle in its saucer. Lying – for whatever reason – was totally foreign to her and she could not bear to continue telling such falsehoods to her innocent, trusting friend. She looked down at her pocket, pretending to

19

search for a handkerchief. 'Verity, there is nothing I would like better than to stay here and talk but I really cannot do so. My parents will be wondering where I have got to and we have so much to do since we leave at dawn tomorrow. I'm sure you will understand.'

'But of course I do, dearest!' Verity declared, rising to her feet. 'How selfish of me to monopolize your time when you have so little to spare. I shall come tomorrow to see you off! Do you sail from Tilbury?'

'No, from Southampton,' Charlotte said quickly. 'That is why we leave London tonight. We shall spend the night in Southampton; so, lovely as it would have been to have you there, you cannot see us off.'

Seeing the look of disappointment on Verity's face, Charlotte felt close to tears herself. This meeting with her erstwhile friend was bittersweet, reviving so many happy memories and highlighting how simple and easy and luxurious her life could have been were it not for . . . She pulled herself up sharply. Somehow she must persuade Verity that she would prefer to take a hansom cab home rather than ride in Lady Hardcastle's coach. Even if she were to pretend a prestigious address, rather than the dingy street where she really lived, the elderly coachman might all too easily wait for the non-existent butler to open the door for her. A hansom cab would cost her far more than she could afford but there was no alternative. Maybe Madame Hortense would allow her a little extra for modelling the bronze gown. If not, she would just have to go to bed hungrier than usual.

Despite Charlotte's efforts to conceal them, Verity quickly noticed the tears glistening on her lower eyelids. 'Dearest, please don't look so unhappy or you'll have me weeping too!' she murmured, folding Charlotte in a fond embrace. 'We shall not lose each other again, I promise. Just as soon as you send me your address from India I shall write to you. We were like sisters once and I've never had a friend so dear to me since we parted. Your papa's posting to India cannot be for too long, and once you are back in England, we shall visit each other. I long for you to meet my darling Guy, and

20

my two little daughters, and who knows, by then I may have a baby son to tempt you back to the idea of marriage and family life. You are far too pretty to remain a spinster. Doubtless you will find a husband in India before we meet again.'

Hurriedly, Charlotte wiped her eyes. Ignoring the expression on the maid's face as she helped her into her shabby coat, she put on her hat and gloves and kissed Verity goodbye.

'I'm comforted by the thought that it's only goodbye for a little while,' Verity said, smiling as she helped Charlotte into the hansom cab now waiting at the front door. 'Bon voyage, dearest!'

'Where to, Miss?' asked the cab driver as he took up the reins.

'Rutland Gate!' Charlotte said, hoping that this would be the last lie she need ever tell. As the tears flowed silently down her cheeks, she reflected sadly that there was no comfortable London home awaiting her, only her cold, cheap, threadbare lodgings; no smiling parents excitedly preparing for a new life in India; no beautiful clothes being packed for her in a cabin trunk.

The thought of clothes brought Madame Hortense to mind and, since they were now out of sight of the house in Eaton Square, Charlotte lent forward and called out to the cab driver that she had changed her mind and now wished to be taken to the couturier. For one thing, the ride would be shorter and therefore not so costly; for another, she could count on young Alf to be somewhere nearby waiting for the chance to earn a few pence. The ten-year-old urchin with the cheerful grin was only too happy to escort Charlotte back through the far from savoury streets to the comparative safety of her lodgings. A young woman walking on her own with a parcel under her arm was fair game for thieves and pickpockets. Madame Hortense's luxurious gowns – albeit only half completed – would fetch a good price as Charlotte had learned to her cost when she had first begun working for Madame Hortense. Young though Alf might be, his presence was enough to keep his like at bay, for there was a certain honour among thieves. Charlotte's pennies paid for Alf to escort her and were often the only earnings that kept him from the ever present threat of starvation.

The thought of food reminded Charlotte of her own aching hunger. There had been a mouth-watering array of iced cakes and egg and cress sandwiches served up by Lady Hardcastle's parlourmaid but Charlotte had not dared take any for herself. It was so long since she had eaten such delicacies and she was so hungry that she had not trusted herself to take dainty, ladylike bites, fearing she would cram them one after another into her mouth.

Quickly Charlotte wiped the tears from her cheeks. This mood of self-pity was one which she always tried to combat. It was best not to think of the cold, of her hunger, of the rats that sometimes emerged from the rotten skirting boards of her dismal, shabby room; of the unpleasant smells that emanated from the other lodgers' rooms. To be with Verity as she was this afternoon had revived a hopeless longing to turn the clock back to the years before her poor father had amassed those terrible debts. Now that he was in another world she could remember him with pity and less bitterness; remember how as a small girl she had adored him and thought him godlike in his looks and character. When events had revealed his innate weaknesses, her disillusionment had made the change in her circumstances even harder to bear. Visiting her father in Pentonville, realizing how hard he strove to pretend he was well treated and content, she had felt both pity and admiration for his courage. She had done what she could to cheer him up, pretending that she and her mother were managing quite happily.

Now it was she, Charlotte, who needed cheering up, she told herself with a rueful smile. The totally unexpected meeting with Verity had proved more than a little unsettling. It had forced her to face the bleak emptiness of the life she now led; to become aware once more of the poverty and squalor that she had begun to take for granted.

She must try to forget Verity, forget those memories she had revived of carefree days gone by, and continue with the colourless routine that, if nothing else, kept her from starvation and allowed her to keep her pride. Verity would never know the truth. There was much to thank her employer for, Charlotte told herself. Not only did Madame Hortense provide Charlotte with desperately needed work, but she had always treated her fairly when she might so easily have exploited her situation. Now Charlotte had further reason to thank her for her tactful handling of the meeting with Verity this afternoon.

But try as she might, Charlotte could not so easily forget her friend's loving companionship and the carefree way of life they had once shared.

Two

April 1887

'**P**lease, I beg you my darling, don't go on crying like this!' Guy Conniston's voice reflected his very real concern over his wife's distress. This depression was so totally foreign to her usual behaviour. One of the reasons he had fallen in love with her had been the constancy of her happy nature. Her violet-blue eyes were almost always bright with laughter and she seemed to have an extraordinary ability to see the sunny side of life as well as the best in others. As a consequence, people were instantly attracted to her, as indeed he had been.

Ignoring the presence of the attendant nurse, Guy lent over the bedside and put his arms round his wife's shoulders. He could feel her subdued sobbing through the soft lawn of her nightgown. 'There will be other babies, Verity,' he murmured. 'Dr Freeman did not *entirely* rule out the possibility!'

Verity made a further effort to stem the tears that had been flowing continuously down her cheeks since she had regained full consciousness from the comforting whiff of chloroform only to be told that she had suffered yet another miscarriage. To make matters worse, this baby had been the boy she had so much wanted for Guy; and to provide the *coup de grâce*, Dr Freeman had told her it was unlikely she would carry another child full term. The fact that she had produced two healthy little girls soon after her marriage was of no relevance. In his opinion, her womb was no longer strong enough for child bearing.

'I will try to believe there is still some hope,' she murmured through her tears. 'I'm so sorry, Guy. I had so

much hoped . . . And Nurse said it was a boy, and . . .'
She was once more overcome by weeping and the nurse
stepped forward to indicate to Guy that it would be best
if he left. With a deep sigh he kissed his wife's forehead
and went out on to the landing. He could do with a drink,
he thought. His wife's unhappy frame of mind was to some
extent a reflection of his own. For Verity's sake he had
made light of Freeman's warning that there might be no
more children. It was not simply that, like any normal
man, he would have liked at least one son. That was only
a part of his discomfort, for very soon he would have to
face his father who would unquestionably be awaiting his
presence in the library. Equally without question, Dr Freeman
would have been thoroughly interrogated by the old man as
to Verity's condition, and his father would know that the
future held little hope of the grandson Guy was supposed to
provide.

Had Guy been a less conventional man, he would have
admitted that he actively disliked his father, Sir Bertram
Conniston. Although he himself had been born and reared
a gentleman, his father was a self-made man who had
more or less bought his knighthood in his early fifties
by way of very generous donations to the Liberal party
funds. His title had done little to curb his domineering
manner; his quick temper and his refusal to ever listen to
anyone's view but his own. That ruthlessness had been the
cornerstone in his father's business success, Guy had long
since realized. Single-mindedly, Bertram Conniston, son of
an affluent builder, had set out to raise his position in society,
first with money and then, once his fortune had been made, by
an extremely advantageous marriage to an aristocratic young
woman through whom he had hoped he would have entrée to
the very best circles.

Part of the marriage settlement had been regarding her
ownership of Kneepwood Court, the beautiful Georgian
manor house left to her by her grandparents. Immediately
following their marriage, his father had moved from a
comparatively small, ugly stone villa near one of his factories

in the Midlands into the luxurious home that he intended to make the foundation of the Conniston line.

Unfortunately this part of his plan would never come to fruition. His wife had died shortly after giving birth to Guy – her untimely death being something he never forgave her. As a consequence, he took little interest in the boy, responsibility for whom he had handed over to his then housekeeper, Enid McLeash, a not uncomely Irish woman in her early thirties. Denied the pleasures of his late wife's body, first by her pregnancy and then by her death, Sir Bertram was still virile enough to notice the buxom attractions of his housekeeper.

With her own plans for betterment, Enid McLeash quickly became pregnant and suggested to her employer that marriage, whilst offering him no social advantage, would provide him with permanent access to her bed, as well as a capable and reliable stepmother for his child. Sir Bertram was soon persuaded to this easy solution and his subsequent title had taken care of his social acceptance by the neighbouring gentry. No matter what opinion they had of Enid, she was astute enough not to be an obvious embarrassment to him.

Six months later their child was born and christened Matthew. Unlike Guy, Sir Bertram's quiet, somewhat delicate first-born, Matthew was a thickset, healthy boy who quickly become the apple of his father's eye. Spoilt by both parents, the boisterous, egotistical child grew into a shrewd, domineering man. Resembling his father in more than mere physique, Matthew was as ambitious as he was acquisitive. More than anything in the world he wanted Kneepwood Court and its four thousand-acre estate. His father was now an elderly man and, when he died, the magnificent Georgian house and its surrounding parkland and farms were destined to go to his elder brother, Guy, whose mother had owned it. Matthew was determined that since Kneepwood Court was not an entailed property, the house and estate should be left to him instead of his half-brother.

Unfortunately for Matthew, the sickly child had grown into a tall, handsome man and Sir Bertram had perforce come to respect his first-born who now managed the estate efficiently and profitably. He knew Guy to be passionately devoted to his home and it did not occur to him to think of changing his will in Matthew's favour, until he had his first major disagreement with his eldest son. Bertram had for some time been secretly planning for Guy to marry Eleanor Sinclair, daughter of a neighbouring gentleman farmer. The girl was what he coarsely termed 'a brood mare' – 'a wide-hipped sturdy wench' who would be sure to provide Guy with a healthy family, thus ensuring the continuation of the Conniston line.

When Guy first announced that he had fallen in love with the pretty little Mademoiselle Verity Duprés and was about to propose to her, his father had been apoplectic. The girl was too young, too delicate, too aristocratic and, moreover, a foreigner. He forbade such a marriage, but Guy refused to listen. There was an urgency to his proposal, since Verity's parents lived in Canada and were staying in England only until the completion of their daughter's debutante year. Within months the Duprés family would be returning to Canada where their ancestors had emigrated after the Revolution.

Bertram Conniston had counted on the fact that Comte Duprés would never allow his seventeen-year-old only daughter to marry in such indecent haste without even a period of betrothal. He didn't allow for the girl's influence upon her father, who could deny her nothing. They were married a week before the Duprés' return to Canada.

As Guy paused outside the library door, his mind was filled with memories of those days shortly before his wedding, when his father had shouted and threatened to disinherit him. Privately Guy had been appalled at the thought of losing his beloved home and the estate that constituted his life's work, but he did not believe his father would carry out his threats. For one thing, Comte Duprés was a man of singular influence in society, and had even been a guest of the Prince of Wales during his year's sojourn in England.

No, Guy had not been disinherited on his marriage, and his relationship with his father had become one of mutual tolerance until after the birth of Guy's two daughters and Verity's subsequent series of miscarriages. Then the old abuses had begun once more, with frequent references to the fact that Guy should have followed his father's advice and married Miss Eleanor Sinclair.

With a conscious squaring of his shoulders, Guy opened the door and stood facing his ageing parent. Sir Bertram was sitting in his customary wing chair, a decanter of whisky on the table beside him and his leg propped up on a footstool to ease his gout. His heavily jowled face was a mottled red and what wisps of hair he had left barely covered the freckled skin of his bald head. Both beard and moustache were white, tinged with brown from the constant smoke from his cigars. His beady black eyes narrowed as he surveyed his son.

'Took your time coming to see me. Mooning over that useless French wife of yours, I suppose. And don't try to defend her. I'll say what I damn well please in me own home. You'd have done a great deal better to have listened to me. Knew what I was talking about when I told you not to marry into the upper classes. Did it myself and what happened? Your mother turned her toes up giving birth to you! Too inbred, the lot of them. "Delicate", Freeman called that wife of yours and that's about the truth – not fit for child bearing. Well, I'm telling you this, Guy, she'd better pull herself together and produce a grandson for me, or I'll do what I said I'd do and hand everything over to Matthew.'

Guy's jaw tightened. 'Dr Freeman has not said it is impossible for Verity to have another child, Father. Naturally she is terribly upset, as indeed am I, and I understand that you want to see another generation before too long. I do appreciate your impatience but these things can't be hurried. Dr Freeman suggested we wait at least a year before trying again. As to your handing the management of the estate over to Matthew, I cannot believe you would really do such a thing. You know Matthew has no love for the land – he's only interested in his horses and stables. Why, I doubt if he knows the name of even one of our farmers. I doubt, too, if his financial management would be remotely reliable.'

28

'And what gives you the right to criticize your brother, eh?' the old man thundered. He was all the more angry because he knew there was a great deal of truth in what Guy was saying. Matthew was not entirely trustworthy where money was concerned. He'd borrow if he was short of funds but not always remember to pay it back. Less serious and far less conscientious than Guy, the son Enid had borne him was a strong, sturdy fellow – traits he shared with his equally good-looking younger brother, Ket. But where Ket was a happy-go-lucky adventurer asking no more than to enjoy life with his friends, Matthew was keenly avaricious. He wanted money and the power that came with it. Living in what had been built as a dower house – a present to him on his marriage to his wife, Monica – he had taken over the Kneepwood stables and slowly built them into a stud. Racing had become his life and he was determined to breed a Derby winner. He insisted that all he needed to improve his stock was more money, but it was his brother, Guy, who managed the purse strings and Guy refused to give him funds that were needed for the estate.

There was a great deal he could tell their father about his half-brother's feckless nature, Guy thought, but he'd never do so unless he were forced to it. Even as children, when Matthew had thrown Ket's puppy in the lake and nearly drowned it, or locked his younger brother in the coal cellar overnight, Guy had not betrayed him to their father. As for his stepmother, she so doted on her eldest son she would not have believed anything to his discredit. She and Sir Bertram had become equally besotted with their grandson, Bertie. Sometimes Guy wondered if Matthew's naming of his first-born after their father had been to gain extra favour with the old man. Sir Bertram certainly doted on the six-year-old boy, who had been carefully coached by his parents to always be polite and affectionate to his grandfather and to declare a fondness for him which he certainly didn't have.

Guy turned his attention back to the immediate problem of placating his father. 'Since you handed over control of Kneepwood farms and land to me, you have never had cause

29

to complain, Father,' he said forcefully. 'On the contrary, they have thrived, as you well know. The apple and cherry orchards are really healthy and, if we don't have a late frost, should crop well. The hop fields, too, have survived the winter and there are numerous shoots of young growth already.'

His father grunted in grudging approval and Guy continued: 'I know you want to see another generation growing up to succeed me, Father, but as far as Kneepwood is concerned, there really is no hurry. I'm sure Verity will produce a boy for us in due course. In the meanwhile if I had no heir, I suppose there is always Matthew's boy, young Bertram.'

His father caught the faintly derogatory tone of Guy's voice and he banged his fist on the arm of his chair as his temper rose. 'You're just jealous because Matt has managed to choose a better breeder than you did – just as I predicted. Five brats in six years – and if I'm not mistaken, there's another bun in the oven. And don't you turn your face away just because I call a spade a spade. Your mother used to do just that, God help her. Thought she'd married beneath her and I suppose she did – wouldn't have done if her father hadn't wanted my money. Well, for all your fine looks and manners, Guy, you obviously haven't got it in you to sire a healthy boy. Better pull your socks up, my lad, or . . .' he gave a coarse chuckle '. . . better pull your trousers down and get that hoity-toity wife of yours in the family way again. I meant what I said – I'll will everything I've got to Matthew and that boy of his. Now be off, I'm tired of talking to you.'

Sickened by the tone of the conversation, although he'd expected little different, Guy went out through the garden door on to the York stone terrace. As he had known it would be, the view across the gardens to the fields and woods beyond was a balm to his spirit. No matter the time of year, he loved this Kentish countryside and appreciated the perspicacity of the architect who had chosen this position for building Kneepwood Court. Now, in April, the lime green of the new-leaved chestnut trees on either side of the drive

30

up to the house was the perfect complement for the sea of wild yellow daffodils swaying beneath the lower branches. Beyond lay the rich brown earth touched with leaf green where shoots of the winter wheat were showing through. Blackbirds, thrushes, sparrows and robins were busy in the dark green hedgerows which would soon be covered in palest yellow and white honeysuckle. In the beech woods down by Eighty Acre farm, the first of a carpet of violet bluebells would be thrusting up through the whitewood anemones.

Everywhere nature was busy renewing itself, Guy thought with a trace of bitterness as he recalled the unhappy state of his young wife. In the meadows lambs frisked about in play, cows were calling to their calves and down in Matthew's stables there were two new colts. Only this morning at breakfast his six-year-old daughter, Kate, had regaled him excitedly with news of the farm cat who had six new kittens and the trip Nanny had promised her and her sister, Lottie, to Home Farm to see the tiny pink piglets.

Why should the simple act of birth be so difficult for his beloved Verity? he wondered. It was not as if she was sickly in other ways. When she was not with child, she could ride with him around the estate without tiring, or dance the night away like a young girl. He drew another sigh. Apart from his deep disappointment at the loss of this last baby, he could not bear to see the tears on his wife's cheeks. His love for her was total and enduring and he wanted her happiness far more than he desired his own.

The sound of wheels on the gravel drive drew Guy's attention to an approaching carriage drawn by two horses. It was unusual for there to be visitors at this time of the morning and, since the doctor had already been and gone, Guy's curiosity was aroused. As the vehicle stopped outside the house, the coachman jumped down and opened the carriage door for its occupant. Guy's face broke into a welcoming smile as he recognised the figure of Ket, the younger of his two half-brothers. Here at the very time he was needed was this most cheerful, amusing and agreeable of fellows – the very person who could bring a smile back to Verity's unhappy face, and indeed to his own.

He hurried across the terrace to greet his brother. Ket was younger by four years but Guy often thought the gap was greater. Where he himself was hard working, serious, industrious and methodical, Ket was a sunny-natured, madcap adventurer. As he shook Guy's hand warmly he announced that he had returned from an obscure village in Guiana full of savages and, that very morning, had crossed the Channel and docked at Dover from where he had just journeyed.

'Fascinating place, Guiana!' he told Guy as, arm in arm, they walked into the house. His dark brown eyes were alight with happy enthusiasm as he entered the hall. 'All the same, there's no place like home, eh, old man? A few home comforts will be more than welcome. How's everyone?'

Grainger, the butler, came hurrying through the service door to take Ket's coat, hat and gloves. 'I'm afraid I didn't hear your arrival, Sir,' he said. 'May I say welcome home, Master Ket, Sir?'

His voice was filled with genuine warmth and Guy reflected that this would be the reaction of all their staff, friends and the whole family. Even their father was unable to resist Ket's laughing, sunny nature and, albeit reluctantly, would give him sufficient funds to go on his next wild escapade whilst voicing disapproval of the last.

As Guy preceeded Ket into the morning room, he said apologetically: 'I fear there won't be much of a celebration for your safe return. My poor Verity suffered a miscarriage in the early hours of this morning. She is distraught – the more so because the infant was a boy . . . and you know how Father is insistent that I should give him a grandson. He's not so much upset as angry – as if Verity could help it, poor darling. Maybe you can cheer her up, Ket. She's always so pleased to see you.'

'I'll do my best, old chap!' Ket said, lowering his lanky frame into one of the armchairs and stretching out long, booted legs in front of him. 'What rotten luck! But better

32

luck next time, eh? No good being pessimistic in this life – look on the bright side, is my motto!'

'Yes, well, there might not be a next time,' Guy said, his grey-blue eyes clouded with anxiety. 'Dr Freeman seems to think it unlikely. Anyway, let's talk about something more cheerful. How long are you home for? You're looking very fit.'

And extremely handsome, Guy thought, wondering why his younger brother had not been snapped up by one of the many pretty girls who vied for his attention at local dances. Possibly because their mothers would not consider Ket to be 'a good catch', firstly because as the youngest son he had no money, and secondly, his reputation for wild adventuring was well known.

Ket's rather finely curved mouth had widened into a grin. 'I'll be staying for as long as it takes me to get Father to put his hand in his pocket! I met a chap in Guiana who had recently returned from Egypt. He made friends in Port Said with some fellow travellers who were sailing back in their Arabian dhow along the Suez canal to the Red Sea. They'd stopped off at several ancient sites and these chaps had seen some fantastic things. If I can get Father to cough up, I thought it sounded an amusing way to spend a few weeks, don't you think?'

Guy smiled. 'Doesn't sound quite to my taste!' he said. 'But I can believe you'd enjoy it. How was Guiana?'

Ket's expression glowed with remembered enthusiasm. 'Unbelievable! And, of course, incredibly primitive in places. In one village I stayed in the tribe practised *couvade* – a weird kind of ceremony where when a woman gave birth, her husband was put to bed and treated as if *he* were the one who'd produced the child. The unfortunate wife goes back to work while he lies in his hammock for weeks being looked after by the women. There's a long list of things he mustn't eat or do, such as smoking, washing himself, touching weapons and so on. Extraordinary! And in some places, the father actually has to buy the child from his wife!'

Guy drew a deep sigh. 'Interesting though that is, Ket, maybe it would be better not to relate it to Verity, who I know loves to hear stories of your adventures. At the moment the very thought of childbirth reduces her to tears.'

Ket nodded sympathetically. 'We must do all we can to cheer her from her melancholy,' he said. 'As soon as she is about again we'll take her out in the carriage. The countryside is quite beautiful as I noticed on my way here from Dover. There is no place lovelier than England in the spring, and we shall ensure dearest Verity will have the chance to enjoy it.'

But without knowing why, Guy felt the stirrings of foreboding. It was as if some sixth sense were warning him that his beloved young wife was not going to be consoled so easily.

Three

M adame Hortense took the parcel of dresses from Charlotte and led her into her private office. Daybreak, her adored tiny Pomeranian, jumped out of its basket, its shrill yapping belying its minute size as it welcomed its doting mistress.

'Sit down, my dear!' she said, putting the finished gowns on a table beside her. 'I won't keep you long, but there are two things I wish to discuss with you. First, I have to tell you I have had a second letter about you.'

Colour flared momentarily into Charlotte's pale cheeks. 'From . . . from Mrs Conniston?' she asked, for there was no one else in the world who might have written, let alone addressed such a letter to Madame Hortense's establishment. 'Was she asking once again if you had my address?'

'Exactly! But this time, there is an enclosure for you. Your friend is a little desperate, I fear – or, should I say, not thinking very clearly. Even supposing you had really departed to India as you led her to believe, it is most unlikely you would have advised me – a mere dressmaker – of your whereabouts and not advised her, a dear friend. But I digress – I think you should read it at once since it is marked MOST URGENT.' She held out the letter, the envelope covered by Verity's rather childish scrawl and smelling very faintly of lavender.

Charlotte felt tears stinging the backs of her eyes, for the news it contained was heartbreaking. Poor Verity had still not recovered her health and spirits since her miscarriage in April, she had written. Her beloved Guy and her dear brother-in-law Ket, home from his travels, had tried unsuccessfully to cheer her, and soon Ket would be departing once more for foreign climes. No less distressing was her increasing loss of hope that Charlotte's promised letter from India giving Verity her address might yet arrive. At first she had told herself it had been lost in transit. Now she was asking herself if Charlotte had once more forgotten her.

> *My darling Guy is sweet and kind and loving but, much as I adore him, I cannot confide in him as once you and I confided our secrets to one another, dearest Charlotte.*

Verity had continued in a postscript penned in even more illegible handwriting. There was little doubt that by this time she had been in tears for the ink was smudged in several places.

> *I wrote in June to Madame Hortense, hoping against hope that you might have written to her and she could give me your address, but alas, she did not do me the courtesy of replying. Guy said I should make one last attempt to reach you since I placed such importance on your companionship, and so I have asked Madame either to forward this to you if she is able, or else return it to me. If it should reach you, my dear friend, please, please reply to me . . .*

Seeing the tears now running softly down Charlotte's cheeks, Madame Hortense's voice was gentle as she said quietly: 'On the last occasion, you begged me to leave Mrs Conniston's letter unanswered. Do you wish me to do so again?'

With an effort, Charlotte wiped her tears away. 'I don't know what alternative there can be!' she murmured. 'If I were to tell her I was back in England, I would have to confess the truth – all of it. How could I expect her to maintain a friendship with the daughter of fraudster – a criminal! For that is what my poor father became, Madame.

36

Had you known the truth when I first asked you to give me employment, Madame Hortense, would you have employed me? I think not, even though I was as ignorant as my mother of my father's wrongdoing.'

Somehow Madame Hortense managed to conceal her astonishment. She had known that the girl was of good family and had fallen on hard times, but she had had no idea that Charlotte's father had been – of all things – a convict! No wonder the girl had been desperate for work, even badly paid work as a seamstress. No wonder she could afford no better than the slum lodgings where she lived. And no wonder she had 'disappeared', leaving no address for her former friends such as Mrs Conniston.

She lent forward and patted Charlotte's hand. 'You have no call to be ashamed!' she said. 'Maybe you are right to say I might not have given you employment had I known about your father, but that only goes to show how narrow-minded and bigoted we all are. Suppose I were to tell you and my clients that my father was employed washing pigs' stomachs for butchers' tripe? You may smile, my dear, but I do not think the image of a French couturier is evoked by pigs' intestines!' She drew a deep sigh before adding: 'I grew up in the slums, so no one knows better than I how easy it is for a man to fall foul of the law and find himself in prison. But perhaps such understanding is too much to expect of a delicate young lady such as Mrs Conniston. On the other hand, a true friend would overlook what has no bearing on your personal reputation. Is it simply pride that won't permit you to tell her the truth?'

Charlotte did not attempt to hide her surprise, astonished as she was by Madame Hortense's understanding as much as by her family background, but she was also moved by her compassion. 'I suppose it's partly my pride,' she admitted. 'But that's not the only reason. Whilst I believe Verity might still wish to be my friend, I can't believe her husband, his family or hers, would approve such an association between us. She would be put in an intolerable position, would she not? Torn between loyalty to me and obedience to her husband, who sounds a very kind and charming man. It breaks my heart to hear how badly she needs me but for her sake I think you will have to return her letter saying that you've had no word from me.'

Madame Hortense drew another long sigh. Life could often be cruel, she thought. She had known Charlotte for four years and had grown surprisingly fond of her. At first she had felt a jealous antipathy to this aristocratic young girl with her perfect articulation, her natural grace and good manners, her porcelain skin and refined bone structure. The young woman asking for employment was the epitome of what Doris Briggs would like to have been, instead of which she was big-boned, with large hands and wide, long feet. No matter how well she dressed – and she was astute enough to follow the French fashions avidly – she knew she would never be taken for a lady, for anything but 'trade'.

Gradually, Charlotte's shy smile and uncomplaining willingness to work overtime won over her prejudice. One winter's day when Charlotte had, for the first time ever, failed to arrive on time, she had gone to Charlotte's lodgings and found her seriously ill with pneumonia. Without hesitation she had taken it upon herself to send and pay for a doctor; had brought food and delicacies which she had fed to Charlotte. It was only when Charlotte was recovering that Madame admitted to herself that the girl had come to feel like a daughter to her – the daughter she had dreamed of but now knew she would never have.

Charlotte had been intensely grateful for Madame's attentions and she both liked and trusted her. But as she understood it, their relationship was that of employer and worker and she would have thought any further familiarity on her part to be taking advantage of Madame's kindness. Her reticence kept Madame's inclination to reveal her affections at bay and, although it was Madame who paid Charlotte's wages, it was the older woman who treated the younger with an instinctive respect.

Madame lent back in her chair, her ample hips and bosom spreading either side of her despite the restraint of her heavily boned corset. 'Have you ever given serious thought to your future, Charlotte?' she asked thoughtfully as she bent down to lift Daybreak on to her lap. 'You are twenty-two years old, am I not right? I don't wish to be disheartening but I'm sure it must have occurred to you that your chances of marriage are very slim.'

Charlotte gave a wry smile. 'You may be truthful and say "non existent"!' she declared. 'Even were some eligible man to fall in love with me at my age – and how would I meet such a man in my present circumstances? – he would withdraw any proposal when he learned of my family background. No, Madame, I have long since resigned myself to a life of spinsterhood. There is no alternative for me.'

Madame lent forward in her chair, her small, black button eyes searching Charlotte's face as she said tentatively: 'That may not be the case, my dear. I've been waiting for a moment such as this to put a proposition to you – one I realize will surprise, even shock you – but I feel it would be remiss of me not to at least mention it to you.'

Seeing the look of incomprehension on Charlotte's face, she gave a half smile. 'Perhaps I shouldn't beat about the bush but relate the facts, however unorthodox they might appear.'

'Please do,' Charlotte said quietly. 'No one knows better than I what a kind person you are, Madame. Whatever you have to say will cause no offence.'

'Then I will be quite honest. There is a certain gentleman of my acquaintance – my solicitor, to be precise – who has expressed considerable interest in you. You have met him on two occasions – once quite by chance when you were delivering work and he was selecting an evening bag for his niece's birthday present. On the second occasion, a casual meeting was arranged by me at his request. I asked you to serve tea to us in my office and we detained you for a short while in conversation. Do you recall the incident?'

Charlotte nodded, her expression bewildered. 'Why, yes! At the time, I did wonder why your maid or young Sally had not served the tea, but as I was in no hurry, I was pleased to help out since you seemed short-staffed.'

'That was merely a ruse to keep you with us. You see, Charlotte, this gentleman had taken an instantaneous fancy to you. As he put it, one brief glance was enough to "smite him like a thunderbolt". Those were his very words!' Madame smiled at Charlotte's expression which was both disbelieving and close to laughter. 'Believe me, Charlotte, this is no laughing matter. He is immensely in earnest – and I have to tell you, he's not only my solicitor, but he recently came into some money left to him by a maiden aunt and he considers himself a relatively wealthy man.'

Charlotte tried to curb the smile that was still turning the corners of her mouth. 'Then may I know the name of this admirer who was smitten like a thunderbolt? Your solicitor, did you say?' Memory told her he was a middle-aged bespectacled man of somewhat insignificant appearance.

Despite herself Madame, too, was smiling but her expression soon regained its seriousness. She had momentarily forgotten how unworldly, how innocent Charlotte was. It was quite possible that the girl, with her limited experience of life, would know nothing of mistresses or kept women. Nevertheless she had promised Mr Samuels that, given a suitable opportunity, she would relay his proposition which – not unnaturally – he was too embarrassed to put forward himself.

'His name is Theobald Samuels,' she told Charlotte. 'He is, he tells me, nearing fifty years of age but is still young at heart. He has a large country house in Surrey where . . . where his wife, his mother-in-law and her sister live; and a smaller bachelor house in Hampstead which he makes use of during the week when he works in the City. It has a pretty garden and overlooks Hampstead Heath – a healthy and pleasing environment, so he relates.'

'That all sounds very pleasant, but what has it to do with me?' Charlotte asked.

Madame Hortense was relieved to be given an appropriate entrée to what she must now say. 'The fact is he badly needs a hostess – someone to entertain his business friends in London. His wife is a semi-invalid and will not leave their home. He also wishes to have an attractive companion to lighten his evenings in Hampstead where he is often alone. In short, Charlotte, if you were to consider going to live with him as his . . . er . . . companion, you would be able to treat the house as your own, employ such servants as you wish and have an extremely generous allowance with which to run the establishment and buy whatever took your fancy.'

What colour there was in Charlotte's face now receded, leaving her even paler than normal. 'You can't be suggesting that I should agree to live with this man?' she said in a low voice. 'Why, he is old enough to be my father, if not my grandfather! And I know nothing of him, and even were I to like him, I could not for one moment consider being required to . . . to live with him merely to enjoy the luxuries of his home and freedom from financial cares.'

Madame took Charlotte's hand in hers. It was very cold and she could feel her trembling. 'My dear child, it's not his intention that you should live there as his daughter but as a wife. During history lessons were you not told about kings who had mistresses? It is not uncommon amongst men who can afford two households, I do assure you. Even our good Prince of Wales has Lilly Langtry, does he not?' She drew a deep sigh. 'I can see you are shocked, my poor Charlotte – as I warned Mr Samuels would be the case, but he is in no hurry for you to make up your mind. In fairness to him, I had to tell him a little about your unfortunate background but he waved this aside. He insists that you will grace his home with your beauty and your refinement, and that you will be treated with the utmost respect.' She put her other hand beneath Charlotte's chin and gently raised it so she could look directly into her eyes. 'I know you have been raised to the highest standards of moral and ethical behaviour by your mother, but she could not know how cruelly life was to treat you. Consider your future, Charlotte – alone, often hungry, without enough money to replace one of your old pretty dresses, without the opportunity to go the opera or the ballet, which you once told me you used to enjoy more than anything else. You have no friends, no family – nothing but work until you grow old and grey and die. Don't look away, for I am telling you the truth, ugly as it is. You are still young, and very, very pretty. I don't wonder Theobald Samuels is so enamoured. You could do a lot worse than permit him to give you a home and a release from the daily drudgery of work, Charlotte. To be a man's mistress is not totally demeaning, you know.'

Charlotte's expression changed once more as she said apologetically: 'As you said a little earlier, Madame, my experience of life is very limited. Before my father's misfortunes I was raised like any other girl of good family. That is to say, until my coming out dance, I spent most of my time in the nursery with my governess, and gossip such as the prince's adultery would never have reached my ears. As you know, I was a debutante with Verity – Mrs Conniston. Subsequently we left our home and I was never in society as an adult. As a consequence, I know only the life my parents led when I was a child. I was aware that they were totally devoted to one another and retrospectively, from the books and poems I've read, I realize that they were lovers as well as husband and wife. I would need to be similarly devoted to a man in order to share my life with him.'

Madame sighed. She understood what the girl was saying. In no way could her middle-aged solicitor be called attractive. Only five foot six in height, with hair already beginning to go grey, his neatly trimmed moustache concealed a somewhat thin mouth. His one redeeming feature – heavily fringed dark blue eyes – were concealed by bottle-lensed spectacles. No, he could not be said to set a young girl's heart a-flutter, although clearly he was a highly responsible, kind, methodical and good individual who might be trusted to take life-long care of Charlotte and would, in all probability, spoil her with love and attention.

'Were I in your shoes and it was me our friend Mr Samuels wished to protect, I would not be here talking to you, Charlotte!' she said bluntly. 'I've had to work hard all my life to achieve even this modicum of comfort. Believe you me, it is easy enough to scorn money when you have plenty, but I grew up all too well aware of poverty and there is nothing I would not do to ensure that I never return to that life. Think well before you look this particular gift horse in the mouth, my dear child. I have known Theobald Samuels for many years and I know he would take care of you.'

Madame Hortense rose to her feet, unseating the little dog, and started to unfold the garments Charlotte had brought with her. She nodded approvingly over the neat stitching while Charlotte replaced Verity's letter in its envelope and handed it back to Madame Hortense.

'I think this will reseal quite unnoticeably if you can use a little gum,' she said standing up. 'I hate to disappoint Mrs Conniston in this way but I love her too much to try to take advantage of her friendship. But this time perhaps it would be kindest to reply to her when you return her letter and say simply that you didn't expect to hear from me after I had gone to India. I doubt if either of us will hear from her again. As for Mr Samuels, I suppose I should say I am grateful for his interest but regret that, despite your advice which I know was well-intentioned, I have no wish for him to put such a proposition to me as I could not possibly accept it.'

Madame Hortense looked at her intently. 'But you will think about his offer, Charlotte? I don't imagine for one moment that he expected you would easily be won, and I am certain that he has no one else in mind. He was quite besotted by you in a manner surprising in a married, middle-aged solicitor! But then there's no knowing how men will behave when their passions are aroused! I will see you next week when you return Lady Armitage's tea gown. Be sure to take great care with her lace jabot, my dear, although I know I've no need to caution you as you have never yet failed me.'

She walked over to her desk, unlocked a drawer, and removed a purse. 'Take good care of yourself, child, and since I have detained you unduly, you are to take a cab back to your lodgings, for which I shall pay.' Disregarding Charlotte's protests, she pressed a florin into her hand and gently ushered her out through the door.

Alone once more, Madame Hortense picked up Verity's letter. The flap of the envelope was still unsealed and, without any hesitation, she drew out the sheets and read them. When she had finished, she replaced them and, gumming the flap of the envelope with great care, she sealed it and penned one of her own in which to enclose it. She felt only a moment's compunction as she did so, fearing lest Charlotte would see her action as betrayal. Hopefully Mrs Conniston would be grateful enough not to reveal who had told her of Charlotte's whereabouts. In a brief note, she outlined the reasons for Charlotte's 'disappearance' and the struggle she was having merely to survive. If Mrs Conniston truly cared about her friend, she wrote, she would ignore her unfortunate family's disgrace and, if such a thing were possible, transfer her back to the world in which she so clearly belonged.

As soon as she had drunk the tea her maid brought in to her, she put on her dolman cape and firmly secured a black satin toque on her head with a jet hat pin. Tucking the letter into her embroidered handbag, she put on her gloves and went out into the street to post it. The sooner the letter was on its way, the better. Were she to have left it overnight, she might have lost her nerve and never sent it. At worst, she thought, Mrs Conniston would be too shocked and nervous to renew the friendship and stand by her friend. If that was the case, at least Charlotte would never know it, and maybe in time she would succumb to the attentions of the solicitor.

She would invite Mr Theobald Samuels to visit her again in the near future. She would tell him a white lie and say that, in her opinion, his cause was not entirely lost; that given both time and patience he might yet win Charlotte for his mistress. It would do him no harm to hope.

I'm a wicked old schemer! Madame thought with a satisfied grin as she hung the finished gowns that Charlotte had returned in the cupboard in the salon. There was little she could do now to improve her own lifestyle so there was nothing to stop her putting her surplus energies into trying to improve Charlotte's. After those dreadful years of visiting the pathetic wreck of a man in Pentonville prison followed by

44

a further desperate year nursing her sick, heartbroken mother, if anyone deserved a break it was this lovely, brave young girl. One way or another, Doris Briggs told herself, she was going to see that Charlotte received it.

Four

'Ah, Charlotte, I wonder if you would be so kind as to deal with a slight problem for me?' Guy Conniston's strong, handsome face was turned in her direction as she walked towards him across the deep-piled Turkish rug covering the library floor. As had been her custom ever since she came to Kneepwood Court three weeks ago, she had taken her breakfast alone with Verity in her bedroom, and Guy's message asking her to attend him downstairs had been a surprise.

'I do hope nothing is wrong, dearest!' Verity had said, the ever ready tears filling her eyes. Although Guy insisted that his wife's spirits had greatly improved since Charlotte's arrival, at times it hardly seemed so.

'I'm sure it will prove to be of little importance,' Charlotte had replied reassuringly as she kissed Verity's pale cheek and went downstairs. Now, however, she was not so sure. Although both Verity and Guy had sworn on oath that they were indifferent to her father's disgrace and wanted nothing more than for her to remain at Kneepwood as Verity's companion, Charlotte was still secretly fearful that something would go wrong and mar this incredible change in her fortunes.

That, of course, was due to dear Madame Hortense, who she now knew had taken it upon herself to reveal her where-abouts and the reason for her reduced circumstances. Verity had lost no time in hurrying to London where she insisted Charlotte should return to Kneepwood Court to live with her for an indefinite period. She had swept aside Charlotte's

46

family disgrace as being of no consequence and vowed Guy would make welcome any such dear friend of hers.

Charlotte, knowing full well that Madame would be sorry to lose her services and had therefore acted only in her best interests, had instantly forgiven her for breaking her promise. They had parted as friends, Madame whispering in Charlotte's ear as she kissed her goodbye, 'If ever you are in trouble or for some reason do not wish to remain with your friends, you can always come back to me!'

There was no likelihood of that, Charlotte knew, for no one could have been made more welcome than herself. In particular the younger of Guy's two half-brothers, Christopher – known to the family as Ket – went out of his way to be friendly and attentive. Even Verity's bad-tempered father-in-law, old Sir Bertram Conniston, had been civil enough for he liked a pretty face, according to Verity! As for his wife, Verity informed Charlotte that Lady Conniston had been quite shockingly obese and with her arrival as Guy's wife she had handed over the responsibilities of chatelaine to Verity and retired to her rooms. Verity had soon realized that Lady Conniston, having been the former housekeeper, had never been accepted by the staff as their mistress, so this arrangement suited everyone, including Sir Bertram who had no further use for her since she had lost her looks. When, eighteen months ago, she had died from a massive heart attack brought about by her weight, he'd barely observed the conventions of mourning.

Charlotte's addition to the household was a matter of indifference to Guy's older half-brother, Matthew, although when he called at the house for a meal or to visit his father he was civil enough. His wife, Monica, however, was unduly critical and unnaturally curious about Charlotte's background. It was as if she guessed there was something suspicious about it, her questions bordering on the impertinent. Where was Charlotte's family home? When had they ceased to live in India? Where had she been living in London? Was she acquainted with the Warwicks? The Granvilles? The Ansons? Indirectly the older woman implied that someone of Charlotte's age and background would normally by now have found a husband and, since that was not the case and she had said her parents were dead, she must have private means with which to support herself.

It was Ket, the youngest of the three brothers, who had rescued her from this interrogation, telling his sister-in-law in a laughing, teasing fashion that curiosity killed the cat and that Monica had no right to put their guest in a witness box since – as far as he knew – Charlotte had committed no crime. His reproach had been so light-hearted that Monica had not been able to take offence, but she had not offered an apology and Charlotte felt it unlikely that the older woman would ever be a friend.

Monica was tall and thin, her angular body topped by a narrow face with a long, pointed nose and a thin unsmiling mouth. Her whole appearance was very much in contrast to her heavily jowled, round-faced, paunchy husband whose reddened, mottled nose indicated his fondness for the bottle. He lacked all Guy's physical attributes, Charlotte decided. By contrast, Verity's husband bore a strong resemblance to his aristocratic mother, whose portrait hung in the dining room. Most attractive of all her features were her eyes – a dark grey fringed with black lashes – and her wide, curving mouth which had a sweet gentleness about it. That sensitivity was reflected in Guy's total devotion to Verity. It was clear to everyone that husband and wife adored one another.

'No need to look so worried, my dear!' Guy said now as Charlotte approached his desk. 'The problem for which I need your help is a simple domestic one concerning one of the housemaids. For some reason our housekeeper, Mrs Barker, seems reluctant to tell me about it or, indeed, deal with it. Normally, she would refer such a matter to my wife but, as you know, we have all been anxious to keep any worry, however small, from Verity. If you are agreed, I will ring for Mrs Barker who will take you to her sitting room and explain her difficulty.'

'Of course I'll go!' Charlotte said. 'I'll be pleased to help if I can.'

She presumed, as had Guy, that this was a simple domestic matter that could be quickly sorted, or at worst, that one of the housemaids had transgressed in some way and Mrs Barker did not wish to take the responsibility of dismissing her without Verity's approval. But it transpired that the girl was pregnant and the problem was complicated by the identity of the baby's father.

'I don't like to trouble Mr Guy,' Mrs Barker said to Charlotte, 'he having quite enough worries with Madam so poorly; but someone's got to help the poor girl – stop sniffing, Daisy! – as none of it were her fault.'

'Not her fault?' Charlotte repeated, looking at the swollen-eyed, wet-cheeked girl in front of her. Every now and again Daisy would wipe her eyes on the corner of her apron, now a crumpled mess. Her reddish hair straggled damply beneath her mob cap and the overall impression she gave was of a buxom, tearful fourteen-year-old.

'Daisy's not yet fifteen, Miss!' Mrs Barker said as if divining Charlotte's thoughts. 'And her mother's a God-fearing woman I've known since she were a girl. I have to believe Daisy when she tells me what happened were dead against her will. She didn't tell no one at first, hoping it weren't ever going to happen again. Then after a few weeks, she started sickness and knew enough from her mother's pregnancies to guess what had happened.'

Charlotte drew in her breath sharply. 'So Daisy was . . . seduced? Forced against her will? But by whom, Mrs Barker? He must be punished – severely so.'

'Yes, Miss Wyndham, but we can't rightly report him to the authorities, he being who he is.'

'I don't care who he is,' Charlotte broke in firmly. 'He must not go unpunished. This could ruin Daisy's life – her chances of marriage. Besides, there's the expense. No, he must be apprehended, Mrs Barker, and made to recompense Daisy financially.'

Mrs Barker put a motherly arm around the shaking shoulders of the now sobbing Daisy. Her expression was grim. 'It were Mr Matthew, Miss Wyndham. You hadn't yet come to live at Kneepwood Court the night it happened. It were Mr Ket's welcome home dinner the night he got back from his travels. Mr and Mrs Matthew were guests and, although Madam was still far from well, she made the effort for Mr Ket and there was quite a party, a lot of wine at dinner, and after the port the gentlemen retired with the brandy. As far as I can make out from Daisy, Mr Matthew could hardly stand up when later that night he burst into her bedroom what she shares with Dolly, only Dolly had a day off to go home as her Mum was ill. So there wasn't a soul to help Daisy and he had his hand over her mouth so she couldn't shout for help.'

Charlotte's mouth was dry, and for a moment she couldn't speak. When she did so, it was in a quiet, firm voice which disguised her inner shock. 'You were right wanting to keep this from Mrs Conniston,' she said. 'Nor must this become generally known. However, I can promise you this much, Daisy, you will not be left destitute. I am sure the family will see that you receive enough money to keep you and your child from starving and, if it can be arranged, with enough over to tempt some young man to marry you, give your child a name. I will see what can be done. Now tidy yourself up and go and pack your things. I shall personally take you back to your parents and explain the circumstances.'

'Oh, Miss, you'm ever so kind!' Daisy said shakily. 'Me Dad 'ud kill me if he thought it were me own doing. You telling 'im 'stead of me will make all the difference. It's right good of you, Miss!'

'Well, I am going to ask something in return!' Charlotte said. 'I won't ask you to tell any lies, but no benefit can be derived from telling all the truth. May I tell your father that "an unnamed gentleman" dishonoured you without revealing it was Mr Matthew?'

Daisy nodded, her tears ceasing now she felt she wasn't going to be punished and that her problem was in other hands. Charlotte, however, was the one who now felt as if a huge dark cloud hung over the family. First and foremost, Verity must know nothing of this. Secondly, she must report the facts to Guy who couldn't fail to be deeply embarrassed

50

by and ashamed of his brother's behaviour. Charlotte knew from exchanges of confidences with Verity that neither she nor Guy liked Matthew, but Sir Bertram was well aware of the rivalry between the half-brothers and took no trouble to hide his preference for his second son whose somewhat coarse, baser nature was in keeping with his own.

Charlotte had learned these facts from Verity in the long hours they had spent walking in the beautiful grounds during the lovely October weather; sitting by her bedside in the evening when Guy was enjoying a game of billiards with the soon-to-be-departing Ket. That they would all miss Ket when he left was indisputable, Verity had declared, and none more than Guy, for the two men were as close as if they had been full brothers. Now she would have to add to Guy's concerns, Charlotte thought regretfully as she made her way back to the library.

Guy's response to Charlotte's account was one not so much of surprise as of resignation. 'I take it you believe the girl was telling the truth,' he said, his words a statement rather than a question. He drew a long sigh. 'I'm afraid to say this is not the first time this has happened, although not to a girl in our employ. I shall go to see her father myself so you need trouble yourself no further, Charlotte. I am sorry I involved you in this unsavoury business and, though you may think me disloyal for saying such a thing about my brother, I have to confess he has no moral sense whatever. Dammit, Charlotte, the man is the father of five children and, although I don't much care for my sister-in-law, Monica is a good wife to him.'

He broke off as if aware that he should not be revealing such feelings to a mere stranger. Or, if not quite a stranger as she was an old friend of Verity's, she had only been living at Kneepwood for a short while. As with an understanding nod of her head Charlotte left the room, Guy reflected how quickly and unobtrusively she had merged into the household. Verity had told him of Charlotte's impoverished state and he supposed that in such circumstances for her to be offered a home such as Kneepwood as his wife's companion must seem like a blessing from heaven. He knew that despite her quiet, self-effacing manner, she was by no means without spirit for it must have taken some degree of courage for a girl of her breeding to support herself and her mother when her father was imprisoned and left them panniless. Perhaps in due course, he and Verity might be able to find a husband for her, despite the fact that she was nearly twenty-three. But for the time being he was more than happy to see all her attentions centred upon his beloved wife. Between Charlotte and dear old Ket he had every hope that Verity would overcome the deep depression that had engulfed her since her last miscarriage and be her sunny-natured, happy, companionable self once again.

The butler drew the heavy brocade curtains across the eight casement windows of the drawing room and, having enquired whether Guy, Ket or Charlotte required anything further, silently left the room. Ket's wide velvet brown eyes were sparkling with laughter as the door closed behind the man. He stretched his long legs out in front of him and leaned forward to talk to Charlotte.

'I know I shouldn't laugh but Grainger always reminds me of Mr Punch!' he said. His voice was low-pitched and husky with subdued amusement. 'Poor old fellow has been with us for donkey's years and ever since I can remember he's had this disastrous effect on me. My apologies, Miss Wyndham.'

He didn't look in the least remorseful and Charlotte smiled. 'I'm sure he's an excellent servant and should not be made fun of!' she declared in mock reproach. 'And I do beg you to call me Charlotte. Surely it is only fair if I am to call you Ket as you requested at dinner.'

'Touché!' interjected Guy from his wing chair by the unlit fire. It was a soft October evening and it was only when darkness began to fall and a crescent of white moon appeared behind the chestnut trees that the four young people had left their seats on the terrace to retire indoors. Verity had decided to go to bed but refused to allow Charlotte to accompany her.

'Nora will see to my needs, dearest,' she had said. 'Stay

here and keep these two rascals from finishing that decanter of whisky. A little feminine company will do them both good!'

She had been smiling as she spoke and when Guy returned to his chair having escorted his wife to the door, he turned gratefully to Charlotte. 'You can have no idea how greatly my wife's health and spirits have improved since you came to stay with us, Charlotte. She says that you've agreed to remain with us indefinitely and, if she continues to improve at the same rate, we can all be confident of her total recovery.'

Although Guy and Verity knew the true facts about Charlotte's father, to safeguard Charlotte's pride, as well as her reputation, they had invented the sudden death of Charlotte's parents in India necessitating her unexpected return home. This fabrication also explained Verity's earlier failure to make contact with her.

Now, looking across from Guy to Ket, Charlotte knew neither could possibly gauge the degree of happiness she was feeling. It came not only from the ability to sleep once more in scented, smooth linen sheets; to bath in steaming hot water whenever she wished; to eat perfectly cooked, delicious meals; to wear beautiful clothes which dear Verity had given her, but also from the knowledge that Verity's depression was almost a thing of the past, her tears remaining only for when she spoke of the baby boy she had lost. She had even laughed outright in animation when, before dinner, she had insisted upon giving Charlotte a certain dress to wear.

'You remember, dearest? You were trying it on in Madame Hortense's salon that day when I found you. I am too pale now to wear that chestnut colour and I recall that it became you quite perfectly.'

Conscious that she did indeed look well in the evening gown, Charlotte felt a renewed confidence at the dinner table when Ket engaged her in a fanciful debate about the merits of women playing tennis and riding safety bicycles for exercise. She had enjoyed, too, Guy's description of the unexpected emergence of Queen Victoria, now aged sixty-eight, from her self-imposed seclusion in Balmoral, culminating in her spectacular Golden Jubilee last June – an occasion Ket had missed during his travels abroad. In the brief half hour when she and Verity had left Sir Bertram and his sons to their port, Verity had whispered in her ear: 'Ket is quite taken with you, dearest. Of course, he is a dreadful flirt and cannot be trusted for two minutes, but he is very attractive, don't you agree?'

Charlotte had felt her cheeks burning, as they did now at the memory. In appearance, there were many similarities between Ket and his half-brother. Both had the same straight Grecian noses and dark hair, but whereas Guy's hair was parted neatly in the middle and he sported a heavily waxed moustache, Ket's black hair curled in an unruly fashion, despite his valet's efforts to subdue it. It gave him a somewhat piratical appearance at odds with his wide, laughing mouth and eyes that seemed alight with inherent but harmless mischief.

As the brothers began to discuss the pending adventure upon which Ket was to embark at the end of the week, Charlotte realized that those attractive family characteristics she admired in Guy were magnified a hundred times in his half-brother. When Ket laughed, his eyes holding hers, she experienced a sinking feeling in the pit of her stomach as if she had just jumped off a high cliff. When he touched her hand as he held out a dish of bonbons, her skin seemed to burn. Even stranger things were happening to her, for as he shook his head in denial of something Guy had said to him, she found herself longing to reach over and run her hands through his unruly curls.

'So you will be leaving us early on Saturday, old fellow?' Guy was saying. 'I suppose there is no use trying to dissuade you. The old man has agreed to fund this expedition, I presume.'

Ket gave a deep, amused laugh. 'It wasn't too difficult. I think Father can only relax when I'm in foreign climes and can't get up to mischief in his environment.' He turned to Charlotte, adding with a sigh, 'I expect you've heard tales of my terrible misdeeds as a child – broken greenhouse, fire in the stables, a hunter's stable door left open, that kind of thing. Pranks, really, but Father used to get a bit choleric if neighbours were involved.'

'I should think so too!' Guy said, but with a friendly smile. 'It's about time you grew up, old chap. What are you? Twenty-six? I agree with Father, it's high time you got yourself married and settled down.'

Ket stood up, his back to the fireplace and flexed his arms above his head. 'I've nothing against marriage as you and Father seem to think. Just haven't met the right girl. Now if someone like Miss Wyndham . . . Charlotte, I mean . . . would overlook my juvenile behaviour and disregard my wanderlust, as well as the fact that I have no means to support a wife, I would gladly take upon myself the matrimonial garb.'

Charlotte felt herself blushing a deep red but neither man seemed to notice.

'Don't you believe a word of it, my dear!' Guy said with a rueful smile. 'Ket may have the best seat on a horse I've ever seen and a delightful way with children and dogs, but as a husband, no woman in her senses would give him even one chance to prove himself capable of a modicum of responsibility.'

Ket's eyes were twinkling as he dropped down on one knee and lifted Charlotte's hand. Her skin felt as if it were burning when he pressed his lips to her fingertips and declared in a deep, theatrical tone: 'I sense you have a kind, loving and tolerant nature, Miss Wyndham. You do not think ill of me, do you, despite what my uncaring brother has said to my discredit?'

Somehow Charlotte found her voice. Forcing herself to sound light-hearted, she pronounced in the same theatrical tones: 'Sir, I cannot comment upon your character, for I have but recently met you and therefore would not presume to judge you. As to marriage, I have long since resigned myself – by preference I hasten to say – to a life of spinsterhood. Therefore, neither on my account nor on yours, would I consider marriage to any man, be he rich or poor.'

Ket rose to his feet and stood looking down at her, the laughter gone from his face. 'I say, Charlotte, you weren't being serious, were you? About resigning yourself to a life of spinsterhood? That would be a most heinous waste if I may say so. Guy, we must do something about this state of affairs!' He was smiling once more as he added, 'As soon as dear Verity is quite better and I am home again, we must have a ball here at Kneepwood, don't you agree? We shall invite all the most eligible bachelors in the neighbourhood and I . . .' He resumed his theatrical voice and stance as he waved one arm in the air. 'I, sweet lady, shall do battle with them for the honour of tying your prettiest scarf about my lance.'

'Ket, will you stop this nonsense? Can't you see you are embarrassing Charlotte? Moreover, whilst she is under my roof, she shall never be made to do anything against her wishes. In this way, if in no other, I can show my gratitude to her for giving her time and friendship so readily to my dear wife.'

'Hear, hear!' said Ket as he sat himself down on the sofa beside Charlotte. 'You must forgive my nonsense,' he added softly. 'I'm not usually quite so silly but in the presence of someone as pretty as yourself, I am compelled to show off. Am I forgiven?'

I think I could forgive him anything, Charlotte thought as she nodded, returning his smile. He is everything he says – childish, silly, impertinent even – but his smile melts my heart and his touch sets it on fire. Mad, impossible, inconceivable though it is, I fear I have fallen hopelessly in love with Ket Conniston, the man Verity says is a born flirt, an innate adventurer and a Casanova who in a hundred years would never encumber himself with a wife.

'He has no need of one!' Verity had told her with a smile. 'Whatever her age, every woman falls in love with him. Why, even my little Kate and Lottie fight for his kisses and cuddles! Maybe I, too, would have fallen for his charms had I not met Guy first. Guy is the most wonderful husband and father and I love him with all my heart. There is nothing in the whole world I wouldn't do to make him happy. That's why I have been so desperately unhappy about the loss of this last baby. It would have been the boy he wanted, and oh, Charlotte, I couldn't give it to him! But you have given me new hope. Despite what Dr Freeman says, I shall try for another baby and this time I will not let it be miscarried. You will help me, won't you, dearest? With you to look after me, I will nurture my unborn baby impeccably until it's born.'

Yes, she would stay, Charlotte promised, for now that she knew she had a really useful part to play in Verity's life it was easier for her to accept her charity, and there was nothing in the world she wanted less than to go back to her lodging house in the London slums or to endure the endless repetitive hours of work sewing for Madame Hortense.

She would write to Madame, she told herself as she bade goodnight to Guy and Ket and went up to bed. Madame would be pleased to hear how happy she was back in her old, rightful environment. And but for Madame Hortense, she would not be here.

But her last thoughts before sleeping were not for her old life but for the new one, and for the bitter sweetness of her new found love for Ket Conniston. Simply to live here at Kneepwood beneath the same roof as Ket was all she felt justified in wanting, but that too would be denied her. The day after tomorrow he was leaving for Africa, and no one, least of all Ket himself, knew how many months – or even years – would elapse before she saw him again.

Five

At breakfast Ket announced that he would be overseeing Guy's valet, who was packing his luggage, after which he would be ready to go with Guy on a last ride round the estate. 'On such a perfect autumn day my inclination to leave England tomorrow is sadly reduced,' he said. 'There's nothing more beautiful than the Kneepwood woods when they are glowing golden and brown in the October sunshine.'

'I can't for the life of me understand this obsession of yours to go adventuring,' Sir Bertram said gruffly as he helped himself to a second plate of kedgeree.

Ket gave his father a friendly grin. 'I'm educating myself, Sir!' he said. 'I was never much interested in geography when I was at school. Besides, what would I do with my time here at Kneepwood in the winter?'

'A bit of hard work wouldn't do you any harm, my boy!' Sir Bertram grunted and proceeded to enlighten his family for the umpteenth time as to how hard he himself had been obliged to work as a boy.

When he finally finished his diatribe as well as his breakfast and left the dining room, Ket turned to Charlotte with a wry smile. 'I dare say you have not heard Father's favourite speech before, and might even have found it interesting. In point of fact, although he runs down my "adventuring", as he calls it, I think he rather envies me. Now, as it is my last day at home, won't you indulge us and come riding with Guy and me this morning? I would greatly enjoy your company.'

Charlotte felt her heartbeat quicken. 'I haven't ridden

since I was a child,' she said truthfully, 'so I must decline your offer.'

Ket looked crestfallen. 'I'm sure Guy could find you a reliable, safe mare, could you not, Guy?'

'No, I should curtail your enjoyment,' Charlotte broke in quickly. 'In any event, I have other tasks to take up my time.'

As the men departed, and Verity went up to the nursery to see the children before they started lessons with their governess, Charlotte made her way to her bedroom where she sat down at the window and leant her head on her arms.

I must stop this introspection, she told herself. Ket's suggestion I should ride with him was no more than a friendly gesture. The fact that I've fallen so hopelessly in love with him is misleading me into thinking he might care a little. Verity warned me he flirts with every female and that every female falls in love with him, so I should know his attentions are meaningless. Tomorrow he will be gone and, unless he is to see how desperately I wish he wouldn't leave, I must find some way to avoid being in his company.

The arrival of the morning post and a letter for Charlotte from Madame Hortense provided her with a legitimate excuse for absenting herself. Explaining to Verity that Madame was not very well and greatly wished to see her, Charlotte arranged for Gregory to take her to the station where she could catch a fast train to London. After a few hours with Madame, she could get the afternoon train back to Kneepwood in time for tea. She could then plead exhaustion and retire to bed, thus avoiding Ket's company for the rest of the day.

On the train from Tunbridge Wells to London, Charlotte was torn by conflicting emotions. Her plan to absent herself from Kneepwood did relieve her from the strain of being in Ket's company. Contrarily, she could hardly bear the thought that tomorrow he would be gone for an unknown length of time and she would have no hope of seeing him, hearing his cheerful teasing voice, his full-throated laughter, of watching the ever-changing expressions on his handsome face.

With an effort, she made herself think of other things –

not least that she was fortunate enough to have the money to undertake this journey to London. Moreover, it was money Verity had made possible for her to earn. During the summer she had made two beautiful party dresses for Verity's daughters – a cream voile and lace with a silk sash and accordion-pleated skirt for Kate and, for Lottie, a yoked dress of blue and white muslin, with rows of smocking edging the bodice and cuffs. The little girls had been delighted, as had their mother, and Verity had insisted that she reimburse Charlotte for her time and trouble. When Charlotte had attempted to decline the payment on the grounds that she lived without payment at Kneepwood, Verity refused to listen. 'You sew quite beautifully, dearest, else Madame Hortense wouldn't have employed you, would she? So now it's I who wish to employ you if you are agreeable. You shall make me an evening dress for the ball I intend to arrange for Guy's thirtieth birthday next month.'

Verity had had sent from London a dressmaker's dummy adapted to her measurements so that Charlotte could use it to design and fit the new gown. When it was finally completed, she pressed into her hand a velvet purse containing a half sovereign, part of which Charlotte had now drawn on for her train fare.

Although these thoughts successfully banished Ket from her mind for the rest of the two-hour journey to Charing Cross station, Charlotte was not long at Madame Hortense's establishment before his name came involuntarily to her lips. There was a luminous look about her which Madame insisted could only mean there was someone or something very special in her life. Was it possible Charlotte had fallen in love? she enquired as they lunched together in the discreet tavern adjoining the salon.

Surprised by Madame's perspicacity, Charlotte felt her cheeks flaming, leaving Madame in no further doubt. Within minutes, Charlotte was pouring out her heart to her former employer's sympathetic ears.

'From all you tell me, my dear, you are following the right path in refusing to take this young man's flirtations

60

seriously,' she told Charlotte gently. 'Nevertheless, I don't see your situation as being quite as hopeless as you say. There will come a time when this charming adventurer will tire of his wanderings and wish to settle down. I see no reason why he should not want you for his wife. You have become a very beautiful young woman, Charlotte. The life you are now leading has restored you to perfect health. Your figure has filled out and rounded most delightfully. I'm not in the least surprised to hear that your precious Mr Ket Conniston has been flirting with you. You would be mistaken, in my opinion, to reject any advances he might make.'

Charlotte managed a half-hearted smile as she ate the chicken galantine Madame had ordered for their luncheon. 'Maybe I should have come to seek your advice sooner,' she said wistfully, 'for Ket leaves in the morning for Egypt. I doubt we shall see him again for a year or even longer.'

'Then you might suggest you exchange letters,' Madame replied quickly. 'Letters that would keep him up to date with affairs at home. You don't have to lay bare your true feelings, for with clever wording you could indicate that all of you at Kneepwood miss his cheerful company. That would keep open the door for him to reply that he misses *you*.'

For a moment, Charlotte's spirits soared. Madame was assuming that a relationship between Ket and herself could be possible. But she knew it was not so. 'Ket is penniless like myself,' she said. 'Verity – Mrs Conniston – told me he must eventually marry a girl with considerable means, if not an heiress. Even if by some miracle Ket were to fall in love with me, I have nothing, as you well know, to offer him. Nor is my family background impeccable. There is no way I could enhance his life. He is entirely dependent upon his father's goodwill and generosity and I am in no doubt that both would be withdrawn were Ket to tell Sir Bertram he wished to marry me!'

Madame Hortense frowned. 'I am surprised to discover you're a realist rather than a romantic, Charlotte,' she declared. 'Have you not heard the proverb "love conquers all"?'

Charlotte sighed. 'Love did not conquer all for my parents,' she said sadly. 'Much as my father loved my mother, he couldn't save himself or her from poverty and shame.'

Madame nodded, covering Charlotte's hand with her own. 'I fear your father's first love was his gambling,' she said gently. 'But you mustn't let those past events mar your future, my dear. I will give you another proverb to take home with you – "whilst there is life, there is hope". Now, tell me other news of your life. Has Mrs Conniston recovered fully from her miscarriage?'

On the train back to Kneepwood, Charlotte found herself in a very different mood from the despairing one that had accompanied her to London. Despite the total improbability of Madame's optimistic prophecies, she had somehow convinced Charlotte that her love for Ket might yet be reciprocated. So far she had given Ket no encouragement to believe she held him in any special regard. There would still be a few hours left this evening if, instead of hiding herself in her room, she went down to the evening meal in her most becoming gown and flirted with him as outrageously as he flirted with her. Although he would be gone the next day, at least he would take away a more exciting memory of her.

Almost as if he were aware of the change in Charlotte's outlook towards him, it was Ket, not the coachman, who met her at the railway halt in the family waggonette.

He jumped down from the driver's seat and hurried to meet her, a huge welcoming smile on his face as he took her bag and helped her up on to the seat beside him. 'I thought your train was never going to arrive,' he said. 'I trust you had an enjoyable day in London? I myself have been quite miserable without your company, although I have to admit that Kate and Lottie tried to cheer me up. For a last treat, I took the pair of them to Matthew's stud to see the new foal. Needless to say they wanted to take it home but settled instead for a ride on Bertie's Shetland pony.'

'I'm surprised Bertie allowed it!' Charlotte commented wryly.

Ket smiled. 'I instructed the groom not to ask the boy's

62

permission, since knowing Bertie's nature, I too doubted it would be given.'

For a moment, he gave his full attention to the horses and then turned his head once more to look at Charlotte. 'Did you really have to go to London today?' he asked in a low voice. 'I had the feeling you did so to avoid me. Had you forgotten it was my last day?'

Wordless, Charlotte shook her head.

'Then take off your pretty bonnet and let me see that beautiful chestnut hair of yours.'

Startled into obedience, Charlotte removed her hat but in doing so dislodged several of the pins securing her hair. As she sought to pin it back in place, Ket stopped the horses and laid one hand lightly on her arm.

'Will you do me yet another favour?' he said softly. 'Take out those other pins and let me see you with your hair down. I know I shouldn't be asking this but we are in a very secluded part of Green Lane. There is no one to see but me, and I shall be able to go to far-off lands with a beautiful portrait of you in my mind.'

Charlotte's hesitation was only brief. With her heart thudding fiercely and the colour deepening in her cheeks, she did as he asked. A moment later, she saw him leaning towards her, his eyes a liquid brown, his expression deeply tender, then she felt his lips against her hair. It was the lightest of touches – one he could deny if he wished, swearing she was imagining the kiss. But he did not do so. Turning back to gather up the horses' reins, he sat silently for a moment whilst she repinned her hair and replaced her hat. Then he said, 'Have I shocked you, Charlotte? I didn't mean to. Will you forgive me for such presumption?'

'I made no protest!' she replied honestly. 'If there is blame needed, it is as much mine as yours.'

Ket gave a sudden unexpected laugh. 'I do love the contradictions that are so much part of you, Miss Charlotte Wyndham. One moment you are quite prim and formal and I decide you have a heart of ice, and then you smile in that warm, entrancing manner and I sense a heart as impassioned as my own.'

'I'm flattered that you have given my character such thought,' Charlotte rejoined, 'and more than a little pleased that you haven't concluded I'm a prudish old maid.'

Ket threw back his head and gave a great bellow of laughter. 'That would be impossible,' he said. 'I'm not much given to literary quotations or proverbs, but I am minded of that one which states "still waters run deep", for that is you, I think.'

'Enough of me!' Charlotte delared. 'Let's talk of you. You spoke just now of having "an impassioned heart". Would I be wrong in correcting that to "flirtatious" or "philandering", perhaps?'

'I don't care to have you call me a Lothario,' Ket broke in with mock anger, 'for I am no libertine. My trouble is I fall in love with every pretty woman I meet.'

By now they were driving through Kneepwood village. The warm daytime air had cooled and darkness was beginning to fall. Oil lamps were being lit in cottage windows and a warm orange glow shone through the doorway of the King's Head tavern. Ket slowed the horses to a walk as a figure appeared at the inn doorway and waved frantically to them to stop.

'Ket? Ket Conniston, is it not?'

The man's portly figure did not allow him to run but he approached the waggonette as quickly as he could, his top hat held in one hand, his cane in the other. His face scarlet from his exertions, he gazed up at Ket and Charlotte with a jovial grin.

'Thought it was you, old fellow!' he gasped. 'Haven't seen you in a month of Sundays. Your brother told me you were abroad.'

'I will be as of tomorrow,' Ket replied, smiling. 'Charlotte, this is my old school chum, Mr George Morrison. George, may I introduce Miss Charlotte Wyndham.'

Charlotte leaned across Ket to shake George Morrison's outstretched hand. It was now almost dark and a chill breeze ruffled the men's uncovered hair.

'Look, it's far too cold to stand out here chatting,' George said, his breathing now steadier as he pulled a muffler round his neck. 'Tell you what, why don't you come along to our house this evening, Ket – and Miss Wyndham, too, if she'd care to? My parents are giving an informal dinner party for local friends to celebrate Cynthia's engagement – Cynthia's my younger sister,' he explained to Charlotte. 'Do come, jolly the evening up a little, you know what most of the neighbours are like, Ket, old chap. The parents won't mind – remember how Mater favoured you when we were small boys?'

Ket laughed. 'Except when we were caught playing some forbidden prank – then it was always *I* who led *you* into mischief.' He turned to Charlotte, his face glowing. 'You will come, won't you, Charlotte? You'll love Cynthia – she's a sweet girl, and remember, it is my last night. If you are certain we will not be *de trop*?' he added to the waiting George, who promptly insisted that Charlotte must accept the invitation.

As Ket drove the last couple of miles home, Charlotte felt her heart beating with a mixture of excitement and anxiety. To go to a party as Ket's partner was like some improbable dream about to come true; but at the same time, she felt anything but self-assured. Although since living with Verity she had been to the occasional soirée and to small dinner parties at neighbouring houses, she had always gone with the family. Never had she been alone and unchaperoned, as would be the case this evening with Ket.

Verity calmed Charlotte's nerves with the assurance that for her to attend alone with Ket would not be considered improper, since Mrs Morrison and other ladies would be at the party. 'Besides, dearest, does it matter what some old-fashioned fogies might say? You are bound to have a lovely time at the Morrisons – they're a delightful family, and Ket will take care of you.'

As Verity's maid, Nora, helped Charlotte into one of the lovely dinner gowns Verity had given her, she surveyed her reflection in the mirror and felt a small thrill of excitement. The dress had a low, square-cut décolletage with a deep collar of cream lace. As Charlotte twisted to see the dress better, the apricot silk of the tightly corseted bodice and overskirt shimmered where it was pulled back in folds over the bustle, falling in a short train at the back. The underskirt was of a paler shade of creamy yellow and was decorated with ribbon bows entwined with silk roses and falls of lace. For once the sleeves were short, capped over her shoulders and held by more apricot ribbons, leaving her arms bare. Verity had lent her long white gloves and a fan to complete her ensemble.

Nora fixed a feathered ornament in Charlotte's burnished copper hair. 'You look ever so pretty, Miss Wyndham – enough to turn all the gentlemen's heads!'

Despite her determination not to allow such crazy thoughts to linger in her mind, Charlotte silently replied to Nora: 'But am I pretty enough to turn Ket's head?' Had he not only an hour ago told her that he fell in love with every pretty woman he met? Had Verity not warned her a hundred times not to take Ket seriously? As she made her way downstairs, her evening cloak over her arm, she knew those warnings were meaningless matched against the power of her heart. She was hopelessly in love with him and, because there was no denying it, she had no alternative but to hope that Ket might reciprocate her feelings.

'I wish you were coming with us, Verity,' she said as Grainger announced that Gregory was at the door with the landau. Verity shook her head. 'Dear George is Ket's former school friend, not Guy's, and we would be *de trop* at young Cynthia's party. Have a lovely time, dearest. You look radiant – doesn't she, Ket?'

He had come into the hall quietly but now as Charlotte turned her head she was hard put to restrain a gasp, accustomed as she was to seeing him more often in day or riding attire. Splendidly turned out in a black cutaway dress coat and black, tight fitting trousers, he was wearing a white waistcoat and a white bow tie and his starched shirt front, with its fashionable standing collar, had a row of mother-of-pearl and diamond dress buttons adorning it. He now threw a black opera cape over his shoulders and drew on white

66

gloves as Grainger handed him a tightly furled umbrella. He looked like a dark-haired Apollo.

'Have I kept you waiting?' he enquired of Charlotte. 'Henry couldn't get my shirt studs fastened, poor chap. Well, I suppose it's time we were on our way, else George will think we aren't coming.'

He reserved the compliments he wished to make on Charlotte's appearance until they were in the carriage. Tucking the fur travelling rug more securely about her knees, he said: 'I can hardly believe my luck having you here beside me. To be honest, when George asked me to bring you tonight, I never thought you would agree to come. You look quite entrancing, Charlotte, if you will permit me to say so. I shall be very proud to have you on my arm this evening.'

For once, Charlotte did not suspect that he was being flirtatious. Verity, Guy and Nora had all told her how lovely she looked and the mirror had left her in no doubt that she looked prettier than she ever imagined possible. The new gown Verity had given her flattered her figure and her mood enhanced the sparkle in her eyes and the colour in her cheeks. There was no pretending that she was other than excited, confident, all her customary caution thrown to the winds. She might well have no future with Ket, she reasoned; he was leaving the country in the morning and may have forgotten her before his next visit home. But for a few hours she would think of nothing else but being happy, of enjoying this one magical evening as his partner.

Ket was not the only person to find Charlotte attractive. His friend, George Morrison, was in constant attendance on her. She couldn't help but like the jovial, portly bachelor, whose jocular comments kept her laughing. She was flattered, too, by his extravagant compliments. Moreover, she decided as he escorted her in to dinner, he seemed to find her light-hearted rejoinders amusing and quick-witted.

'Damned if I can understand old Ket,' he said as, seated beside her at the dinner table, a footman refilled their glasses for the third time.

Slightly befuddled by so much unaccustomed wine, Charlotte

enquired: 'What is it you don't understand, Mr Morrison? Ket's character seems quite clear to me.'

'That's just my point,' her companion replied. 'Ket never could resist a pretty female, yet here you are, the most beautiful of God's creations, living under his very roof, and the fellow has not yet proposed. Not only that, he is voluntarily going off on another of his madcap adventures, leaving you behind to be snapped up by some other chap.'

'Ket is a free spirit, isn't he?' Charlotte rejoined as both of them looked across the dinner table to where Ket was sitting beside an elegant middle-aged lady and a pretty young blonde girl who was gazing up at him with adoring eyes. He was dividing his attention between his two dinner guests but suddenly looked up and met Charlotte's eyes. It was not a friendly glance – more a disapproving one, she thought as she quickly turned back to George. Had she been laughing a little too loudly? she wondered. The very last thing she wanted was to have him ashamed of her.

When dinner was over and the ladies had repaired to the bedroom to refresh their appearances whilst the men enjoyed their port, a girl of Charlotte's age came over to the dressing table where she was seated. She gave Charlotte a friendly smile. 'I hope you didn't think me rude, staring at you at the dinner table,' she said, 'but I was certain you and I had met before.'

Charlotte's heart missed a beat as she replied quickly, 'I don't think so. I'm sure I would have remembered.'

The girl held out her hand. 'I'm Annabel Hope,' she said. 'Do forgive me but it's your beautiful hair that reminds me of one of the debutantes in my season. I remember now – Charity Wyndham.'

The colour drained from Charlotte's face as her brain worked furiously for a disclaimer. 'I know who you have mistaken me for . . . my cousin,' she said. 'She has the same coppery-coloured hair as mine. She came out in the same year as Verity Conniston. I was in India with my parents then so I never actually did the Season.'

Annabel Hope gave yet another friendly smile as she said:

'That explains it then. I was sure I'd seen you somewhere. Do forgive me for enquiring, but I think it would have bothered me for days if I hadn't. By the way, I do really envy you your lovely hair!'

With a murmured 'How kind of you to say so!' Charlotte put down the hairbrush. As quickly as she could politely do so she excused herself and went downstairs. Her heart didn't slow its beat until the men returned from the dining room and the party reassembled in the drawing room and George's sister, Cynthia, sat down at the piano to entertain them with her very accomplished playing. To Charlotte's disappointment it was George and not Ket who asked if he could sit beside her. A little later, Cynthia was accompanied by her fiancé who had an agreeable baritone, but Charlotte could not concentrate on their performances. She was conscious only of Ket's eyes, fastened upon her from the opposite side of the room. He was frowning slightly and once more she began to wonder what could be wrong. Was her hair or her gown in disarray? George, however, warmed by the copious amount of wine and the balloon glass of brandy that had followed the meal, became even more complimentary – even a little amorous, allowing his knee to touch Charlotte's leg as the piano playing came to an end.

Charlotte excused herself and, in company with several other ladies, retired to the guest room again to check on her toilette. Other than a stray curl which had escaped Nora's pins, she could see no reason for Ket's disapproving glances. When she rejoined the party, he quite deliberately ignored her and the happiness that had buoyed her at the start of the evening now gave way to a feeling of despair. She could think only of her foolishness in ever supposing that Ket had any special feelings for her. He seemed to be making it quite plain that the opposite was the case.

When at midnight the guests began to leave and Ket came over to suggest that it was time for them to go, she felt close to tears as he helped her into the landau and the horses began to move down the drive. Somehow George's whispered wish for a future assignation only added to her sense of failure. Much as she liked him, it was only as a friend.

For five minutes, neither Ket nor Charlotte spoke. When Ket finally broke the silence it was to say in a low, pointed tone: 'I've no need to enquire if you enjoyed your evening. Clearly you did so.'

Unaware of the reason for his unfriendly tone of voice, Charlotte said: 'Wasn't I supposed to enjoy myself? Isn't that why you suggested I should accompany you?'

'*I* was supposed to be your escort for the evening – not Morrison!'

Ket's angry tone as well as the implications of his accusation took her breath away. 'Then why were you not as attentive as George?' she countered, angered by the unfairness of his criticism.

'Because it became clear to me quite early on in the evening that you were thoroughly enjoying Morrison's company.'

It was on the tip of Charlotte's tongue to reply that yes, indeed, she had found George's jolly conversation both entertaining and, at times, flattering. But she bit back the words as it struck her suddenly that Ket was jealous. Her heart soared at the thought that he cared enough about her to resent her interest in someone else. Her voice softened as she turned to look at him. 'Must we quarrel, Ket? I had such a lovely evening thanks to you. I found your friend an amusing companion but I don't think I could ever feel anything other than friendship towards him.'

Ket's expression relaxed somewhat as he said dourly: 'He obviously felt a great deal more for you. It wouldn't surprise me if he came calling at Kneepwood in the very near future.'

'I would be happy to see him,' Charlotte replied, but swiftly added, 'But only ever on a friendly basis. If he were to suggest a deeper attachment then I would have to put an end to any such visits.'

Moonlight was flooding into the small window of the landau, and by its light Charlotte could see the sudden smile that transformed Ket's face. 'I'm delighted to hear it,' he said. 'I should hate to return to Kneepwood to find you had left home to marry poor old George – not that he would be a bad husband, I suppose. Our family have always thought of him as the proverbial bachelor who would never marry. If ever he should propose marriage to you, Charlotte, did you mean you would not accept him?'

'No, no I would not!' Charlotte replied. 'You can be certain I will still be at Kneepwood when you return, Ket.'

Ket leant closer to her and took one of her gloved hands in his. His voice was teasing but husky as he said: 'Supposing I were to be away for a year or more?'

'I will never leave Verity – not as long as she needs me,' Charlotte told him.

'Not even to get married? Have a home of your own? Children?'

'Kneepwood is my home now, and in any event, I have no wish to be married,' Charlotte replied quickly.

Unless it were to Ket, she thought silently.

'Nor I!' Ket said. 'I've always thought that matrimony would restrict my favourite occupation – travelling. But people do change their minds, Charlotte. Sometimes I find myself envying Guy his closeness to Verity and the love they share. Don't you feel envy when you see them together, so very devoted and entirely of one mind?'

Before Charlotte could answer, Gregory turned the horses' heads into the long drive up to Kneepwood Court. They were both suddenly aware that they were almost home; that their time alone together was quickly running out. Without warning, Ket placed his hand beneath Charlotte's chin and, lifting her face up to his, he bent his head and kissed her on the lips. It was only a fleeting kiss, yet it was enough to cause a tumult of emotions in Charlotte. She caught her breath in a gasp.

Supposing he had shocked her by such unconventional behaviour, Ket made a swift apology. 'Forgive me, Charlotte. I'd no right to do that; but you looked so beautiful, so inviting in the moonlight, I simply forgot myself. Please tell me I am forgiven.'

Unable to speak, Charlotte could do no more than nod. She was filled with regret and dismay as the landau came

71

to a halt outside the big front door of the manor house –
dismay that this magical evening had come to a close and
a desperate regret that, for an indefinite period, there would
be no opportunity for Ket to kiss her again.

Six

December 1887–1st January 1888

'We shall have to take great care they don't set the tree alight!' Verity said as Charlotte affixed the last of the tiny tin candle holders to a branch of the large fir tree standing in the corner of the drawing room. She placed a little white candle in the holder and stood back to admire the Christmas tree. Her face was radiant.

'The children will think it quite magical,' Charlotte said as she, too, stood back to appreciate their handiwork. It was the Queen's late husband, Prince Albert, who had introduced the Germanic tradition of bringing a fir tree into the house to add to Christmas decorations. Later that afternoon, Matthew and Monica would be bringing their children over to join Verity's two little girls for tea when they would all place their Christmas presents under the tree. Charlotte had volunteered to play on the pianoforte for some carols, after which carol singers from the village could be expected to arrive at the front door.

Verity drew Charlotte down beside her on to the velvet-buttoned sofa. She gave a sigh of pleasure. 'Six months ago I didn't believe I could ever be happy again!' she said. 'In so many ways, I have you to thank for my present contentment, dearest.' She squeezed Charlotte's arm affectionately. 'You are such a peaceful person to be with – and so very sensible!' she added. 'I know myself to be feather-brained and quite stupid at times and I am so fortunate that my darling Guy says he wouldn't have me any other way.'

'All any of us want is that you should be happy!' Charlotte interposed. She was aware that Verity was once more with child, although she had not as yet confided this news to anyone else – not even Dr Freeman. She had missed only two periods and had decided to wait another month before admitting that she was pregnant. She had chosen to discard Dr Freeman's warning that she might never again be able to carry a child full term. 'Doctors are not infallible!' she had said to Charlotte. 'And my instinct tells me that all will be well this time.' So only Charlotte knew the true reason why all traces of Verity's long-lasting depression had disappeared and she was her old, sweet, sunny-natured self once more.

'If only Ket could be here for Christmas, our cause for celebration would be complete!' she said now. Seeing the colour staining Charlotte's cheeks, she gave her hand another squeeze. 'And don't pretend you are not in agreement. I have not forgotten how pleased you were when he sent you his "fondest regards" in his last letter!'

Hurriedly, in order to divert Verity's attention, Charlotte withdrew from the pocket of her blue and fawn striped dress a pretty Christmas card she had received that morning from Madame Hortense. It depicted a stable scene and when held up to the light the infant Jesus appeared in the manger with an angel above. 'Wasn't it kind of Madame to remember me?' she commented to divert Verity's thoughts.

'I'm certain she is quite genuine when she says how much she misses you,' Verity commented. 'And not just as a seam-stress. She must have cared very much for your happiness when she wrote to tell me of your unhappy circumstances.' She leant forward and looked deep into Charlotte's eyes. 'You *are* happy living here with us?' she enquired. 'I don't know what I should do if you felt the need to go elsewhere; but if it was for your greater happiness . . .'

'I couldn't possibly be happier elsewhere!' Charlotte inter-rupted. 'I know you've forbidden me to express my gratitude to you and Guy for giving me a home, but the fact is you have given me back my life. Before . . . Since my poor parents died . . . life was merely an existence. Now I wake in the mornings eager for the coming day and my last thought before sleeping is thankfulness for the day gone by.' She gave a deep sigh. 'If only there were some way in which I could repay all your kindness!' she said. 'If ever there is anything – anything at all I could do for you and Guy, you would tell me, wouldn't you?'

Verity clasped Charlotte in her arms. 'Dearest, it's thanks enough to have you living here as my friend and companion. Much as I adore Guy, he is very much a man with a man's interests and concerns. I understand his love for his home and don't begrudge the time he spends out on the estate or in conference with his bailiff. Did you know that Kneepwood used to belong to Guy's mother? He never knew her since she died soon after his birth, but he found a diary of hers in one of the attics written when she was a girl. Although she did mention other things, mostly it contained ecstatic references to her grandparents' home where she often stayed as a child; to the gardens where she played; visits to the farmsteads on the estate; descriptions of the trees, the haymaking in the fields, the bluebells in the woods. I think this is one of the reasons Guy so loves Kneepwood – it's the only link he has with his mother. I do believe Kneepwood means nearly everything to him and I hold only a small part of his heart.'

Charlotte looked shocked as indeed she sounded when she protested, 'How can you say such a thing, Verity? It is plain to everyone that he adores you.'

Verity smiled. 'Oh, I know I have nothing to fear from competition with other women. My Guy has no roving eye; nor is he attracted to the gaming tables and race courses which are Matthew's temptations. But Kneepwood – therein lies a part of himself; something which has been there all his life, whereas I have been only a part of it for the past seven years! That is why I simply must give him a son. You must start praying as I do every night that this baby I am carrying will be a boy.'

Charlotte hesitated. It worried her that Verity was seemingly taking it for granted she would carry her child full term, despite Dr Freeman's warning. Even were she by some miracle to do so, there could only be a fifty-fifty chance that it would be a boy. If it were not . . .

'Do you really believe Sir Bertram would carry out his threat to disinherit Guy?' she asked. 'Surely he knows how devoted Guy is to his home; how much work he puts into it? Why, if your brother-in-law were to become its manager there would be no benefit since he dislikes all forms of paperwork and has little interest in the land except as fodder for his horses!'

Verity was smiling despite herself. 'You have hit the nail very surely upon its head as far as Matthew is concerned!' she said. 'I try not to think too badly of him because he is, after all, Guy's half-brother, yet I wonder how it's possible that two men could be so opposite, not to mention Ket who is Matthew's full brother. Were ever two characters less similar?'

Charlotte nodded, afraid to speak lest the tone of her voice betrayed the emotion she felt whenever Ket's name was mentioned. He had written twice from the places where his latest adventure had taken him – once from Beirut and once from Crete. His letters to his half-brother and sister-in-law were fascinatingly descriptive of his surroundings, yet nevertheless revealed his light-hearted, enthusiastic approach to life and to his fellow travellers. He seemed entirely content with his nomadic existence, only in the last paragraph of each missive saying that he thought often of them all at Kneepwood, trusting they were well and adding that 'the charming Miss Charlotte' must be included in his heartfelt wishes for their good health and happiness. It was Guy's habit to read Ket's letters aloud at the breakfast table, and on each occasion Verity had turned to Charlotte with a knowing smile, saying: 'There, dearest, I told you Ket was not going to forget you in a hurry!'

It was madness to hope, Charlotte told herself now, yet more and more often she found herself daydreaming, lost in imaginary situations where, bored with his adventuring, Ket would return home wanting only to settle down to married life. Or appearing in his carriage hotfoot from Dover, filled with impatience to see her again! To fall on one knee and propose! To tell her that he had fallen hopelessly in love with

76

her and could not wait another minute to learn if she loved him in return. She was ashamed of such ridiculous thoughts and the undoubted insanity that prompted them. Ket had done no more than send her his good wishes! And prior to that, his friendliness had only once taken on a more intimate meaning. She could think of no logical reason for even the slightest supposition that he could consider her worthy of his serious attentions. Tossing and turning sleeplessly in her bed at night, Charlotte harshly reminded herself that she was now twenty-three years old and a spinster who should be well past the stupid, romantic dreaming that belonged to girlhood. Love and romance had long since passed her by and pretending otherwise, even momentarily, could bring her nothing but disillusionment and unhappiness.

Such stern cautioning did nothing, however, to stop her heart fluttering fiercely when, a week later at breakfast on New Year's Day, Guy held up a long, thin envelope with an unusual collection of heavily franked foreign stamps on it.

'In excellent time for Ket to wish us all well for 1888!' Guy said, smiling as he slit the envelope neatly with a knife.

'Though a trifle late for Christmas!' Verity said, returning Guy's smile. 'I suppose he won't yet have received my letter telling him how much we all missed him during the festivities.'

'I doubt *he* missed *us!*' Guy said with a wry lift of his eyebrows. 'Just listen to this eulogy from my fond brother!' He proceeded to read the first of four closely written pages. They contained a detailed account of his journey by boat up the Nile from Port Said; the ancient sites he and his fellow passengers had seen around Cairo; the astonishing stroke of luck that had enabled him to make this part of his journey in the utmost comfort and luxury:

I had the good fortune to meet my delightful companions by chance in Cairo. My American host, Mr John Copley, was enjoying a Mediterranean cruise in his yacht, Sunbeam *– a magnificent vessel that could accommodate ten times the numbers in his family*

who were travelling with him. I had befriended his
son, John Junior as he is known, who had managed
to lose himself in the bazaars in the medieval part of
the city. John introduced me to his family who, when
they heard I was intending to go to Port Said via the
Suez Canal, insisted I travel with them.

Guy stopped reading for a moment to look at his wife.
'Trust our Ket to land on his feet!' he said dryly. 'Next thing
we'll be reading that this Copley family have decided to sail
on to India in order to accommodate the fellow!'

'And why not?' Verity rejoined. 'Ket's such good company, I could well believe he'd be a most welcome guest –
don't you agree, Charlotte?'

Nodding, Charlotte rose to her feet, trying to hide the
heightened colour in her cheeks as she hurried to the sideboard to pour herself another cup of coffee.

'It would seem you're right, my dear!' Guy said as Charlotte
sat back down at the table. 'Listen to this next page.'

My new friend, John Junior, is a most agreeable
fellow and we enjoy many similar activities. On most
occasions we are accompanied by his twin sister,
Naomi, who is equally good company. She is also
a very handsome young woman with a surprisingly
independent manner, due in part to her upbringing
in the United States but also to her father's indul-
gence. Since childhood she has insisted upon the same
freedoms as her twin brother, and Mr Copley cannot
say her nay. The three of us have, therefore, been
able to enjoy many excursions without the tedium of
a chaperon.

John Junior has twice warned me that Naomi has
told him she intends to marry me and what Naomi
wants, she nearly always gets! However, I have made
it plain to him that I'm a hopeless adventurer with
no inclination to settle down to matrimony even if I
could afford it. It seems that there have been a goodly

*number of suitors for Naomi's hand, not just because
she's a very attractive girl but because of her dowry.
But I'm the first eligible man in whom she has shown
the slightest interest.*

*Of course, this is all very flattering but other than to
give you the excuse for a good laugh, I cannot believe
this affair can be of much interest to you. Nevertheless,
I can hear you, dear Verity, saying: 'But what does she
look like, Ket? Is she tall, short, dark, fair? Would I
like her? Is she elegant? What would your father think
of her?' And so on, so to satisfy your feminine curiosity,
I will enlighten you. Naomi is dark-haired, dark-eyed,
slim, fashionably dressed, neither short nor tall – if
anything, not unlike Miss Charlotte but a deal more
outspoken! I suppose Father would approve of the fact
that I'd be no further drain on him financially were I
to marry a rich wife. He once told me I should go out
and find one since I showed no inclination to earn my
own living!*

Here Guy broke off reading as Sir Bertram came into the
breakfast room. Guy knew instinctively that Ket wouldn't
want their father to read his letter; that Sir Bertram would
disapprove of the somewhat facetious tone in which it was
written, for Ket wrote without restraint, as freely as he
talked. Madcap he might be but he was always totally frank,
totally honest.

An hour later, when breakfast was over and Verity had
joined Guy in the study where he kept the estate books, he
read her the remainder of his brother's letter.

*I shall be remaining in Suez for the best part of a week
and then Mr Copley has decided to sail Sunbeam down
the Gulf of Suez. John Junior and I, and perhaps Naomi,
plan to explore where we dock on the way, after which
we hope to go on to the Red Sea. Naomi has just come
into the lounge and insists I send her kindest regards to
you all although she doesn't know you! She is going to*

*insist her father brings her to England before the end
of the year to meet you.*

'It sounds as if this girl is really serious about Ket!' Verity
said, frowning. 'She may be very nice – and very rich, too!
– but somehow I hope nothing comes of this.'

Guy looked at his wife in surprise. 'Do young Ket the
world of good to settle down,' he said. 'Surely you, of all
people, have no prejudices against the Americans? Why, you
even speak with the trace of an American accent!'

Verity flung herself into his arms. 'I know you're teasing
me, Guy, but if I do have an accent, it's Canadian, not
American. Anyway, darling, as far as Ket is concerned, I'll
let you into a secret. I want him to come home and marry
Charlotte.'

'Charlotte!' Guy echoed, kissing the tip of her nose. 'But
surely she is hardly the kind of girl to whom Ket is usually
attracted?'

'That's exactly it, Guy. She's different, special, and she'd
be wonderfully good for Ket.'

Guy's arm encircled her shoulders as he drew her closer.
'And you are matchmaking!' he said smiling, but his tone
became more serious. 'Don't count on Ket behaving as you
would wish,' he counselled. 'He may protest that this Naomi
girl is simply a "good friend" and "fun to be with", but the
two of them are going to be thrown together for quite some
time – and Ket is susceptible, even if he isn't the marrying
kind. If the girl handles him right – doesn't hold him on too
tight a rein – he could get to like the lifestyle she leads. But
I may be wrong. We'll just have to wait and see.'

'I hope you're wrong, dearest!' Verity said as, with a
sigh, she made her way to the door. Meanwhile, it would
perhaps be best to warn Charlotte that Guy thought this
friendship could come to mean something more serious. Guy
hadn't noticed, but she had seen Charlotte's blushes when he
had read out Ket's glowing report of the pretty fun-loving
American heiress.

80

Seven

February 1888

S taring out of Verity's bedroom window across the white
blanket of frost covering the lawns and flowerbeds,
Charlotte reflected that the weather duplicated her own and
Verity's spirits. The bitterly cold wind that now and again
swept small clouds of frost into angry swirls might as well
have been assaulting her heart, despite the heavy panes of
glass separating her from the elements.

I've no right to be feeling such self-pity! she reproached
herself. Not only had she been indescribably stupid to ever
imagine that Ket Conniston felt something deeper than friendship for her, but she had no right to be thinking of her own
unhappiness when poor Verity was so distraught – and
with good cause. She had yet again miscarried, and the
doctor had flatly forbidden her to conceive again. It was
highly dangerous for her to do so, he had reiterated, and
in fact he considered it somewhat of a miracle that she
had become pregnant this last time. He had repeated his
opinions to Guy who must now face the fact that he would
never have a son.

What right had she, Charlotte, to feel equally desolate
because she'd fallen in love like some silly schoolgirl with a
man whom she should have realized could never have loved
her. This very morning, Guy had received a further letter from
Ket, despatched from somewhere in India, announcing that he
and Naomi Copley were now engaged to be married.

Quickly, Charlotte brushed away the tears that were poised
to fall from her brimming eyes. It was high time she stopped
thinking about herself and did what she could to comfort

her friend. Pale, exhausted by her recent ordeal, Verity lay with her eyes closed, the epitome of despair. As Charlotte approached the bed to put a comforting arm around her, she began to sob quietly.

'I can bear the disappointment for myself but not for Guy!' Verity wept brokenly. 'I'd do anything in the world to make him happy yet I cannot give him the one thing in the world he wants!'

'I understand your feelings, dearest,' Charlotte whispered, 'for I would do anything in the whole wide world to make *you* happy, yet I cannot do so!'

Whilst the two young women clung to one another, seeking what comfort they could from each other's warmth and sympathy, downstairs Guy, too, was close to despair. Stretched out in one of the big leather wing chairs in the library, Matthew was puffing uneasily on one of his father's Havana cigars.

'Father said I should see you, Guy, as soon as you'd finished upstairs with Verity. Have to say I'm sorry she's lost another one. Still, there's always Bertie to keep the Conniston line going.'

'Bertie!' Guy echoed in a tight, furious voice. 'God forbid he ever has charge of Kneepwood. And don't try to defend him, Matt. This time he has gone too far and I hope you've seen fit to give him a good thrashing. Just don't let him near me for a while else I'll thrash him for you!'

The previous afternoon, Nanny had taken their two little girls, Kate and Lottie, to tea with their cousins at the dower house. Before tea the children had been permitted to put on their coats and go down to the stables to see the kittens, one of whom was promised to Kate as soon as it was old enough to leave its mother. From Kate's hysterical account later, it transpired that Bertie had put a match to this particular kitten's tail, then dropped it into the water butt and held the lid down until the wretched animal had drowned.

'All boys show off a bit at his age!' Matthew had tried to excuse his son. But he knew as well as Guy that it was by no means unusual for his son to exhibit signs of extreme

82

cruelty, shooting birds with his airgun and leaving them to a slow death with broken wings; throwing frogs on to the bonfire to see them explode; stealing into his younger siblings' night nursery and frightening them half to death with ghostly groaning and tales of terrible tortures awaiting them in the darkness.

'Come on now, Guy, you know as well as I do, boys will be boys – although as you have only girls perhaps you aren't aware of all the problems!'

In the light of the recent loss of Guy's last child, Matthew's jibe was indeed below the belt, and quickly he sought to lessen the barb. 'But you mustn't think I'm not sympathetic towards young Kate!' he said quickly. 'I've asked my valet, Bellamy, to go out this very morning and find the girl another kitten that she can have right away – soon make up for the loss, don't you know!'

'I hope you're right!' Guy said wearily. As usual Matthew had entirely missed the point, which was that Bertie should be obliged to acknowledge his behaviour for the cruel, sadistic action that it was. But to expect such compliance from the boy's father was a waste of time, for had Matthew himself not been similarly inclined when they were children? Since Guy had been older and therefore stronger, Matthew had not dared to bully him as he had once bullied young Ket. But before long his younger brother had learned how to defend himself and to give back as good as he got.

Matthew was now, once again, demanding a further loan, his voice placating as he quoted their father's agreement to it. For once he had the grace to look penitent as, in answer to Guy's direct questioning, he catalogued the debts he had recently accrued.

'Honestly, old chap, I only agreed to put money into the nag because she was a dead cert – that's to say, Carruthers convinced me she was bound to be a winner with her form. I was a bit short at the time or I'd never have signed that promissory note.'

'You've already used that excuse in the past!' Guy broke in wearily. 'When Father upped your allowance last year, it was on the clear understanding that you must manage on it. There simply aren't the funds to bale you out again!'

'Papa said there'd been an excellent harvest last summer and that there was plenty of money in the estate account!' Matthew protested forcibly. 'You're so damned tight-fisted, Guy – always were.'

Guy's mouth tightened. 'You've no right to say such a thing. I'm responsible for the running of Kneepwood, and whilst it's perfectly true that we had an exceptional harvest, that money has been earmarked for repairs to the cottages at Hollowbrook. You may not know it, but there's not one whose roof doesn't leak, and I've given my word . . .' He broke off, knowing he had little choice but to comply with his father's dictates. Yet he could hardly bring himself to write out the cheque. He had personally given his word to their tenants that repairs would be carried out this coming spring. The Horsham stone slabs had already been delivered and it awaited only the better weather to start work. How was he going to pay for the roofing now? From his own pocket by the look of it since the incomes from the farms would not carry that expense as well as Matthew's debts.

But it was not this particular debt of his brother's that was causing Guy such profound anxiety. It was the thought of the future. Once his father learned that he, Guy, would now never have a son, he would undoubtedly carry out his threat to bypass him in his will and bequeath Kneepwood to Matthew. What would then become of the place was beyond Guy's horrified imaginings. Even were Matthew to die prematurely, it would be his odious child, young Bertram, who would inherit. The thought was unbearable, yet must be borne, Guy realized.

Once Matthew had left, gleefully clutching his cheque in one large sweating hand, Guy knew he should go up to see his wife again and offer such comfort as he could. But for the moment he was too much in need of comfort himself. To lose Kneepwood would be to lose what he valued most in his life – valued even beyond his much loved family. Verity and the little girls had been a part of his life for a few years only whereas he had been born a part of Kneepwood. He knew every brick and stone of the house; every tree, hillock, ditch and coppice on the land. His rapport with his tenant farmers was one of deeply affectionate trust and he would have died rather than betray any one of them.

Unable to bear his thoughts Guy went down to the stables and when his black stallion, Nightwind, was saddled, he rode off at a gallop to the furthest edge of the estate where the pine forest fringed old Jim Collins' land. In its cold, dark interior he hoped he might find solace.

Although Charlotte was aware of Guy's precipitate departure when she went at Verity's request to find him, she tried to keep the nature of his absence from her. But Verity guessed immediately that he was avoiding her.

'He wouldn't be so cruel, Verity!' Charlotte protested. 'There must have been some other reason for his hurried departure.'

'No, Charlotte, Guy doesn't mean to be cruel. It's because he is afraid of hurting me by revealing his pain, his disappointment, that he has gone. He will be back this evening, you'll see, and he'll behave as if it is of little consequence that I have failed him yet again.'

Charlotte grasped her friend's hand and held it tightly. 'You haven't failed, dearest. You must never think that. It's not your fault – it's God will.'

'Don't speak to me of God!' Verity said bitterly. 'No one could have prayed more devoutly than I. Yet on each occasion I have either produced girls or been unable to carry the baby full term.'

'Guy loves his daughters, just as you do!' Charlotte protested.

'That is indisputable – but it's a son he needs; a son he *must* have if he is to keep Kneepwood. You don't know my father-in-law as I do, Charlotte. He doesn't love Guy – not as he loves Matthew and that odious boy, Bertie. They're like him, you see, whereas Guy resembles the mother Sir Bertram hated. He once told me she had cheated him by dying when she did! That she was a weak, useless female who had never learned how to pleasure him in bed. Can you imagine any father-in-law, no matter how deep in his cups, saying such a thing to his son's wife? It was as if he was challenging me to "pleasure" Guy – and since I have given Guy only daughters, he has treated us both with ill-concealed contempt. That Guy and I love one another so deeply is of little consequence to him. He wants a clutch of strong, lusty grandsons who take after him.'

It was on the tip of Charlotte's tongue to retort: 'Well, let Matthew give them to him!' but she bit back the words. That was all too likely to happen and then Guy would lose Kneepwood.

With a deep sigh, she sat down on the edge of the bed and looked into Verity's tragic eyes. 'You know, don't you, that there is nothing in the whole world I wouldn't do for you if it were within my power. It breaks my heart to see you so unhappy and to know there's nothing I can do.'

A wry smile twisted Verity's mouth. 'I do believe you, dearest, but there's only one thing in the world I need to make me happy – a son, and that you cannot give me.'

The bitterness in her voice cut Charlotte to the heart. 'I would give you my own son if I had one!' she declared, close to tears herself. 'If I could bear a child for you I would do so, not only because I love you dearly but also because I owe both you and Guy so much. I'd give everything I have to be able to say to you both: "Here is the little son you both want and need".'

Tears of emotion rolled down her cheeks as, surprisingly, Verity's tears dried. She was regarding Charlotte's face with deep intensity. 'You really mean that, don't you?' she said in a soft, questioning tone. 'For a moment, I felt a surge of hope – that somehow you and I might arrange for you to have a child for me . . . It would be a boy, of course – and Guy could go to his father and say: "You will never be able to deride me or my wife again. You will never again need to threaten to take Kneepwood Court and estates from me and hand them to my worthless half-brother. You . . ."' As suddenly as she had begun, her voice failed and she dissolved once more into quiet sobs. 'What madness ever to suppose for a single instant that such a thing was possible!' she whispered. 'And even were it so, it would be beyond all bounds of friendship for you to contemplate such a thing.'

Charlotte's tears had ceased and now her eyes were bright with a burning excitement. 'Why shouldn't I bear a child for you if I can do so?' she said earnestly. 'I shall never marry – I have told you this many times – and so I shall have no children of my own.'

Momentarily the light left her eyes and she looked desolate. Not more than a few days ago, she had secretly nurtured the hope that Ket might one day fall in love with her – maybe marry her, take her with him on his travels. That dream was instantly shattered when Guy had read out the news of Ket's engagement to Naomi Copley, the rich American heiress. Verity couldn't know it, but Charlotte's life had no purpose now. Were it possible for her to devote herself to making Verity and Guy happy, she would gladly do so.

As she repeated this to Verity, she could not fail to see the renewed hope in her friend's eyes even whilst she reiterated that she could never allow Charlotte to make such a sacrifice.

'And what is it I would be sacrificing?' Charlotte asked. 'If I were to have a child for you to present as your own, we would have to arrange matters with total secrecy. No one should ever know that I was with child and you were not; that I had given birth and you had not. As long as this secrecy were possible, we would have nothing to fear.'

Verity drew a long, trembling breath. 'I do believe you are serious about this, Charlotte. Can we really even be thinking about such a thing? Besides, I couldn't keep it from Guy – and I doubt if he would ever approve of . . . of what would unquestionably be deceit . . . to his father . . . to Matthew. I suppose it would depend how great his love for Kneepwood is – how little the degree of responsibility he feels for his father, for Matthew. Sir Bertram wants Guy to have a son so that the family name is established in direct line. It's no fault of Guy's that my body is too weak to carry a child full term, but you are strong and healthy, Charlotte, and would not miscarry as I have done.'

The brief flash of excitement in her eyes faded suddenly as her thoughts took an opposite turn. She grasped Charlotte's hand. 'This is madness. I believe I'm truly a little insane to be thinking such thoughts. It's wrong of you to be encouraging me, Charlotte. It is *madness*! How can you look so sane, so normal? I'm beginning to believe I'm dreaming.'

It was a moment or two before Charlotte could bring herself to reply. Her own thoughts had carried her in a different direction. When she had said she would bear a child for Verity, it had not immediately occurred to her that she would need a man to father that child; *that for it to be a Conniston, it must be Guy's child.* Could Verity have realized that her beloved husband would have to take her, Charlotte to bed and . . . Her thoughts ceased at this point, for she had no idea how a child was conceived – only that the man and woman must lie together. She knew it wasn't necessary for them to love one another, for wasn't Daisy about to produce Matthew's child, born not of love but of drunken rape? Perhaps Verity was right and this idea was beyond all reason; that Guy, for one, wouldn't contemplate such a deception. And even if he did, how could the necessary secrecy ever be achieved? Maybe for a few months no one would guess that she was with child and that Verity was not. She could go away once it became obvious that she was pregnant. Verity could far less easily conceal the fact that she was *not* carrying a child. Her maid who dressed and undressed her would know. The doctor would most certainly know. She and Verity would have to go away – far away, abroad perhaps, only returning to England after the baby was born. And after all that, what if it were not a boy but another girl?

As if her own thoughts had been travelling the same route as Charlotte's, Verity said: 'If by some miracle Guy were to agree, Charlotte, and yet despite all our caution you gave birth to a girl, I would still take care of it, bring it up as my own. You would never need to fear that I would desert you or the child.'

Charlotte managed a weak smile as she put her arms round Verity and hugged her. 'Of all the misgivings I might have about this crazy notion,' she said, 'I would never doubt your integrity, dearest.'

Verity returned her embrace but her eyes quickly clouded once more. 'Suppose you were to bear the infant and discover that you couldn't contemplate parting from it? I don't think I could have given away either of my little girls once the midwife had placed them in my arms. We would have to make some arrangement so that we could share the child.'

She paused, her tears drying as she concentrated upon this new problem. Then, forgetting her former misgivings, she looked up at Charlotte excitedly. 'Why, I can think at once of what we could do. I could make you the children's governess. That way you would never have to be parted from your child. It would mean I could always look after you – know you would always be part of our family.'

She paused for breath, her face now bright with animation as it had not been since she had miscarried. It was at this juncture that there was a knock on the bedroom door and Guy came into the room. His face barely concealed his relief as he bent to kiss her forehead.

'So you are feeling better, my sweetheart?' he enquired. 'Charlotte has managed to cheer you a little?'

Verity grasped his hand and held it tightly between her own. 'Oh, Guy, we've had such a wonderful idea. We have been planning . . . a madcap plan, you will call it . . . but it could work, Guy, my darling. I really believe it to be possible. The loss of this baby wouldn't be quite so terrible, and it would mean everything would be all right if you would but agree. You may think it insane, impossible, unreasonable, unethical, but even if it is all these things, *it could work if you were agreeable . . .*'

'Hush, my love, you are becoming overexcited,' Guy said, noting her flushed cheeks and feverish speech. 'You mustn't worry that I will disagree with anything you want, my darling.

My only wish is that you should be happy. I can't bear to see you weep, as well you know. Just to see the sparkle back in your eyes is enough to fill me with joy. So, whatever this madcap scheme is that you two girls have devised, I shall support you if it's humanly possible. Does that promise please you?'

With increasing bewilderment, he looked from Charlotte's anxious expression to the concern in his wife's. Without being aware of it he held his breath as he waited for one or other to speak. It was Verity who did so. 'It's only fair that you have the right to know what we have been planning *before* you give your agreement,' she said quietly. 'So I won't hold you to your promise.'

Guy attempted to lighten the tension in the room. 'And what is so earth-shattering that you feel obliged to release me from my word?' he enquired, looking from Charlotte to Verity. Charlotte remained silent, biting her lip. Verity, however, drew a deep breath as she said in a rush of words: 'Our plan concerns you, Guy. You see, darling, you have to give Charlotte a child and she will give it to me – it's to be hoped it will be a boy. No one but the three of us will ever know the truth and, most importantly, your father will believe it is ours. It's a wonderful, perfect plan and I'm so excited by the thought of it! Charlotte has agreed and if you, too, will agree, my darling, then what seemed like a crazy dream can become a reality. So will you still promise to support us, Guy?'

It was a moment before he spoke. Then he stood up and said quietly: 'I'm going to send Nora for the doctor, Verity. I think you are feverish and unwell.'

Disregarding Verity's cry of protest, he went quickly to the door and closed it firmly behind him, leaving Charlotte and Verity in no doubt that there was no way he would ever give his consent to their preposterous scheme.

Eight

T o Verity's dismay, Guy did indeed send for the doctor. Whilst awaiting his arrival, Verity swore Charlotte to secrecy about their plan although she had no need to do so. Having seen Guy's reaction, Charlotte herself was having doubts as to Verity's state of mind – and indeed her own. It was not that she was any the less willing to bear a child and give it to Verity if it were possible; it was the thought of what must be done to achieve that; the lies, deceit, duplicity, intrigue. And not least, it would mean that she must lie with a man who was not her husband, thereby forcing him to commit adultery with his wife's best friend. Even if Verity believed her motive was to give Guy his heart's desire, that made it no less immoral.

Beseiged by doubts, she questioned whether the time might come when Verity would regret having encouraged Guy's adultery, no matter what the purpose. Perhaps she might turn against the child. And would she, Charlotte, despite her present beliefs, find herself unable to give up the baby when it was born? Moreover it was time she faced the fact that, however unlikely the possibility, there could never be a marriage for her when this deed was done. Was she really ready to confine her future to spending the rest of her life as a governess in the Conniston household?

Charlotte's thoughts returned inevitably to the life she had spent working for Madame Hortense and living in poverty in those freezing, threadbare rooms in Clerkenwell on the brink of starvation. To be a governess for Verity and Guy and live beneath the same roof as the child she might give them, was surely not far short of heaven by comparison. And it was to Verity she owned the miraculous change in her fortunes – a debt she might now be able to repay.

The doctor could find nothing seriously wrong with Verity other than a slightly heightened fever. He prescribed rest and complete quiet. Guy would hear of nothing less and refused even to consider renewing the discussion that had precipitated the doctor's visit. 'I can't believe that you were in your right senses when you propounded your scheme to me, my darling,' he said, bending to kiss Verity's cheek as he prepared to leave the room. On the doctor's instructions, Charlotte had drawn the curtains so that the room was in semi-darkness. Guy cast a quick, puzzled glance at Charlotte.

'I trust you've done your best to discourage my wife from voicing such a fanciful – indeed, I would say hysterical – idea. I think it might be best if we both now leave my poor darling to sleep.'

Verity reached out and caught the sleeve of Guy's morning coat. 'You must go if that's your wish, Guy, but don't take Charlotte from me. I don't want to be alone and Charlotte is such a comfort to me.'

Guy gave a reluctant sigh. 'Very well! But I want no more crazy talk of births and inheritances and the like. Talk of jollier subjects. Charlotte, I have here a letter I received today from Ket which I've not yet had time to read. You may read it to Verity who I know will find it vastly entertaining.'

As he bent to kiss his wife's forehead, neither of them saw the colour which had yet again flooded into Charlotte's cheeks. Crazy as it seemed, even the touch of Ket's letter was enough to evoke a breathless expectancy. Not many weeks since, his hand had touched these very pages. His thoughts had been of home, of his family – perhaps even once or twice of her. She couldn't wait to read the words, yet when Guy had left the room, Verity took the letter and laid it on the counterpane.

'We don't want to waste time hearing what darling Ket has been up to. I dare say his letter is full of his precious Miss Naomi Copley. Men are such bores when they fall in love . . . unless . . .' She gave a mischievous smile. 'Unless it is oneself with whom they have fallen in love! But enough of Ket – what of our scheme, Charlotte? You haven't let Guy's reactions bring about a change of heart, have you, dearest?'

Charlotte drew a deep sigh as she walked to the window and opened the curtains a little way so that the sunshine could lighten the room somewhat, and perhaps by some miraculous association, lighten her heart. 'It's not Guy who has made me wonder if we would be doing the right thing, Verity, it is the ethical implications. Have we the right – you and I – to deceive the whole world, even the child itself who could never know the truth? I share your dislike of your father-in-law and indeed, of Matthew and Bertie, but would we not be unprincipled, to say the very least, if we were to deceive them in such a manner and disinherit not only Matthew but his worthless young son?'

Verity was listening with a profundity unusual to her. 'I understand what you're implying, Charlotte, and I do agree with you in part. Our purpose, though, isn't to benefit ourselves but to save Kneepwood; to give Guy the security of the future. No one could disagree that he would make the better custodian of Kneepwood – and that, after all, is what my father-in-law wants far more than he wants to please his favourite son. He blinds himself to Matthew's faults, but one day those faults in his character will reveal themselves in such a way that Sir Bertram will see him for what he is – provided he lives long enough to do so. That's a gamble no sane person would want to take. If only Guy's mother had lived until six years ago, the new Marriage Act would have allowed her to will Kneepwood to Guy. As it stood when she married, her estate of course became my father-in-law's. So, Charlotte, it must not go to Matthew. If it's within my power, I *have* to secure Kneepwood for Guy.'

'Is there . . . no other way?' Charlotte asked tentatively. 'Has the doctor really ruled out any chance of you having another child?'

Verity nodded, her lips trembling as she whispered: 'He is in little doubt. I might conceive again but he maintains

93

my womb will not support a baby beyond a few months' development. Oh, Charlotte, if we could only transfer my baby into your body! But what's the purpose in crying for the moon. There's no other way than the one we have thought of.' Her voice became almost a whisper as she added, 'If you don't wish to make this enormous sacrifice, I shall understand. I have no right whatever to ask it of you. After all, why should you sacrifice your future for Guy and Kneepwood?'

Charlotte was silent. It was not a sacrifice she was making for them, she thought. For the most part it would be for Verity who had given her a new life when the alternative might have been poverty and the drudgery of working for Madame Hortense until she died, or worse still, she might have become the mistress of Madame's middle-aged solicitor whose name she couldn't now remember. No, she would have no regrets about renouncing either such future now that she knew the one man she might have married was engaged to someone else. On the contrary, planning and carrying out such a scheme might give some real purpose to her otherwise inconsequential life. The misgivings she now had were of the vastness of the deception their plan necessitated. Did Verity not feel as apprehensive as herself about this deceit?

'I'm trying not to think about that side of it!' Verity declared honestly. 'Don't you see, dearest, that our duplicity will pale into insignificance beside the need to secure Kneepwood for Guy.'

Charlotte bit her lip. 'I doubt if Guy wants Kneepwood at such a price!' she said.

Verity's flushed cheeks paled. 'I fear you may be right – he has such high morals. But I believe I can persuade him, Charlotte. He might not agree for his own benefit but he desires my happiness above his own. He's already aware that I always blame myself for failing to produce a son for him; and for the fact that I quite shamelessly stole his heart from poor Eleanor Sinclair who he might well have married had I not set my heart upon him! Did you know that Eleanor married the new vicar at Withyham on the rebound when Guy

94

married me and has already borne him four sons? Sir Bertram reminds me of this each time I miscarry!'

'But that's so cruel!' Charlotte protested. 'How could he do such a thing?'

'Quite easily!' Verity replied sadly. 'You may have noticed that he never asks Nanny to bring Kate and Lottie to see him although he often requests visits from Matthew's brood. When he passes my girls in a corridor or in the garden, he barely greets them other than to say: "You must be from Guy's stable – pity he can only breed fillies!" Poor little Kate asked me not a week since why her grandfather disliked her, for it was clear to her that he did.'

Charlotte could say nothing to comfort Verity since she had seen for herself that Sir Bertram never tried to conceal his likes or dislikes. He fawned over Bertie and made light of the boy's sadistic inclinations. Cutting off a frog's leg in order to see it trying, unsuccessfully, to jump was no more than a scientific investigation, he had argued in the boy's defence. And as for Bertie shooting the garden birds, how else was the boy to practise the use of firearms unless with a moving target? A year or two on, Bertie would be taking part in his grandfather's shoot and Sir Bertram intended to be proud of him.

'I know how little Sir Bertram seems to care about Guy,' Charlotte said, 'but what of Ket? Didn't you tell me that his father infinitely preferred Ket to Guy?'

'Yes, indeed, but not in quite the same way as he idolizes Matthew who is most like him both in looks and character. It was different with Ket who refused to be intimidated by his father. He never cried but would laugh off his punishments if he couldn't talk his way out of them. Guy told me Ket's boyhood at Kneepwood was relatively easy for him. Everyone loved him – all the staff, his siblings, his mother. Sir Bertram, like all bullies, respected the person whose character he realized was stronger even than his own.'

'But as their father, Sir Bertram must have had total power over all his children, including Ket.'

'Yes, that was so, but he didn't have power over Ket's

95

spirit, which remained totally free. As soon as Ket had completed his schooling – and he was an excellent scholar and enjoyed his school days – he went off adventuring. When Sir Bertram refused to fund his adventures, Ket found work to finance himself. Once Sir Bertram realized he couldn't control Ket's adventuring by financial deprivation he relented and gave him an allowance – not from any altruistic motive, but because he didn't want a Conniston selling his labour and giving people the impression his father was too poor to indulge him.'

Charlotte went over to the side of the bed to sit down in the chair she had earlier vacated. 'It sounds as if your father-in-law is ashamed of his roots,' she said thoughtfully.

'Undoubtedly so!' Verity agreed. 'His life has been spent creating a new dynasty – the Conniston dynasty – and it must all be perfect. That was why he married Guy's mother. I can't understand how he came to marry his housekeeper when Lady Conniston died – perhaps by then he believed himself rich enough to be above local gossip. Enid had the good sense to stay out of society, or else Sir Bertram persuaded her to. In any event, I or Monica have acted as hostess for him when he entertained. If the poor woman lived, I suppose she would have had to come out of her seclusion in order to see her younger son married. I hope Ket's wedding will be soon, Charlotte, so that we need not delay our plans. I should hate to be in Europe and unable to see darling Ket wed his American heiress.'

Charlotte clasped her hands tightly together to disguise their shaking. Could she bear to see Ket watching his adoring American bride walk up the aisle towards him? However charming, sweet, intelligent and attractive, could Charlotte ever like the woman who had captured Ket's heart? And what madness possessed her to think in such a fashion! Ket had never been hers; had never given her one reason to suppose that he might want her for his wife, unless it was that single stolen kiss after the Morrisons' party. Quite possibly these strange, violent emotions that churned inside her were a mild form of insanity. To have imagined for one instant that Ket's kiss was borne of love was in itself insane.

'Charlotte, I'm frightened by the look of distress on your face.' Verity's urgent tone was indicative of her genuine concern. 'I think we should forget everything we've talked about . . . about you having a baby for Guy and me. Guy is right – it's madness and I hate myself for being so selfish as to have ever considered it. Please forgive me, dearest.'

It was at that moment Charlotte realized how truly her friend cared about her. For her sake, Verity was prepared to set aside the wish closest to her heart – and the declaration had not been lightly made. She forced a smile to her lips. 'It wasn't madness, and you weren't being selfish, my dear friend. It was I who suggested I give you a child. It's what I want to do; what will give me, as well as you and Guy, great happiness. You need have no doubt that it's my wish to carry out our plan – if Guy can somehow be persuaded. You think you can prevail upon him but I don't share your certainty. I know how much he loves you but he is a man of great probity and . . .'

'And we talk in circles,' Verity said softly. 'Don't worry about Guy. I *shall* persuade him. I'm so happy that you, at least, are really willing to undertake this adventure – for that is what it will be, dearest. I have been thinking about how we could manage matters once the baby begins to show. We can take a trip abroad to Switzerland perhaps, or to France, where it would be near enough for Guy to visit. He wouldn't want to leave Kneepwood for any great length of time but we would have to remain abroad until the baby was born. So, one of us could be struck down with some mysterious illness prohibiting our return from our holiday. Guy could visit us and, on his return home, announce that I was once again with child and a foreign doctor had insisted I remain in bed. Oh, Charlotte, it will all be possible – even easy – don't you see? I hardly dare say so but I am beginning to be so excited.'

Perhaps the part of the plan Verity had described would be easy, Charlotte thought, but she had ignored what must come beforehand – the making of the baby. Even in the unlikely event that Guy were to put his principles to one side and agree to the project, would he be willing to make her pregnant? Perhaps it was time for her to pay Madame Hortense another visit. Madame would be able to tell her what took place between a man and a woman that made a baby. Verity would tell her if she asked, but that would be an embarrassment for them both. No, if Guy were persuaded to go along with Verity's plans, she would go and see Madame.

As Verity lay back against her pillows, she said, smiling: 'I am so happy, Charlotte. It's as if the past shadows have left me and I can look forward to the future again. I think I might even sleep a little while. But you look pale, dearest. You must take a walk in the garden and put some colour back into your cheeks whilst I rest. Here, take Ket's letter with you – it is several pages long. You can read it and later tell me a shortened version of his news.'

Charlotte had no choice but to do as Verity suggested lest she suspect that Charlotte was very far from disinterested in her brother-in-law's affairs. *No one must ever know*, she vowed silently as she went along the landing to take a warm ulster coat and hat from her wardrobe. Although the sun shone, she knew she would need gloves and a muff as well as her overcoat if she were to remain outdoors for long.

There was no sign of Guy in the hall and she supposed he had retired to his study. The library door was closed, behind which Sir Bertram would undoubtedly be taking his afternoon nap. Apart from a parlourmaid scuttling through the green baize door to the kitchens there was no one to be seen. Nor was there a sound from Verity's children, who would most probably be enjoying a perambulation with Nanny.

The thought of the two little girls brought Charlotte's mind sharply back to the child she might one day be carrying. Quickly she put the topic out of her mind. She would do as Verity asked, which she now admitted she herself desired to do. She would go down to the summerhouse by the shrubbery and read Ket's letter. Even knowing that it could only distress her, momentarily at least it would bring him close, for he wrote very much as he spoke – delightfully so.

My dear family,

I can't give you an address since we are constantly on the move. Mr Copley decided not to sell Sunbeam *and we sail in her daily from one port to another. John is a most restless fellow and is always pressing his father to up anchor and set sail for another new experience.*

I trust this does not give you the impression that I like the fellow any the less than I did on first meeting him. He is the jolliest companion, as is Naomi who, perhaps because she is John's twin, quite often behaves as if she too were a boy. She swims faster even than her brother but has not yet been able to outdistance yours truly! We have been hill climbing and Naomi will hitch up her skirt and petticoats and fasten them in such a manner you would think them pantaloons. The servants who accompany us are clearly quite shocked but she pays them no heed and is invariably in good heart at all times.

There followed an account of all the towns and countries they had visited, the sights they had seen, the curios and mementoes Mr Copley had purchased that filled three packing cases, and the clothes Naomi had bought but openly confessed she might never wear.

It's a constant source of amazement to me how indifferent Mr Copley is to the cost of things, but I suppose he has no need to enquire a price since he can afford whatever takes his fancy. Naomi and John are no different and all three are so generous that I have to keep my wits about me to maintain my independence. Naomi tells me I should forget my stupid English pride but, although she doesn't understand, I know you will. As far as I can, I must pay my own way.

I looked for a letter from home when we were in Port Said but alas, there was none. Was I silly to hope that little Miss Charlotte might have sent me an account of herself? Has Guy found a horse for you so you can start riding again? I can picture you looking most becoming in a riding habit with a black top hat, silk scarf wrapped around it, atop your chestnut hair. Guy should give you Copper to ride, for you would make the most excellent match.

Charlotte pressed the pages against her heart, her eyes closed as she tried to conjure up the image of Ket's laughing eyes; the serious note of his voice when he had insisted she took up riding again so that when he next returned to England she could go out hunting in the season. 'It's wonderful sport!' he had declared with boyish enthusiasm. 'Except perhaps at the kill – but you needn't stay to watch that if you prefer. Why, I almost wish I weren't going abroad so soon and I could teach you myself!'

Had she been deluding herself to believe that Ket was a little attracted to her? Charlotte asked herself now. Had he been merely flirting, or was it just his natural friendliness? There was no purpose speculating on the past, she told herself sharply. Ket made no secret of his feelings now. He loved Naomi Copley and was engaged to marry her. There had been no mention as yet in his letter of a possible wedding date but, as she read on, she gathered that the Copley family intended to end their tour next autumn when they would sail to England and – the Connistons and God willing – would spend some time at Kneepwood as Ket's guests.

I can never repay their hospitality, but I know you will all make them very welcome and we must, of course, have a big party so that I can introduce Naomi to our friends. I know she will love you all and you will not fail to love her, for she is such tremendous fun and so jolly to everyone she meets.

Hot tears welled on to Charlotte's cheeks. It wasn't fair, she wept childishly. She, too, might have been 'tremendous fun' and 'so jolly' if her life had been as diamond-studded as Naomi Copley's.

Through the blur of her tears Charlotte could see in a corner of the summerhouse the set of croquet mallets and hoops which would be in evidence again once the summer sunshine had dried the croquet lawn. Guy, Verity, Ket and herself had enjoyed such fun during late autumn afternoons. The two brothers had been fiercely competitive and urged Verity and herself to stop laughing and take the game seriously, but they, too, had been laughing. Once the game was over, if she and Ket had been victorious, he would drop his mallet and, putting his hands round her waist, would swing her around in a victory whirl, showering her with compliments for her excellent play.

Oh, Ket, she thought now as she tried to stem the tears that were still falling down her cheeks, it was such fun and I loved you so much. Was I misleading myself thinking that you, too, were a little in love with me? Or was it just that we were all so carefree and happy?

Suddenly Charlotte stopped crying as the tiniest glimmer of hope crept into her mind. Ket had said in his letter that they wouldn't be coming to England until next autumn – that was a long, long time away. They wouldn't be setting a wedding date before he had introduced Naomi to his family. Wasn't it possible that between now and then the two might find they were not so compatible after all? That Miss Copley might decide she disliked Ket's flirtatious ways with other females? That they might quarrel? That she might find someone she fancied more than Ket?

Unlikely though these hopes might be, an engagement was not binding and things did go wrong between betrothed couples. With a fiercely beating heart, Charlotte decided that she must confess to Verity the secret love she felt for Ket. Verity would understand then why she could not at present further their plan for her to have Guy's child, since it would put paid to any hope she might have of Ket falling in love with her.

Slowly, Charlotte rose to her feet and, smoothing her skirts, began to make her way back to the house. Strangely, she did not regret the offer she had made Verity, nor was she any less willing to go through with it. But now it must be conditional so that she could continue for a little while longer believing that, however much Ket loved Miss Naomi Copley, he was not entirely indifferent to her.

Verity might be momentarily disappointed, Charlotte warned herself, but almost as if the two girls' emotions were working in harmony, whilst Charlotte had been away Verity herself had had second thoughts. When Charlotte had first declared that she would more than willingly have a child for her, it had seemed as if the dark cloud of depression and hopelessness had been miraculously dispersed and light had come back into her heart and mind. It wasn't as if she had ever wanted this next child for herself – only for Guy, who she would always feel she had failed. Other than for Guy, she hadn't even wanted the baby she had just lost. The fact that it had been the boy Guy wanted had devastated her for his sake rather than her own. If Charlotte were now to have a son for them it would be the perfect solution, since it would still be Guy's child if not her own.

Unaware of the tears Charlotte had been shedding in the privacy of the summerhouse, as the hour passed new and unwelcome thoughts began to seep into Verity's mind. Much as Guy wanted a son and heir, he was not a man to whom deceit and duplicity came easily, however necessary they were. Somehow she would have to persuade him that the welfare of Kneepwood and all its tenants must be his first concern. He owed nothing to Matthew and to his father. Even if Guy could be persuaded, what of Charlotte's future? If their plan succeeded, no one would know she had borne a child, but a husband would know at once that she was not a virgin. Charlotte had the right to have children of her own to love, and to love and comfort *her* in her old age. And although in her capacity as governess Charlotte could love and care for the child she would have for Guy and herself, that child would never know Charlotte was its mother or call her such by name.

The extreme selfishness of their plan now struck Verity with such force that the moment Charlotte came back into the room she burst into tears. As Charlotte hurried forward to take her in her arms, she confessed her disgust with herself for even momentarily accepting Charlotte's offer. 'The whole scheme was totally unfair to you, dearest,' she wept. 'I'm so ashamed of myself for considering it.'

For a moment Charlotte couldn't find words to express her feelings. Verity's change of heart meant that for the time being she needn't confess why she must see Ket once again or see him married before she would irrevocably jeopardize her future. Nevertheless, she realized what it must be costing Verity to relinquish what had appeared to be the perfect solution to her problems.

'Look, Verity, mightn't it be sensible for us to postpone any decisions at this moment? You are still weak and perhaps not thinking as clearly as you should be for such a momentous undertaking. We must take time to consider this very carefully. First you must get well, then we'll have to plan the timing of such a venture. In the autumn for example, should we decide to go ahead, Ket said he would be coming to stay with his fiancée and her family. That's no time for us to be "holidaying" abroad. Then you will have to persuade Guy to agree. Don't you see, Verity, so many people would be affected by what we want to do; not just you and me, but Guy, your little girls, your father-in-law, Matthew and his family, even the child itself. And not least we should consider the possibility that we might be discovered in our enterprise.'

Verity's face was very pale, her eyes enormous as she returned Charlotte's gaze. 'You're right, dearest, we mustn't be impulsive. I will never again allow myself to forget that it would be I who would gain and you who would be the loser. Both Guy and I have said that we want to see you safely married with a happy future ahead of you. I still want that and even if you don't agree now that such a possibility exists, I am certain you would agree were you to meet the right person. Let's see what can be done during these next six months – a year maybe – to find you a husband of your own.'

For the first time that day, Charlotte smiled. 'Dearest Verity, I don't want you to find me a husband. Have you forgotten that I am twenty-three years of age? I'm perfectly content living here at Kneepwood with you and Guy and the children. If you allow me, I shall continue to do so until I am an old maid.' Or unless by some miracle Ket were to break his engagement and fall in love with me, Charlotte thought. Knowing how absurd such a thought was the expression on her face became instantly wistful.

She would have been a great deal sadder had she been able to anticipate Ket's next letter home. Mr Copley had been called back to the States on urgent business. They were cancelling their plans to travel on to Ceylon and would be going directly to America instead. Ket had written to Guy:

> *Naomi thinks it might be a good idea for us to get married from her home this coming summer. Her father would be delighted to send all of you tickets to travel out on the* SS Etruria, *including the children. I think he'd quite enjoy chartering the whole ship if you needed it! You'll be getting official invitations soon but thought I'd drop you a line and forewarn you of events. Can you believe that in less than three months your nomadic brother will be a married man?*

Charlotte did not read the rest of Ket's long letter. As far as she was concerned, she had read all she needed to know.

Nine

March–October 1888

'**M**y dear child, I shall not ask you to betray any confidences, as I'm well aware you are far too ethical to do so.' Madame Hortense's words were softly spoken but nonetheless emphatic as she continued: 'These questions you have just asked me on behalf of this so-called friend are in fact for yourself, if I'm not very much mistaken.'

She looked at the horrified expression on Charlotte's face and felt a second wave of deep concern. '"How do a husband and wife beget a child?"' she quoted. '"If this performance is accomplished, would the wife conceive of a certainty? Are there special times in this monthly cycle you talk of when a child might not be conceived or definitely will be?" And so on and so on. What sort of questions are these, Charlotte, for a young unmarried girl to be asking? Why, I ask myself, can this "friend" not enquire for herself? Surely if she is married, as you say, she must know by now how married couples are united?'

Her voice, which had risen, now softened again. 'Don't take me for a fool, Charlotte. Believe me, I am truly your friend and I am flattered that you should come to me for advice, but I would prefer you treat me as an honourable confidante who you may trust absolutely.'

Charlotte felt close to tears. For days now she had tried to steel herself to visit Madame Hortense and ask her advice. There was, after all, no one else to whom she could turn. It seemed indelicate to ask Verity, of all people, what her husband actually did when he went to her bed. It must be awful enough for Verity to know that the man she loved was intending to lie with another woman. No, it would not be akin to adultery, Verity had insisted. It would merely be a transaction between consenting adults with no emotion involved. It would happen only once in some insignificant, unknown hotel where Charlotte would stay the night. At some time that night, Guy would come to her room. There need be no lamp lit, no words spoken and he would leave her afterwards as surreptitiously as he had arrived.

It was all very well for Verity to make everything sound so simple, Charlotte thought, but now, thanks to Madame Hortense, she had a very good idea of what would happen and she was appalled. With little knowledge of the facts of life, Charlotte had given no serious thought to the physical aspect of their plan. Unwilling to dwell on this new and disturbing information, Charlotte turned her thoughts back to the woman sitting opposite her. They were seated either side of the fireplace in Madame Hortense's apartment above the shop. Her Pomeranian dog, Daybreak, lay curled on her broad lap snuffling as it slept whilst Madame stroked its thick orange coat absent-mindedly. She had been delighted to see Charlotte again and they had enjoyed a really happy reunion until after they'd finished tea and Madame had enquired as to the reason for her visit. In her letter Charlotte had said that she needed advice 'on a rather delicate matter'.

'I don't want to lie to you, Madame,' Charlotte said now, 'so I won't deny that it is for myself that I ask these questions. I pretended otherwise only because I feared you would not give your approval to my intentions and would of a certainty try to dissuade me from them.'

Madame Hortense frowned, only with difficulty hiding her anxiety on hearing Charlotte's admission. 'Do I detect a fear that I might succeed in dissuading you from them, Charlotte?' she enquired.

Charlotte shook her head vigorously. 'No, that wouldn't be possible, for I have agreed wholeheartedly to go through with this plan which, in point of fact, was of my own devising.'

Madame Hortense could certainly do or say nothing to prevent her having a child for Verity if it were possible,

Charlotte thought. Only Ket could have done that – and Ket was on the verge of marriage to the American girl. Although the Conniston family's planned visit to the United States for Ket's wedding had had to be cancelled because of the sudden tragic death of Naomi's grandmother, Ket and Naomi were still going to be married after a suitable interval – very quietly, of course, with only a few friends and relations present. Ket had written at length of the tragedy and its aftermath.

Not only Mr Copley but my poor Naomi and John are deeply distressed and shocked by old Mrs Copley's passing, which was unexpected. She had the very best doctors, as you will suppose, but it seemed she suffered a massive stroke and lasted only three further days, never regaining consciousness.

As you can imagine, this isn't a very happy household in which to be residing and there is so little I can do to comfort them. Naomi agrees that I should absent myself – pay a visit to Canada perhaps which I have always wanted to do – and return in six months' time when we can be quietly married and begin our life together. She hopes that her father will be sufficiently recovered to allow her to come to England with me for our honeymoon. I cannot wait for you all to meet her . . .

Memories of Ket now, as always, brought stinging tears to her eyes. As Madame Hortense's arms went round her, she felt an overriding need to confide in more detail. There was no one else she could talk to of her hopeless love for Ket.

Madame managed only with the greatest difficulty to contain her horror as she listened to Charlotte's outpourings. Too wise to voice her dismay, she said gently: 'Charlotte, my dear, believe me I do understand how enormously grateful you are to your friend – to dear Mrs Conniston. And how sorry you are for her having these dreadful miscarriages. But what you plan to do – even were it to succeed, which I think highly unlikely – is to put in jeopardy the whole of your future, your chances of marriage—'

107

The colour had risen to Charlotte's cheeks and her voice trembled as she interrupted. 'I will never marry now, regardless of whether I bear a child for Verity or not. I will never love anyone but Ket or wish to spend my life with another man, however kind and affectionate. Verity has promised that I shall always have a home with her and I truly believe we have become as near to sisters in our affections as it's possible to be.'

'That's no substitute for a home and husband of your own – *children* of your own,' Madame said forcibly. 'You make no mention of the children that you might otherwise have; and what of this one you intend to have for Mrs Conniston? Do you really believe you will simply be able to hand it over to her, saying "here, this is your child, I don't want it!" Suppose when you give birth to it you find you love it intensely? That happens with many women – and even with men who had no wish to be a parent.'

Despite her intention to remain calm, Madame's voice rose several tones as she declared emphatically: '*You cannot do this, Charlotte!* The obligation you feel to Mrs Conniston should not demand the sacrifice of the rest of your life. This is not something that will disappear in time. Do you realize that for as long as you live, you would never be able to claim your child once you had given it away to your friend? And think of the consequences to everyone if ever the truth were to be discovered! This is truly madness, Charlotte, and I am deeply surprised that Mrs Conniston – let alone her husband – have persuaded you to assist them in this iniquitous and unprincipled scheme!'

Charlotte's tears dried and her cheeks flushed a deep pink. 'You are mistaken, Madame. Verity and Guy did not try to persuade me – I am the one who has persuaded them to the idea! As for it being wicked, who would we be harming? What law exists to say that I can't give my child away to whom I please? Rather I am hoping to prevent a miscarriage of justice, for Guy's half-brother, Matthew, is an evil man who could only bring shame and misfortune to Kneepwood and its dependents. As for Guy's father, Sir Bertram, he is

108

the one who has been so horribly insistent that Guy should beget a son.'

'And if your child is a girl?'

For a moment, not unnoticed by Madame Hortense, Charlotte hesitated. Then she said firmly: 'Mrs Conniston – Verity – has said she would still keep it as her own; that it could grow up as a sister to her existing little girls. Nor will I be parted from it for she would employ me as governess if I felt the need to supervise and influence its upbringing.'

Madame gave a deep sigh. 'It seems as if the three of you have decided upon all aspects of this madcap scheme,' she said. 'But no one can take fate into account. Suppose, despite your denial of the possibility, you were to meet a gentleman who managed to find a way into your heart; who, but for your past, would dearly love to have you as his wife and mother of his children. Would you leave him in ignorance of the fact that you had lain with another man; had his child and, not least, given it away?'

The colour left Charlotte's cheeks and her expression became rigid. 'Since I can't be married to the man I love, I shall never wish to marry anyone. Even as I speak of Ket, I'm forced to remember my past, my poor father's criminal record. What man would wish his good name to be connected by marriage to my wretched family? No, Madame, I have no such illusions as to my future prospects, and since my life cannot be otherwise, at least I can put it to good purpose by helping Verity who I love dearly.'

She leaned over and covered the older woman's hand with her own. 'It was never my intention to burden you with these revelations!' she said. 'You must forgive me, since I can see you are worried on my behalf. I do assure you there is no need. I haven't entered this agreement lightly, without forethought. You are so kind that I know you will wish me well despite your disapproval, and I am grateful to you for the . . . the enlightenment you have given me. It will greatly help me to play my part appropriately when the time comes.'

Madame took Charlotte's other hand in hers so that she was holding tightly to her. 'My dear child, of course I wish

109

you well, but I must be honest and admit that I wish you would give this idea a great deal more time for reflection. It doesn't seem to have occurred to either you or Mrs Conniston that a single night abed with her husband may not guarantee a conception. If there had to be many more occasions, how would you, or indeed they, feel about it? Mrs Conniston loves her husband and whilst once may be something she can accept, repeated acts of intercourse between you and Mr Conniston could cause her to feel both jealousy and dismay, to say the very least.'

This wasn't a possibility Charlotte had envisaged nor, she supposed, had Verity. But she put it hurriedly from her mind. Seeing the determined expression returning to Charlotte's face, Madame sighed and then added: 'All I can ask is that you do give very serious thought to what I've said. I believe your plan has unforeseeable dangers as well as difficulties, not to mention the irreparable harm you would be doing yourself.'

It was not, however, either the difficulty or danger of the plan which kept Charlotte awake following her visit to Madame Hortense. It was the thought of the intimacy she must share with Guy Conniston. She found it hard to meet his eye at meal times or indeed to talk to him at all and she sensed that he, too, viewed what was to happen as a highly embarrassing duty. Conversely, Verity seemed to be in unnaturally high spirits – enough for Matthew's wife, Monica, to remark upon her sudden emergence from the former doldrums.

'It's a quite unnatural transformation!' she declared to Charlotte. 'I was saying to Matthew that only a week or two ago, I thought it might be necessary to call in a specialist doctor. So deep was Verity's depression, we even thought she might have to be locked up for her own safety!'

'Really, Monica,' Charlotte had protested. 'You're exaggerating Verity's state of mourning for her last miscarriage. Anyway, I'm sure you will agree that it's wonderful to see her so cheerful once again.'

'How could I be less than happy!' Verity said when they

were once more alone. 'I know you've warned me that you might not conceive, although you are in excellent health and we know of no reason why you shouldn't do so, but surely you realize that you have given me renewed hope? I know my darling Guy doesn't approve of our plans, but only last night he told me how happy he was to see me smiling once more. Between us, we shall ensure that he, too, is smiling when he holds his son and heir in his arms at last.'

'Verity, darling, you *must not count upon it*,' Charlotte said anxiously. 'Supposing I don't conceive? And even if I do, we have only one chance in two that it will be a boy.' She did not add that, were the baby a girl, she didn't think she could go through the proposed procedure a second time. Nor, she suspected, would Guy be willing to do so. He had insisted that she and Verity should have six months' sober reflection before they went ahead with their plan, without which he himself would not consider it.

The summer passed pleasantly enough with croquet games at Kneepwood, tennis parties with local friends, picnics with the children by the nearby lake, horse riding through the leafy beech woods down by the river bordering the south boundary of the estate.

There were letters from Madame Hortense asking her to visit, but Charlotte was unwilling to travel to London, fearing Madame's blatant disapproval of their plan. She herself had begun to dread the night that was coming ever nearer. Verity was intending to book a room in a small hotel near Marble Arch for a fictitious Mr and Mrs Kent for the tenth day after Charlotte's last monthly illness, Verity having once been advised by Dr Freeman that this was the most auspicious time to conceive.

Charlotte wasn't the only one to have misgivings. One night at the end of September, lying in the darkness of their marital bed, Guy said in a low, despairing voice to Verity: 'I can't bear to be a disappointment to you, my darling, but try as I might, I am unable to rid myself of the fear that we are wrong to allow Charlotte to undertake this for us.'

As Verity's body stiffened and she tried to sit up, Guy put a restraining hand on her arm. 'Please, my darling, listen to what I have to say before you comment. For a moment we won't discuss the ethics involved – merely the execution. Have you seriously given thought as to how this child is to be conceived? Loving you as I do, how can you expect me to go in cold blood to another woman's bed – a virgin at that – and have intercourse with her? Maybe for Charlotte it's not such a problem since she would have naught to do but lie there, but I . . . Well, I suspect I will almost certainly be impotent – a terrible disappointment for you; a humiliation for poor Charlotte; an embarrassment for me.'

In the darkness, Verity's lower lip trembled and her voice shook as she said fearfully: 'But the room would be in darkness, Guy. I've told Charlotte she is to go to bed as soon as she has taken her evening meal and to turn off the light. That way you can pretend it is me lying there. Oh, Guy, I don't think I could bear it if, after all our discussions, the plan was to be discarded. You know how many problems it would solve . . . and it would be *your* son, Guy. You would truly be its father.'

Guy's voice was no less emphatic as he said: 'We both know that the child might not be a boy. But even supposing that the Fates were kind, do we really have the right to pretend to my father, to Matthew, that the boy is my legitimate heir?'

'But Guy, we've talked about this so often. If you have a son, your father will leave Kneepwood to you instead of to Matthew, who you know would only bring the estate into disrepute – if not penury. You've said you would do anything – *anything* to avoid such a disaster. How can you even think of cancelling our plans now at this late stage? Why, Charlotte goes up to London next Wednesday and—'

'But is this fair to her?' Guy interrupted hoarsely. 'Have you forgotten that when Ket was last at home, we agreed we would introduce her to society and find her a husband? We are condemning her now to a life as a companion or governess – a life of spinsterhood.'

For a moment, Verity did not answer. Guy made Charlotte's future sound so barren – and yet it would not be entirely so. She would have borne a child; would be able to watch it grow; enjoy its affections; bestow her affection on it. She would be secure for the rest of her life, since Verity would never, ever allow her to return to the dreadful life of poverty from which she had rescued her. Somehow she would make up to Charlotte the fact that she was without a husband – which would have been the case anyway had she never given her a new life at Kneepwood.

'It was for Charlotte to make her own decision, Guy,' she said quietly. 'I wouldn't have tried to persuade her against her will any more than you would. Don't forget that it was her idea. It was Charlotte who offered to do this for us. Don't you recall her words: "This will enable me to return just a small part of the joy you have given me." She feels very indebted to us for bringing her here to live and no one cares to be always on the receiving end of charity.'

Guy drew a long sigh. 'Your arguments are convincing, my darling, yet I'm still not entirely convinced that we are acting with honour. Were that so we would be announcing quite openly that Charlotte was to provide a child for you since the doctor has said you cannot carry another yourself. Imagine the horror on everyone's faces, no matter how practical and sensible the idea. I am not even sure if the act of surrogation is not a criminal offence.'

'But Guy, women often employ wet nurses to suckle their infants. Aren't they acting as substitutes for the mothers?'

'Perhaps!' Guy agreed with a brief smile at his wife's ingenious arguments. 'However, we wouldn't be needing to act with such secrecy if to substitute an illegitmate child for a legitimate one was within the law.'

'Guy, darling, I beg you not to give way to these doubts at this late stage. I don't think I could bear the disappointment. Can't we leave the moral, ethical side of this to fate? After all, Charlotte may not conceive, and if she does, she may, like me, have only girls.'

It was several moments before Guy spoke. Then he said

quietly: 'Have you thought how you would feel if Charlotte were to have this infant – a boy possibly – and feel such maternal love towards it that she couldn't bear to give it to you – despite all her vows to the contrary?'

In the darkness, Verity nodded. 'Yes, I have thought of it. She denies such a possibility but I've borne a child and she has not, so I recognize how a woman feels when her newborn infant is placed in her arms. Nevertheless, I don't think this will happen. If it did, then I could do naught else but release her from her promises and agree that she must keep it. But how would that be possible, Guy? She has no home, no money, no parents. What could she offer her child? We can trust her, Guy. She will never betray us and I will never abandon her.'

Guy drew another deep sigh.

'It's late, and I think between us we've said all that can be said. I will argue no further if you'll agree one thing – that we never tell another living being what we are about to do. It could affect the lives of too many people, and once done cannot be undone. You and Charlotte have taken six months for reflection as I requested. Since you're both still of the same mind and as I can't bear to disappoint you, I will do my best to fulfil my part. It won't be easy, my darling, for I love you too much and want no other woman but you.'

Verity drew his face down to hers and kissed him passionately. 'It is because I know you won't be unfaithful to me in your thoughts that I can bear to think of you and Charlotte—'

'Hush, sweetheart, let's not talk of it. Let's think only of what you and I are about to do. I love you so much, my darling wife.'

'And I love you with all my heart!' Verity whispered as Guy's mouth closed over hers and he moulded her slender body to his own.

A week later, Guy felt his way in the near total darkness to the bed where he could see faintly the outline of Charlotte's body. The London hotel room was hot and Charlotte had

114

opened the windows which were hung with velour curtains, the shabbiness of which mercifully could not be seen.

Silently, he removed his clothes and, lifting the bedcovers tentatively, he slid between the sheets, muttering an awkward apology as he did so. Charlotte made no reply but lay silent and rigid beside him. He could feel her trembling and realized that she was even more nervous than himself. His sudden pity for her nullified his own nervousness and he said gently: 'Try not to be afraid. I will do my utmost not to hurt you. Perhaps if we both think only of Verity and what we are trying to achieve for her, it will be easier for us.'

At first Charlotte heeded his advice but gradually it dawned on her that Guy's voice as he gave her gentle instructions was almost identical to Ket's. She hadn't noticed it before because she had always seen his face when he spoke to her. But now – in the darkness as she felt Guy's movements – her body began to react in a way she had never experienced before. Despite the initial pain as she was penetrated she felt herself respond in a way that was new, and yet it was as if she had always needed it – familiar, exciting, arousing and stirring in her a deep yearning for Ket. It was not Guy but Ket who was now thrusting into her, Ket's voice in her ear saying he hoped he was not hurting her. She felt the male body above hers shudder and then become still and realized that, after all her fears, she had not wanted this act to end. Her body was still hungry, wanting, needing more.

Whilst waiting for all the wakened nerves in her body to subside, Charlotte lay perfectly still as slowly Guy raised himself and eased out of the bed. She felt his face touch her cheek very briefly in a kiss which seemed more like another apology. The frustration she felt gave way suddenly to pity. Poor Guy, who had not wanted her any more than she had wanted him! What he had just done was intended as a gift for the woman he loved. And as for herself, she hadn't once thought of Verity – only of Ket, the man she loved who could never now be hers.

Ten

S tanding outside the door of the day nursery, Verity tied
a large gentleman's silk handkerchief round Charlotte's
eyes. Her voice was childishly excited as she said: 'No
peeping, dearest! I've promised the girls that you won't
look until you are in the centre of the room.'

'Very well, I promise not to look!' Charlotte replied,
returning Verity's smile. It was such a pleasure these days
to see her dear friend quite restored to her former high spirits
and gaiety.

Verity knocked on the door and Charlotte heard Lottie's
high-pitched voice calling to her sister. 'Quick, Lottie, Mama
and Aunt Charlotte are here. Nanny, will you light them
quickly, please?' There was a brief pause and then the door
opened. Verity took one arm and someone who Charlotte
assumed to be Kate took the other. A moment later, Verity
removed the blindfold and Charlotte understood the reasons
for all the secrecy of the last five minutes.

In the centre of the large nursery, the scrubbed wooden
table was now covered with a white cloth. In the middle of
the table stood a pink and white iced cake with six candles
on it. Around the cake were several small packages none too
well wrapped but tied with pretty ribbons.

'Happy birthday, Aunt Charlotte!'

'Happy birthday! We wanted to surprise you.'

'Please open your presents.'

The children's excited voices were accompanied by tug-
gings at Charlotte's skirts as they urged her forward towards
the table.

'Now girls, please don't maul Miss Wyndham in such an unladylike manner!' Nanny's voice bore a note of authority recognized instantly by her two charges. Then it softened as she smiled at Charlotte. 'Happy birthday, Miss Wyndham.'

'Thank you, Nanny!' Charlotte replied. She was fond of the old woman who had once been Verity's nanny and was now nearing retiring age. With her grey hair tied back in a bun and half hidden by her starched white mob cap, she reminded Charlotte of her own nanny who she had loved so dearly.

The little girls, fair-haired and blue-eyed like their mother, were staring up at her expectantly. Kate, now seven years old and the elder by three years, said with adult seriousness: 'We're very sorry we couldn't put on the right number of candles but Mama wouldn't tell us how old you are!'

'Kate, darling, that is not a question you should ask grown-ups,' Verity said gently. She turned to Charlotte. 'I do believe you had quite forgotten that December the twelfth was your birthday, am I not right?' As Charlotte nodded, Verity laughed. 'It's because we've all been so busy preparing for Christmas!' she said. 'Come now, dearest, do open your presents. I think the girls are agog to see if you approve. And Dolly will be here presently with the tea, which we are to enjoy with the children today, so we must soon clear the table. Charlotte, I think you should blow out the candles now before they drip wax on to Cook's pretty icing!'

'You're all spoiling me!' Charlotte said reproachfully, but her eyes were bright with happiness. She loved Verity's little girls almost as much as she loved their mother, whose kindness to her was unending. Now she was almost certain she had conceived, for she had missed her monthly period twice since the one time she and Guy had been to London – something which had never happened to her before, even when she had been so ill and Madame Hortense had saved her life with food and care.

'I sewed it all myself!' Kate's voice broke into her thoughts as she took the last piece of wrapping paper from a pink satin pincushion, which was the child's much-prized present to her.

'It's beautiful, Kate,' Charlotte said quickly, bending to hug the little girl. 'And I really do love the lace frill. How clever of you to choose my favourite colour.'

'Is it your favourite?' little Lottie enquired in a despairing voice, which Charlotte quickly took to mean that *her* present was another colour.

'It's my favourite for some things like pincushions!' she improvised. 'But I wouldn't want my vegetables to be pink, would I?'

The children giggled and Lottie's expression changed quickly from despair to hope. 'Open my present next, please Aunt Charlotte!'

Obediently, Charlotte did so to expose a sky-blue velvet bookmark with a somewhat wobbly letter C embroidered on it.

'It's just exactly what I need to mark the page in my diary, where tonight I shall write down what a lovely birthday I'm having. And do you know, Lottie, blue is my very favourite colour for bookmarks!'

Later, as they made their way downstairs, Verity said to Charlotte: 'You're so good with the children, dearest. You are a natural mother . . .' She broke off, well aware that this could be a tricky subject she had broached by accident. Verity hugged the thought to herself. It seemed almost certain that the miracle had happened and that Charlotte was indeed carrying a child, Guy's baby. Was it possible Charlotte really didn't mind that she would never be acknowledged as its mother nor hear it call her Mama?

As if aware of Verity's thoughts, Charlotte said: 'You mustn't allow any misgivings. If I'm truly with child, it alters nothing we agreed all those months ago. I want to have this baby *for you*. I shall never permit myself to imagine that it's *mine*, or wish it so. But now it seems likely that I have conceived, shouldn't we be making serious plans as to how we are going to bring about this . . . this deception?'

Verity slipped her arm through Charlotte's and led her into the morning room where she knew they would not be interrupted. Guy was in the study and Sir Bertram in the

118

library, and it was unlikely there would be any visitors so late in the day.

Sitting by Charlotte's side on the window seat, Verity said quietly: 'If our hopes are well founded, dearest, you will show no sign of your pregnancy until February. It's then we must go away. Guy says we must go to Europe on a prolonged holiday – that I must pretend I'm not very well and can't face the English winter weather. Guy would come with us, of course.'

Charlotte frowned, knowing how conscientious Guy was about caring for matters of the estate. 'Will he wish to be abroad for so long – several months at least?'

Verity smiled wryly. 'Whether he wishes it or not, he is greatly in need of a holiday, Charlotte, for he has not really recovered his strength since that heavy chest infection he had last month. I shall persuade him that such a holiday will be for my good rather than his own, and then he'll be willing to come!'

'If this baby is to be born in July, surely we can't holiday for *all* the months prior to the birth?' Charlotte said, trying to remain practical, for she had given much thought to the future and she feared that Verity had given little, if any.

Verity, however, had worn Guy's nerves to shreds with her ever changing ideas as to how Charlotte could have her baby undetected by anyone they knew, and how she herself could suddenly produce a healthy baby without anyone having seen that she was with child again. Finally, for the sake of peace, Guy had agreed that she and Charlotte must go abroad to somewhere quiet and unfrequented by tourists; and far away from the health spas, cities and seaside resorts favoured by the rich. They might take a few weeks' genuine holiday before finding a villa somewhere where they could enjoy the sun as well as the necessary privacy.

Verity now suggested that, after a month abroad with them, Guy should return home with the news that she was with child and the doctors had insisted that she stay in bed and under no circumstances undertake the journey home until she was a great deal stronger.

119

'Wouldn't it seem strange if Guy left you alone abroad at such a critical time?' Charlotte enquired now. 'Everyone, as well as Guy, would suspect a threatened miscarriage.'

'Then Guy must tell them that it's precisely to avoid such a thing I have been confined to bed.' Her face broke into a smile. 'And why should Guy worry when he has left me with someone as capable as you to look after me? Of course, Guy will come out again to visit us, and finally, when the baby is due, he will be on hand and there to bring us home. Don't you see, dearest, it will all be quite simple?'

Verity's plan sounded feasible but throughout the remainder of the evening, Charlotte's doubts remained. Feasible it might be but it wasn't without many inherent dangers. Suppose they were to run into someone Verity knew? Suppose the foreign registrar was not prepared to accept that she, and not Verity, was Mrs Guy Conniston? It was unlikely that Sir Bertram would be suspicious, for he took little interest in his daughter-in-law's activities, or even Guy's.

Monica, however, was a different matter altogether. Not only was she an inveterate gossip and made it her business to know what was happening to everyone on and off the estate, but in particular she would try to insinuate herself between Verity and Charlotte. She made no attempt to hide her dislike of Charlotte, who she treated with barely concealed contempt as she might have done a poor relation. She never lost an opportunity to make some oblique reference to Charlotte's past and was clearly furious that Verity would not tell her what had happened in Charlotte's life before she'd brought her to Kneepwood. She had even gone to the trouble of writing to a number of her friends in an attempt to discover more about the Wyndham family, so far with no result.

Monica, Charlotte decided, might justifiably be suspicious of this plan of Verity's. She would be jealous of the fact that, whereas Matthew was always in debt, Guy had been left money by his late mother with which he planned to finance this long holiday. Such suspicions as Monica might sustain would be more than trebled when Verity eventually returned home with a healthy son and heir.

Perhaps it wouldn't be a boy, Charlotte thought uneasily, yet the whole reason behind all this was in order to have it so. Perhaps she had not conceived after all. But there could be little doubt that she had done so, after just that one to-be-forgotten night. Each morning she felt a strange nausea which passed off quickly only to be repeated the following morning. But despite these positive signs, Charlotte couldn't bring herself to believe she was any different from usual – on the contrary, she felt remarkably well. Clearly her condition was beneficial to her she had decided that morning, surveying her reflection in the cheval mirror. Her chestnut hair shone as she brushed it, her eyes were bright, her skin clear and glowing – so opposite from poor Verity, who had looked pale, fragile and sickly from the earliest month of pregnancy.

Such thoughts continued to plague her until after she changed for dinner when her maid Mary chose the chestnut velvet gown for her to wear that evening. She was reminded of Madame Hortense and was thinking of the letter she must write to her when she joined Verity in the drawing room.

'Guy will be down in a few minutes,' Verity said. 'How pretty you look, dearest! Tomorrow . . .' Verity broke off suddenly, her fair head tilted to one side. She appeared to be listening to something outside the door.

'Is it the children?' Charlotte enquired, for they were to be brought down to the drawing room by Nanny after their supper to say goodnight to their parents.

'No, it's a man's voice!' Verity said. 'I think . . . Oh, Charlotte, I do hope I'm right. If I'm not much mistaken, that voice is my darling brother-in-law's – Ket's.'

As if on cue, the door opened and Ket Conniston strode into the room. His caped ulster was spattered with rain, as were his breeches and top boots. His eyes were alight with mischievous laughter. 'Grainger said I'd find you both in here. He wanted me to divest myself of these wet clothes before I joined you, but I simply couldn't wait a moment longer. Verity, my much loved sister-in-law, how are you?' He swept her into his arms and kissed her on both cheeks. Releasing her, he stood for a moment, his head turning to look at Charlotte. Once more, he

121

gave a broad smile. 'Why, you look even more beautiful than I remembered!' he declared, and before she could withdraw the hand she was holding out in welcome, he took it in his own and, turning the palm upwards, placed a soft, lingering kiss in the centre and closed her fingers over it. 'I hope you haven't forgotten me!' he said softly. 'I suppose you won't believe me if I tell you that you are one of the reasons I have abandoned America and come home?'

In the confusion that followed this extraordinary statement, Charlotte's blushes were not observed. The footman who had followed Ket into the room now took his wet coat, hat and gloves. The footman was in turn followed by Grainger with a tray holding a decanter of whisky and several glasses. Behind him strode Guy, his face alight with pleasure as he put his arm round his brother's shoulders.

'If you'd sent us warning that you were coming, old chap, I would have told Grainger to put a couple of bottles of champagne to chill,' he said. 'Sit yourself down and tell us what has brought about your change of plan. We understood from your last letter that you'd completed your adventures in the wilds of Canada and were returning to the Copleys' mansion in Boston to follow up your postponed nuptials.'

Ket sank into the cushions of the drawing room's large sofa. He leaned forward, stretching his arms towards the flames of the log fire to warm his hands. 'Devilish cold outside!' he murmured. 'I took the train from London to Tunbridge Wells and then hired a nag at the Black Boar to bring me here. Half froze to death, although I suppose it was far colder in Canada. Temperatures there were already minus ten degrees when it was only October.'

Guy shook his head despairingly. 'You're a glutton for punishment, Ket. Why in the name of heaven didn't you send a boy from the inn up here and we'd have told Gregory to fetch you in the brougham?'

'Never gave it a thought!' Ket said, laughing. 'Grainger is sending the fellow to the station to collect my luggage. Worry not, my hearties, I am rapidly thawing and immensely glad to be here!'

'You have yet to tell us why!' Verity reminded him.

'Ah, yes, indeed!' Ket replied, the glint of amusement leaving his eyes as he turned his gaze back to meet his brother's. 'As I told you in my letter, when poor old Mrs Copley died, I made myself scarce and went off to Canada. Amazing place . . . and where I ended up, there were only a handful of people – trappers mostly – mountain folk. Nothing in the whole wide world could have been more different from the life I'd been leading in Boston and on the Copleys' yacht. Theirs is a world of "You like it, you have it" – money no object. I suppose I was seduced by the incredible opulence of my life with them.' He paused to take a drink from the whisky tumbler Grainger had given him before continuing with a more serious expression. 'As you can imagine, Guy, life in the Canadian mountains was a question of survival; of using your wits to acquire your food, keep warm, stay alive. In the winter for example, temperatures could drop to minus twenty degrees.'

He turned now to face Charlotte. His eyes were brilliant as in a low, enthusiastic tone he described how those six months of getting back to nature had changed his whole attitude to life. 'I am not suggesting that it's the way I would always want to live,' he stated. 'But it did show me what a very shallow and selfish existence I'd hitherto been enjoying – simply filling each day with a new amusement but to no real purpose at all. Can you understand what I'm saying? I hoped that when I returned to Boston, Naomi would understand and appreciate that I now wanted more from life than one long round of enjoyment; that I wanted to put something back into it so that when I grow old I wouldn't feel as if my life had been completely meaningless.'

'And Naomi didn't wish to change her way of life?' Verity's voice was gentle as she prompted Ket to continue his explanation.

'No, I suppose she could see no reason to do so. In a way, I realize I was wrong even to ask her to give up the merry-go-round she enjoyed so much. She'd been brought up in the very height of luxury since her babyhood and, not unnaturally, her parents had spoilt her so that she was accustomed to having everything she wanted and having it her way.'

'Poor old fellow!' Guy said sympathetically. 'So you had to tell the unfortunate girl at the eleventh hour that you no longer wanted to marry her?'

To everyone's surprise, Ket grinned. 'Well, not quite. As it transpired, to cheer her up after her beloved grandmother's demise, her father had bought her a superb Arab filly. It was a bit feisty and Naomi had never done much riding. So Mr Copley arranged for a neighbour, who was an experienced horseman, to come round and give her and the Arab some training. There's no doubt that this chap, Willoughby, fell head over heels for Naomi and . . . well, I was away and she was lonely and by the time I returned, she was no longer at all sure she wanted to go through with the wedding. She said that, feeling as she did about Willoughby, it wouldn't be fair to me.'

The anxious expression left Verity's face. 'So the engagement was called off by mutual agreement!' she said. 'I suppose I shouldn't say this, but I'm really glad, Ket. I hated the thought of you going to live in the United States where we'd so seldom see you. Now what are you going to do? Is it back to Canada?'

Ket shook his head. He turned suddenly to Charlotte. 'What would you recommend, dear Miss Charlotte, for a not very broken heart? Can I hope that your charming company will help to heal the scars? You've not become betrothed in my absence, I trust?'

Somehow, Charlotte found her voice. Her hands were trembling but she clasped them tightly together in her lap. 'I'm afraid I shan't be here for long enough to be of any help to you,' she said, astonished that her voice could sound so cool and steady. 'Guy is taking Verity and me to Europe for a holiday just as soon as he can make adequate travel arrangements. Verity has relations awaiting her visit in the south of France, have you not, dearest? But first we may spend a day or two in Paris.'

There was only a momentary pause before Verity found her voice. As Charlotte had been speaking, she'd realized that for obvious reasons her friend would wish to avoid Ket's companionship, lest somehow he guessed her condition and asked awkward questions. Both she and Guy had decided that in no circumstances was anyone – even Ket – to know what they were doing. She hurried to Charlotte's assistance. 'Yes, indeed, these French cousins have come to Europe all the way from Quebec and will be returning in the spring, so we are planning to make the effort to meet them in February shortly after we arrive in France or else we shall miss seeing them altogether.'

Ket looked momentarily dismayed but then he smiled. 'As you won't be leaving until after the new year, your plans could suit me very well. I could accompany you to Paris, could I not? I've no doubt you'd welcome a little help with the ladies, eh, Guy?'

Guy nodded uncertainly. The last thing he wanted was to depart to the continent so soon after Ket had come home. But having seen the look that had passed between Verity and Charlotte, he assumed that their previously unannounced plan to leave Kneepwood so soon must be tied up in some way with this baby exchange. He'd had several months to think about that and, with each passing day, he'd come closer to the conclusion that he'd been mad ever to agree to such a wild notion. When nearly two months had passed, he congratulated himself on the fact that nature was not after all to be manipulated so easily. Then suddenly, a few days ago Verity had flung herself into his arms in a whirlwind of excitement saying that Charlotte was almost certainly with child – in fact it could be said to be virtually definite.

'Of course, Charlotte might miscarry as I did!' Verity had announced, seeing that Guy did not share her happiness in the news. 'We agreed, didn't we, dear heart, to leave this in the hands of fate?'

'I neither can nor will do anything to negate the plan,' Guy had said sombrely, 'but I still can't rid myself of the belief that it is totally unethical.' On the other hand, he told himself,

125

since it so clearly brought happiness back to his beloved wife, he was prepared once more to put his concerns to the back of his mind and try not to dampen her enthusiasm with his doubts. He looked now at Ket's face and wished he could share his brother's enthusiasm to join them, but he was far from sure Verity could maintain the necessary secrecy over a period of time.

'We may well stay in Paris for a week or two and I fear you'd quickly become bored with our tea parties and sightseeing, old chap,' he said. 'But that's not to say we can't spend a night or two together in Paris if you have reason to go abroad with us.'

Ket seemed unabashed. 'I have every reason. I was talking at length with a fellow traveller on the ship coming home and was most taken with the tales he related about the new winter sport of skiing. The good fellow told me that there is already a ski club in Munich in Germany and that this year there is to be a winter resort in Chamonix in France. I could travel on to Chamonix from Paris, could I not?' His face lit up with an eager smile as he glanced from Guy to Verity and then to Charlotte. 'Why don't you all join me? I'm told that skiing is the greatest fun, more so than skating; and at this time of the year there should be plenty of snow.'

'I'm not fond of the cold weather!' Verity said quickly. 'That's why we plan to travel on from Paris down to the south where it will be so much more pleasant than here in England.'

Ket turned to Charlotte. 'And you, Charlotte, wouldn't you enjoy skiing? To glide over the snow on wooden slats sounds the greatest fun. Doubtless we would fall a great deal at first but we could hold each other up.'

Charlotte took a deep breath and swallowed, as if by doing so she could more easily blind herself to this glimpse of heaven. 'No, I would much prefer to join Verity and Guy in the sunshine!' she lied. Her thoughts and emotions were in turmoil – so much so that she had unwittingly bitten the inside of her lower lip. She could taste the blood on her tongue. Not even Verity could know what this sudden sight

126

of Ket and the knowledge that he was not going to marry the American girl after all, and appeared eager for *her* company, was doing to her.'

Ket's woebegone expression may have been a trifle exaggerated but his sentiments were genuine enough as he said: 'It seems as if you two ladies are none too anxious for my company.' He drew a deep sigh. 'But never fear, I shan't follow you to the south of France, however tempting the prospect. I shall go to Chamonix and seek other amusement there.'

Verity sat down on the sofa and hastened to put her arms round him in a hug. 'Darling Ket, of course we would have loved your company, but I for one know only too well how bored you would become. Don't look so crestfallen, you rapscallion. We both love you dearly, don't we, Charlotte?'

As Charlotte nodded obediently she could not look at Ket. Verity of course was happily unaware how close she was to the truth.

Ket turned away from Charlotte's downcast head and gave his attention back to his brother, but his thoughts were not entirely concentrated on what Guy was telling him about the estate. He was experiencing an unusual feeling of disappointment. On the boat travelling from Boston to Tilbury, he'd found himself thinking less and less about Naomi Copley and the life they might have shared and more often about his sister-in-law's baffling companion. From the first, Charlotte had intrigued him, and not just because Verity refused to enlighten him about Charlotte's family history. Verity had told him nothing other than that she was of good family, was orphaned and penniless, and she'd chosen to befriend her. He'd not considered Charlotte particularly pretty in the way that the fair-haired, blue-eyed Verity's china doll appearance had enslaved Guy. Nor did Charlotte have Naomi's vivid, extrovert vivacity and striking Latin American colouring. But there was something captivating about Charlotte which had not allowed him to forget her. Intelligent yet shy, she had hidden depths which challenged him to unravel them.

This evening, however, he sensed that Charlotte was turning her back on all his attempts at friendliness. During the journey home, he had looked forward immensely to her peaceful undemanding companionship, for she was the very antithesis of Naomi, who had demanded his constant attention and unceasing activity. He tried to recall now if when he'd last seen Charlotte he had somehow given her cause for offence, but he could think of no ill-chosen word or action. On the contrary, they'd enjoyed a delightful light-hearted verbal flirtation which he'd hoped to renew, so long as she'd not become betrothed in his absence. Perhaps, he told himself, that was exactly what had happened, for it would explain her coldness towards him. When Guy paused in his description of the new engine-driven grass-mowing machine he had recently bought, Ket said, as casually as he could make his tone: 'Surely it hasn't been all work and no play? Haven't you had any parties whilst I was away? Haven't you seen the Granvilles? The Emersons? The Morrisons? Hasn't that admirer of hers, George Morrison, come to call on our lovely Miss Charlotte? Or perhaps that new young doctor, John Forfield, has been paying his addresses?'

'Ket, would you stop teasing poor Charlotte who, as you might remember, had no time for the pompous Dr Forfield when we last invited him to Kneepwood. Moreover, if there's any matchmaking to be done for Charlotte, Guy and I will do it. But we've other things on our minds with our wonderful holiday pending, as, indeed, has Charlotte. Am I not right, dearest?'

With a look of intense relief, Charlotte rose swiftly to her feet. 'You're quite right, Verity, and you've reminded me that I still have some sewing to do for our holiday that can't wait. If you'll excuse me, I'll leave you all in peace until dinner.'

As Guy and Ket rose politely to their feet, Guy said: 'Before you leave, Charlotte, I must wish you many happy returns for your birthday. I had intended to offer my good wishes at breakfast but you didn't put in an appearance.'

Charlotte remembered the sudden bout of nausea which had afflicted her that morning. Ket now stepped forward and, before she could guess his intention, he once more took possession of her hand.

'My most sincere wishes for your future happiness!' he said, and for the second time that afternoon, he pressed a kiss into her palm. 'That will have to do for a birthday gift, Charlotte!' he said, his brown eyes smiling as he looked into hers.

Charlotte quickly withdrew her hand from his and, not daring to return his gaze, she turned and hurried from the room as quickly as she could. Only when she reached the privacy of her bedroom did she allow the hot, stinging tears of regret to fall.

Eleven

'Are you feeling a little better now, Charlotte?'
Ket's voice, filled with concern, only deepened Charlotte's misery. Fortunately, the now customary bouts of early morning nausea had not assailed her during the train journey from Tunbridge Wells to Dover, but once on board the ferry carrying them across the Channel to Calais, she had been prostrated. Fortunately, the kindly steward who attended her assumed she was suffering from seasickness. And fortuitously the sickness had ceased as they boarded the train to Paris and the colour had returned to Charlotte's cheeks.

'I'm afraid I'm not a very good traveller,' she said in answer to Ket's question. It was yet another lie she was telling him, she thought as she picked up the book on her lap and pretended to read. For the past three weeks, whilst Guy had been organising their 'holiday', Ket was in constant attendance, inviting her to accompany him to go skating on the lake; to play cribbage or backgammon with him; to take his nephews and nieces to the pantomime in Tunbridge Wells. Even the obnoxious Bertie behaved with Ket in charge, and Charlotte could see only too clearly how well Ket managed the children, how much they all loved their uncle and enjoyed his company.

As did she, Charlotte thought unhappily, for in different circumstances she would have welcomed Ket's interest with an enthusiasm she had never imagined possible. Not only did she so much enjoy his company, but she was finding him dangerously attractive – the way his hair curled over his forehead; the sparkle in his dark eyes; the way his mouth turned up at the corners and his eyes crinkled as he laughed. She had noted the breadth of his shoulders; the casual way in which he crossed one long leg over the knee of the other when he was seated.

For the hundredth time since Ket had returned so unexpectedly from America, Charlotte tried to force herself to stop feeling this physical awareness of him; to stop thinking how hopelessly in love with him she was. To allow such truths was to admit her agonizing regrets. Despite Verity's loving attentions and the glow of happiness which surrounded her, Charlotte couldn't subdue the cloud of bitterness that engulfed her whenever she allowed herself to consider how different her response to Ket might now have been. Lying awake at night, unable to find the oblivion of sleep, she recalled Madame Hortense's warnings. *'It is the whole of your future life you are putting in jeopardy . . . your chances of love, of marriage.'*

How certain she had been when she sat facing her former employer that she would never marry, since Ket was beyond her reach! How emphatically Madame Hortense had insisted that there was no substitute for a home, a husband and children of her own. No one, she had insisted, should fail to take fate into account . . . and how right she had been proven! Who could have believed that Ket would change his mind about marrying Naomi Copley? And still less might anyone have believed that on his return to England, he would show such interest in herself!

Watching the changing expressions on Charlotte's face from behind his newspaper, Ket's thoughts were likewise centred upon his interest in her. Charlotte, he reflected, could not have been more opposite to Naomi in looks or character, yet now he was finding himself as attracted to her as he had once been to the volatile American girl. Was he really so fickle that he could change hearts this easily? Or was he merely intrigued by Charlotte because she so clearly discouraged his advances? Thinking back to his last visit home the previous year, he'd had the impression that Charlotte welcomed his attentions. She was not by nature

131

flirtatious, but she had smiled and often blushed when he was openly flirting with her. Sometimes in the ensuing months, when he had been all day in Naomi's company and was a little wearied of her constant laughter and activity, he had thought of Charlotte, so quiet, so tranquil, so serene, and astonishingly found himself wishing he could lay his head in her lap and feel her small white hands soothing his face and forehead. Without just cause, he had imagined her happy and content to do so. But now she seemed almost to be ignoring him; or if that were not possible, to respond only so far as good manners demanded. It was a challenge – one which Ket was unused to, since nearly all the females he encountered, young or old, appeared only too willing to welcome his attentions.

An hour later the train drew into the Gare du Nord where one of the many porters hurried to take their luggage to a waiting *fiacre*. A second hackney coach was hired for Charlotte and the Connistons and they were driven through a melee of traffic to the Rue Rivoli where Guy had booked rooms for them in the Hotel Wagram. There was a large suite for Verity and Guy overlooking the Tuileries, and comfortable rooms each on the same floor for Ket and Charlotte.

Left alone briefly in order to unpack and change her clothes, Charlotte was glad of the respite. She was finding it next to impossible to ignore Ket's presence. In the carriage he'd sat beside her, his leg warm against her skirts, his arm only an inch away from hers. Once, when the cab had swerved to avoid a careless pedestrian, he'd caught hold of her arm and held it safely against his body.

Sitting on her bed, Charlotte stared across the room at her reflection in the dressing table mirror opposite. The girl staring back at her did not look like herself, she thought, for she was immensely chic in the new fur-trimmed emerald-green jacket and tartan overskirt Verity had insisted upon buying for her. A month before their departure, she had sent to Madame Hortense for a complete wardrobe to be made up for Charlotte for their travels abroad.

The thought of Madame brought a frown to Charlotte's

forehead. She hadn't been able to bring herself to write and confess her condition, knowing only too well that Madame thought her demented even to be thinking of undertaking such a commitment. She was far from sure she could write convincingly of her pleasure at having pursued their plan. Ever since Ket had returned from the United States, unattached and seemingly anxious for her company, she'd had to force herself not to wish with all her heart the night with Guy undone and the baby she carried never to have existed.

Verity came hurrying into Charlotte's room. She stared at the unpacked valise on the bed and threw up her hands in exaggerated dismay. 'Dearest, you have no *femme de chambre* to assist you! I will send you the maid the hotel has provided for me. Are you feeling all right, Charlotte? You still look very pale!'

Charlotte forced a smile. 'I'm in the best of health!' she said brightly. 'I do assure you, Verity, you have no need to worry about me.'

Verity put her arms round Charlotte's shoulders. 'Nevertheless I do!' she said softly. 'Oh, Charlotte, you can't believe how happy I am – and Guy, too – now that we are all here in Paris. It's as if Guy has decided to enjoy this holiday after all, despite his misgivings about what we are doing. Not that any of us could be miserable in Ket's company. Don't you agree, dearest, that he's the very best of travelling companions? I do so wish we could tell him our secret but Guy has forbidden me ever to tell a soul – and that includes our dear Ket.'

She paused briefly to peer in the mirror and adjust an ornamental comb in one of the rolled curls at the back of her head before turning back to Charlotte. 'I'll leave you now to change your clothes. Guy is going to take us all out to dine and afterwards, if we are not all too tired, Ket wishes to take us to the Moulin Rouge where there will be a cabaret and perhaps we can dance.'

Charlotte bit back the instant refusal that rose to her lips. To dance the waltz with Ket would be a dangerous intimacy which might all too easily betray her emotions. As it was,

Verity had no idea that she was hopelessly in love with Ket – nor must she ever know, since that could only result in a dreadful feeling of guilt. Not that this whole unfortunate plan was of Verity's devising, for it was she, Charlotte, who had first volunteered to have a child for Verity and Guy. No, she had no one but herself to blame for her situation. Only Madame Hortense had anticipated what might be the cost to herself, but even now Charlotte was determined to go through with it to its conclusion without complaint.

To do so was all but impossible, Charlotte realized as their first evening in Paris neared its end. Ket was in the best of spirits, laughing, joking with each of them in turn, but always at Charlotte's side, cajoling her into smiles, a dance, a shared joke. With Verity and Guy in equally good heart, Charlotte couldn't remain sombre and, halfway through the evening, she had abandoned caution and finally given herself over to enjoyment.

On reaching the hotel, they travelled up in the rickety *ascenseur* to the third floor, seeing Guy and Verity to their suite then, with Ket's arm tucked through hers, walking along the corridor to Charlotte's room. Ket was eulogising about the spectacular cabaret music at the Moulin Rouge and seemed unaware of the fact that he was now holding Charlotte's hand. When they reached her doorway, he turned her palm over and, as he had done before, pressed it to his lips. 'I've had such a splendid evening,' he said softly. 'I do hope you, too, have enjoyed yourself, Charlotte? It's very important to me that you should be happy.'

Somehow, Charlotte found her voice. 'I've had a wonderful evening, mainly thanks to you, Ket,' she said truthfully. 'But now I really am tired and ready to retire.'

Ket was at once solicitous. 'How selfish of me to wish to keep you with me any longer!' he said, taking her key from her and opening the door to her room. 'But I shall see you in the morning, won't I? Guy is insisting I accompany him to this new tower which is to be opened for the May exhibition. I doubt we will be allowed to ascend it but Guy tells me that Monsieur Gustave Eiffel has built it so high that visitors will be able to see all of Paris from the top. I wish you were accompanying us, Charlotte!'

Somehow, she managed a smile. 'Verity is determined to take me shopping!' she said. 'But we shall meet again for lunch, I think.'

'Most definitely!' Ket replied, handing her back her key. 'I only hope the weather will improve. Spring is the time to be here, not February. You should be seeing Paris when the chestnut trees are out and people can sit outside the cafes, drink their wonderful French coffee and watch the pretty girls pass by.'

'A picture I can see quite clearly in my mind!' Charlotte said, smiling, but Ket's face was serious.

'Yes, sweet Charlotte, I too can picture it. I would sit with my legs stretched out to the sunshine and a glass of Pernod in one hand, and with the other, I should wave to you as you came towards me. You would join me at my table and, because it was Paris in the springtime, we would talk to each other and flirt a little, and before long, we should fall in love.'

'And out of love an hour later, I dare say!' Charlotte replied as evenly as she could. Forcing a light-hearted smile, she edged past Ket's tall frame and went through her doorway. Entering the comparative sanctuary of her room, she managed to keep her voice calm and casual as she said: 'Goodnight, Ket, and thank you again for making the evening such fun.'

Reluctantly, he watched the door close behind her. The evening had been fun, he told himself as he went down the corridor towards his own room. In fact, most of the day had been enjoyable except when Charlotte had been so ill on the boat. Later, she had proved to be an interesting conversationalist during dinner. And despite the fact that she had drunk very little of the excellent champagne the rest of them had savoured, she'd suddenly relaxed her guard and matched his jolly mood perfectly. Verity had noticed the transformation and, whilst Guy was deep in conversation with Charlotte, she'd told him that he was proving the perfect tonic for her.

'I've not seen Charlotte so animated since the last time you were home,' she had told him. 'But you must take care not to break her heart, Ket. I wouldn't want Charlotte to think you had fallen in love with her.'

'And why not, my sweet sister-in-law?' Ket had queried, laughing. 'What if I have fallen in love with our lovely Miss Charlotte? She isn't betrothed to another. We could be well matched were it not for the fact that both she and I are penniless!'

He couldn't now recall what Verity had replied – something to do with the fact that he would be off to Chamonix soon and doubtless be fancying some other pretty female with whom he would imagine himself in love. Far more important than that had been her additional comment – that Charlotte had expressed her determination never to get married, however eligible the suitor.

As he made his way into his own room, Ket found himself remembering Verity's declaration and he questioned it now as he hadn't done at the time. Had Charlotte had an unfortunate dalliance with some man who'd put her off the male sex? Or was it perhaps because her father had brought such misery upon her family? Verity had finally told him how it came about that Charlotte lived with them at Kneepwood. Or was it simply because she had never yet fallen in love and could see no reason to give up her freedom into the hands of another?

He was still pondering the enigma of Charlotte as he turned out the gas lamp above his bed and tried to settle himself to sleep. Try as he might, he could not put her image out of his mind – the sweetness of her sudden smiles, the soft timbre of her voice, the rounded curves of her body. Least of all could he forget the haunting scent of roses that had emanated from her when he sat so close beside her in the *fiacre*.

He turned on his side and, with an effort, tried instead to think of the itinerary they had planned for the morrow. First the visit with Guy to see the extraordinary 984-foot iron edifice called the Eiffel Tower and then, as the weather was still wintry and cold, they planned to visit the Louvre where he particularly wished to see the Egyptian antiquities.

Lunch at Maxim's and afterwards they had tickets for a matinee performance starring Sarah Bernhardt at the Vaudeville Theatre. With the exception of the morning, Charlotte would be with them for the whole day and he would have ample opportunity to break down that invisible barrier she seemed so anxious to keep between them. With a sigh, Ket realized that his thoughts had come full circle back to Charlotte and he knew that, despite Verity's warnings, he was a little in love with her.

Throughout the following week Ket never left Charlotte's side, often linking his arm through hers, taking her hand, leaning so that his shoulder touched hers. They visited the palace at Versailles, viewed Whistler's paintings at the Salon, went to an exhibition of Meissonnier, attended Benediction in the beautiful cathedral of Notre Dame. They had been to the Folies Bergère, taken tea at Rumplemeyers and dined at the Café de Paris.

It was an exhausting schedule but one which was immensely exciting for Charlotte. For one thing, she had never been to Paris before, except as a very young child with her parents. Too young to remember much of that visit, she could recall being taken for walks in a perambulator by her nanny in the Bois de Boulogne. How different was the visit this time – not least because their activities had all been in the company of Ket Conniston. On their last night dining at the Côte d'Or, Charlotte was filled with a feeling of desolation so intense that tears sprang to her eyes as Guy paid the maitre d'hotel and they stepped out on to the rainswept street. She was achingly conscious of Ket's warm side as he sat next to her in the *fiacre* taking them back to their hotel.

'We shall all miss you terribly, Ket,' Verity said, snuggling against Guy's shoulder as the *fiacre* rumbled over the cobbles. 'We've had such fun, the four of us, haven't we, darling?' she appealed to Guy. She glanced at Charlotte's taut face and thought better of suggesting they might stay a further week.

It occured to her that perhaps it hadn't been such a good idea to allow Ket to accompany them to France, however agreeable a companion he had proved to be. When he had confided on the night of their arrival that he might be falling in love with Charlotte, she had assumed he was far from serious. Had she not warned Charlotte again and again that Ket was the most outrageous flirt and that no female should ever take his attentions seriously? Although now in no doubt that his admiration of Charlotte was perfectly genuine, she and Guy both thought his increasing attentions to her were prompted by the manner in which she kept him at arm's length. She recalled the many pretty girls who Ket had romanced in his youth, and realized now that his behaviour with Charlotte was quite different.

Later that night as she and Guy prepared for bed, he made light of Verity's concerns. 'Ket will have forgotten all about Charlotte by the time he reaches Chamonix,' he said as he climbed into bed beside her. 'I know my young brother, my dear, perhaps better than you do.'

Verity drew a long sigh as she snuggled down against his warm shoulder. 'But what of Charlotte?' she questioned. 'I think she's head over heels in love with Ket. And don't shake your head like that, Guy. I watched her at dinner tonight and every time he spoke to her, she blushed. And in the *fiacre*, I saw Ket try to hold her hand and she wouldn't allow it.'

Guy gave his wife an amused, quizzical look. 'So if she is in love with him as you are suggesting, why should she refuse such approaches? I somehow doubt it's in Charlotte's nature to play hard to get. She's the last person to be coquettish!'

Verity beat a small fist against Guy's chest. 'You are thinking like any other insensate male!' she chided. 'Don't you see, it is because she's in love with him that she has to avoid his advances? Guy, you can't have forgotten, she is with child – your child. She knew when she agreed to have the baby that she was jeopardizing her future. She's in no position to encourage Ket's – or any other man's – advances.'

In the light of the bedside lamp, Guy's face showed the distress he was feeling. 'Then our own selfish desires have perhaps ruined two people's chances of happiness,' he said thoughtfully. 'I do wish . . .'

'No, Guy, I beg you, don't say you wish we had never agreed Charlotte should have the baby. *I'm* the one who is guilty, not you, because your heart was never in it from the beginning. I was the one who wanted it. I wanted it for you. I couldn't give you the son you needed, but Charlotte could. And remember, Guy, she wanted to do it for us. There were lots of times when I asked her if she wished to change her mind and she always said no. We both insisted she wait six months before making a final decision so we could be sure it wasn't a spur of the moment mistake that she might regret.'

'I know, I know, darling. Don't distress yourself, I beg you. After all, we cannot be sure Ket is in love with Charlotte, or that Charlotte is in love with him. He will almost certainly forget her in time and she . . . well, she will have other things to distract her.'

Charlotte was thinking the same thoughts as the young French *femme de chambre* undid the last of the buttons on her gold and cream striped evening dress. As she stepped out of it on to the thick carpet of her hotel room, there was a knock on the door. The maid handed Charlotte her *peignoir* before hurrying to open the door as the knocking sounded a second time.

Charlotte's heart missed a beat as she heard Ket's voice demanding in a low, imperious tone to be admitted. The girl came hurrying back to Charlotte. It was a Monsieur Conniston, she informed her, her sparkling eyes barely able to conceal her excitement at such unconventional behaviour from the handsome Englishman. She was well aware that Verity and Guy were a married couple; that the younger gentleman was unmarried, as was the young lady she was now attending. This might well be *une affaire de coeur*.

'The Monsieur wishes to speak to you, Mademoiselle!' she told Charlotte in French. 'I told him you were *déshabillé* but he insists . . .'

'It's quite all right, I'll see what he wants!' Charlotte broke in.

The girl bobbed a curtsy as she said in a low voice: 'Now

139

I have removed your gown, you will not need me any longer, will you, Mademoiselle?'

Charlotte was tempted to tell her to stop grinning so suggestively and remain in the room until Ket left. But, realizing that Ket would almost certainly dismiss the girl anyway, she told her she could go. She pulled her *peignoir* more tightly across her body, sat down on the dressing table stool and picking up her hairbrush, busied herself brushing her long chestnut hair. The *femme de chambre* bobbed a further curtsy, this time to Ket, before leaving the room and closing the door as she did so.

'So, at long last we are quite alone!' Ket stated as he came to stand behind Charlotte and regarded her reflection in the mirror.

She did not look up to meet his gaze as she said, in as matter of fact a tone as she could manage, 'I understand you have something to say to me, Ket. What is so urgent it can't wait until the morning? As you can see, I'm preparing for bed and this is no time for you to be here.'

'I'm well aware of that, Charlotte, but you know my train leaves early tomorrow and quite possibly I shall be gone before you are up. This may be the last chance I have to talk to you alone – indeed, the first chance, since we've always been in company with Guy and Verity,' he added in a disgruntled tone.

Conscious of the fact that Ket was standing very close to her and causing her heart to beat painfully fast, she turned on her stool, thus obliging him to step backwards. 'Since you are here, you had better sit down. There's a chair over there by the window.'

Ket made no move towards it and instinctively Charlotte pulled the edges of her *peignoir* more firmly together, her head bent as if to see what she was doing so that she need not look up at him. The gesture was useless, for now he caught hold of her hands and pulled her to her feet.

'Charlotte, look at me!' His voice was soft but nonetheless insistent. 'You can't go on avoiding me. Don't you under-stand, there is no time left for prevarications? You must know by now that I'm quite hopelessly in love with you. I have to know whether I'm right in believing you do care a little for me?'

Charlotte's hand went to her mouth as if to prevent the words that had sprung to her lips: *'I don't just care a little, Ket, I love you with all my heart!'* But the words remained unspoken.

'What's wrong? Why do you shut me out in this fashion? You've been doing so all week and yet . . . yet there have been moments when I was quite certain you wished me to kiss you as greatly as I wished to do so. Am I wrong? Don't you care at all?' He drew her hand away from her mouth and lifted her chin so that she was forced to look at him. His eyes were luminous and his tone so appealing, Charlotte felt her resistance weakening. She drew a deep breath, striving for calmness.

'Of course I care about you,' she said in as calm a tone as she could muster. 'I'm deeply fond of you, Ket, and I dare say you are right, there have been moments during this wonderful holiday when I did wonder for a moment or two if our friendship might include a kiss or two. Paris is such a romantic city, isn't it?'

For a moment Ket didn't speak, then he took hold of her arms and drew her against him. 'Then kiss me now, Charlotte! Give me one of those "friendly" kisses engendered by the romance of Paris.' His voice, deep and husky, sounded challenging and Charlotte knew at once that he meant it so. Somehow, he seemed to know that if she allowed him to kiss her she would have no choice but to return his kisses. She tried to turn her face aside but Ket would not permit it. 'You shall not elude me any longer, Charlotte. I love you – and what is more, I think you love me!'

Without further words, his face came down to hers and his mouth, burning hot, pressed against her closed lips. She felt his hands, no longer holding her arms, reaching round her waist and pulling her even tighter against him. Her legs trembled as the heat of his body set fire to her own. The stiff resistance of her limbs gave way to a melting yearning and

141

she made no protest as he pulled her down on the bed so that they were lying entwined. Ket's kisses became more ardent and she no longer tightened her lips against him but pressed her mouth to his. Only when he reached one hand to cover her breast did she draw away.

'Don't, Ket! Please don't!'

His eyes, dark, intense, searched hers. 'You do love me! I know you do! Why do you pretend otherwise? I want to marry you, Charlotte. Do you understand what I'm saying? I love you and I want to marry you.'

Ket was not to know how bittersweet his words were. She struggled to renew her resistance and drew away from him. Sitting up, she said: 'So perhaps I do love you a little – in one way. I mean, I don't deny that you are a very attractive man and . . . well, I'm not immune to your . . . your attractions . . .' She was stumbling on her words which, whilst in part were true, were very far from the admission of love she longed to make. 'And naturally, I'm very flattered that you should think you love me . . . ask me to marry you. But, strange as it may seem to you, I don't want to be married – ever. I . . . I don't want to belong to someone else. Do you understand, Ket? I value my independence.'

By now he too was sitting up. As she fell silent, he got to his feet and stood looking down at her, his expression inscrutable. 'Have I understood you correctly, Charlotte? Are you as good as saying you find me sufficiently attractive to welcome me as a lover but not as a husband?'

If he had intended to shock her, he had failed, Charlotte thought, for his accusation was nearer the truth than he could realize. Yes, she longed for him to kiss her, hold her, touch her. Remembering how she had lain with Guy and longed for Ket, she longed now for him to possess her, to make himself a part of her. Her whole body ached with that yearning.

The unbidden memory of that night in the hotel with Guy, and the reason for it, once more stiffened her resolve. However difficult, she had to make Ket believe she didn't really love him; that she would never marry him. 'I'm really sorry, Ket, if I've misled you,' she said as, needing to put distance between them, she walked towards the door. 'This isn't the first time I have been accused of leading a man on and then letting him down. I . . . I may not look as if I am that kind of person, but now and again I feel the need to . . . well, to enjoy a little flattery from the opposite sex, a few personal attentions. I . . . Truly, I didn't mean to hurt your feelings.'

Ket walked across the room and stood with his hand on the door knob, his face perilously close to Charlotte's. There was a totally unexpected half smile touching his mouth as he said: 'I've understood what your *kisses* told me and I've listened to what you have told me and frankly, Charlotte, I don't believe a single word you have said. However, I appreciate the fact that, whatever your reasons, at the present time my proposal and my love are not wanted. But we will most surely see each other again when we both return from our travels. Therefore I shall now say goodnight – and for the time being, goodbye as well, since I shall not expect you to be about when I leave for Chamonix in the morning.'

He brushed her lips lightly with his own and, turning on his heel, went out through the door without a backward glance. Charlotte's heart felt close to breaking as he closed the door behind him. Throughout the remainder of the night she lay awake, trying to overcome the feeling of desolation that was far greater even than when her beloved parents had died.

It was not until the first light of dawn appeared through the half-open curtains that she regained her former self-control. Today, she told herself with a sigh of relief, she, Verity and Guy would be leaving Paris for Italy. She now knew without any doubt that she could never stay in Paris again without the memories of Ket tearing at her heart. Today, she would revert to the person who had been happy to know she was with child. It was pointless to allow herself the folly of regretting what was irreversible. Even had it been, she reasoned, what possible future could there be for her and Ket? Moreover, it was more than possible that he hadn't really fallen in love with her. They had been thrown together intimately in this romantic city, and Ket was on the rebound from his broken engagement to Naomi Copley. The American girl was the kind of wife he needed, and she would have fulfilled Ket's need for excitement and adventure. Even had Charlotte not been with child, she had nothing whatever to offer him other than a small talent for painting watercolours, and a very able talent for sewing a neat seam.

Thoughts of Madame Hortense and those poverty-stricken years she had spent at the Maison in Hill Street helped restore the intense feelings of gratitude which had prompted her to lend her body to Verity. Once the baby was born, it would cease to be part of her and she would be free to live as she wished for the remainder of her life. The fact that she had borne a child out of wedlock and thus put herself beyond the possibility of marriage would make her no different from the Charlotte who had worked for Madame. During those years, she had resigned herself not only to spinsterhood but to a spartan, friendless old age. Then Verity had appeared like a fairy godmother and transformed her life; promising that she would be loved and cared for for the rest of her days.

No, Charlotte vowed, never again would she allow herself to regret that by giving Verity her heart's desire she had forever denied herself the joy of love.

Twelve

'Do you realize, ladies, that Monsieur Eiffel's tower in Paris is nearly four times higher than the edifice you are now gazing at?' Guy was pointing a gloved finger at the Campanile – the bell tower of the beautiful thirteenth-century Florence cathedral – its fantastic marble facade dappled by the early spring sunshine. 'Now I don't know about you two intrepid tourists, but I'm too tired after all this morning's sightseeing to go into the *Duomo*. I suggest that we repair to that rather nice looking tea shop adjoining Calmano's Antiques just off the Piazza del Duomo.'

Whilst Charlotte gave a sigh of relief, for she too was foot weary, Verity smiled as she tucked her arm beneath Guy's. 'I don't think they have tea shops in Florence,' she said gaily. 'But I do agree we are all in need of a rest.'

As the three of them made their way back towards the Palazzo Vecchio, she happily listed the sights they had seen since their arrival in Florence two days previously. They had booked into a small but pleasant hotel where they knew they were unlikely to encounter any of their acquaintances. Yesterday they had devoted first to the Church of San Lorenzo with its beautiful Medicean chapel, and then to the Santa Maris Novella's frescoes. That morning they had visited the national museum in the palace of Il Bargello; admired the famous Ponte Vecchio over the River Arno, and not least, the fantastic view of the whole city of Florence from the Piazzale Michelangelo.

It had been an exhausting schedule but, tired as she was, Charlotte had insisted that it should not be curtailed on her account. Although quite quickly fatigued, she welcomed any activity that would distract her from thoughts of Ket; of what he might be doing on the snowy slopes; of what activity she might have been sharing with him had it not been for her condition.

As they drank delicious Italian coffee in preference to the proffered weak tea, Guy took out his phrase book and learnt some words which he hoped might enable him to find a really nice *pensione* for Charlotte and Verity to live in when he returned to England. So far, his enquiries at their hotel had borne no result, but now Verity suggested they make enquiries at the antique shop adjoining the cafeteria. The owner, Signor Calmano – their waiter informed them in barely recognisable English – sold antiquities for people *di nobile origine*, translated by a laughing Verity as 'of noble birth'.

'Then I shall go and enquire if he has any noble clients who might be prepared to let their property to us,' Guy said, 'whilst you two girls enjoy another patisserie, or whatever they call their cakes in Italy!'

Verity watched with a loving gaze his tall figure weaving a way between the tables towards the door. 'I'm so happy to see Guy in such good spirits!' she confided to Charlotte as they drank their coffee. 'I must confess that there was a time when I began to think I'd been wrong to persuade him to do something so completely against his wishes. Do you know, Charlotte, when he agreed to meet you that night in London, I'm convinced it was only to put paid to my entreaties, and that he never once believed you would conceive as a result.'

She paused while a German tourist and his wife settled themselves at an adjoining table, then continued in a quieter tone. 'Although Guy tried hard to hide it when I told him the wonderful news that you were with child, he couldn't entirely conceal his dismay. He's such an honourable, upright man and despite knowing Matthew's true worth – or lack of it – I know Guy hates the thought of deceiving him. Perhaps I'm more ruthless than I appear, for I have no such compunction. As you well know, Charlotte, what we hope to do is for

Sir Bertram's good, for the tenant farmers, and, indeed, for Matthew and his family too, since Kneepwood would soon cease to exist under his guidance. Now I truly believe Guy has come to see our deception in that light and is as anxious as we are for our plan to succeed.'

'That's excellent news,' Charlotte said warmly. 'All has gone well so far, and now we've only to find somewhere safe to conceal ourselves until the baby is born. Had you thought, Verity, what we would do if . . . if Ket decided to pay us a visit? After all, if we are to remain here in Italy we shall not be very far from France, and when Guy returns home and tells everyone the fictitious story that you are more or less confined to bed here in Florence, what is more natural than that Ket should want to come to visit you?'

For a moment, Verity was silent. Then she smiled. 'I think you'll agree, dearest, that I'm becoming exceedingly skilled in the art of deception,' she said, 'for I have an excellent solution. If Ket were to announce his intention to visit us, he can be told that we have gone to Rome to see a maternity specialist and it isn't known when we will return.'

Charlotte nodded, her head bent over her coffee cup so that Verity should not see her expression. Verity's idea was a good one but it highlighted the fact that she would not see Ket again for a very long while. Which was all for the best, she told herself firmly.

Guy's return to their table put thoughts of Ket from her mind. He was beaming and clearly had good news. 'We are most fortunate,' he enthused. 'Quite remarkably so. Only yesterday one of Calmano's regular customers paid him a visit. The gentleman brought with him a painting of a Venetian scene by Carpaccio which the antique dealer was delighted to purchase from him.'

The Conte dell'Alba was a charming man from a distinguished family, the antique dealer had told Guy, adding in a low, confidential tone that in recent times, the *conte* had become somewhat impoverished due in part to the high taxes levied in Italy this past decade. His wife, the *contessa*, had died quite recently and the *conte* had decided to take their only child, a boy, to Rome to live with his aunt whilst he took a prolonged holiday abroad.

'Calmano was more than happy to elaborate,' Guy continued cheerfully. 'I gathered that many of the servants at the villa have already been discharged, only the old retainers being kept on. As Calmano understood the situation, unless reliable caretakers could be found, the *conte* might close the house altogether. He has given me the location of the Villa dell'Alba, which is some distance out of Florence in the countryside. It is quite isolated but stands in a lovely garden shaded by cypress trees and with a beautiful fountain and priceless marble statues scattered around.'

He paused while the waiter brought him some fresh coffee, then turned back beaming to his wife and Charlotte. 'Calmano thought I should waste no time going out there to see the *conte* and discuss the possibility of renting the villa for six months. It does sound ideal for, although it is isolated, you would be within five kilometres of Florence where there are excellent doctors, Charlotte – even a hospital should you need it. If you agree, Verity, I shall go there first thing tomorrow morning and, as tactfully as I can, put a proposition to this gentleman. If he will agree to let us his house for the next six months at a low rate, I propose to conclude the arrangement then and there. I have little doubt, my dear, that the villa will be to your liking.'

When, two weeks later, Verity and Charlotte stared out of the windows of their hansom cab, they agreed at once that Guy's eulogies were well founded. The long, straight drive leading up to the house was flanked on either side by tall dark green cypress trees pointing up to a postcard-blue Italian sky. At the end of the drive stood a large stone-carved three-storied house, fronted by a round, green lawn. In the centre of the lawn was a fountain sending sprays of sparkling water cascading down the flanks of a bronze horse into a circular basin.

Seeing the object of their scrutiny, Guy relayed the information the Conte dell'Alba had given him about this mythical winged horse. The sculpture was a copy of part of the

148

dell'Alba family crest and, when the fountain had been installed in the last century, the family motto had been inscribed beneath it: TERRAM SPERNO, SIDERA PETO. 'I scorn the earth, I seek the stars', Guy translated proudly.

'The count will be leaving for Rome soon after we arrive,' he told them as they left their hotel in Florence. 'I think he wishes to meet you both before he goes so there is no avoiding an introduction. Don't forget, Charlotte, that you and not Verity must play the part of my wife. In fact, from the time of our arrival at the Villa dell'Alba, it will be necessary for the two of you to exchange identities.'

As a result of Guy's cautionary advice, it was Charlotte rather than Verity who stood at his side and Verity a little to their left as they rang the great iron doorbell of the villa. The late March day was sunny and warm enough for them to be wearing short dolman capes over their walking out dresses. Pretty beribboned hats covered their heads. The count himself opened the door to them. He was a man in his forties – tall, thin, very much of aristocratic bearing.

'Please be welcome to my home, Signora Conniston!' he said, bending over Charlotte's gloved hand which he raised to his lips. His dark eyes were unsmiling as he bowed to Verity before returning his gaze to Charlotte. 'My housekeeper, Luisa, will show the rooms to you. I am sorry that she does not speak very much of your language, Signora Conniston.'

'I'm sure we shall manage quite well, Sir!' Charlotte said quickly, seeing that Verity was about to speak. 'May I introduce my companion, Signorina Wyndham?'

The arrival of a further coach with all their luggage put an end to the formalities and, having assured himself that his new tenants were quite happy to be left to their own devices, the count excused himself, explaining that he would be leaving for Rome within the hour.

Luisa, the plump elderly housekeeper, came hurrying down one of the two magnificent staircases which curved upwards to a minstrels' gallery. The walls on either side were hung with oil paintings of the dell'Alba ancestors. The woman was smiling broadly as she curtsied to each of them in turn.

'*Venga a vedere les cameres!*' she said, leading the way from the hall into a large, very beautiful room she called *il salotto*. The six tall windows were partially shuttered but it was still light enough for the new arrivals to see the magnificent, if very slightly faded, furnishings. Deep violet-coloured brocade curtains hung from ceiling to floor either side of the six windows. Two sofas of the same colour with carved, gilt backs stood at right angles to a vast fireplace carved in pure white marble. On the mantelpiece stood a pair of gold candelabra and a Venetian clock decorated with china cupids and gold, turquoise and pink flowers. Over it hung a magnificent fragile glass mirror.

'What a beautiful room!' Verity said, her eyes darting from one lovely piece of antique furniture to another. She put her arm round Charlotte's waist and hugged her. 'We're going to love being here, aren't we, dearest?' She turned to Guy excitedly. 'How clever of you to find this place, darling. I always thought the drawing room at Kneepwood was one of the loveliest rooms anyone could have but this . . .' She pointed to the domed ceiling which was painted like that of some of the churches they had seen in the city. 'If only you were to be staying here with us, I think I could happily live here for always!'

Conscious of Luisa's presence, Guy refrained from the impulse to hug his excited young wife to him. Instead, he linked his arm through Charlotte's. 'We shall have plenty of time to further our admiration,' he said. 'We must let Luisa show us the rest of the villa.'

Verity, however, was busy studying a large, gilt-framed portrait of a dark-haired, very Italianate woman, her head covered in a delicate lace mantilla, an exquisitly painted fan in one slender beringed hand.

The housekeeper stepped forward. '*La Contessa!*' she said in a low voice. From their limited understanding of Italian, they were able to comprehend a few of her next words. '*Morte . . . l'influenza . . . convulsioni . . . ospedale.*' The old woman's eyes were full of tears as she explained the death of her employer's late wife. To divert her from her

150

sad memories, Charlotte suggested they go upstairs to sort out their bedrooms. As they went up the wide staircase, she explained as best she could, with much use of sign language, that Guy snored very loudly and had to have a room of his own, since she could not sleep for the noise. Quite rightly, she had feared that the housekeeper would show her to a double bedroom for herself and Guy. Behind her, she could hear Verity giggling as if she were a young girl again.

Nodding her head in understanding, Luisa led them along the gallery where she stopped outside one of the rooms. Opening the door, she indicated to Charlotte that she should go in. At first, the interior seemed dark and gloomy, but Luisa hurried forward to open the shutters. Brilliant sunshine flooded the room and Charlotte gasped. Not even at Kneepwood, or any of the Connistons friends' big country houses, had she seen anything like this bedroom. Not only was it huge – nearly as large as the *salotto* below – but it was like a bridal suite. Everything in it was white and gold – the brocade cover of the big double bed, the white muslin curtains round the frame of the four poster and hanging floor to ceiling from the six large windows. The white tiled floor reflected the white and gold ceiling. A beautiful table stood in the centre of the room, its top inlaid with brilliantly coloured semi-precious stones. Against the walls stood two dark wood wardrobes intricately carved and highly polished.

'You should be having this room, Verity!' she whispered, for clearly it had once been the master bedroom for the late *contessa*.

'It is lovely but I'm sure I shall be perfectly happy with any room in this gorgeous house,' Verity said cheerfully.

Guy was offered the adjoining room to Charlotte's and Verity the next one along the gallery. Verity was laughing again as Luisa went downstairs to instruct one of the servants to bring up their luggage.

'Will I creep along to your room or you to mine?' she asked Guy, her eyes sparkling. 'We mustn't shock poor Luisa by being seen in bed together.'

Despite his dislike of all the secrecy, Guy was nevertheless

151

delighted to see Verity sparkling with happiness – something that had been missing for so long. A little of her excitement was infectious, and later that evening he stole along the passage like some secret lover to his wife's bedroom. More soberly furnished and decorated, it was almost as large a room as the white one and the bed amply big enough for them both.

'If only you could stay longer with us!' Verity whispered as he took her in his arms. 'Don't you love it here, Guy? Promise me you won't hurry back to Kneepwood too soon.'

'I promise!' Guy said tenderly, but although no date was mentioned that night, both knew it would not be much longer before he felt obliged to return to his duties at home.

A week later, Guy departed to England, promising to return before the end of April.

'I'll miss him dreadfully,' Verity confided to Charlotte as they strolled along one of the many stone-walled terraces in the Villa dell'Alba garden. The villa had been built on the hillside and from the terrace they could make out in the far distance the domes and towers of Florence. Near to hand, they looked down on the beautiful lake fed by a nearby mountain stream, the water shimmering in the late afternoon sunshine. The air was filled with the scent rising up from the *limonaia*, the orchard of lemon trees not far from the entrance to the villa. Juan, the old head gardener, had proudly shown them round the estate not long after their arrival, and every morning he brought baskets full of flowers for Luisa to decorate the house with.

'We shall have to get used to being on our own!' Charlotte replied.

Verity bent to smell the scent of one of the many rose bushes adorning the terrace. 'Well, we have very quickly become accustomed to our new identities!' she said, smiling. 'Do you think when we go home we'll forget to change back?'

Charlotte doubted it, wishing she could share Verity's amusement at what seemed to her to be an entertaining game. But try as she might, it was impossible to put out of her mind the fact that, were she not carrying a child for Verity and Guy, Ket could be here on holiday with them. At night, striving to find sleep in the exotic white bedroom with the moonlight streaming in through the unshuttered windows, she could not put Ket out of her mind. Somehow the fateful night with Guy had let loose the dormant physical side of her nature. Had she been asked beforehand what the wedded bliss Verity referred to might be, it would not have crossed her mind to think of sharing such intimacies with a lover. Now there was no unknowing what passed between man and woman, and she had only to think of herself in Ket's arms in her bedroom in Paris to understand the needs and passions such intimacy evoked.

With difficulty, Charlotte now forced herself to think of other things, to listen to Verity who was recalling, with much amusement, the visit paid to them by a female friend of the absent count. Not knowing he had removed for an indefinite period to Rome, the imperious old lady called upon them without warning a few days after Guy had left. A flustered Luisa announced the visitor's arrival to Verity and Charlotte with a whispered warning that *il Conte* always avoided her because she was such a hopeless *chiacchierone*. By her sign language, Verity successfully translated this as 'chatterbox'. But it was too late to avoid the visitor who sailed into the *salotto* where the girls were drinking lemonade.

Having introduced herself, she proceeded in faultless English to tell Charlotte that she lived only a few kilometres away and would be delighted if they were to visit her. She addressed her remarks entirely to Charlotte, believing her to be the lady of the house and Verity a mere paid companion. Verity had found the situation vastly amusing and somewhat overplayed her hand, dancing attendance upon Charlotte as if she herself were the next best thing to a servant. Fortunately, it turned out that the old lady was something of a recluse and had only come calling because she'd heard her servants gossiping about the English tenants of the Villa dell'Alba. It seemed she was well aware of the count's impecunious state

153

and, although at first shocked that he had resorted to allowing paid tenants into his family home, she was practical enough to appreciate the necessity for it.

'I greatly enjoyed her visit, didn't you, dearest?' Verity said to Charlotte as they made their way slowly back towards the villa. 'We're so good at pretending to be each other I doubt Sarah Bernhardt would better us.' She drew a deep sigh. 'All the same, I suppose we should try to avoid meeting visitors lest they ever came to England and saw us in our true guises. At least, from the way that snobbish old lady was talking, it seems she will never come to England since she considers our climate "*assoluto impossible*".' Verity's imitation was so good that despite her sombre mood Charlotte smiled.

'I've been thinking, Charlotte,' Verity continued. 'If you're feeling well enough, why don't we go to Florence after our siesta? We could buy ourselves one of those marvellous straw bonnets we saw when we were on our way to the *Duomo* and darling Guy would not permit us to stop! We could put on our black dresses and wear veils as if we were in mourning; then if we did meet anyone we knew, they wouldn't recognize us.'

Despite the fact that she was nearly in her sixth month, Charlotte felt remarkably well. The morning sickness had stopped and she was sleeping very well, except for the nights when she dreamed of Ket. The dreams were tormented – she saw Ket in a group of people but as she went towards him, he turned and disappeared into the moving crowd; or he was leaning over the rail of a ship as it drew slowly away from the quayside where she was standing. She always awoke from such dreams with a terrible sense of loss and tears running down her cheeks.

'I think your idea is an excellent one,' she said now to Verity. 'Only this morning Luisa said that Georgio, the coachman, would be very happy to drive us anywhere we cared to go. As far as I could understand, she wants us to explore the surrounding country before the baby makes it difficult for me to take a lot of exercise. She kept smiling and pointing to my stomach and saying "*incinta*".'

'That's not unlike the French word for pregnant, *enceint*,'

Verity said, hugging Charlotte's arm as they entered the villa. They stopped only momentarily to dip their hands into the cool water of the fountain. 'Perhaps during these next few months I could learn Italian and surprise Guy when he visits us,' she added.

'Guy will be home by now,' Charlotte remarked as they went into the big dining room for lunch, during which Verity speculated as to what her husband and children might be doing. But as they enjoyed Luisa's delicious meal of veal with a salad of grilled aubergines and tomatoes, followed by local cheeses and crusty Italian bread, Charlotte's thoughts remained elsewhere. Would Guy have received a postcard from Ket from Chamonix? she wondered. Would Guy write to Verity and remark upon it if he had? Might such a postcard or letter contain a message for her, or had Ket by now ceased thinking of her?

I must stop this, she told herself sharply. The sooner I put Ket completely out of my mind, the better it will be for me. I must try to think more about the child I'm carrying. There was no pretending she was not *incinta*, she thought wryly, since for some time now she had felt the baby move. Although clearly a part of her, somehow she still didn't think of it as hers, only as the child she was carrying for Verity – the much wanted son. Charlotte was certain that it would be a boy although she had no reason to believe it so. When she and Verity talked of it, it was Verity's baby. 'I shall call him Edward after my father,' she declared. 'Tomorrow I shall write to my parents and tell them I shall be presenting them with a grandson in July. They will be a little shocked that I'm not resting at home but I shall tell them they mustn't think of coming to England until little Edward's christening, since to do so when I've had so many miscarriages would be tempting fate.'

Charlotte knew Verity would have loved to buy some of the beautiful handmade baby garments they saw that evening in a shop in Florence, but she cautioned her not to tempt fate herself. 'I see no reason for it but I, too, could miscarry,' she warned Verity.

Such a possibility, however, seemed highly unlikely. The

155

Conte dell'Alba had given them the name and address of his family doctor in Florence who he highly recommended, and as Charlotte and Verity were in the city, they decided to call upon him and make an appointment for Charlotte. If all was in order, Charlotte hoped to give birth at the villa with a reliable midwife in attendance.

Il dottore – an elderly doctor by the name of Benelli – was not busy when they called and, at his suggestion, he examined Charlotte immediately in his consulting room.

'You are in excellent health and condition, Signora Conniston!' he told her. 'From the dates you have given me I think it most unlikely you would miscarry now and your infant should be born early in July. May I suggest you call to see me again in four weeks' time? Or, if you prefer, I could call on you at the Villa dell'Alba?'

He asked for news of the *conte*, which they were unable to give him, and with much bowing and shaking of hands, they said their goodbyes.

If it were possible, Verity's spirits rose even higher after the doctor's good news, and although Charlotte tried to emulate her joy, she couldn't rid herself of a feeling of dismay. No doctor had previously examined her; told her there were no complications and when to expect the baby to be born. Signor Benelli's pronouncement brought home to her the fact that what had begun as little more than an incredibly risky venture had now become an inescapable reality.

Trying to find sleep later that night as the moonlight flooded through the unshuttered windows, Charlotte tried desperately to feel pleased – if not for herself, for Verity and Guy. But although she did manage to be glad for their sake, she was devastated for her own. Were it not for this baby, she might even now be in France with Ket discovering the joys of winter sporting in the snowy mountains. It was even more heartbreaking to remember that he had genuinely wanted her to join him.

Aware as she had never been before of the hopelessness of her situation, Charlotte was no longer able to keep at bay the bitter pain of regret.

Thirteen

May 1889

T he intense heat of Italian summer had yet to come, but
nevertheless the temperature was in the mid-seventies
and both Charlotte and Verity were wearing wide-brimmed
straw hats and frocks of Indian muslin. Downstairs, Luisa
was supervising the preparation of a picnic lunch to take
with them on their proposed outing to the village of Sant'
Andrea. According to her, Sant'Andrea was not too far for
a pleasant carriage ride and, if Signora Conniston was not
'*troppo stanco*' on arriving there, they could continue to the
small hill town of Montespertoli. When Charlotte assured her
she was unlikely to be too tired, Luisa explained that it would
be cooler in the hills and the scenery would be '*bello*'.

'We mustn't forget our parasols!' Verity said as she turned
from the mirror to look at Charlotte. She lent forward and
gave her an affectionate hug. 'You look so pretty, dearest!'
she continued. 'And so slim! No one would ever guess that
you are now in the seventh month. I was like a mountain with
Lottie. Are you quite sure you feel well enough to undertake
this picnic?'

'Of course I do!' Charlotte said truthfully. 'I'm looking
forward to it. We've only left the villa once or twice since
Guy went home.'

Guy had arrived for three weeks at the end of April, much
to Verity's delight. He gave them news of Kneepwood and
the children, who appeared to be quite settled with their new
governess – a retired Scottish school teacher who Verity had
engaged before they departed to Paris. He also told them
angrily that Matthew had totally neglected the affairs of the

157

estate and as a result, the corn merchant, having received no order for seed, had failed to deliver it for the spring sowing. Furthermore, Matthew had taken it upon himself to sack the head groom who Guy considered an excellent fellow, for no better reason than that he hadn't permitted young Bertie to ride Verity's mare.

'I can't remain too long with you, much as I would love to, my darling.' he had told Verity. 'I know I don't have to tell you that Matthew is simply not to be trusted. At least I was able to reinstate Hanworth, albeit with a substantial rise in his wages and a personal guarantee that no one but myself should be allowed to give him notice!'

'And what of Monica?' Verity had enquired. 'Was she at all surprised when you announced that I was pregnant again – and remaining here in Italy?'

Guy had thought his sister-in-law disinterested. If anything she was relieved to have Verity out of the way and to be in charge, he'd said wryly. She had taken it upon herself to come in every day and interfere with the running of the house and disrupt the housekeeper's and Cook's wishes. Guy had brought with him two postcards from Ket addressed to 'The Family'. Quite naturally, Verity had taken them from him to read them first, but she had passed them on to Charlotte with a teasing smile.

'See how he hasn't forgotten you, dearest,' she'd said. 'Each one has a postscript saying "Please give my fond regards to Charlotte".'

Charlotte tried not to think about the cards, but when Verity discarded them in a waste basket for Luisa to burn, she had secretly retrieved them, feeling guilty as she did so.

'If you are seeing or writing to Ket, please give him my best wishes!' she had said to Guy when he left for home. However, Guy thought it unlikely Ket would return to Kneepwood but would probably travel further afield when the weather became too warm for his new sport of skiing. Guy had not given anyone the address of the Villa dell'Alba, saying that Verity and Charlotte would almost certainly be returning to England as soon as the doctor pronounced Verity well enough to travel.

One place Ket would not be was here in Italy, Charlotte thought as Georgio, the coachman, turned out of the driveway and headed the horses in the direction of Sienna. Had it not been so far away, both she and Verity would have loved to visit that medieval walled city with its spectacular cathedral. Instead, they would be turning westward soon after leaving the villa and driving to Sant'Andrea.

Poor Guy! Charlotte thought as their coachman drove the horses at a gentle pace past small farmsteads with their olive groves and vineyards covering the hilly countryside. How he must have hated the lies he'd had to tell!

They had been travelling a little less than an hour before coming upon a coach not unlike their own, stranded on the side of the road with a broken wheel shaft. Two ladies, one portly and the other stick thin, stood by their conveyance frantically waving their parasols. Their coachman was struggling to lift the heavy wheel from a ditch bordering a rundown vineyard. The plumper woman, resplendent in a plum coloured *poult-de-soie* travelling costume and heavily decorated hat, came hurrying over to their carriage and addressed Georgio, who had pulled his horses to a halt. Waving a small phrase book in one hand, her parasol in the other, in execrable Italian she asked Georgio for his help. Her accent was so Americanized that Georgio didn't understand a word she said. He climbed down from his seat, opened the carriage door and put down the step so that Verity could get out.

'We are English,' she said. 'Can we be of assistance? Perhaps our coachman could be of help to your man.'

The American lady's face went an even deeper red than heat and anxiety had already rendered it, this time with pleasure and relief. She only just restrained herself from hugging Verity. 'Oh, my dear!' she exclaimed, her Southern drawl even more pronounced. 'You just can't know how thankful I am to meet you. When our coach broke down here, miles from anywhere we know, I despaired. There has not been even a farm cart passing by.'

She seemed to suddenly recall that she was addressing a

159

stranger. 'Why, I've not even introduced myself,' she said. 'My name is Euphemia Hammel and I'm from Georgia in America. The lady standing beside the coach is my friend and companion, Miss Frances Austin. We're on our way to Sienna but after this misfortune, I fear it's unlikely we shall ever get there!'

Charlotte had by now joined Verity and the American lady, and Verity introduced them both, remembering just in time to give them their changed names.

'I'm sure Georgio and your own coachman will be able to repair your carriage, Mrs Hammel,' Charlotte said. 'Perhaps whilst we wait, you and your companion would care for a cool drink? We have a picnic with us and our houskeeper has packed plenty of lemonade wrapped in wet cloths to protect the bottles from becoming too warm.'

'You are just too kind, Mrs Conniston,' the American replied, beaming. She beckoned to her friend and further intoductions were made. Georgio went to help Mrs Hammel's coachman and the four ladies sat down on a rug on the grass at the side of the road. As soon as the drinks had been poured and distributed, Mrs Hammel began to ply her rescuers with questions. Had they, like herself, come from Florence? Where were they staying if not in the city? Were they tourists like herself and Frances? They were 'just crazy' about ancient buildings and artefacts. Were Verity and Charlotte also going to Sienna? Where was Sant'Andrea?

Fanning her perspiring face vigorously with a lace handker-chief, she put down her glass and dived once again into her reticule, producing a dog-eared *Baedecker* guide which she offered to lend Charlotte and Verity.

Miss Austin said very little, which was not surprising since Euphemia Hammel never stopped talking. However, in one of the rare silences, she said to Charlotte in her quiet, less strident voice: 'Do you by any chance have relatives in America, Mrs Conniston? When Euphemia and I were in Boston, we met someone of that name. Do you recall him, Euphemia? That tall, dark young man who was staying with your friends, the Copleys.'

160

'Great Scott, that must be Ket!' Verity said excitedly. She was about to add the words "my brother-in-law" when Charlotte broke in quickly.

'That might well have been my brother-in-law, Christopher Conniston!' she said. 'What a small world, Miss Austin.'

'Well, fancy you remembering that young man's surname, Frances!' Euphemia Hammel declared. 'I've always said you have a remarkable memory, my dear. I do recall Mr Conniston now – such a good-looking young man, and so charming. You were quite taken with him, Frances, if I'm not mistaken!'

Her companion blushed and looked quite embarrassed. 'Don't be so silly, Euphemia. I must be at least twice the young man's age.'

Obviously not over-given to sensitivity, the older woman continued her teasing until Verity said, as she had so often in the past, to Charlotte: 'Nearly every female falls for Ket's charm. Indeed, I quite fancy him myself, do I not, Verity? Mrs Conniston is married to Ket's elder brother, Guy,' she continued with a mischievous smile at Charlotte.

She saw the American woman glancing at Charlotte's figure and added, 'They have two delightful little girls and are expecting an addition to the family quite soon.'

Euphemia, as she now insisted she should be called, turned to Charlotte. 'That's just too wonderful!' she gushed. 'And I must say, my dear, I do admire your courage driving out in these remote places in your condition without a man to protect you.'

'Are you not doing likewise? And much further afield than we are going!' Verity challenged.

'Well, yes, dear, but not in Mrs Conniston's condition.'

To Charlotte's relief, the conversation was brought to an end by the arrival of Georgio with the news that the coach was now repaired. Farewells were exchanged, Verity and Charlotte only barely able to sidestep Mrs Hammel's request for their address in England.

'Not that I intend to go there, since we visited your country last year!' she said. 'And there are so many other countries we have yet to explore. Now we can't thank you enough for your man's assistance, can we, Frances? Do please take care of yourselves and be sure we shall never forget your kindness.'

With typical American generosity, she took her purse from her reticule and withdrew a number of notes. These she handed to Georgio who beamed happily at the unexpected tip.

'Very much!' he said as he escorted Charlotte and Verity back to their own coach. '*Americana signora molto lire.*'

'I think he means Mrs Hammel is very rich!' Verity said, laughing. 'I saw her giving him a very handsome tip for assisting her coachman.' She squeezed Charlotte's hand. 'I think we carried that off very well, don't you, dearest? Except when Mrs Hammel spoke about Ket. I was just about to say he was *my* brother-in-law and might have given the game away if you had not interrupted. Not that we shall ever meet them again since they have already "done" England. Just fancy them being friends of the Copleys and you and I meet them in the middle of Italy!'

For the next five minutes Verity reminisced, pondering Ket's engagement to Naomi Copley. She was unaware of the emotions that the sound of Ket's name and his near marriage to another woman aroused in Charlotte.

'Look, Verity, we have reached the crossroads where we turn right for Sant'Andrea,' she interrupted. 'We should tell Georgio to slow down a little for that road surface looks even worse than the one we have just been on. We don't want a breakdown like poor Mrs Hammel!'

Diverted from memories of Ket, Verity called up to Georgio to slow the horses since they were in no great hurry to reach their destination. The air was redolent with the smell of orange blossom and lemon flowers, and everywhere there were beautifully coloured butterflies enjoying the sunshine.

'This is such a lovely country!' Verity exclaimed. 'No wonder so many artists came to live and work here. We must pay a visit to Rome before we go home. I was reading in our *Baedecker* that the city is two hundred miles from Florence. Maybe Guy will take us there for a short stay after the baby is born. We could take the train home from there instead of from Florence.'

She turned to give Charlotte a quick hug. 'I'm so very happy, dearest, and all thanks to you. At one time, our plan seemed like an improbable dream, yet here we are with you carrying Guy's son for me.'

Charlotte attempted a smile. 'I wish you weren't so convinced the infant will be a boy. All we have planned will be for nothing if it should be a girl.'

Verity's face took on a look of deep concern. 'I would feel so guilty if that happened,' she said. 'You've sacrificed so much for Guy's and my happiness. Sometimes I wake at night and imagine you in a bridal gown about to be married and I ask myself how on your wedding night you could confess you were no longer a virgin and—'

'Verity, stop this nonsense, please!' Charlotte broke in. 'You've absolutely no cause to feel any guilt. I told you when first I proposed our plan that I would never marry. I am twenty-four years old as well you know, and should have been married long since had that been my intention.'

Verity frowned. 'I know you consider yourself too old, dearest, but you are very pretty and you have attracted the attention of that nice friend of Ket's, George Morrison, for one. I've no doubt that if you had given him any encouragement he would have proposed. I know he is not as handsome as Guy or Ket but—'

'No buts!' Charlotte interrupted. 'Even were I free, I have no wish to be married to someone like George, no matter how nice a man he is.'

Verity regarded her friend curiously. 'You are such a warm-hearted, caring person, dearest, it seems strange that you have never wanted to marry.'

To Charlotte's intense relief, she was saved having to reply by Georgio indicating the village of Sant'Andrea ahead of them. Almost at once, they were surrounded by a horde of young children, nearly all barefooted; the babies carried by their elder sisters were bare-bottomed. Smiling shyly, they ran along beside the walking carriage horses, gazing at the foreigners, their large brown eyes wide with curiosity.

Charlotte indicated to Georgio that they should stop beneath the shade of a large cypress tree in order to eat their picnic lunch, but the coachman shook his head, pointing to the children. He made pretence of cramming food into his mouth and Verity ceased smiling.

'I think he means the children will be hungry and eager to share our picnic!' she said. 'It's easy to forget how dreadfully poor the peasants are.'

She reached in her reticule and drew out a handful of coins. These she gave to Georgio to throw down to the children who now fell over one another to scrabble in the dust for this unexpected bounty.

Aware they would now be followed by the children, Georgio urged the horses on through the cobbled streets of the village and out into the countryside in the direction of Chiesanuova. Only when they had driven through this next village and had turned left uphill towards Montespertoli did he draw the sweating horses to a halt.

'*Mangiare qui!*' he told them, smiling.

'And why not eat here? It looks a delightful spot!' Verity said to Charlotte as she climbed down from the carriage and helped Charlotte to do the same whilst Georgio spread a rug on the rough grass and lifted down the picnic basket. He himself moved into the shade of another tree some short distance away and proceeded to unwrap the small bundle of bread and cheese Luisa had given him for his lunch.

'I expect Luisa told him to keep an eye on us!' Verity said, amused. 'I suppose she thinks two foreign ladies on their own without a man might be easy prey for brigands – if such exist in this beautiful countryside.'

Georgio had indeed been instructed by Luisa not to take her English *signoras* too far from the villa. They had taken time to see the home of the sixteenth-century writer, Niccolo Machiavelli, and the fourteenth-century triptych and marble font in the church of Sant'Andrea. Now Georgio shook his head when they suggested they continued a further mile to see the eleventh-century Pieve of San Pietro in Mercato. Pointing to the pretty enamel fob watch Verity was wearing, he said: '*Sono le tre meno un quarto, Signoras. É tardi!*'

'Goodness, it's nearly three o'clock already!' Verity said, looking at her watch. 'Georgio is telling us it's time to go back.' She looked at Charlotte, noticing that she did look pale. 'I think we have done quite enough exploring,' she said. 'Let's just sit back and enjoy this truly magnificent scenery as we go home.'

Charlotte was tired, but not unduly so, she reassured Verity as Georgio turned the horses' heads downhill.

'Maybe there'll be another letter from Guy waiting for you!' she said, for mail seemed to be delivered at any time on any day of the week except Sunday.

'Oh, I do hope so!' Verity said, sighing. 'I so long to see him. He must visit us again soon. Perhaps he will bring letters from the children. I miss them, too. Wouldn't it be lovely if we could have them all out here with us at the Villa dell'Alba?'

There was no mail for Verity on their return, but two days later she received a long letter from him.

> *My dearest dear!*

he had written in his neat italic script.

> *You may picture me in the library writing this letter to you whilst Ket is out riding with Matthew and can't enquire, as is his wont, if the address to which I shall send this is now a permanent one. It's best he does not know that I am writing to you, my darling.*
>
> *I know you will be as disappointed as I am to hear that I may not be coming to see you next week, nor have I any idea when that will be possible. The problem is that Ket has come home from France and is determined to come to Italy with me when next I go. Understandably, I suppose, he's of the opinion that I must know where you are residing if I am to travel to Europe to see you!*

The only solution that comes to mind, so long as Ket lingers on at Kneepwood – so unlike him, is it not? – is that you have come upon some of your French Canadian relatives and have succumbed to their pleas for you and Charlotte to stay with them. He is talking of going to north Africa for a few months and I'm hoping he will decide to further these plans soon. It is quite strange that, for the time being at least, he seems to have lost some of his wanderlust and is anxious, he tells me, for another jolly sojourn such as the four of us had in Paris. Frankly, it surprises me that he found those few days so entertaining.

Well, my darling, I trust that the letter you will now write will have the desired result and I shall be able to book my passage across the Channel without further delay.

Please give my very best wishes to dear Charlotte, who I trust remains in excellent health and isn't finding her condition too onerous. We are both so indebted to her are we not? I wish I could think of some magical method of repaying her for the selfless way in which she is helping us. To be truthful, my darling, there are times when I regret most deeply the ever increasing number of lies I have to tell. Deceit does not come easily to me and sometimes I wonder if dear old Ket believes a word I say, since I can't speak with any conviction.

There followed yet another page with news of their two little girls, who could talk of nothing else but the hound puppy Matthew had given them – *'probably because Monica refuses to have another dog in their house'*, Guy had added. Fortunately both Nanny and their governess liked dogs so the animal was allowed up to the nursery quarters. The children had asked if they might accompany Guy on his next visit to 'dear Mama', but Guy was happy to say that they seemed quite settled without her – unlike himself, for he missed her most dreadfully.

When Verity had finished reading Guy's letter for the

second time, this time aloud for Charlotte's benefit, her mood was subdued.

'Do you think we've been wrong to ask Guy to act against his nature?' she asked Charlotte. 'I know we've planned all this for his benefit rather than mine, so that he can inherit Kneepwood, but is this all too big a price to pay? And for you, too, dearest. I am suddenly filled with doubt.'

For a moment, Charlotte couldn't reply. When she did so, it was to say: 'You mustn't allow such doubts to torment you now. We can't undo what is already done and we must face the fact – Guy, too – that it's too late to wipe the slate clean.' In a rare gesture, she placed her hand over her stomach. 'This is Guy's baby in here, and according to that nice Dr Benelli there is no reason to suppose it will not be born fit and healthy. You know, Verity, I feel these movements inside me all the time now, and yet I never think of the baby as mine – it's as if it doesn't belong to me, and I know this is as well for all of us. I shall not want to hold it when it's born – only to be told that it's a perfectly formed, healthy child – and I pray every night that it's a boy.'

Verity was smiling happily again. 'Edward!' she said softly. 'Oh, Charlotte, as darling Guy said in that letter, we both owe you so very much. If only we could think of something as wonderful to give you in exchange.'

But it was not possible for them to give her the only thing in the world she wanted – the love of Ket Conniston, the man whose love she had forfeited forever.

Fourteen

May 1889

L ulled by the successful manner in which they had exchanged identities for the benefit of the American ladies in the hills, Verity and Charlotte were sitting in the garden one afternoon the following week, recalling the incident with some amusement. Hearing their girlish laughter from the vine-covered terrace where she was sitting at a garden table polishing the silver, Luisa smiled. In the two months since their arrival, she had grown fond of the two delightful English ladies, although she failed to comprehend why the husband of Signora Conniston was not with them more often. As she understood the current situation, he was due to arrive any day but such had been the Signora's expectations for the past three weeks.

The sound of a bicycle bell ringing by the kitchen quarters alerted her to the unscheduled arrival of a tradesman's boy, or perhaps an unwanted hawker or knife grinder. The sun was blazing down from a cloudless sky and, as she wiped the perspiration from her forehead with the corner of her apron, Luisa sighed. All sensible people would be enjoying their siesta at this hour, she told herself as she put down her polishing cloth and shuffled round the side of the house.

Recognizing the English postage stamp and guessing correctly that this was most probably from Signor Conniston, Luisa hurried across the terrace to where Charlotte was seated. Addressed as it was to Signora Conniston, Charlotte was obliged to take it although she realized it was intended for Verity. As Luisa returned to the kitchen, Charlotte handed the letter to Verity.

'Is it from Guy telling us when he will be arriving?' Charlotte asked as Verity opened the letter. But the look of happy anticipation on Verity's face gave way to a cry of dismay.

'Charlotte, listen to this, it is quite terrible!' she exclaimed. 'I will read it to you.'

It was my intention to be with you by the 14th, Ket having booked his passage to north Africa two days ago. Last night he informed me that he was determined to see Charlotte before he absents himself for so long and has announced he will travel with me to Italy as he can join his ship at Leghorn.

I have been unable to dissuade him, so it is imperative that you and Charlotte leave the villa immediately. I have postponed my own visit for a week pleading matters of the estate, but seven days is the longest time feasible.

I have just received your lovely long letter telling me of your encounter with the two American ladies. You might, therefore, advise Luisa you are visiting them, but of course leave no address nor indication when you might return from this hypothetical visit.

It is imperative that you leave word for me at the main post office in Florence as to where I might contact you, which I shall do as soon as Ket is obliged to leave to join his ship.

I have looked at the map and see that Sienna – which you said you both wished to visit – is only sixty miles from Florence and think this would be a safe distance from the Villa dell'Alba and my determined young brother.

I urge you both to leave the villa without delay as I do not wish Ket to suspect you are doing so to avoid him. He is already questioning the oddity of you remaining abroad so long in what he thinks is your condition, as indeed are Matthew and Monica.

I am as disappointed, as I know you will be my

169

darling, that we shall not be together as planned next
week. Do please take the greatest care of yourselves.

Charlotte's face had whitened as, instinctively, her hand
went to the all too obvious bulk beneath her skirts. There
was no possible way at this stage of her pregnancy that it
could be concealed from Ket. Guy was right to suggest the
only way out of this predicament was for her to go away
with Verity.

'I suppose Guy dare not risk us staying in a hotel in
Florence,' Verity said sadly. 'Sienna will be safe. I will
get Georgio to drive me into town this very afternoon
so that I may go to the railway station to discover suitable train times and see if they will book us into a suitable hotel.'

Charlotte tried to keep her mind on Verity's planning but
her thoughts were chasing one another like squirrels in a cage.
What had prompted Ket to take the extraordinary decision
to postpone his plans to travel to Africa? To avoid such a
thing happening, Guy had agreed never to advise Ket when
or where he might be going to meet Verity and herself.
Supposedly with Ket's steamship ticket booked for a specific
date, Guy had thought it safe to reveal his own travel plans,
whereupon Ket . . .

Charlotte's heart missed a beat as she guessed, with rea-
sonable certainty, that Ket was determined to see her whatever
the disruption to his arrangements. Were it not for the
baby . . . She bit her lip fiercely, determined not to allow
her thoughts to take her further into what might have been.
Turning to Verity, she said calmly: 'I will invent some story
for Luisa's benefit – a dying relative in England or some
such. We can't give her an address which she could pass
on to Ket and Guy. I will pack some suitable clothes, but
for what length of time will we need to be away, do you
think? A week? Two weeks?'

Verity frowned. 'We can only guess. Guy will discourage
Ket from staying. After all, there is nothing for him to do at
the villa and for all Ket knows, we could be away for a month.

170

When he finds us gone he will certainly want to resume his own travels.'

She rose swiftly and helped Charlotte to her feet. Her face was once more clouded. 'It will be unbearable to know Guy is here and I cannot be with him,' she said, sighing, as they returned to the house to find Luisa. 'And he will so hate this further subterfuge as much as he will hate my not being here.' She gave another deep sigh and attempted a smile. 'We've no right to complain, have we, dearest, when you are making so many sacrifices for us.'

'We should leave by midday tomorrow at the latest!' Charlotte changed the subject quickly. 'Although Guy said they wouldn't get here until Thursday, we daren't risk them arriving earlier than planned.'

To have Ket see her in this condition was certainly more than she could endure, she thought. They must say nothing to Luisa about Ket's and Guy's arrival for then Ket would realize they were being avoided deliberately.

Charlotte informed the housekeeper that she and Signorina Wyndham would be returning to England next day to see Signorina Wyndham's aunt – her only relative – who was very ill. Naturally, they were sorry to leave when the weather was so beautiful, but hopefully they would be back within a week or two – unless, of course, in the unfortunate event of a funeral. But they would give Luisa plenty of warning so that she could air the beds and prepare food.

'But here is much food already prepared!' Luisa cried. 'Who shall eat it all?'

Guy and Ket, Charlotte thought wryly, but pretended not to have understood Luisa's protestations as she went slowly upstairs to pack.

Unlike his older brother, Ket spoke fluent Italian among several other languages. It was he, therefore, who questioned Luisa when, on their arrival at the villa, they discovered that Verity and Charlotte had departed two days before.

'But why? Where have they gone? Surely they told you something of their plans?' he said, his disappointment so

171

acute he spoke far more sharply than he might otherwise have done.

Luisa shrugged her shoulders despairingly. 'It was the letter,' she told him. 'The letter from England which arrived two days ago. The signorina told me the relative was very ill – perhaps dying.'

Ket turned to Guy, frowning. 'I thought Verity said Charlotte had no relatives.'

'*Zia! Zia!*' Luisa repeated when Ket questioned her further.

He turned back to Guy, his disappointment so obvious that Guy was filled with dismay at the thought of all the lies he had told Ket.

'I'm afaid I don't know too much about Charlotte's background,' Guy muttered, glad to be able to speak the truth for once. He was aware, of course, that the dying aunt was fictitious and that, if the girls had taken his advice, they were somewhere in Sienna. His heart had been in his mouth when the hired coach had brought them from the railway station to the villa. He hadn't been one hundred per cent certain that his letter warning them of his arrival with Ket had ever reached Verity; or that they had managed to do as he suggested and find themselves somewhere to hide out in Sienna. As soon as he could, he wanted to go back into Florence to call in at the post office and see if there was a message from her. He hoped it would say that they were in good health and were just awaiting word from him as to when they could return. He was as desperate to see Verity as Ket appeared to be to see Charlotte.

It was causing Guy no little concern that Ket's feelings for Charlotte were not as transient as he and Verity had supposed. He had been quite shocked when, at the eleventh hour, with his luggage packed and his ticket safely in his keeping, Ket had suddenly announced that he was not going to leave next day after all but, since Guy now had an address for Verity and Charlotte in Italy, he would go there with him and continue his journey to Africa at a later date. Nothing Guy had said – without it being too obvious he did not want him along

172

– had dissuaded him. On the contrary, the more difficulties Guy raised, the more Ket's determination to go with him increased.

In desperation, Guy had sent the letter when Ket had turned to him suddenly and said: 'It seems to me, old fellow, as if you aren't too keen on me paying my addresses to Charlotte. I know Verity thinks I'm not really serious in my intentions and that I'll end up breaking Charlotte's heart. Well, I can tell you here and now, I'm very much in earnest. I know I'm not much of a catch but I do love her and I think she might care a little for me, despite what she says.'

Deeply disturbed, Guy had argued, 'You've often thought yourself in love before now, Ket, and it's come to nothing. What about Morrison's sister? Only last month—'

'I was on the rebound from Charlotte!' Ket interrupted. 'She and I had had such a wonderful time together in Paris and then . . . well, she said she wasn't interested in me, and when Amelia set her cap at me, I thought for a little while I might get over the way I felt about Charlotte – but I couldn't. I can't. I do love her, Guy, and I'm going to ask her to marry me. That's why I'm coming to Italy with you.'

Luisa was far from happy. Delighted to have Signor Guy back at the villa, and charmed by his handsome brother, she wished almost as much as they did that Verity and Charlotte were not so unfortunately absent. As she told the younger Signor Conniston, the ladies really had not given her any inkling as to how long they would be away – only that they were going to England. Signora Conniston had implied they might be back quite soon so long as the poor English lady did not die and they were obliged to remain longer for the funeral.

'So there is really not much point in you hanging around, old chap,' Guy said to Ket. 'They could be weeks – and who knows, they may decide not to come back at all. If Verity is well enough, they might return home.'

'I thought the doctors had told her she mustn't travel until after the baby was born,' Ket said thoughtfully. 'She must be a great deal better if she has gone to England with Charlotte.

173

Why hasn't she gone back to Kneepwood in any case, Guy? It doesn't make sense.'

Nor did it, Guy thought miserably. One lie so easily led to another. Were there no one else but himself to consider, he would then and there have told Ket the truth, although it could only make him even more unhappy. But he had no right to betray Charlotte who would no more wish Ket to be told than would Verity.

'Maybe that is exactly what the two of them plan to do,' he replied to Ket. 'We shall just have to wait and see.'

Sighing, he tried to relax whilst he waited for news, and more urgently waited for Ket to leave. For three days, his brother prowled round the house and gardens like a caged lion, becoming increasingly restless. Guy suggested a day in Florence visiting the cathedrals, art galleries, museums, but Ket would have none of it. He wished only to remain at the villa where he was expecting the girls to return at any minute.

'Since they are unaware we are here, they have no reason to return in a hurry,' Guy said. 'It's not as if they were expecting my arrival, still less yours, old chap. I dare say if we have heard nothing by the end of the week, I might well return home. Of course, you must do as you please.'

Slowly, Ket's disappointment gave way to resignation. At least, he consoled himself, if Charlotte were attending a dying aunt in England, she was not on the point of promising herself to someone else! Maybe he was being too impetuous. Whatever was happening now, Verity would certainly be going home after the baby was born, and undoubtedly Charlotte would be with her. He could ask Guy to send him a telegram advising him they were safely back at Kneepwood and then he could curtail his Africa trip and return at once to see Charlotte.

Much relieved by this suggestion, Guy agreed at once that this new plan of Ket's seemed the best possible idea, and the following day he himself drove Ket into Florence, putting him on a train to Leghorn where he would link up with his original itinerary.

174

With a certainty that his brother posed no further danger of discovery, he hastened to the post office. Finding the promised letter from Verity advising him of their whereabouts, he decided to go to Sienna first thing the following morning to bring them back to the villa.

Before going home he called in at Calmanos where the old man greeted him with a beaming smile. The signor must stay and take coffee or perhaps a glass of wine with him. Maybe the signor would like to look around the shop and see if there were some small trinket or objet d'art which the signor would care to purchase as a little surprise for his charming young wife.

'Such a beautiful face! Such *bella cappello* – the colour of *castagna* – which Guy interpreted from the man's miming was chestnut. With a small shock, he realized that the antique dealer was referring to Charlotte rather than Verity and, wistfully, he reflected that he could not be happier than when this whole unfortunate scheme was behind them. He knew that his beloved wife and her friend had devised this mainly for his benefit – if not entirely for him – in the hope that his father would soften his prejudice against him and leave Kneepwood to him. Matthew, he thought as he glanced round the antiquities in Calmanos' shop, was without doubt a wastrel, a ne'er-do-well, and a dishonest one at that. He'd not paid his farrier for a year and was denying he owed the fellow the sum he was demanding. Guy had paid it, of course, for he knew the man well and was in no doubt at all that he would not have claimed payment for services he'd not made. Matthew had been gambling on the fact that, if it came to a court hearing, it would be his word against the farrier's and he'd be given the benefit of the doubt. When Guy had reprimanded his half-brother, Matthew had merely shrugged his shoulders and said "it was worth a try". There was little Guy could do to change his attitude other than to threaten to tell their father – at which point Matthew had laughed, knowing Sir Bertram would never take Guy's side against his.

Would the advent of a son really safeguard Kneepwood and all its tenants? Guy wondered as, feeling obliged to do

175

so, he purchased a pretty Italian brooch he thought Verity would like, and a less costly bracelet for Charlotte. Whilst he was in the shop, he decided also to buy presents for his two little girls – a tiny silver and enamelled pendant for Kate and a pretty marcasite brooch for Lottie.

Having paid for his purchases, he returned to the villa where he informed a delighted Luisa that he expected his wife and Signorina Wyndham to be returning the next day. As he sat down to eat the meal she had prepared he experienced a gamut of emotions: relief that Ket was finally out of the way along with a certain uneasiness that this was the first time in his life he'd ever been pleased to see his much-loved younger brother's departure. Then there was the overwhelming feeling of relief that, for the time being at least, there need be no more lies other than the one they were still living; a fierce determination that never again would he allow himself to become enmeshed in such deception. But overriding all these concerns was the impatient longing to see his cherished wife again; this last emotion tinged only with the disturbing thought that it was for his sake that Ket would always be denied his chance to marry the woman he seemed so genuinely to love.

Fifteen

'The new nurse seems very competent!' Verity remarked as she and Charlotte settled themselves comfortably in the coach taking them and their luggage to Kneepwood. The nurse with her luggage, the baby and the baby's paraphernalia was following behind. Guy had gone on ahead to prepare the staff for their arrival.

He had engaged the woman temporarily to meet the boat train at Dover and take charge of the infant until Nanny took over at Kneepwood, his wife having discharged the Italian nurse at Calais. Competent though she had been, the reasons for not bringing her with them to England were twofold. Firstly, Verity and not Charlotte would once again be Mrs Conniston on their return, and secondly, the Italian girl who had looked after the baby since its birth at the end of June was apprehensive at the idea of living abroad.

'Guy said this woman has excellent references,' Charlotte replied, her voice listless. Verity regarded her anxiously. 'You're sure you are feeling well?' she enquired. 'I'm certain you have lost a great deal of weight since the baby was born.'

'The *dottore* said I was in perfect health!' Charlotte reminded her. She let her thoughts roam back to the day after the birth when the doctor had found her in tears. He had been immensely kind, despite the fact that he couldn't have known the real cause of her despair, supposing it to be her obvious disappointment that the infant was a girl.

'Such a beautiful little *principessa* you have, Signora Conniston. Another time you have the *figlio*, no? You have much good health and you will have many sons. No more tears, Signora, eh?'

For the best part of a week, Charlotte had been unable to stop crying. She realized Guy and Verity were worried about her and did their utmost to hide their own disappointment, but nothing either one said to reassure Charlotte could assuage her feeling of failure. Verity had been so certain she was carrying a boy! That, after all, had been the whole point of the plan.

At the end of that first week, when she had steadfastly refused even to *look* at the baby let alone hold it, Guy and Verity had come to see her with the announcement that if she had changed her mind and wanted to keep the child, they would not stand in her way. Moreover, Guy would arrange for Charlotte always to have sufficient funds to support it and herself. But it was the very last thing Charlotte wanted. She had never once looked upon the baby as hers. She'd merely been the bearer for Verity and Guy. Surprisingly, both seemed taken with the infant, which they, Luisa and the doctor all remarked looked like her father. Finally, Charlotte had visited the nursery and seen for herself the baby's grey-blue eyes and the wisps of brown hair. Even the slight quirk of one eyebrow was a replica of Guy's. She could see nothing whatever of herself, nor had she felt an urge to hold the baby, to reclaim it as part of herself.

Now, on their way back to Kneepwood after an absence of six months, they were returning home. Verity was glowing with excitement, longing to see Kate and Lottie again and to show them their new sister. The baby was to be called Florence, 'to remind them of their happy sojourn in Italy', she had announced to Charlotte. It did not occur to either of them to suggest Charlotte choose a name. Somewhat to their surprise, it was Guy who doted on the child who, he said, reminded him of a little cousin who had died of consumption when he was barely out of petticoats himself. It was as if she had been returned to him, he had declared.

'I suppose I shall receive the usual disparaging remarks from my father-in-law!' Verity commented as the coach headed across the Kent countryside towards Ashford. 'He

178

takes pleasure in humiliating me. Not that I shall let it worry me. I'm more concerned about Monica's comments. From what Guy has said, she is highly suspicious of our prolonged stay abroad and the consequent separation between Guy and myself. Knowing how devoted we are, I suppose it must have seemed very strange to her.'

'But she can prove nothing by her suspicions,' Charlotte said reassuringly.

'It's as well Ket is away,' Verity said. 'I think he might have asked a few searching questions that we can do without. I wonder how he's enjoying Persia. Very much, I don't doubt, for he always enjoys his travels. Guy thinks he's unlikely to be home before Christmas.'

For which she would be truly thankful, Charlotte thought, knowing she couldn't live under the same roof as Ket without falling even more deeply in love with him. She had determined to use all her strength of will to put him out of her heart and mind, for only that way lay peace.

The excitement and bustle of their return to Kneepwood did temporarily put all other thoughts from her mind. Sir Bertram was once again laid up with gout and was at his most disagreeable. He criticized Guy for having gone away for yet another month, as he had done in order to be with Verity and Charlotte at the time of the birth. The old man blamed Guy for the many things which had gone wrong in his absence – nearly all of which had been due to Matthew's mismanagement.

'You know very well Matty has had little experience in managing the estate!' he'd said to Guy. 'You're supposed to be in charge, but you go gallivanting off to some barbaric country for no purpose other than to enjoy yourself.'

Guy made no attempt to argue with his father's criticism when he returned home, and Matthew, who was present, made no attempt to shoulder any of the blame. Nor was Charlotte able to do so when Sir Bertram decided to take his bad temper out on Verity.

'The usual story!' he ranted. 'When you and Guy do manage to propagate, all you can do is produce yet another

179

useless filly. For God's sake, why can't the pair of you beget a son like Matthew here?'

White-faced, Guy now did stand up to his father. 'Kindly show a little more respect to my wife, Sir!' he said in a cold, hard voice. 'And since you have chosen my brother as an example, may I remind you that he has also produced "fillies" as you prefer to call them.'

Sir Bertram banged his fist down upon the table beside his chair so that his whisky glass shuddered and the liquid slopped over the rim. His face was scarlet as he shouted: 'Don't you dare bandy words with me, you young whipper-snapper. Now get out of the room, the lot of you; and don't let that nanny of yours bring the child near me. That's an order!'

As they went upstairs to supervise Nora's unpacking of their trunks, Verity said sadly to Charlotte: 'Poor darling little Florence – first you don't want to see her and now it's Sir Bertram who refuses to do so, although he's no surprise. Never mind. I shall make it up to her.'

There was little need for her to do so, since both Kate and Lottie were already the infant's adoring slaves. When Verity went up to the nursery, it was to find Nanny sitting comfortably in the nursing chair feeding the baby with a bottle whilst the two little girls argued as to who might be first to undertake this duty. The governess, Miss Armstrong, was also gazing at the blue-eyed infant with undisguised admiration, and Dolly had stopped laying the table to gawp at her.

'Oh, Mrs Conniston, what a beautiful baby – and so like her father, if I may be permitted to say so,' Miss Armstrong gushed. 'We were all so concerned for you out there in a foreign land – and with your medical history, well, we did wonder if you would ever manage to bring back a little brother or sister for the girls.'

Verity lent over and touched the baby's cheek. 'You mustn't forget that I had Miss Wyndham to take care of me,' she said as she turned to drop kisses on the heads of her little girls. 'But for her we might not have our little Florence!'

And that was the truest word she had spoken since she had arrived home, she told herself as she went in search of Guy. As she entered their bedroom, he appeared out of his dressing room where he had been changing for dinner. He hurried towards her and enfolded her in his arms.

'I'm very sorry Father was so abominably rude to you!' he said. 'I suppose it was stupid of me to hope he would give us a happier homecoming.'

Verity raised her face to receive his kiss. 'Believe me, my darling, I am not in the least put out. I have just had a lovely ten minutes with the girls and they're really thrilled to death with the baby. I think she has quite superseded the puppy, Gladstone, who was banished from the nursery in case he harmed the infant.' She raised her arm to brush back a lock of brown hair that had fallen over Guy's forehead. 'It's so lovely to be home. Do you know, darling, were it not for having failed you, I could even be perfectly happy. I really love that baby, despite—'

Guy put a hand gently over her lips so that she couldn't voice the fact that it was not her infant but Charlotte's. 'She is *our* baby!' he said. 'And we must thank the good Lord that Charlotte has no wish to make claim to her. I find it hard to understand her disinterest.'

Verity drew a deep sigh. 'From the very first, Charlotte never wanted a baby for herself. She wanted it for us – for me. I don't think she ever allowed herself to think of it as hers. Had there been any such risk, she would never have suggested she have a baby for us. As to you loving little Florence, could I presume to think it's because everyone says she's the image of you?'

She smiled briefly as she hugged him. Then her anxious look returned.

'Had you thought, dearest, that since the baby is not the boy we so desperately wanted, all this year's escapade may have done is to make your father even more certain to allow Matthew to inherit? Maybe we should let a little time go by and then ask Charlotte if she would consider trying again? She is so generous I'm certain that she would do so.'

Guy drew back from Verity's embrace. In a cold, sharp voice, he said: 'No, Verity! Don't for one single moment consider it, for I shall never agree – not even though I know I shall ultimately lose Kneepwood. I couldn't go through these past months again. Little though the love is that I have for my father, I still shudder at the thought of deceiving him; of having to lie to everyone; even old Ket who I know would trust me to the end of the earth. No, darling, I cannot and will not do such a thing ever again. Frankly, with hindsight, I don't think we should ever have done it.'

Verity's eyes filled with tears. 'Oh, Guy, I had no idea you felt so deeply. I know in the beginning, when Charlotte and I first devised the plan, you didn't want to participate in it; but later, you agreed and . . .'

'Only because you were so dispirited, my darling. I realized that you felt you had failed me when you had your last miscarriage, and that this wild idea would rectify everything. But of course, there were always pitfalls, not least that the child might be a girl. I didn't appreciate quite how much I would dislike the scheming, the lies, the deceit; or, my dearest one, how much I would hate being parted from you.'

His arms tightened around her once more as he confessed: 'After Ket went off to north Africa and I didn't have his company to cheer me, I was so lonely and downhearted here without you that I realized my love for Kneepwood was nothing beside my love for you. So you see, my darling, now that you are back home with me, that's all I care about. In a way, I'm almost glad the baby is a girl and that we can now put this last year behind us and live openly and honestly again.'

'Oh, Guy!' Verity whispered through her tears. 'If you are happy, despite everything, then I shall be too. I just wish I could be sure that Charlotte has no regrets. Like you, I find it hard to believe she has no feelings for the baby. Why even I, who am not her real mother, love her dearly and always will, for she is part of you. Charlotte will not even go near the nursery.'

'We must allow her to do as she wishes,' Guy said. 'On

the boat coming home she was telling me how much she had loved Italy, the country and the people; that she would like to go back there. She said she could understand now why people so loved to travel, and that she might wish to do so herself one day.'

Verity's eyes filled once more with tears. 'I'm so devoted to her, Guy. She is like a sister to me. I should be quite miserable if she went away.'

'But you wouldn't try to dissuade her, would you, dearest? I would make any wish she had financially possible. In fact, I have decided to arrange a regular income for her so that she can be quite independent of us. We are so much in her debt, it's the very least we can do.'

Verity blew into the handkerchief Guy had given her and drew a deep breath. 'You are right, of course. I won't be selfish – in fact, I will suggest to her that she might like to take a short holiday away from us all.'

Nevertheless, when she approached Charlotte that night as she was preparing for bed, it came as a shock when Charlotte at once fell in with the suggestion that she might like to go away for a while.

'I was intending to tell you earlier, Verity, that there was a letter waiting for me from Madame Hortense,' Charlotte said. 'She has been quite ill and said she would really love to see me. I think I told you that once, when I was so ill I was close to death, she came to my rooms and nursed me back to health. In those days, I was only her employee and no one could have blamed her for ignoring my predicament. But for her, I would almost certainly have died. I would like to go to London and reassure myself that she is having proper care. She let slip that Sally, her maid, now takes her little dog Daybreak for his outings twice a day. That was one of her most enjoyable occupations, so I fear things may be worse than she wanted me to believe.'

With an effort, Verity concealed her dismay. 'But of course you must go, dearest! When you have decided upon the day, we will ask Cook to prepare a basket of nourishing foods to

183

take with you – some calves-foot jelly, perhaps, and a jar of her best beef broth.'

It was perfectly true that Madame Hortense had asked Charlotte to visit, but her former employer was not the only reason Charlotte wished to go. Nor, as Verity might have supposed, did she wish to put a distance between herself and the baby. It was the association of Kneepwood with Ket, who she was trying so hard to forget. Sooner or later, one of the family would mention his name, even the odious young Bertie, who hero-worshipped the uncle who had taught him on his last visit not only to fish but to ride his new rubber-tyred safety bicycle as well.

The following morning, there was yet another long letter from Ket, who had been exploring the Holy Land.

'Gets around, that boy, don't he!' commented Sir Bertram half admiringly next morning as the family sat around the breakfast table.

'When will Uncle Ket come home again, Grandpa?' asked Kate, who had been called downstairs with Lottie to receive their uncle's postcards.

'Your guess is as good as mine, young lady!' Sir Bertram replied. 'If the boy isn't enjoying himself too vastly, I daresay he'll be back sometime this autumn.'

'In time for Florence's christening, I hope!' Verity said. 'I want him to be her godfather.' She had wanted Charlotte to be one of the godmothers, but Charlotte had declined quite forcefully saying she preferred to remain completely detached from the baby.

As talk of the proposed christening continued round the table, Charlotte made an unobtrusive exit and hurried to her room. The thought of Ket as godfather to the baby had been strangely disturbing. He didn't know that she had birthed the little girl. How horrified he would be were he to know that Florence was born as a result of a liaison between Guy and herself. No matter how worthy her motives, he would see her as wanton, dissolute, and judge Guy and Verity, as well as herself, to be deceivers. Which indeed they all were, Charlotte told herself unhappily, and all because she had been first to think of the plan to provide a son for Guy. And even that she had failed to achieve. Perhaps if she had been able to give Verity a little boy she would not feel so inadequate, so ineffectual as she did now.

The need to get away from Kneepwood was even more urgent now than it had been before Guy had read Ket's latest letter. Verity had been talking of having the infant christened in October and that was only two months away. If Ket were to return home for the occasion, Charlotte could not bear to be present.

There was a knock on Charlotte's door and Verity came into the room. She looked quite beautiful, Charlotte thought, as she sat down on the ottoman at the end of the bed and arranged the pleated folds of her cornflower-blue skirt. In her beringed hand she held a folded white piece of paper which she now handed to Charlotte.

'It's an enclosure for you from Ket, dearest,' she said. 'Guy saw the opening address and realized it was personal. He didn't think you would want him to read it aloud at the breakfast table.'

Charlotte's face had turned first red and then a deathly white as she stood up from the escritoire by the window. Her hand was trembling as she held it out to take the folded paper from Verity. Seeing her agitation, Verity said gently: 'I'll leave you to read your letter in peace,' and without further comment she left the room, closing the door softly behind her.

It was a full minute before Charlotte could bring herself to unfold the paper. She realized it was unlikely to contain a further description of Ket's travels, for such accounts were impersonal and could have been included in the family letter. Suppressing her agitation, Charlotte started to read.

Dearest Charlotte, for that is what you are to me, believe it or not – probably not, for I can see you frowning, shaking your lovely head and saying, 'What nonsense is that man talking now?' But it is not nonsense, Charlotte. I have already told you that, when I parted from Naomi Copley, you were in my mind, and more so on the way home when I found myself hoping that you had not become engaged to marry another.

Those next weeks at Kneepwood and in Paris were wonderful in that I could spend time with you and enjoy your company every day – and yes, I still enjoyed them although you so often rejected my attempts to attract your approval and repelled any advances I dared to make.

Charlotte, I have never forgotten that wonderful afternoon when I met you off the train at Kneepwood Halt and you took your hair down and you allowed me to kiss you.

I think that is when I first thought there might really be some hope for me, those hopes only to be cruelly dashed when you seemed to be so taken with dear old George Morrison at their party. And afterwards . . . afterwards you let me kiss your lips, Charlotte, and it was then I knew you did love me a little, even although you strove so hard not to let me know it. In Paris, too, you tried to hide it until that last wonderful night when you allowed me to come to your room and just for a little while, you responded to my loving.

Oh, Charlotte, why then did you run away from me, hiding yourself in Italy for so many interminable months? I know I'm not in the least what is called 'an eligible bachelor', I have none of the prerequisites for a husband. Is this why you turn away from me, Charlotte? Is there really no hope for me? Is it my adventuring that you dislike? If so, I would try to set it aside.

When Guy told me he was uncertain when you and Verity would be returning, I decided that I must try a little harder to put you from my heart and mind. I hoped here in the Holy Land to recover my spirits, but I have not succeeded. So I shall come home in time for the christening of Verity's new baby which, I pray for Guy's sake, is a boy and that he was born safely. When

186

*I return, Charlotte, my sweet, sweet girl, I shall ask you
to marry me. No matter how ill-advised you might be to
say yes – and I have no doubt you would receive such
advice, since I have nothing but my love to offer you –
I beg you not to refuse me too hastily.*

*I think of you in my waking hours, darling Charlotte,
and you are always in my dreams.*

Charlotte sat down on the edge of her bed and, closing
her eyes, pressed the letter to her heart which was beating
furiously. For a moment or two she could think of nothing
but that Ket loved her. She didn't doubt for one moment the
validity of the emotions he had so eloquently expressed. *He
loved her.* He was going to ask her to marry him. If she were
to accept, she could be his wife. She could live with him,
share every day and night with him . . .

The thought of nights spent in Ket's arms, of being his
lover, being loved by him, brought the colour rushing to
Charlotte's cheeks. Memories of what had happened between
her and Guy in the London hotel were superseded by imaginings of Ket lying beside her as Guy had done, holding her,
invading her . . .

Then sanity returned. It was almost a year now since she'd
put herself beyond Ket's reach forever. Not only could she
never betray Guy's and Verity's secret or reveal the baby's
true illegitimate status, but she could never confess to Ket that
she had already had intercourse with a man – still less with
his own brother. To do so would be to lose forever the love
and respect he now had for her. Though she had forfeited the
right to claim it, at least he would remember her as someone
worthy of his love. He would not despise her.

That she could deceive Ket by not telling him the truth
until after their marriage flashed across her mind, but the
possibility was instantly rejected. She loved him too much
to delude him in such a manner and to risk his subsequent
scorn when he discovered her deception.

Two days later, Charlotte left for London. Verity was openly weeping as she said goodbye, but not even to comfort her would Charlotte promise a date when she would return. Nor had she gone up to the nursery to see the baby who, by all accounts, was thriving in Nanny's care. She had sent a telegram to Madame Hortense advising her of her arrival but had not received a reply.

On the train to London, Charlotte momentarily forgot her concerns at Kneepwood. Madame Hortense's letter had been written two weeks before their return from Italy and Charlotte realized there was a possibility that her former employer's health might have seriously deteriorated. When finally the hansom cab pulled up outside the Maison Hortense the door was opened for her almost upon her pull at the bell by a woman Charlotte assumed to be Madame's charwoman. With a strong Cockney accent, she greeted Charlotte effusively and all but dragged her indoors.

'I been awaiting you ever since your telegram arrived!' she said, beaming. 'Madam is ever so glad you're visiting. You will stay, won't you? She's been right poorly and the doctor's been in and out like nobody's business. You is Miss Wyndham, ain't you, Miss?'

Before Charlotte could reply, the woman took her portmanteau and beckoned her to follow her upstairs to the little spare room in Madame's flat above the salon.

'There now, Miss, I've made the bed up for you like Madam said and put a stone bottle in to make sure the sheets is aired. You tek orf your 'at and coat and I'll put the kettle on, it being nearly tea time and I dare say as 'ow you could do wiv a cuppa, yes? Then I'll 'ave to be on me way. I've 'arf a dozen young 'uns be wanting their tea at 'ome, but I didn't want to leave Madam without someone 'ere to tek care of her.'

With considerable anxiety, Charlotte made her way to Madame Hortense's bedroom. She was shocked to see the figure propped up against her pillows who, despite her welcoming smile, looked haggard and white-faced but for two red spots on her gaunt cheeks betraying a fever. Ignoring the tiny dog curled up on the bed at Madame's feet, Charlotte bent to kiss her forehead.

188

'Don't look so concerned, my dear!' Madame said in a husky voice. 'I know I've lost a bit of weight but I'm much better now, and all the better for seeing you. You're not looking all that perky yourself!'

After the charwoman had left a tray of tea for them and they were on their own, Madame Hortense probed further. 'No need to tell me what you've been up to!' she said, sighing. 'You've disregarded my advice and had that baby, haven't you, you silly girl!'

Charlotte tried to smile. 'I'm twenty-four years old and no longer the girl you once knew. Yes, I did have a baby – it turned out to be a little girl.'

Madame took a sip of her tea and regarded Charlotte speculatively. 'I suppose you kept your word and gave the infant to your friend. Now, I suppose, they don't want it because it's not a boy and—'

'No, that's not it!' Charlotte broke in. 'Verity adores the baby – she looks just like Guy. He loves it, too.'

Madame Hortense sighed. 'I see! And you're breaking your heart because you want the child yourself?'

Again Charlotte shook her head. 'No, on the contrary. Not even when I was carrying the baby those months we were in Italy did I ever feel it was mine. After its birth – which was far more painful than I had expected – when the midwife handed it to me, I made Verity take it from me. It didn't seem to be part of me any more and that is the truth even though it may sound most unnatural.'

Perhaps because even at birth, the infant looked exactly like Guy. Had it looked like Ket . . . She stifled the thought, fearing that her regrets might render her unable to conceal her tears.

'Let's not talk about me,' she said in a falsely bright tone. 'I'm here to discover what has been wrong with your health. In your letter you said you had been ill since June. Has the doctor given a name to your indisposition? It must be more serious than you told me since you've closed the salon and are confined to bed.'

'Oh, you know what doctors are – they hum and haw and

keep changing their minds. A bout of pneumonia seems the most likely verdict. Anyway, I'm better than I was and all I need is a little longer to regain my strength.'

'And the salon?' Charlotte enquired. 'Won't you lose customers if it remains closed too long?'

Madame sighed. 'Quite possibly, my dear. But who could I entrust to run it? Another couturier would in all probability steal my clients and I couldn't trust the business to an unknown. Now, if you were here . . .'

Charlotte caught her breath. It was as if Madame Hortense had understood the true state of her emotional life and was offering her a way to escape from Kneepwood and its associations with Ket. She believed herself quite capable of running the salon to Madame's satisfaction. It would keep her busy without too much time to think about the way she had ruined her life and destroyed all chances of a happy marriage to the man she loved. There was no doubt whatever that Verity and Guy would allow her to remain under their roof for the rest of her life, free of financial or any other responsibility. Guy had already spoken to her about giving her an allowance so that she could travel if that was her wish; to be independent. But that seemed to her as if she was being paid for what she had been through this past year; for trying to give them the son they wanted. Now, if she took on the salon for Madame Hortense, she would be earning her independence and not having it as a charity.

For the next two hours, until Madame visibly tired and needed to rest, they enlarged the plan, Madame with relief and Charlotte with a growing enthusiasm. It seemed there was a young woman, not unlike the girl she had once been, who Madame would have employed had she herself been up and about and there to supervise. She would now give the girl the job of assistant whilst Charlotte took charge.

'But as soon as you are well enough, I shall hand back the reins to you, Madame!' Charlotte said. 'I'm agreeing to this only as a temporary measure.'

'I understand, my dear, and I can't tell you how grateful I am for your offer. You can live here with me unless you wish otherwise.' She paused to stroke the silky coat of the tiny Pomeranian dog beside her. 'Daybreak will be pleased to have some extra company, and perhaps you could find time to take him for short walks in the park occasionally. I shall so enjoy your company, my dear, but won't you miss the gay social life you enjoyed with Mrs Conniston?'

She did not fail to notice the shadow that clouded Charlotte's face as she replied: 'Later, perhaps, when you are feeling stronger, I will tell you all about my life with the Connistons and why I have no desire to stay with them any longer. But that can wait. The fact is, your offer has come as a great benefit to me and I can only say how glad I am that it will be of benefit to you, too.'

It was agreed that Charlotte should return to Kneepwood the following day to pack up her belongings and explain her plan to Verity. A week later, when it came to their parting, Verity was in tears and Charlotte had a lump in her throat as she said: 'It's only until Madame is well enough to take charge again. Then I promise I will come back, even though I can't promise I will stay. We'll write to one another, shan't we? And you can come to London to visit the salon. Only the other day you were saying you needed a new tea gown and a walking out dress for the autumn, as well as something very special for the christening. Madame will be delighted that you're once again patronising her salon.'

Verity's tears ceased as she gave Charlotte one final hug. 'Now I know it will only be a for a few weeks before you return, I am not quite so sad. Don't forget, dearest, that now and forever more you are like the sister I never had. Come back soon for I shall miss you sorely.'

But soon it was not to be. Neither Charlotte nor Verity were aware that a considerable time would pass before Charlotte would see Kneepwood Court again.

Sixteen

For the first few weeks after Charlotte had reopened the Maison Hortense, she was too busy to write the letter she knew she must compose in reply to Ket's proposal. She was by now aware of the seriousness of Madame's illness and had been advised by the doctor that she was unlikely to live beyond six months. Well aware how much store Madame Hortense set on her beloved establishment, Charlotte had given her promise that she would remain in charge until Madame was better and able to take charge herself. If Madame was aware that this could never happen, she gave Charlotte no indication that she did.

During daylight hours Charlotte had little time to think of her own misfortunes. Clients who had been unable to order garments from their favourite dressmaker returned eagerly once the doors of the Maison were opened again. Apart from the novice assistant Madame had had in mind, Charlotte was obliged to employ two extra, experienced seamstresses. Then there were the walks Daybreak so much enjoyed in nearby Hyde Park. They were not long but nevertheless took up even more of her time. It was only in the evenings, when she sat by Madame Hortense's bedside stitching a hem of a skirt or sewing lace on to the neckline of a bodice for an evening gown, that there was any time to talk.

'No one at Kneepwood knows when Ket will return from his travels,' Charlotte confided in her friend. 'It might not be for months, but on the other hand he could turn up at any time. He's very impetuous and when he learns I am not at Kneepwood, he will almost certainly come here to London.

192

I cannot let that happen, Madame – I dare not! I must reply to his letter so that it awaits his homecoming . . . leaves him in no doubt that I cannot . . . will not marry him. But . . .'

'But you know that your letter of rejection will be the end of your relationship,' Madame finished for her. Seeing the tears gathering in Charlotte's eyes, she added gently: 'Are you quite, quite certain that your young man wouldn't be able to overlook your lost virginity? You wouldn't be the first bride to intimate a fall from a horse as the cause!'

Despite her misery, Madame's deviousness brought a brief smile to Charlotte's face, but it became deeply serious as she said emphatically: 'I love him too much to lie to him, to cheat. Even if I were to tell him he was not the first man who I had lain with and he was prepared to overlook it, there is the child . . . Yes, it looks exactly like Guy at the moment – everyone says so – but suppose, when it grows up, Ket were to see a likeness to me . . . No, Madame, I have always known that the child was something he could not overlook.'

Madame's eyebrows were raised ironically. 'I seem to recall you telling me the baby is a girl, Charlotte – *she*, not *it*. However, I appreciate the fact that your mind is made up and you don't intend to give poor Mr Ket Conniston the choice as to whether or not you are a fit person to marry.' She gave a deep sigh. 'I can't recall any occasion when you have taken my advice about your life, so I shall refrain from giving it now, Charlotte. I do understand that in the circumstances you don't feel you can live with your friends at Kneepwood any longer, and I'm more than happy to assure you that you have a home here and indeed an occupation, for as long as you need it. You have become like a daughter to me.'

Charlotte lent forward and brushed the grey hair gently from Madame's feverish forehead. 'I'm so very grateful. You rescued me when my parents died and kept me from starvation. Now, when I need you, you are rescuing me again. I can't tell Verity the real reason I can never go back to Kneepwood, for she has no idea I am in love with Ket and were she to guess it, she would feel guilty that it was for her I had put myself beyond Ket's reach. She will be hurt by my decision but I'm sure I can convince her that I need the stimulus, the challenge of my work here.'

'So the decision is made and you will stay with me?' Madame asked.

'Yes, Madame, and I shall write to Verity and to Ket this very evening after I have walked Daybreak and we've had our supper,' Charlotte forced herself to promise.

There were tears in her eyes as she wrote first to her friend informing her that, in view of the seriousness of Madame's illness, it was unlikely she would return to Kneepwood in the foreseeable future.

As for the affectionate sentiments Ket expressed in his last letter to me, she wrote, *I have taken this as meaning no more than light-hearted banter. You know what a dreadful flirt your brother-in-law is! Will you kindly pass on to him the enclosed letter when he next returns home, and when you do so, do please give him my best wishes for his future. In the same way as I look upon you as a dear sister, I have the same regard for Ket as if he were my brother . . .*

The letter she enclosed for Ket was not so easy to compose. She decided to be as matter-of-fact as possible so that he would be in no doubt that she would never agree to marry him.

The sentiments you expressed came as a surprise, she wrote. *Naturally, I am most flattered, although I suspect that the magic of Paris may have prompted the feelings we both experienced there. However, on my part they were of a temporary nature only and, as Verity will tell you, I have returned to London to live with my dear friend Madame Hortense and to the occupation I so much enjoy – running her dressmaking establishment. I am not domesticated by nature and therefore I have never wished to be tied by matrimony to such duties as marriage would entail.*

You expressed a fear that my consideration of your proposal might be affected by your lack of financial assets. I do assure you that this has no bearing whatever on my decision as to my future. Were I inclined to matrimony, I should concern myself only as to the suitability of my proposed husband and myself as partners. I am sure that on reflection you will arrive at the same conclusion as myself that, despite any other consideration, we are not well suited.

Thank you once again for the kind thoughts you expressed, and please believe that I shall always remember you as a very dear friend with whom I shared many happy hours.

Charlotte was no longer able to restrain the tears as she added her signature to her letter. She left it unsealed until the following day in order to read it in a calmer frame of mind and to assure herself that she had given Ket no encouragement to pursue his attentions. Fearful lest he should decide to come to London in an attempt to dissuade her from her decision, she added a postscript saying briefly that there were no circumstances which would change her mind.

Charlotte now devoted herself to the running of the Maison Hortense and to nursing Madame, who was becoming increasingly frail. The doctor who called on a regular basis wished his patient to go into a hospital but, knowing how Madame Doris (as she had asked Charlotte to call her) abhorred the idea, Charlotte insisted she could manage, although she was becoming increasingly exhausted. It was only when the doctor insisted upon Madame having the attentions of a day nurse that Charlotte was able to relax a little bit.

Verity wrote regularly every week. Although Charlotte had told her she had no wish to be told news of baby Florence, Verity never failed to mention her – how pleased Nanny was with her progress; how greatly the children adored her; how Guy doted on her and how Sir Bertram had still not deigned to see her! The old man had suffered yet another attack of gout and was increasingly bad-tempered – sufficiently so for even Matthew to keep out of his way.

Matthew had squandered his monthly allowance – destined to be spent on the repairs necessary to the roof of his house – on a smart new high-perch phaeton. A pair of perfectly matched greys came as part of the costly package and Sir Bertram was complaining about the additional expense of feeding these extra horses. Not so Monica, Verity had written, obviously with some amusement. Dressed in her finest tailor-made costume with its smart Newmarket jacket, her sister-in-law never missed an opportunity to ride up beside Matthew when he was showing off his high-stepping equipage in Kneepwood village. Occasionally young Bertie was permitted to ride in his mother's place.

Autumn was nearly over and Christmas was approaching before Verity and Guy had word from Ket. He had found friends in Syria who had persuaded him to travel on to Turkey with them, where they planned to explore some of the ruined Byzantine churches of Anatolia. It was too good an opportunity to miss, he had stated, but he would without question be home for Christmas, a time now set aside by Guy and Verity to have Florence's postponed christening. Verity's letter was pleading.

> *If Madame Hortense can possibly spare you, you must come and stay for the occasion, dearest!* she had written. *I insist that you should be one of the godmothers and I will brook NO refusal over this. Ket, of course, is to be Florence's godfather. I pray Madame Hortense is well enough for you to come and stay for the few days either side of the christening, although I shall quite understand that you would not wish to leave her alone over Christmas itself . . .*

'But of course you must go, child,' Madame Hortense said, her voice now only barely audible. 'We will ask Nurse if she can stay overnight for one or two days, and if not, I can always go into hospital as Dr Groves wishes.'

Charlotte enfolded one of Madame's frail hands in her own. 'Please believe I have *no wish* to go back to Kneepwood. Not only does it hold too many memories, but the occasion of the christening itself is not one I want to attend. I realize I can be made a godmother in my absence so I would rather detach myself totally. No, Madame, with your permission I shall write back and, if you will allow, say you do not wish me to leave you.'

Which was little more than the truth, Doris Briggs thought as she watched Charlotte hurry downstairs to see a client. Not that she would have admitted so had Charlotte wished to go away. Nevertheless, she treasured what little time she had left with the girl she'd all but adopted. Not only was Charlotte caring for her as if she were her true daughter, but she was managing the salon every bit as well as – if not better than – she herself had ever done. This was satisfying in itself, but even more so because she knew the demands of her work kept Charlotte from feeling the terrible regrets that might haunt her had she the time to think.

Doris Briggs turned restlessly in her bed. In a few minutes her capable day nurse would bring in her tea and medicine before washing her and making her bed for the night. Such activities were becoming increasingly tiring and she was less and less inclined to make any effort. She was, she knew, more than ready to die had she only herself to think about. But she worried about Charlotte's future happiness. At least she had ensured that the girl was financially secure. Even if Charlotte didn't wish to continue running the Maison Hortense and deriving an income from it as Doris herself had done for the past twenty-five years, Charlotte could always sell the premises. Its value would have increased greatly since she had purchased all those years ago. Charlotte would then have enough capital to invest in a modest annuity. No, it was not Charlotte's physical well-being but her mental happiness that worried her.

Once or twice in the past, Doris had found herself wondering whether Charlotte would be torn between her promise to give her baby to the Connistons and her own maternal instinct

197

to keep it. But on the rare occasions when Charlotte referred to the baby, she did so as if it were indeed her friend's child and of no concern to her. Doris had long ago decided that only someone as selfless and devoted as Charlotte could ever have contemplated bearing a child for a friend. Not only was there the extreme discomfort and risks of childbirth to be endured, but the risk, too, of their deception being discovered. It was fortunate for all concerned that the baby appeared to take after her father – her appearance something none of the participants seemed to have worried about before the birth.

Wearily, Doris Briggs tried to sleep. From downstairs she could hear the high-pitched tones of one of the clients, followed by the murmur of Charlotte's voice. Poor child! she thought – losing first her parents, then her home, then her child and now her lover. Was she never to find lasting peace, happiness?

Verity regarded the groom's hot, perspiring face with growing apprehension. Since the man's intense agitation had rendered him all but incomprehensible, she endeavoured to keep her own voice quiet and controlled.

'Tell me again, Jackson – you are saying that one of Mr Matthew's greys has come back with a broken rein hanging from its neck but the other horse has not returned?'

'Yes M'm, that's it exactly, M'm. The poor beast is in a right awful lather and them two's never apart of a norm, M'm. Somefink awful's 'appened, I just knows it.'

His voice had risen another few notes and Verity said firmly: 'Could Grainger not find Mr Conniston – Mr Guy?'

'No, M'm. Nor Mrs Matthew neither though Mr Hanworth' – he referred to the head groom – 'said t'was Mr Matthew what went out with the phaeton. He had Master Bertie with him. Jim's ridden out on Star to go looking for 'em, M'm, and said as 'ow if Mr Conniston weren't 'ere, I was to come and tell you.'

Keeping her own voice steady despite her misgivings, Verity said: 'Tell Gregory to take one of our horses and ride down to the village. Hanworth may need help if he has found Mr Matthew. Meanwhile, we must just wait for one of the men to return with some news.'

Realizing that the groom was genuinely shocked by his suspicion of a nasty accident, Verity added: 'Things may not be so bad as you suppose, Jackson. Now find Gregory and then go along to Cook and ask her to make you a cup of strong tea – with a tot of brandy in it.'

As he left the room, Verity herself realized that Jackson had every reason to be worried. For Matthew to have allowed one of the pair of carriage horses to run off, he could only have lost control of the animals or the carriage. And meanwhile, where was Guy? If there had been an accident, his presence was essential, for he would know what to do. Suddenly she recalled that Guy had been riding over to Slaugham to visit his mother's elderly sister. This was a duty he did not enjoy but carried out every year near the anniversary of his mother's untimely death, the old lady having no other living relative. Her house was in a village a good many miles distant and Verity knew Guy could not possibly arrive home before darkness fell.

She had a sudden longing for Charlotte who would without doubt have been a great comfort at a time like this. Charlotte never gave way to panic, which she herself was prone to do in an emergency if Guy were not at hand to back her up. As she paced the floor of the drawing room glancing every now again through the French windows at the darkening sky, she heard the door burst open and, turning, saw Monica pushing past the footman to get into the room.

'Verity, have you heard? Matthew and Bertie have not come home yet or sent word. They must have had an accident. Jim has gone to look for them. One of the horses came galloping into the stable yard covered in lather. You've not heard any news, have you?'

Her face was ashen and although Verity actively disliked her sister-in-law, she felt deeply sorry for her at this moment. If it had been Guy and one of her children who was missing . . .

With an effort, she put a comforting arm around Monica's

bony shoulders. 'I'm sure Jim will be back presently with good news for us, Monica,' she said soothingly. 'I expect it's something quite unremarkable – the phaeton has lost a wheel or some such, and Matthew and Bertie have had to shelter in one of the farms. Doubtless at any moment a messenger will come hurrying up to the house to tell us where they are.'

'But the horses . . .' Monica gasped. 'Matthew thinks the sun rises and sets on that pair of greys. He'd never have let one run off like that with a rein broken and dangling. It could have got caught up and . . .'

'Monica, stop this pessimism immediately. Now sit down and let me get Grainger to give you a little glass of brandy to calm you down. This is not like you at all and I'm sure Matthew would laugh at your concerns.'

'I dare say he would!' Monica said in a sharp, bitter voice. 'If you want the truth, my concern is not so much for him as for my darling Bertie. If anything has happened to Bertie . . .'

Her voice had begun to rise hysterically and Verity went herself to the sideboard to pour a small glass of brandy for Monica from the decanter. In all the years she had known her sister-in-law, she had never seen her lose her self-control. Her own feeling of apprehension deepened. According to Monica, Matthew and Bertie had departed soon after ten that morning, stating that they would be back in good time for luncheon. It was now close on two o'clock. Even Matthew, ill-mannered and inconsiderate as he was, would not have stopped at an inn for his midday meal without sending a lad to advise Monica he would be late. Besides, there was the runaway horse . . .

A further half hour passed before their worst fears were realized. A neighbouring farmer's son arrived on foot leading the second of the carriage horses into the yard. Alerted by the dogs' barking, Verity and Monica hastened to the window and saw Hanworth hurrying the lad towards the kitchen door. A few minutes later, a white-faced Grainger came into the drawing room.

'It's Farmer Pearson's lad, Dick, Madam,' he said. 'I'm afraid he has some very bad news.' He glanced quickly at

Monica and then away again. 'If you would care to question him, Madam, he's in the hall. Shall I show him in?'

Verity laid a restraining hand on Monica's arm as she nodded to Grainger. Dick, his cloth cap tucked under his arm, his face crimson, was pushed into the room by the butler.

'Speak up, boy!' Grainger said as the lad began to mutter.

''Twas Mister Matthew and the little 'un, M'm!' the boy said. 'In the ditch, M'm. The carriage were on top. Me Dad were ploughing four-acre field and saw one of t'orses rearing up and t'other one bolted and next thing, carriage were upside down in ditch. Me Dad weren't strong enough to right carriage so 'e tolt me to run 'ere and 'e'd run to village to get 'elp.'

'The boy – Master Bertie!' Monica shouted as she stepped forward to grab the terrified farm lad by the arm. Her face was twisted by fear and anxiety. 'Did you see the boy? Was he all right?'

'I dunno, M'm, I dunno!' Dick gabbled, fearing the tall thin lady was about to strike him. Verity stepped forward and gently eased Monica's grip on the child.

'Let me find out what else he knows, Monica!' Turning to Dick, she placed a hand under his grubby chin. 'There's nothing to be afraid of, Dick,' she said softly. 'Nobody is going to blame you for whatever is wrong. On the contrary, you have been a very good lad to come to the house so quickly with Mr Conniston's horse. Grainger shall find you a small reward after you have told me all you know.'

The boy's face brightened and he looked at Verity expectantly.

'Did your father tell you if either of the two persons in the upturned carriage spoke to him?' Verity questioned, the casual tone of her voice hiding her own anxiety.

Dick shook his head. 'Not as I 'erd 'im say so, M'm. I'd have asked 'appen I'd knowed you wanted to know, M'm!'

'Yes, of course you would,' Verity replied. 'I suppose if your father had thought one or other of the persons in the carriage was injured, he'd have gone to fetch the doctor, wouldn't he?'

Dick scratched his head, his eyes screwed up in the effort

of working out the right answer to the question. 'Mebbe!' he said at length. 'But mebbe not if 'e thought they was dead. When me grandad died, me dad fetched undertaker, not t'doctor.'

Despite the extreme gravity of the situation Verity could not restrain a smile, which vanished quickly as she heard Monica's gasping sobs behind her. Nodding to Grainger to remove the boy, she turned to her sister-in-law and, in as strong a tone as she could muster, she said: 'You really mustn't give way at this point, Monica. We have no proof whatever that any serious harm has come either to Matthew or Bertie. Clearly the boy knew nothing of any reliability – he was only repeating what he thought his father had seen. Now drink that brandy I gave you and pull yourself together. I dare say some men will arrive at any moment with your two wounded soldiers needing our care and attention. I'm sure I've heard you tell me what a demanding patient Matthew is, and I dare say Bertie will be first to want his mother's attentions.'

And everyone else's, Verity thought but immediately chided herself for even thinking so unkind a thought when the wretched Bertie might indeed be dead. She gave a deep sigh, glancing at the bracket clock over the mantelshelf and wishing the hands had moved on a great deal further so that at any moment Guy would be there to support her.

Guy, however, was still two hours' ride from Kneepwood when the news finally reached Verity and Monica that both Matthew and Bertie were dead, their necks broken instantly when the carriage had somersaulted into the ditch. The vicar was first to inform them, arriving in his dog cart, whereupon Monica fell in a deep faint and was put to bed by the housekeeper. Thus the poor woman missed the gruesome sight when, half an hour later, Farmer Pearson and three other strong men came slowly up the drive pulling a handcart on which lay the bodies of her husband and favourite son.

Meanwhile, Sir Bertram had been enjoying his customary afternoon rest during which no one was permitted – on any pretext – to disturb him. Verity had therefore decided that, until there was any positive news about Matthew and Bertie, he was not be to woken. By now, however, Sir Bertram had woken from his siesta and summoned his valet to explain the meaning of the commotion clearly audible from downstairs. Although well aware of events, the servant prevaricated, pretending he was not too sure what had occurred lest his master flew into one of his violent tempers and berated him. In no good mood, and as soon as he was dressed, Sir Bertram hobbled downstairs, complaining with every step of the painfulness of his gout. Hearing Sir Bertram's angry voice on the stairway, the vicar beat a hasty retreat and it fell to Verity to break the dreadful news to her father-in-law.

Not unexpectedly, Sir Bertram's shock and grief took the form of a towering rage. He had warned Matthew against buying the greys, he ranted. He'd told him not to buy a phaeton from so-called friends who would not be disposing of it had it been of well-built, reliable construction. And not least, he had warned him not to drive 'those confounded beasts so demmed fast'. He then turned his wrath on Monica despite her absence, blaming her for allowing Matthew to ride out on so unreliable an equipage and not least for allowing him to take young Bertie with him.

It was only as the old man mentioned the boy's name that his anger evaporated like a puff of smoke and his face was suffused with grief. Clenching his fist against his mouth, he staggered out of the drawing room into the library, closing the door and locking it behind him.

Shaken to the very core of her being, Verity summoned Grainger and told him to send one of the servants down to the village post office to despatch a telegram to Charlotte. The wording was brief but to the point. Matthew and Bertie had been killed in an accident. Sir Bertram and Monica were prostrate with grief, and she herself had never been in greater need of her friend. Please, please would Charlotte come, if only for a few days, to give her support.

Charlotte showed the telegram to Madame Hortense who refused to listen to any of Charlotte's protestations. She

203

herself dictated the telegram to be sent immediately by one of the seamstresses saying yes, of course Charlotte would come. She would catch the next possible train to Kneepwood.

Seventeen

December 1889

'I will be alighting at Kneepwood Halt,' Ket replied to his travelling companion as the train from London to Tunbridge Wells left the station.

'I know Kneepwood quite well . . . stayed for a weekend's hunting with a jolly fellow by the name of Morrison – George Morrison,' Ket's fellow traveller announced. 'Darc say you know him?'

Before long, the two men were in friendly conversation and in his easy-going manner Ket was soon telling the stranger not only about his recent travels but his plans for the future. 'I'm counting upon this lady accepting my proposal of marriage,' he confided.

His companion, a middle-aged banker residing in Tunbridge Wells, smiled at Ket's handsome face. 'I can see you are very much enamoured!' he said. 'However, I have to confess I am a little confused. Didn't you tell me that you'd been travelling in the Middle East during these past months? What if some other admirer has stepped into your shoes in your absence and won the regard of this matchless young lady?'

The smile left Ket's face and he frowned. 'I'm not usually a coward,' he said, 'but in this instance I do confess I have been fearing just such a possibility.'

Ket was silent for a moment whilst the train went into a tunnel and it was necessary to draw up the window quickly against the cloud of smoke that blew in from the engine. As they emerged into daylight at the other end, he said: 'I have, however, written to Miss Wyndham telling her of my intention to propose on my return to England. I decided, you see, that if she will agree to marry me, I will cease my adventuring abroad and obtain a position of some kind that will afford me an income. I might make an excellent geography master – after all I am very well travelled! Or I might write books about my adventures abroad. But first I must obtain Miss Wyndham's promise to marry me.'

'And you think this lady will agree to do so?' the banker prompted, charmed by Ket's openness.

'Sometimes I believe she will and other times I fear she will refuse me,' Ket replied honestly. 'Now, you must be quite fagged out with my affairs. Tell me, Sir, are you married? Do you have children?'

Whilst he and the banker continued to exchange details of their lives the journey passed quickly and pleasantly. When Ket descended from the train at Kneepwood Halt he was in good heart, his travelling companion's good wishes ringing in his ears. His first hope was that Charlotte would be at home. He had received one long letter from Verity advising him that Charlotte had gone to London for a holiday, but that she was expecting her to return in time for the christening. Furthermore, her letter said that she would never forgive him if he were not home in time for that occasion. His future god-daughter was quite enchanting, she had assured him, and he would be much taken with her.

Ket did not question the fact. He was attracted to all young things – puppies, kittens, colts, lambs, babies. They aroused a strong protective instinct in him and it amused him to see how sentient they were.

A porter came hurrying up the platform with his trolley with Gregory close behind.

'I'll ride up beside my coachman,' Ket told the porter, 'so you can load my baggage inside.'

With the luggage stowed away and the porter duly tipped, Gregory climbed on to his seat beside Ket and touched his whip to the horses. Noticing the black cravat, arm band and ribbon round the coachman's top hat, Ket lent forward and asked: 'Had a bereavement in your family, Gregory?'

The man turned to look at his young master who he

now realized knew nothing of the disaster that had recently overtaken the Conniston family. Following the dreadful accident, he now informed Ket, Mr Matthew's and Master Bertie's funerals had taken place the next weekend. Poor Mrs Conniston, Mr Matthew's wife, had been too distraught to attend and Mr Guy had been obliged to support Sir Bertram, who the tragedy had aged quite markedly, and was now almost unable to walk.

Suddenly realizing that he was talking to the dead man's brother, Gregory quickly busied himself, urging the horses to a trot.

Although Ket had never felt close to his elder brother and was, in fact, a great deal fonder of his half-brother, Guy, he was neverthless shaken by the news of Matthew's death, not to mention that of his young nephew, Bertie.

'Tell me, Gregory,' he said after a minute or two when he'd regained his composure, 'how did this come about? I know nothing of it other than what you have told me and it would be best if I don't arrive at the house uninformed.'

He listened quietly whilst the coachman related the sad details of the accident.

'Mr Guy said it was uncommon bad luck,' the man told Ket. 'There were many a phaeton what had overturned without killing its occupants. Mr Guy thought as how Mr Matthew must have been driving them greys a deal too fast.' As if suddenly aware of his own speed, he slowed his horses to a walk. 'The master arranged a beautiful funeral service which was all the sadder for being so near Christmas,' he continued. ''Tis a blessing you've come home to cheer the poor souls, Mr Ket,' he added as they turned the horses into the drive leading up to the house. 'Cook was only saying at dinnertime how Miss Wyndham being home has helped everyone keep halfway cheerful despite the tragedy. Now you're back, Sir, it will do 'em all a power of good.'

Ket's mood brightened perceptibly at the knowledge that Charlotte was home. Perhaps his unexpected arrival would cheer them, he thought as he greeted Grainger who had opened the big front door for him. It was unlikely that

Charlotte would be too downcast since she had no great liking either for his unfortunate brother or his nephew. Nevertheless, this was not perhaps the most acceptable time for him to be proposing to her. On the other hand, their engagement, if such were to be announced, might prove a welcome distraction for the family. His heart soared anew at the thought he would be seeing Charlotte at any moment.

'Where is everyone, Grainger?' he enquired as he followed the butler into the empty hall.

'Taking tea, Sir, in the drawing room. There have been that many callers wishing to express their sympathy. Sir Bertram isn't receiving as he is still very grief-stricken, you understand, Sir. So Mr and Mrs Conniston have undertaken the duty.'

'And Miss Wyndham?' Ket enquired in what he trusted was not too urgent a tone of voice.

'Miss Wyndham is in the schoolroom, Sir, looking after the children. Perhaps you didn't know, Mr Ket, that poor old Nanny had a stroke when she was told the news about Mr Matthew and Master Bertie. She raised them both as babies as you know. She's gone to live with her sister in Worthing and Miss Wyndham is standing in until Mrs Conniston can engage a new nanny.'

'Then if Mr and Mrs Conniston have visitors, I will go up and see the children,' Ket said.

'Will you take tea in the nursery with the children, Mr Ket?'

'Why not, Grainger!' Ket replied with a smile. 'That will really make me feel I have come home.'

His heart was now filled with a joyous excitement at the thought of Charlotte not only here at Kneepwood but alone upstairs – well, alone but for the children. She would have no reason to hide her feelings when she saw him – feelings which he prayed would be as happy as his own as he bounded up the stairs three at a time.

There was a bright fire burning in the schoolroom grate, around which was a three-sided leather-seated brass fender. Both Lottie and Kate were perched astride it where they had been sitting listening to Charlotte reading them a story. Charlotte was ensconced in a high-backed basket armchair, a baby nestling in the crook of one arm, a storybook held on her lap by her other hand. The firelight added to the glow of the gas mantle, softening the somewhat harsh outlines of the schoolroom table and hardbacked chairs. Wood smoke mingled with the smell of blackboard chalk and drying baby garments which hung on a clothes horse close to the fire. It was a picture of domesticity that might have been carefully posed by an artist wishing to portray the intimate side of family life.

Charlotte, Ket noticed with tender amusement, was even wearing one of Nanny's starched white aprons. Her lovely copper-coloured hair was not tucked into a frilled cap, however, but hung in two girlish braids over her shoulders. Her cheeks were flushed from the heat of the fire but flamed a deeper red as she heard the door open and Ket appeared in the doorway. But for the baby on her lap she would have jumped to her feet, but she remained where she was, the blush on her face fading to white. Ket took a step towards her but before he could reach for her hand Lottie and Kate were upon him, standing on tiptoe, hugging his legs and demanding to be picked up and kissed.

'And there's a nice warm welcome for me!' Ket said laughing as he hugged first one and then the other. But as he did so, his eyes never left Charlotte's face.

'You look quite shocked, Charlotte!' he said standing so close to her chair that she was afraid at any moment he would touch her. 'Didn't Guy tell you I was arriving home this afternoon? I sent him a telegram from Dover when we docked and they assured me it would be delivered by midday.'

'Guy didn't mention it to me,' Charlotte answered, her voice so quiet as to be almost inaudible. 'How long have you been back?'

Ket sat down facing her on the leather-seated fender, the little girls on either side of him.

'But five minutes at most,' he said. 'Grainger told me you

were up here and I could wait no longer to see you. Charlotte, have you missed me?'

Once again, Charlotte's cheeks burned a deep pink. 'We all missed you, didn't we, children?' She avoided a direct reply.

'I mean, did *you* miss me, Charlotte?' Ket persisted.

There was a moment's silence broken only by the baby's sudden snuffling. Ket's face broke into a smile as he lent over and pulled the white shawl away from the infant's face.

'How old is she? She's a pretty little thing – prettier than either of you two were at that age!' he said teasingly to the little girls who broke into cries of protest.

'And she's not *she*!' Lottie insisted. 'Her name is Florence and our governess says it's rude to call anyone "she" because that's the cat's mother.'

Despite herself, Charlotte smiled, her eyes meeting Ket's, which quickly became serious.

'Charlotte, did you get my letter?' he asked in a low, intense voice. 'The one telling you of my intentions when I next came home?'

Charlotte's hold on the baby tightened unconsciously as she replied: 'Yes I did, Ket, but I'm beginning to think you didn't receive mine. Verity promised to forward it to you with one of her own but . . .'

'I had only one letter from her – the one that was waiting for me when I arrived in Persia, although in it she assured me she had written twice previously. Your letter must have been enclosed in one of those. May I ask what news you had to give me – good news, I hope?'

Charlotte bit her lip. It was obvious to her now that Ket had no idea she intended to put an end to their relationship, if such it could be called; or that she fully intended to return to London and run the Maison Hortense for as long as Madame lived – even after that – as a lifetime occupation. She had received several letters from Madame saying that she was being very well cared for by her attendant nurse; that her illness seemed no worse and Charlotte must remain with her friends for as long as they needed her.

Nevertheless, for the past week now she had been longing to leave Kneepwood. She suspected that Verity was deliberately finding fault with every applicant for the post of nanny who came for interview in the hope that Charlotte would grow fond enough of the baby to wish to remain at Kneepwood forever. Now there was an even greater reason for her leaving soon – Ket was home and she had only to be in his company, to look at his engaging figure and loving face to remember how desperately in love with him she was.

'Look, Ket, I don't think this is the time to discuss our . . . our letters!' she said, adding with enormous relief, 'And here's Dolly with the tea. Shall we postpone our conversation until after the children are in bed?'

'Very well!' Ket agreed with a smile. He was quite content to wait an hour or two longer before formally voicing his proposal, especially as his instinct told him Charlotte was much affected by his homecoming. He had a very good idea why she always seemed anxious to keep him at arm's length, for Verity had informed him in a private moment that Charlotte's father was a fraudster who had brought disgrace on his family. Understandably Charlotte must have accepted the fact that no self-respecting family would approve of a son marrying a girl with such a sordid background. Nevertheless, Verity had opined, someone like George Morrison was sufficiently taken with Charlotte that he might well have overlooked her origins had she given him any encouragement.

Ket had kept his counsel at that time, unsure as he was if his feelings for Charlotte were indeed illimitable. He'd thought himself to be falling in love with her when he'd met Naomi Copley and come within a hair's breadth of marrying her. On leaving Paris it had crossed his mind that he might yet again meet someone new and think himself in love. But although on his travels he had frequently met with eligible young females who were obviously interested in him, he'd never found one to change his desire to make Charlotte his wife. It was a conviction even he himself did not fully understand, for she was so different from any other girl he had known –

so quiet and gentle, so lacking in coquettishness, so eager and enthusiastic a companion; and, he sensed beneath that cool exterior there lurked unexplored depths of passion. Again and again she haunted his dreams and he no longer had the slightest doubt that he wanted to spend the rest of his life with her.

As Charlotte prepared the children for bed, and with Dolly's assistance, bathed and fed the baby, tidied the day nursery and schoolroom, her mind was in a turmoil. Ket's friendly, happy chatter during tea and the smiling face he presented every time she glanced at him, left her in no doubt that he never suspected she would turn down his proposal. And why would he? she asked herself bitterly as she kissed the little girls goodnight and turned out their light. Ket was an extraordinarily handsome man with a delightful, sunny disposition and likeable character. It was beyond her understanding why he should think himself in love with her – perhaps because she alone of all the girls he had befriended had not encouraged his advances and she was, therefore, a challenge. At least she could comfort herself with the thought that when she did reject his proposal, it would not be too long before he found some other girl to love. Unlike her own heart, Ket's would not be broken, Charlotte thought bitterly.

Dearly as Ket loved the company of his half-brother and sister-in-law, the evening of his homecoming seemed endlessly long drawn out. Sir Bertram, was pathetically pleased to see him, but before long was overindulging in alcohol – sherry before dinner, red and then white wine, followed by port at dinner and finally brandy, ordering Grainger to leave the decanter by his chair. He became at first belligerent and then maudlin and on several occasions brought the unhappy Monica to tears by miscalling Ket by his dead brother's name.

It was an unhappy atmosphere and when, after coffee, Charlotte said she must go upstairs to make sure Dolly was not having any problems with the children, Ket too excused himself on the grounds that he was sorely fatigued by the day's journeying. As soon as he was out of the room, he

212

hurried upstairs to the third-floor nursery wing where he found Charlotte. She was standing facing the fireplace, her back towards him as he entered the schoolroom. Hesitating only for a minute, Ket walked over to her and, placing his hands on her shoulders, turned her gently to face him.

'Oh, Charlotte, say you really are pleased to see me!' he said softly. 'You have scarcely said one word to me this evening.' He put a hand beneath her chin and lifted her face so that she couldn't avoid looking at him. He took a step closer to her and they were now near enough for him to feel her heart beating against his own. No longer able to control his emotions, he clasped her tightly to him. 'Dearest, darling Charlotte. I don't think you have any idea how much I love you. I've tried so hard to forget you whilst we've been apart, but all the time all I really wanted was to be back here with you. I love you, Charlotte, with all my heart. I want you to marry me. I want you to be my wife.'

It was a declaration Charlotte knew she would never forget as long as she lived. There had been nights when she had lain in her lonely bed allowing herself to imagine occasions such as this where Ket would declare himself; imagine herself forgetting all the dreadful barriers to their love and responding to him as her heart and body dictated. She knew now as she had known then that this could never happen. Perhaps the Fates had decreed that they would fall in love, but Ket had discovered his heart's desire too late, and she had put herself beyond his reach forever.

Only for a single instant did she allow herself to stay there, held tightly in his embrace, before she struggled to break free. 'You don't understand, Ket!' she said desperately. 'I can't marry you. Nothing you say will make me change my mind.'

Ket gave a faint smile, drawing her back into his arms. 'My darling girl, you think I don't know about your father, your background? I do know and it means nothing to me. It's you I want, you I love. I know I have nothing to offer you except my willingness to earn a living sufficient to keep us both. There is no work I won't undertake – and as you may know, I have a small allowance from Father. Even were he to disapprove of my marriage to you and ceased that allowance, I wouldn't care except for your sake. I love you, Charlotte. Do you believe me?'

Unable to halt his urgent speech, Charlotte could not remain unmoved by it. Here was Ket, the happy-go-lucky adventurer, prepared to devote his life to her. Tears sprang to her eyes. She did not know how Ket had come by the details of her family's past. She supposed Verity or possibly Guy had told him. Once she had believed that her father's disgrace would bar her from any suitable marriage. Now she knew that was not so, but there was a far, far greater barrier between herself and Ket – one she could never speak of to a living soul. Almost as if to provide proof of such an obstacle, the baby in the adjoining night nursery gave an audible cry.

'Don't go, Charlotte. Let the nursery maid see to the child. I need you here. I need you to tell me you do love me and that you will be my wife.'

Tears choking in her throat, Charlotte looked quickly down at her clasped hands. She dared not meet Ket's eyes lest he should read the truth there and know that she lied when she said: 'I'm sorry, Ket, but honoured as I am by your proposal, I cannot accept it. I do . . . I do love you dearly but you see, there is someone else in my life you don't know about. He's someone I met in London.' Encouraged by the ease with which the lie had come to her lips, she improvised further, incorporating a few truths amongst the lies. 'He's a gentleman who used to come to Maison Hortense to help his wife decide upon the garments she wished Madame to make. A few years ago, his wife died and when I was last in London he asked me to marry him. I . . . I said I would.'

Ket's face had paled but his hold on Charlotte's arm tightened. 'Then you must change your mind and tell him you don't love him,' he said fiercely.

Somehow Charlotte managed to force herself to tell yet another lie. 'But I do love him, Ket – not as I love you, like a brother, but as I should love my future husband. He is good and kind and loves me dearly. I'm really very sorry, Ket, if

214

unwittingly I have led you to believe my affection for you was other than that of a dear friend, a sister.'

Abruptly, Ket let go of her arms, his forehead creased in a frown, his eyes dark and stormy. 'A sister! So that's all you feel for me – sisterly love? What if I were to kiss you, Charlotte, like this . . .'

Before she could stop him, Ket had put both hands behind her head and forced her mouth to his. Involuntarily, her body melted towards his, offering no resistance as he pressed himself against her. As her nerves awakened, the strength seemed to leave her legs and she was filled with an overpowering need to surrender herself to him. His feverish kisses were now covering her face, her neck and her lips. For a moment, she tried weakly to resist him but, as if her body had a will of its own, she felt herself responding.

'You do love me, you do!' she hear Ket's voice against her ear. 'Give this man up, Charlotte, and marry me. You don't love him, I know you don't. You belong to me.'

'Ket, please, let me go!' Charlotte's eyes were full of unshed tears as she gathered her remaining strength to put space between them. Whilst Ket touched her she was powerless and only as she drew back from him was she able to say, 'Yes, you were right, it's not just as a sister that I . . . I care for you. You are a very attractive man and were my affections not otherwise engaged . . .'

'Who is he?' Ket broke in fiercely. 'Verity mentioned no such suitor. Name him, Charlotte, else I shall not believe he exists.'

Desperately, Charlotte searched her mind for a name – someone Ket could not check on like George Morrison. Suddenly she remembered Madame Hortense's lawyer, Theobald Samuels. He was the man Madame had suggested would keep her in comfort for the rest of her life – as his mistress. He fitted the lie. For all she knew he might indeed wish to marry her since, according to Madame, Mrs Samuels had passed away over a year ago.

'Samuels!' Ket repeated, the fire leaving his eyes as he turned away from Charlotte's desperate face. 'I see. I suppose the fellow has a nice home to offer you; that he will be able to support you as I could not. Well, I wish you good fortune, Charlotte, and I apologise for any embarrassment I have caused you, blundering into your affairs in so cavalier a fashion. I can but hope you'll be very happy. I suppose you will be returning to London soon?'

'I expect so,' Charlotte replied miserably. 'My friend, Madame Hortense, is very ill and I wouldn't have left her so long had she not insisted I do so. I'm sure Verity could have found a suitable nanny for the children long since had she really put her mind to it. Now I shall insist upon it as I'm sure you won't want my presence here at Kneepwood in the circumstances.'

Ket turned an angry, bitter face towards her. 'You mean *you* would find it awkward,' he said hurtfully, implying that he personally would not be much affected. 'Is it your wish then that we should cease to be friends since we are not to be lovers?'

The word took Charlotte's breath away. Ket might so easily have said 'man and wife', yet he had used the word 'lovers' as if to remind her of what might have been. Perhaps her response to his kisses had betrayed the passion she had tried so hard to hide. For one single instant, there flashed across her mind a memory of the only time she had shared a lover's deepest intimacy with a man and how she had thought only of Ket and longed for him to be holding her in his arms.

So intense was her feeling that she took refuge in sharpness. 'Of course we shall stay friends as we have always been,' she said with a well-feigned casual shrug of her shoulders. 'Why ever not, Ket? Although we may not see much of each other if I'm to return to London as soon as I hope. If you should come to London at any time, you must visit me and perhaps I can find an opportunity to introduce you to my fiancé.'

Despite himself, Ket could not let this last remark go unchallenged. 'Your fiancé? You haven't said you were formally betrothed. Verity never said so. And where is your betrothal ring?'

Turning her face aside so that Ket could not see the blush

on her cheeks, Charlotte gave a little laugh. 'How can you be so thoughtless, Ket? Would I wear my precious ring here in the nursery when my hands are so often in water? As to my engagement, it's a secret for the moment whilst Madame is so ill. We shall not announce it until she is better.'

Or rather, until she has died, Charlotte thought miserably. Maybe she would really end her life as Theobald Samuel's wife. She could never again live with the Connistons. Her future would depend upon whether Madame's only living relative – a cousin who lived in Australia – decided to close the Maison down or sell it, since it would certainly be he who inherited it. Perhaps if he sold it the new owner might give her employment, but she was no longer sure if she could bear to live a solitary life again. Perhaps in the end she would find it easier to put Ket and the Connistons forever beyond her reach if she did become Mr Samuel's wife.

'Go to him then and see if it's of any consequence to me!' Ket all but shouted the words as he walked towards the door. 'But I'm warning you, Charlotte, you may live to regret marriage to another man. No other man could love you as I do – and what's more, I still believe that although you may not know it, you do love me.'

As the door closed behind him, the tears that had been gathering in Charlotte's eyes rolled slowly down her cheeks. As if to compound her misery, from next door came the soft crying of the baby who would never know that her conception stood forever between her mother and the man she loved.

Eighteen

December 1889–January 1890

V erity sat on the side of Charlotte's bed, her pretty face drawn with bewilderment. 'I simply don't understand, dearest! We have never had secrets from each other. It hurts me beyond saying that you could become engaged without telling me. Who is this Mr Samuels? Why have you never spoken of him? Had you met him before . . . before . . . ?'

'Yes, I met him a long time ago. He is Madame Hortense's solicitor and he used to come to the Maison with his wife before she died.'

With her head bent over her suitcase as she folded her clothes, Charlotte could lie to Verity with comparative ease. She had been unable to stop Ket telling Verity that he loved her and had proposed marriage, but she could pretend she was indifferent to him except as a friend, a brother. Were Verity to imagine for one instant that Charlotte's offer of surrogacy was responsible for ruining her life, she would be grief-stricken and filled with guilt. She must never know the truth and the easiest way of explaining was for her to endorse the lie she had told Ket.

'So when did his wife die? When did he propose to you? Why didn't you write and tell me?' Verity was close to tears, feeling that Charlotte was shutting her out of her life. She had imagined when they returned from Italy that Charlotte would continue to live at Kneepwood forever; that she might replace Miss Armstrong as governess to the girls, including little Florence. But far from being anxious to bond with her child, Charlotte had been reluctant to stand in for poor old Nanny and ever since had pestered her to engage a professional woman so that she could return to London. She had given, as a reason for the urgency, Madame Hortense's deteriorating illness but now Verity suspected Charlotte might be hurrying back to London in order to see more of her future husband.

Biting her lip, Verity said hesitantly: 'Does he know, Charlotte, that you aren't . . . well . . . unversed in . . . unenlightened . . . ?'

'You mean have I told him that I'm not a virgin?' Charlotte broke in, deliberately explicit. 'Yes, of course, Verity, but rest assured, I made no mention, or ever will, of the baby.'

She was well aware that Verity was hurt that she hadn't confided so important a matter to her. But perhaps this was as well, she thought as she fastened the leather strap round her valise and went to the wardrobe for her chesterfield coat. Since she knew she must put distance between herself and Ket, she knew also that she couldn't continue her close relationship with Verity. Even now she was struggling not to throw herself into Verity's arms and confess her love for Ket and her heartbreak at having to reject his love. For everyone's sake – Verity's, Guy's, the baby's, Ket's and not least her own – she must not return to Kneepwood in the forseeable future.

'Then I shall try to be happy for your sake,' Verity said, rising from the bed and crossing the room to put her arms round Charlotte's shoulders. 'I shall miss you most dreadfully, and poor Ket is, I know, quite broken-hearted. Perhaps you're right, dearest, and he will soon recover from his broken heart when the next pretty girl comes into his orbit. He was ever the flirt, was he not? As for me, since you won't stay here with me, I shall come up to London more often to see you, and naturally I am curious to meet your Mr Samuels.'

Charlotte's heart missed a beat as she pulled gently away from Verity's embrace and reached for the handle of her suitcase. 'I will arange a meeting as soon as possible!' she said quickly. 'You do understand that whilst Madame Hortense is so ill . . .'

'Yes, of course!' Verity broke in. 'And please don't attempt to carry your case, dearest. I'll tell Grainger to send Fred up here to collect it.' She glanced at the fob watch on her jabot and sighed. 'Gregory will have the carriage waiting already. It's time for you to go, Charlotte, if you are to be sure of catching the London train. Shall you go now and say goodbye to the children?'

Charlotte looked quickly away. 'I think not. The girls will only be distressed knowing that I'm leaving them. Please tell them I'll write to them and hope that they will write to me. And wish the new nanny well.'

She walked through the door and, as she stepped on to the landing, a door opened at the far end and Ket came striding towards her. They stood for what seemed an endless moment, staring at one another and then, mercifully, Verity tucked her arm in Charlotte's, saying: 'Come, dearest, we mustn't dally. Charlotte is just leaving, Ket, as soon as Fred has collected her luggage.'

On Ket's handsome face there was the parody of a smile. 'There's no need for Fred. I shall carry it for you – one last small service I can perform for you, Charlotte.'

There was an edge to his voice that bordered on bitterness, and tears sprang to Charlotte's eyes as she felt his hurt. She dared not look at him again although she longed to do so, to imprint his image forever on her mind. She had no likeness of him to take with her, so her memory would perforce have to suffice.

If Charlotte was hoping her departure from Kneepwood would be quick and comparatively painless, it was not to be so. Verity was in tears as she stood in the doorway, Guy's arm around her shoulders, waving goodbye. Above in a third-floor window, Lottie and Kate were calling to Charlotte to come back soon. There was no sign of Ket who she had half hoped would reappear to bid her farewell.

A light rain was falling from a uniformly grey sky as Gregory urged the horses down the drive and set off at a trot towards Kneepwood station. The elm trees were bare of leaves and the grass verges of the lane were besmattered with mud, giving the landscape a look of destitution. It matched her mood, Charlotte thought as she dashed the tears from her eyes. In two days' time it would be Christmas – a time when by family tradition there would be a children's party at Kneepwood involving children from the village and the estate. There would be no annual ball on New Year's Eve as the family were still in mourning for Matthew and Bertie, and Monica had become a recluse in the dower house, but Ket was home and that was a big boost to everyone's spirits.

It was too wet and windy for Gregory to attempt to talk to Charlotte or she to him as the windows of the carriage were closed. She was alone with her thoughts until finally he drew the horse to a halt at Kneepwood station and came to open the door of the brougham for her.

'You're in good time, Miss. Train won't be in for another quarter hour. Will I put your luggage in the waiting room, Miss?'

'If you would, Gregory,' Charlotte replied, stepping down from the carriage. As the coachman disappeared into the little station building, someone dismounted from a chestnut horse where he had been sheltering from the rain under the overhang of the roof. At the rider came towards her, Charlotte recognized him and her heart lurched. It was Ket, a dark shadow in his caped topcoat and brown derby.

'Send Gregory home!' he said in a low voice. 'I need to talk to you alone.'

He took her arm and ignoring her murmured protest, half pulled her under the cover of the station forecourt.

'I can't let you go like this, Charlotte!' he said urgently. 'I laid awake all last night thinking about you . . . us . . . what you said to me. I don't believe you are in love with this man you call your fiancé. Verity said she knew nothing of him. I think you invented him. I think you love me. Say that I'm right. You do love me, don't you?'

His face was so close to hers that Charlotte could see the tiny flecks of brown in his dark eyes. His breath was on her cheek and the proximity of his body, even through their thick outer garments, was sufficient to send her heart racing and her legs trembling.

221

'Ket, please, you're mistaken . . . I . . . I don't love you. If I misled you in Paris . . . If you thought . . . I'm sorry . . . I'm going to marry Theobald Samuels. Why don't you believe me? This is only making it more difficult for both of us!'

Ket gave what almost amounted to a snort of disgust. 'So you are going to marry this Samuels fellow, but not once have you told me that you love him. Perhaps he is very wealthy and has promised you a life of luxury. Is that it? Is it because you were once destitute and he can give you everything you've always wanted and I have nothing to offer you? Is that it?'

Close to a total breakdown, Charlotte grasped the straw he offered. 'Yes, that's exactly it, Ket!' she lied. 'I want a big house like Kneepwood and beautiful clothes like Verity has and servants and—'

'Answer me, Charlotte,' Ket interrupted. 'Do you or don't you love him?'

She drew a deep breath, wondering why she couldn't bring herself to utter the ultimate lie. For no more than two gold pins she would tell him the truth. *No, Ket, I don't love him. I love you. I don't care about the big house and the clothes and servants. I want only you.* But whilst her heart longed to confess the truth, she heard herself say: 'Please let me go, Ket. I'm sorry to have been obliged to hurt you but it would be unforgivable of me to pretend to feelings I don't have and then later to countermand that declaration. In any event, I am promised to Mr Samuels and were it not for poor Madame Hortense's ill health, we would even now be married.'

For a brief moment, Ket was silenced. Then he said, incredulously: 'You mean you might actually have been wed without telling Verity? I thought you were her friend!'

Charlotte bit her lip. She was once more perilously close to tears. 'Of course I'm her friend and she is mine. But I do have a right to some privacy, don't you agree? In the light of the fact that Mr Samuels has been married before, he wishes us to have a quiet ceremony with only ourselves and two witnesses present, and I am in accord with his wishes.'

'Are you then?' Ket said bitterly. 'No beautiful wedding gown? No train? No little Kate and Lottie to throw rose petals

222

at your feet when you left the church? Didn't you want any of these things, my pretty Charlotte? It seems to me your Mr Samuels is not quite the generous benefactor you have indicated. It explains why you don't wear a betrothal ring – the one he has not yet given you!'

'Stop it! Stop it!' Charlotte cried, unable to bear Ket's taunting voice. 'This conversation is of no benefit to either of us. Please go, Ket. My train will be here presently and . . . and I want you to go.'

Ket drew a long inward breath as if to regain his equilibrium. Stupidly, he had clung to the hope that even at this very last minute, if he followed her on horseback to the station and saw her alone, he might yet persuade her he was worthy of her love. He now reflected bitterly that it was true he had nothing to offer her other than promises; that clearly this man she intended to marry was wealthy enough to indulge her every whim. For all he knew, the fellow might be handsome as well as rich, and Charlotte too shy to admit that she found him physically to her liking. Ket was convinced that, unlike some females, Charlotte had hidden fires that would respond to a man's loving. He had sensed it, felt it, when he kissed her.

The reappearance of Gregory from the station gave Charlotte the opportunity to move away from Ket's side.

'Are my bags quite safe?' she enquired unnecessarily, for she could see a porter standing by them on the platform. 'Here is Mr Ket come to wave me goodbye. The weather is so inclement I think you should both go home now. The porter will see me on to the train which I believe is almost due. So I'll bid you goodbye, Gregory, and please accept my very best wishes for the coming year.' She turned to Ket and forced a smile to her lips. 'And my very best wishes to you, Ket,' she said. 'And thank you for coming to see me off.'

For one moment of madness, she stood there in the rain hoping that Ket would disregard convention, the presence of Gregory, the stationmaster, the porter . . . disregard everything she had said to him and sweep her into his arms. She longed almost to the point of faintness to throw her arms round his neck, press her mouth to his and . . .

'Safe journey, Charlotte!' Ket spoke beside her, his voice quiet, casual – as casual as the movements of his body when he turned away and walked over to his horse. He lifted his hat and called a greeting to a late arriving passenger whom he knew, and climbed into the saddle. Eager to return to its warm stable, the chestnut high-stepped over the cobbles and clattered out of the station yard. Not once did Ket turn his head and look back.

From the distance came the piercing whistle of the arriving train, to be followed soon afterwards by the loud hissing of steam. The wind carried the white cloud down the platform, enveloping both Charlotte and the porter as he lifted her bags into the carriage. It filled their throats and nostrils and mingled with the sudden flood of Charlotte's tears.

At first, Madame Hortense had been amused by Charlotte's account of her fictitious engagement to Theobald Samuels, but she quickly realized the corner into which Charlotte had forced herself. Two weeks had passed since she'd left Kneepwood and Verity had written to say she intended to come to London to stay a night with her godmother, Lady Hardcastle, in Eaton Square and do some shopping. Naturally she wanted very much to see Charlotte and could not wait to be introduced to the mysterious Mr Samuels.

> You must bring him to dinner with me at my god-
> mother's. She will be delighted to renew your acquaint-
> ance, dearest, and can be counted upon to make your
> fiancé welcome. Please write by return and name a date
> suitable to you both . . .

'I'm afraid you have either to break off this so-called engagement or else you must ask Theobald if he will agree to be named as your fiancé,' Madame Hortense said with a sigh.

Charlotte looked at Madame's gaunt face, her own aghast. 'You don't think this would risk Mr Samuels thinking I might really wish to marry him? You know I shall never love anyone but Ket.'

'My dear child, I haven't suggested that you love Theobald, merely that you might serously consider marriage to him. Let's not beat about the bush, Charlotte – I shan't live much longer as we both know, and after I am gone, who will look after you? Protect you? You say you will never return to Kneepwood – not even if your precious Ket marries someone else, not even if Mrs Conniston were to write and tell you your own daughter needed you. So . . .'

'Florence is not my daughter, Madame!' Charlotte interrupted. 'She is Verity's child. Verity dotes on her quite as much as she dotes on Kate and Lottie . . . sometimes I think even more so. As for Ket marrying someone else, that would not stop him taking his wife back to Kneepwood for family occasions – weddings, funerals, christenings, Christmas and so on. You may call me a coward but I don't think I would ever be able to face him and behave normally.'

'Then if you don't intend telling Mrs Conniston you have broken off this so-called engagement, and you won't produce Theobald as your fiancé, you will have to find some other excuse to explain his absence.' Madame's voice was weak, her body having become little more than a skeleton as her illness had progressed. The following week she was to be taken into St Bartholomew's Hospital on her doctor's orders. She lay propped up by several pillows in her large brass bed, her faithful little dog curled up at her feet. Charlotte wondered what degree of misery the animal would feel when its mistress went into hospital.

Before that event, Madame now related, she had arranged a final visit from Theobald, who was finalizing her will. She regarded Charlotte's anxious face as she imparted this information. 'So you can't avoid meeting him, my child!' she said with another faint smile. 'He knows you are back in London with me and can't wait to see you again.'

Despite herself, Charlotte smiled too. 'I do believe you are attempting to be a matchmaker!' she said, adding with a sigh, 'Oh, Madame, how simple life would be if I suddenly discovered Ket meant nothing to me after all and I could actually fall for Mr Samuel's charms!'

These were not many she decided when, two days later, she let the lawyer into the apartment and served him a glass of sherry whilst they waited for the day nurse to complete her duties in the sickroom. His figure was still trim and he still had a healthy head of hair despite his age. His best attribute – his deep blue, dark-lashed eyes – were unfortunately all but concealed behind bottle-lensed glasses. His nose was aquiline, his mouth partially concealed by a bushy waxed moustache. It would be difficult to gauge his age, Charlotte thought, were it not for the touches of grey at his temples. He was clearly an educated man who spoke with a quiet, modulated voice and behaved with the utmost courtesy.

'I can't tell you what a pleasure it is to meet you again, Miss Wyndham,' he said as Charlotte sat down in the chair opposite him. 'A great pleasure indeed, albeit in these sad circumstances,' he added. 'As you know, I have been acquainted with Mrs Briggs for more than twenty years, and she has become as much a friend as a client.'

'I am devoted to her, too,' Charlotte said, warming to the man's obviously genuine sentiments. 'Madame has been very good to me and treats me like a daughter. But I expect you know that.'

Her companion nodded and, putting his sherry glass down on the table beside his chair, he lent forward, his hands propping his weight on his knees. 'Mrs Briggs – Doris as she likes me to call her – did inform me when she first employed you of the misfortunes which had overtaken your family, Miss Wyndham. It grieves me that as a young girl you had so hard a time when you should, by right of birth, have taken your place in society. May I say how greatly I admire your courage? Doris tells me you have never given way to despair.'

Somewhat taken aback by this declaration, Charlotte shook her head. 'Believe me, Mr Samuels, there have been times when I have come very close to despair. And since, by your expression, I can see that you don't entirely believe me, I will add that there was such an occasion not very long ago.'

The lawyer sat back in his chair and, taking off his

226

spectacles, took his time polishing them with a snowy white handkerchief. He was unaware that without them he looked ten years younger.

'Would it be impertinent of me to suggest that your present distress concerns a matter of the heart?' he enquired.

He's too perceptive! Charlotte thought, her cheeks flushing. Madame Hortense had surely not betrayed her confidences – nor could she have done since she had only known of her feelings since her return from Kneepwood. Mr Samuels was regarding her apologetically as he replaced his glasses on his nose.

'Forgive me if by chance I have happened upon the truth!' he said. 'The very last thing I would want is to upset you, but when pretty young women such as yourself admit to despair, I think it's true to say that invariably they have been crossed in love. Believe me, it was but a guess and I do apologise most sincerely.'

Aware of the look of distress on Charlotte's face, he added gently: 'May I say that I would be greatly honoured if you would consider me as your friend? If there is ever anything I can do to alleviate your unhappiness, I beg you to call on me so that I may be of help if I can.'

Charlotte had herself once more under control. 'You're very kind, Sir,' she said, 'and I appreciate your concern. However, I'm not sure you would so readily offer me your friendship were you aware how I have misused your good name.' She nearly smiled at the expression on the solicitor's face which was in equal parts astonishment and apprehension. 'Not illegally, I do assure you!' she added quickly.

'That's a great relief!' he replied, not without a dry humour. 'Would it be asking too much of you to enlighten me as to your meaning?'

Why not! Charlotte thought bitterly. She had told so many lies that it would be a relief for once to tell the truth – not that she would ever reveal to a living soul the truth about the baby. Slowly, quietly, she began to speak of her love for Ket, of his for her and how she had had to reject him. Even now she was forced to lie, giving her disgraced family rather

227

than the baby as the reason for her rejection. Her companion was frowning as he listened to this part of her story.

'No man in love would reject his beloved because her family had brought disgrace upon her!' he said with unexpected forcefulness.

'No, I realized that but you see, Mr Samuels, it is I who must reject him. I love him too much to allow him to take on a wife who would inevitably bring him dishonour, disgrace. Besides, I have nothing whatever to offer him, whereas unencumbered he can attract young women of good background and with excellent dowries such as the American girl he was engaged to before he fell in love with me.'

'I see! So you believe this Lothario will soon recover from his broken heart?'

'I hope so. It was to that end that I misused your name. I know it was very wrong of me, but yours was the first name that came into my head.'

Theobald Samuels lent forward and laid a restraining hand on Charlotte's arm. 'Whatever you have said, you must not allow it to distress you, Miss Wyndham, for I am sure I shall not mind it as greatly as you fear. Now tell me, please, what it is you have said about me?'

'Not really about you, Sir – about us!' Charlotte blurted out. 'I said we were . . . we were . . . I said we were engaged to be married!'

A slow smile spread over the man's face. 'Did you indeed! Were that true I should be the happiest of men. So you have betrothed me to yourself without my knowledge!'

Charlotte nodded, unable to find her voice.

'Then if such was your misdeed, I beg you to think nothing more about it, for I can't think of anything I would wish for more than to be engaged to marry you, Miss Wyndham. So you see, there is little harm done, If the truth be known, I am flattered that you should consider me a potential husband even if, as I assume, it's in a fictitious light?' Behind his glasses, his eyes began to twinkle. 'Come to think of it, my dear, I can think of nothing I would like more than for you to agree to be my wife.'

His light-hearted acceptance of what she had done brought a sigh of relief from Charlotte, who now found herself returning the lawyer's smile.

'You are being very kind,' she said. 'I had no right to use your good name in order to get myself out of a predicament. My father used to warn me that one lie nearly always leads to another.'

The lawyer's face became suddenly serious as once more he lent forward. 'I would like to be a great deal kinder!' he said. 'Several years ago, when I first met you, I told Doris that more than anything in the world, I would like to have your affection; that I couldn't marry you since I had a wife but that if you would agree, I would buy a house for you, give you the wherewithal to run it; sufficient money to buy anything within reason that you wanted . . . and not least my devotion. No, let me speak, please. You may consider I was insulting you by even thinking of such a thing, but that was not my intention. I did not expect you to love me or even to have any deep feelings for me. Why should you? I wanted only to take care of you. Now I am a widower, so the Fates have allowed me to ask you to marry me – to be my wife.'

A proposal – such as it was – from Mr Samuels was the very last thing Charlotte had anticipated when she had invited him into Madame Hortense's little sitting room for a glass of sherry. Even now she could barely believe she had heard him make such a declaration. She could only presume that he'd felt her own admission entitled him to be so precipitate. He seemed anxious to assure her that he had not intended to declare himself so soon. Doris, he now told her, had informed him that she was returning to London after an unhappy affair of the heart, since when he had thought of little else but his hope that she might turn to him for comfort. His late wife, he elaborated, had been a worthy woman who had borne him three children, only one of which had survived infancy. His regard for their mother had been dutiful rather than passionate. Therefore, when she had passed away two years ago, her death had not been a great tragedy for him so Charlotte need not think his proposal was in the hope of replacing his late spouse.

Charlotte allowed him to unburden himself without interruption. It was no more than he had done for her. When he fell silent, she assured him that she had not taken offence; that at some later stage in her life she would consider his proposal, although she thought it unlikely she could ever agree to it. It would not be right, she said, whilst all her thoughts and affections were centred on another man.

'Since you are not angry with me, may I dare hope that we can now consider ourselves friends, Miss Wyndham? It would give me the greatest pleasure.'

'I see no reason why not!' Charlotte said. 'For you to be my friend is nearer the truth than you being my fiancé, isn't it?'

He returned her smile. 'As you know, I would much prefer the latter. However, as your friend, if I can ever be of any help, you will advise me, won't you?'

Charlotte nodded gratefully, thankful to have been afforded this unexpected opening to her request.

'In point of fact, I do need your help, Mr Samuels,' she said earnestly. 'It's for a tea party in Eaton Square. I have been invited to attend *with my fiancé*. That's why I invented you – so everyone would believe I really was going to be married and couldn't therefore love someone else.' In her eagerness to make him understand, she covered his hand with own. 'I promise it will only be for this one occasion. If you really will attend the tea party with me, Mr Samuels, as . . . as my betrothed, I will be very greatly indebted to you.'

Looking at Charlotte's bright, eager face, Theobald felt a surge of hope. Without hesitation, he covered her hand with his own. 'If I am to do as you ask, my dear, may I suggest that you begin to call me by my Christian name? Theo would, I think, be appropriate for your fiancé. And you have no need to feel indebted to me. As you know, there is nothing I should like more than be your fiancé, if only for an afternoon.'

He might have elaborated further had not the maid called in to say that Madame Hortense was now ready to see him in her room upstairs.'

Nineteen

February 1890

On her previous visit to the house in Eaton Square, Verity's godmother, Lady Hardcastle, had not been at home and Charlotte had taken tea alone with Verity. What a long, long time ago that now seemed, Charlotte thought as Theobald pulled the front doorbell and linked his arm through hers.

'You are trembling, Charlotte!' he said. 'You understand, don't you, that as a betrothed couple it is right for us to use Christian names? Please be assured that I shall not let you down.'

Nor did he do so. They were shown into the withdrawing room where Lady Hardcastle was waiting to receive them with Verity standing beside her. As soon as they had been announced, Verity ran forward and with a glad cry, flung her arms around Charlotte.

'I am so immensely pleased to see you, dearest. I was afraid some last minute duty would cause you to cancel our meeting. Godmother, you remember my dearest friend Charlotte, don't you? Oh, and forgive me, Mr Samuels, in my excitement, I was forgetting my manners. This is Charlotte's fiancé.'

With a smile and a small bow Theobald stepped forward to take Lady Hardcastle's outstretched hand. Very much a member of the aristocracy, his hostess was elegantly attired in a blue silk moiré tea gown; her silver grey hair was elaborately coiffed. Having given her guests a quick unobtrusive once-over through her diamond-encrusted lorgnette, she nodded approvingly.

'Do sit down, Charlotte, my dear, and you too, Mr Samuels!

May I proffer you my congratulations? If I may be so personal as to remark upon it, my goddaughter told me that you were no longer in your youth, Mr Samuels, which I view with the utmost approval. Far too many young men are engaging in matrimony these days without the wherewithal to support their wives in the manner to which they have been accustomed. I understand that you are a successful professional man and already have a home to offer Charlotte.'

She did not appear to expect a reply, so Verity broke into the conversation, her face glowing as she addressed Charlotte. 'You shouldn't have kept this charming man a secret from us all, dearest. I was quite overcome when she told me of her engagement, Godmother. We all were, and especially Ket. I think my brother-in-law had designs upon Charlotte!' she said, laughing. 'Of course, he has always been a great flirt and it came as no surprise to us when, soon after Charlotte left, he started courting Amelia Morrison. You remember her sister, Cynthia, whose party you attended, Charlotte?'

She paused momentarily to look mischievously at Theobald. 'The Morrisons are neighbours of ours. George Morrison, Amelia's brother, was so smitten with Charlotte that I think he would have proposed had she given him the slightest encouragement!'

'In which case, I should have been very much the loser, Mrs Conniston!' Theobald said, linking his arm through Charlotte's and regarding her fondly. 'I can hardly believe my good fortune in finding so lovely a person still unattached when clearly she has been pursued by many admirers.'

'The girl is right to be selective!' Lady Hardcastle interposed as the parlourmaid brought in the tea. 'Too many girls marry the first man who proposes. Now tell me, Charlotte, do you take milk? Sugar? And you, Mr Samuels, Cook has made a cherry cake especially for you. She is convinced that every man finds cherry cake irresistible.'

'Which indeed I do!' Theobald replied.

Verity took a sip of tea and turned to Charlotte. 'As soon as you've finished, dearest, I want to take you upstairs to show you the new hat I bought today. You can spare her for a short while, can you not, Mr Samuels?'

There was no way Charlotte could avoid this private tête-à-tête with Verity. So far, the little subterfuge of bringing Theobald Samuels with her and passing him off as her fiancé had gone without hitch. But she knew Verity would want more detailed information.

As she had surmised, no sooner were they alone than Verity sat her down on the chaise longue beside her and said: 'He obviously admires you very much, Charlotte, and I do understand that an older man can offer you security and protection, but do you *really* love him?'

'Perhaps my feelings for Theo are not quite so obvious as his for me,' Charlotte broke in evasively. 'They may not be similar to those you feel for Guy, but I have a great respect and affection for Theobald and we suit one another very well.'

'He's a widower with a grown-up daughter, you told me. Will he want a new family, Charlotte? I can hardly bring myself to ask this, but will you . . . Would you want little Florence . . .'

'No! I would not!' Charlotte broke in firmly. 'You know very well that I have never looked upon her as my child. She is yours, Verity. I know you love her and that she is well looked after and, I'm sure, is very happy. Besides . . .' Charlotte had been about to say that she had no intention of marrying Theobald but broke off just in time. 'Neither Theobald nor I want children,' she substituted quickly. 'I'm glad you approve of him, Verity.'

Verity managed to conceal a sigh. 'He seems very nice, Charlotte, although somehow I hadn't envisaged you with someone quite so – so middle-aged. In fact, to be honest, I suppose I had half-hoped you would marry Ket. I know he truly loves you because he told me so after you had left us. He said he might have persuaded you to marry him had it not been for your engagement to Mr Samuels.'

Such was the pain in Charlotte's heart, it was a moment or two before she could speak. Then she said bitterly: 'It hasn't taken him long to recover from his broken heart, has it? You say he has been courting Amelia Morrison.'

'Yes, that's true, dearest, but have you never heard of someone who has been rejected turning to another on the rebound? Anyway, I doubt if Ket will propose to her as, in my opinion, he is far too fond of his bachelor life. He's been talking of returning to the wilds of Canada, and I can't see Amelia Morrison caring for that kind of life, even were her parents to approve such a marriage. She is not self-sufficient and capable like you are, Charlotte. George told us that she fainted the other day when a mouse ran across the room!'

Suddenly, despite the seriousness of their conversation, both girls were laughing and then hugging one another.

'Oh, I do so miss you, dearest!' Verity said as she dried her eyes. 'And everyone missed you most dreadfully at Florence's christening. Even that old bear, my father-in-law, kept asking where you were. Poor Sir Bertram has not been the same since Matthew and Bertie died. The doctor seems to think he may have suffered a small stroke which has affected his brain – the tragedy combined with all that port he drinks. I wouldn't wish the cause of it to have happened but I have to say life is a lot happier at Kneepwood now he has ceased to rage at everyone. He has even started to speak affectionately to my darling Guy – well, if not exactly affectionately, approvingly. He even praises him for the way he runs Kneepwood – and rightly so.'

'Does Guy think that his father will leave Kneepwood to him now there is no Matthew or Bertie to inherit?' Charlotte asked.

'He doesn't talk about it but I'm sure that's what will happen,' Verity said as she stood up and walked across the room to the window. Outside in the square, the pavements were glistening in the steady downfall of rain. The plane trees in the centre garden were bare of leaves and looked dreary and downcast. But despite the bleak outlook, Verity's face was unexpectedly joyful as she turned back to Charlotte. 'I have other good news for you, dearest!' she said. 'At least, I think you will consider it so. I . . . I hesitate to say this and haven't done so to anyone but Dr Freeman as yet – not even my darling Guy – but Dr Freeman thinks I am pregnant.'

It needed all Charlotte's self-control not to cry out in protest. If Verity carried this baby full term, and it was a boy, it would negate the very purpose of all the lies and deceit of the past two years; not least, it made the sacrifice of her future happiness a devastating folly.

It was with an immense effort of will that she leant forward to embrace her friend; to find the right words of congratulation. 'Oh, Verity, that is exciting news, but what does Dr Freeman say? Surely he forbade you to have any more children after that last miscarriage?'

Verity's laugh was like that of a mischievous child. 'Yes, and at first he reprimanded me quite severely for disobeying him, but finally he admitted he might be wrong to have done so. You see, darling, like everyone else, he thinks I gave birth to Florence. You will recall I kept making excuses not to see him when first we returned from Italy since he would have known at once if he'd examined me that I hadn't given birth. I wrote him a little note at Christmas time saying how well I was and that I would call upon him in the new year. By the time I did so last month, I was pregnant.'

Verity caught hold of Charlotte's arms and swung her round in a circle, her eyes shining. 'Don't look so worried, you silly goose! I'll be fine. This time I feel quite different – no sickness, no fainting, no fatigue. Don't I look well?'

Charlotte managed a smile. 'Yes, in fact you do. I shall pray all goes well for you.'

'And I for you, dearest,' Verity said. 'I hope you'll be wonderfully happy with your nice Mr Samuels, although I have to say' – she gave a wicked little smile – 'Theobald is not my favourite name!'

'Nor mine!' Charlotte said, joining in Verity's laughter, but her happiness did not last long. If it were not for Ket, she thought, she would have liked to go back to Kneepwood with Verity, take care of her, be there to enjoy their erstwhile friendship and intimacy. She knew that Verity would be wishing this, too, but would not say so, aware as she was that

235

poor Madame Hortense was so near to death; and that even when her employer had left this world, that Charlotte would be fully occupied preparing for her wedding to Theobald Samuels.

As they returned to the drawing room, Lady Hardcastle turned to Theobald. 'When these two young ladies get together, they behave like school children. I apologise for them!' But she was smiling as Verity went to sit on the footstool and lent against her skirts.

'Were we really gone so long?' she asked. 'I do apologise, Mr Samuels, but we had so much to talk about, did we not, Charlotte?'

The solicitor echoed Lady Hardcastle's smile. 'My hostess has kept me well entertained with stories of her late husband's exploits as a young subaltern in the Crimean war.'

'Yes, indeed,' said Lady Hardcastle, 'and Mr Samuels has in turn been regaling me with theories about that fearful man they are calling Jack the Ripper!'

'A most improper subject for a ladies drawing room!' Theobald said. 'But as I am a legal man, Lady Hardcastle was anxious to hear my views.'

'I most certainly was!' Verity's godmother admitted as Charlotte rose to go. 'Now be sure to send me an invitation to your wedding, dear child!' she added, rising to kiss Charlotte and shake Mr Samuels' hand. 'I have so much enjoyed your visit, and yours, too, Sir. You must come and see me again, both of you.'

As Theobald handed Charlotte into the waiting hansom cab she leant back against the velvet-buttoned upholstery and gave a deep sigh. 'I'm most grateful to you for accompanying me and . . . and for playing your part so well. I hope it wasn't too much of an ordeal.'

'On the contrary!' Theobald said as the cab wound its way through the traffic towards Westminister. 'I found Lady Hardcastle a delightful companion and, if I say so myself, I think she enjoyed my company, too. It was very gracious of her to invite a common or garden solicitor for a return visit. Your friend, Mrs Conniston, was most charming to me, too.'

236

Charlotte drew yet another long sigh. 'I just wish we hadn't had to lie to them,' she said wistfully.

Theobald turned to face her and, without warning, took her gloved hand in his. 'Must it be a lie, Charlotte? I am well aware that your affections are engaged elsewhere, but as we all know, time is a great healer and I believe that in due course you will recover from this disappointment. No, please let me finish what I wish to say. You know already how I feel about your unfortunate family and that this makes no difference to my regard for you. Even before my late wife died, when I first saw you at the Maison, I fell in love with you. Oh, of course I knew it to be wrong since at that time I was still a married man, but I could not put you out of my mind. Now I'm a widower, I am free to offer you a future as my wife.'

Charlotte looked down at her hand, which was still clasped in his. Her companion's impassioned proposal – his second – was an unexpected embarrassment. Obviously her former refusal, despite its being firmly voiced, had not deterred him. Perhaps the time had come when she should admit the truth about her past, after which Mr Samuels would be unlikely to propose again. In a quiet voice she said: 'You were generous enough to say that you would be prepared to disregard my family background, but there is a further disgrace of which you are unaware, Sir, for which I alone am responsible. The fact is, I'm not the flawless character you might think me. I . . . I have had a lover. It shames me to admit it, but it is only right that you should know.'

A full minute passed when Theobald Samuels did not speak. He has every right to be shocked now he knows the truth, Charlotte thought, and doubtless he was now trying to find words to withdraw his offer of marriage. Instead, his grasp on her hand tightened and his voice was condemnatory as he said: 'I can but surmise this lover you speak of took advantage of your feelings for him, but does not love you enough to marry you. Believe me, my poor child, you are well rid of him. Your loss of innocence at least leaves me free to speak more bluntly than I could otherwise have done.

I wish to say, Charlotte, that if you were to agree to marry me, I would not expect you to receive me as your lover as well as your husband. I would be satisfied merely to know that your shared my life, my home. I would hope that with time we might become more intimate, but until you wished it so, I would ask no more of you than your companionship and affection.'

Now it was Charlotte's turn to fall silent whilst her mind was racing with conflicting emotions. There was no longer any doubt that Theobald Samuels really did love her for he paid no regard either to her background or to her lost virginity. Moreover, he was offering her marriage without the usual wifely obligations. As Madame Hortense had said only a short while ago, as a husband he would give her security, protect her, perhaps even a *raison d'être* after she herself had gone. The thought of how near to death Madame Hortense was brought tears to Charlotte's eyes.

'I'm sorry to be so silly!' she said as she took a handkerchief from her pocket and wiped her eyes. 'It's just that today has been a strain and you have been so kind, and I must go now to the hospital to see Madame who is going downhill so rapidly. I cannot think about my future. With things as they are, it is too distressing.'

At once, Theobald was filled with contrition. 'It was most thoughtless of me to speak of my own sentiments at such a time,' he said. 'Please give my proposal no further consideration for the time being. In the meanwhile, if I can be of any assistance during this difficult time, you know I shall be at your call.'

Not half an hour later, Charlotte sat at Madame Hortense's bedside in a ward in St Bartholomew's Hospital. Despite her condition, the dying woman was still mentally alert. 'I know you don't want to talk about my demise, Charlotte,' she said. 'But please bear with me. I have made Theobald my executor and he is aware how I wish my funeral to be conducted. He also has possession of my will. Now don't look so woebegone, my dear. I have had a good long life and I am quite ready to go to my Maker but for one thing.'

Charlotte took Madame's parchment-thin hand and held it between her own. 'Whatever it is, I will try to do it!'

Madame Hortense's gaunt face creased in an ironic smile. 'One cannot "do it" at will, my dear. It's that I cannot be at peace until I know you will be secure. And so I am leaving the Maison to you. If you decide not to marry Theobald – although that is what I would most like to happen – then at least you will have a means of keeping yourself in modest comfort. I am also leaving you the apartment. And you are not to cry or I shall feel my parting gift to you is making you unhappy.'

'Oh, Madame, you must know how immensely grateful I am. As for Theobald, he has twice proposed to me. You are quite right, he is a very kind, nice person who would make an excellent husband. Does it make you happy to know that I did not exactly refuse his offer? I told him I didn't wish to make up my mind about my future just at present. Maybe in time . . .'

Madame's face took on an expression of enormous relief. 'Oh, my dear, I cannot tell you how happy it makes me to know that you will not be alone in the world. It is a great relief to me to know that such a union is a possibility. I know that Theobald will be a backbone of assistance to you in the immediate future. There are so many finalities following a death – the certificates, funeral arrangements, probate, a headstone and a lot more to arrange. I wouldn't want you troubled by such formalities, and Theobald will be able to deal with them for you. I do believe your respect and liking for him will increase and, it's my belief, may well turn to something deeper.'

I could never love him, Charlotte thought, *not as I love Ket*. But seeing how happy such a possibility had made her dear friend, she refrained from saying so.

There remained only the matter of the future of Madame's little dog who, after a week of pining for his mistress, had suddenly ceased to look for her.

'I wondered if you would like me to take him down to Kneepwood,' Charlotte suggested tentatively. 'The children would adore him and he would have the benefit of a large garden and country walks.'

'Oh, my dear, you cannot imagine what a relief that is. My only worry apart from you was for my darling Daybreak. If you really think Mrs Conniston would agree to give him a home, I'd be quite at peace.'

With these two concerns no longer on her mind it seemed as if she gave up any wish to prolong her life, and two weeks later Madame Hortense died.

As she had forecast, Theobald was a tower of strength to Charlotte, even to the point of being in the hospital waiting room to offer comfort and support to her when she had bidden her good friend her last farewell.

'She was indeed a friend to you, Charlotte!' Theobald told her after the funeral as they drove back to the empty apartment. 'Since her one living relative, her cousin in New Zealand, cannot be present, I shall now read her will to you and the maid who are the only beneficiaries.'

As Charlotte already knew, the Maison and the apartment above it had been bequeathed outright to her, including all garments finished and in preparation, and all accessories that might be in the showroom at the time. There was an outright gift of a hundred pounds to the maid, Sally, who promptly burst into tears for she had been genuinely devoted to her late mistress.

'And what you may not know, Charlotte,' concluded the solicitor, 'is that Doris Briggs has left you an annuity of eight hundred pounds, which should give you a moderate standard of living for the rest of your life.'

For a moment, Charlotte was too overcome to speak. When she did so, it was to speculate how it had been possible for Madame to afford such an astonishing bequest. 'As far as I'm aware, she always lived very modestly,' she said to Theobald. 'And surely, with such a large amount of capital at her disposal, she had no need to work?'

Theobald dismissed the tearful maid who departed to the kitchen to fetch a light meal that had been prepared for them to eat after the funeral. Other than themselves, there had been only the two new seamstresses and one of Madame's oldest customers present, and they had declined to return to the apartment with Theobald and Charlotte for the wake, the seamstresses glad to have a half day's holiday. Charlotte did not intend to reopen the Maison until the following day. Now, according to Theobald, the annuity Madame had bequeathed her would obviate the necessity for her to maintain the dressmaking establishment if she didn't wish to do so. She could sell the Maison and live a life of leisure – perhaps travel abroad if she had the temerity to do so alone. She suddenly remembered Ket telling her of two intrepid middle-aged English ladies who alone had travelled a thousand miles through Egypt some fifteen years ago.

The return of Sally with a tray of food brought Charlotte's attention back to Theobald. 'Forgive me,' she said. 'I was quite lost in thought.'

He smiled forgivingly at her, thinking how charming she looked in her tight-fitting black mourning dress, albeit she was far too pale and her eyes were puffed by her weeping. 'I am not sure if you knew, Charlotte, and if not I'm certain Doris would not mind me telling you that she came from very humble beginnings. She resolved to work her way up in the world, educating herself as best she could by reading at night in the public libraries and working by day as a seamstress. She had one talent – that of drawing – and it soon became known to her employer that she could design quite beautifully and creatively. To cut a long story short, she earned better wages, saved whenever she could and was finally able to buy her own establishment – a modest little shop in Bermondsey. Within five years, she was able to buy this house and turned the ground floor into the Maison Hortense as you know it. She was by then in her early forties and the habit of working and saving had become ingrained. She could no more sit back as a lady of leisure than leap off the roof of the Crystal Palace!'

Charlotte listened to this story without much surprise but with a great deal of sadness. 'So Madame never had time to enjoy the fruits of her success?' she murmured. 'That seems so sad.'

Theobald put down his plate and lent forward for emphasis. 'She was not an unhappy woman, Charlotte, I do assure you. Although I was not her accountant, she often spoke to me of the small fortune she was accumulating and how it was invested. That knowledge gave her the feeling of security she needed – and she did enjoy the accolades of her customers who appreciated the lovely garments she made for them. Many of those clients were – indeed are – titled ladies like your friend's godmother, the charming Lady Hardcastle. Although by virtue of her profession Madame was still "trade", she knew she could pass as their equal. But her greatest pleasure in later life came from you, Charlotte. Even during the time you lived with the Connistons, she still thought of you as a daughter and, when I came to visit her, she talked of little else but yourself.'

'I am very touched to hear this,' Charlotte said as he paused. 'I owed her so much – she once saved my life, you know – and so when I went to live at Kneepwood, I always wrote to her every week unless I was actually visiting her.'

Theobald nodded. 'She often read parts of those letters to me, especially when you were in Italy with Mrs Conniston and had so much of interest to relate. It was because of her that you were back with gentlefolk of your own class, she told me proudly, although she never said how she had achieved this.'

Charlotte smiled. 'By giving my friend, Mrs Conniston, my address when I had expressly forbidden her to do so!' she said. Then her smile faded. 'Do you know if she was disappointed in me when I told her I was returning to London for good and wanted my old job back working for her?'

Theobald stroked his chin thoughtfully. 'I am not certain if disappointed is the right word, Charlotte. I think it would be more true to say she was worried. You see, she knew by then that she would never recover from her illness and she was concerned for your future. You were too conscious of your family's disgrace to consider marriage, she told me, and she hated to think of you as quite alone in the world. That is when I confessed my own deep regard for you and, although it was perhaps unseemly to be saying such things not a year since my poor wife's death, I told Doris that I could wish for nothing more than to have the right to look after you, and that it was my intention to propose marriage as soon as an appropriate occasion arose.'

Charlotte gave a little sigh. 'Yes, Madame went out of her way to prepare the ground for you!' she said with a faint smile. 'I think she genuinely admired you as a person as well as a solicitor.'

'We shall both miss her, will we not!' Theobald pronounced. 'Now I must leave you, Charlotte, for there is much to be done, and you, I know, have many letters to write to those customers who will have read of Madame's death in the newspaper and wish to know what is to happen to their favourite dressmaking establishment.'

Theobald was right, Charlotte thought as she accompanied him to the door. Letter-writing would keep her occupied and keep her grief at bay. She could hardly bear to go into Madame's room, see the empty bed, the curtains drawn, the half-opened book by her bedside which would now never be read. At least Daybreak's empty basket was not too distressing because the little dog had been taken home by Sally, the maid, who was caring for it until Charlotte could take it down to Kneepwood.

Tomorrow, she thought, she would have to steel herself to empty the wardrobe, the chests of drawers, the bureau. Primrose, the youngest of the new seamstresses, could help her pack the clothes into parcels and take them in a cab to the Distressed Gentlefolk's headquarters. But now she must go to Madame's bureau and get down to work. Her first letter, she decided, would be to Verity, whose weekly letters never failed to enquire about Madame's health. Verity would be sad on her behalf but happy too to learn of Madame's unexpected and very generous gift to her.

I shall miss her most dreadfully, she wrote, *but meanwhile, I don't want you to worry about me. Theobald is shouldering most of the tiresome details appertaining to a death. But you and Guy will know of these, having dealt with the aftermath of poor Matthew's and Bertie's deaths.*

Is Sir Bertram any better now? And has Monica recovered yet from her decline? Most important question of all, how are you keeping? Is Dr Freeman happy that all is still progressing smoothly?

Please give my love to the children and tell them Daybreak is well and looking forward to coming to live at Kneepwood. I shall bring him down as soon as I can arrange a visit. It's so good of you, dear Verity, to offer him a home.

As she finished the letter and laid down her pen, just for an instant Charlotte's hand reached beneath her desk and lay on her stomach. It was quite flat, with no movement within, yet her mention of Verity's coming child had inexplicably reminded her of her own.

With a shake of her head, Charlotte reached for the blotter and carefully dabbed the wet ink. *No, not my child,* she told herself. Florence had never been hers. Even when she had felt the baby move inside her, it had been Verity's and Guy's baby. There would never be another one. Even if she did end up marrying Theobald, she would never want his child. In fact, she could never want any child . . . Unless it were Ket's.

Twenty

March–May 1891

With only two days to go before the Maison Hortense closed for Easter, it was with a sigh of relief that Charlotte shut the doors behind the departing seamstresses. It was ten o'clock on March 29th and everyone was exhausted from the effort of finishing work on the last of the Easter orders – a magnificent evening gown for Lady Cynthia Verlaine to wear at the Carlton House masked ball. Incredibly detailed, everyone including Charlotte had had to work on it, stitching tiny beads on to the bodice. She herself was now delivering it, not trusting so important and valuable a garment to one of her staff.

The London streets had been washed clean by the afternoon's downpour and in the late evening the weather had turned cold with a hint of frost in the air. Charlotte shivered, her body chilled as much from the draughty cab as from her mood of depression. This was not just caused by tiredness but by a number of additional, less curable factors which she had been too busy to consider before now. With Lady Cynthia's gown duly delivered, she sat back in the cab home and allowed a number of concerns to occupy her mind.

First of her problems was Theo. For the past year he had been constantly in attendance. After Madame Hortense had died, she'd welcomed his frequent visits and the way in which he had taken the burdens from her shoulders – having the lease of the premises and ownership of the Maison put legally in her name; seeing to probate of Madame's will; renegotiating accounts with suppliers; even writing in his neat script letters to Madame's clients informing them of the change of ownership and Charlotte's plans to continue the establishment.

On occasions, when they had been working late, Charlotte would cook a simple meal for him. At other times, he would take her to a concert or to the theatre; or on a Sunday, if it was warm enough, to listen to the band in Hyde Park. He was an attentive, undemanding companion but Charlotte was increasingly aware that his manner towards her was becoming ever more proprietorial. He'd promised her that he wouldn't speak of marriage again until a year after Madame's death, but that year had passed and Charlotte was no nearer being desirous of marriage to him, agreeable although he was.

She had now reached the conclusion that she did not wish to spend the rest of her life working from eight in the morning until sometimes late in the evening managing the Maison Hortense, as it was still called. Those years living with Verity at Kneepwood had opened her eyes to very different, wider horizons, not least the fascination of foregin countries. She'd dearly loved Italy, despite her condition and the reasons for she and Verity to be living there. They'd had far too little time to explore the antiquities of Rome; to visit such places as Venice, Milan and Naples. She longed to go back to Italy but could see no likelihood unless she were to close down the business and find the courage to travel alone.

There was no possibility that Verity could accompany her, even for a week or two, for in October she had given birth to a healthy baby boy. Although she had an excellent new nanny to take care of the infant, her delighted parents had come over from Canada to spend Christmas with the family and were still with her. The advent of their little son was the miracle Verity and Guy had never expected to happen, and they were overjoyed. Although Charlotte was thrilled for her, there were moments when she could not control the feeling of bitterness that she need never have offered to have a child for them; that with hindsight she should have listened to Madame's cautionary advice. Verity's letters were ecstatic and because Charlotte had been too busy to visit Kneepwood, Verity had come

246

to London with Nanny and the new baby to pay a brief call on her.

'I know you love running Madame Hortense's shop and you'll soon be marrying your Theobald,' Verity had said then. 'But don't you sometimes long to do other things? You will surely stop working when you are married, won't you? Then you and Theobald could travel together – perhaps go back to see the Villa dell'Alba?'

Charlotte had not the slightest desire to go there with Theobald, but Verity's remarks had put the thought in her mind that she could go without him. Madame had left her enough money for her to take such a holiday if she wished, although she would have to live frugally in a *pensione* rather than in an establishment like the Villa dell'Alba!

During that visit, Verity had shown her the latest letter she had received from Ket, who had spent the last nine months on an expedition to Persia. He had somehow managed to get himself invited to one of the Shah of Persia's six palaces and been entertained by some of his most beautiful concubines. He was intending to travel from the mouth of the Karun river to Ahwaz, which had only that year been opened to foreign steam travel. As for poor Amelia Morrison, her hopes of marriage to Ket dashed by his departure, she was now being courted by Dr Freeman's son. Verity had said, laughing, 'How many more hearts will our Ket break?'

Determined not to give Ket another thought, Charlotte found time the day after Verity's visit to go to the travel agent, Thomas Cook, and enquire if a six-month holiday could be arranged for her, a single woman, to go sightseeing in Florence, Milan, Venice and Rome, as well as the likely cost. She was told at once that both travel and accommodation could be booked in advance should she wish to proceed and they would notify her of the cost once she was more certain where exactly she wished to go and at what time of year.

On her return from Lady Verlaine's house in Lowndes Square, when the cab drew up outside the Maison Hortense, Charlotte paid the driver and, unlocking her door, made her way upstairs to her apartment. As always on entering she was painfully aware of Madame Hortense's absence. Although most of her personal belongings had gone, somehow her presence was still there and Charlotte missed her quite painfully. Now, however, she lit the small coal fire and seated herself in the armchair opposite the one where Madame used to sit.

'If you were here now, how would you advise me?' Charlotte asked aloud, as if her benefactor were really present. 'Would you want me to keep on the business? Since I've been in charge I have never lacked for clients and I think you would be proud of the way I have managed. Was it to keep me busy so I wouldn't grieve for you that you willed the Maison to me? Or were you thinking of it only as a temporary measure to occupy me before I married Theobald? Did you really and truly want me to marry him, even though I don't love him? Would you think me ungrateful, irresponsible, imprudent to put both the Maison and Theobald behind me and go away by myself whilst I'm still young enough to travel? I know you would tell me such a plan takes no account of my old age and that it would be reckless of me to abandon the security that, as a single woman and without a family, I would need. But I am so tired of responsibilities, of knowing what each tomorrow will bring. I am twenty-six years old and since I was seventeen I've had no chance to be young and carefree.'

Many, many years later, Charlotte remained convinced that somehow Madame Hortense found a way to send her the reply she wanted, for at that moment the door of the room clicked shut. The movement sent a tiny draught of air towards the fireplace and from the mantelshelf something disturbed by the slight breeze fluttered to the floor. Sighing, Charlotte bent to pick it up, noticing as she did so that the writing on the back of the postcard was discoloured by smoke from the fire. Turning it idly in her hands, she gave a small gasp. The picture was of the Palazzo Pitti in Florence, the cathedral with its magnificent tower in the background. Turning over to the writing, Charlotte recognized the postcard as one she had sent to Madame from Florence two years ago. There were tears in her eyes as she deciphered the message she had written.

*This whole city is quite magical and I don't think
I could ever weary of sightseeing. Italy is beautiful
and I am taking your advice and enjoying life to
the full as best I can, because as you said, one is
only young once! Nothing else matters but happiness, you told me and I am so pleased to be able
to say I am very happy as I sit here writing this
to you . . .*

Charlotte was too level-headed not to realize that it was the
draught from the closing door which had blown the postcard
off the mantelshelf at the very moment she'd been asking
Madame's advice. Nevertheless, the timing was such that it
seemed like more than a coincidence. An envelope falling . . .
perhaps. A postcard, possibly. But a postcard of Florence,
Italy? And with the quotation of Madame Hortense's advice
written unarguably on the back?

Perhaps no one else would be influenced by such super-
stition, Charlotte told herself, knowing that this small, insignificant happening was nevertheless sufficient to resolve her
uncertainty. Her mind was now made up and immediately
after Easter she would go back to Thomas Cook and ask the
travel agent to arrange for her to go to Italy in the middle
of May.

Meanwhile, she would ask Theobald to lease the downstairs rooms comprising the Maison Hortense for a year.
Perhaps at the end of twelve months she would have tired
of travelling; wish herself back in London with her old
occupation, and could reopen the Maison. It might take
a little time to build up her clientele again but some of
the older clients would almost certainly return, and others
would follow. As for the girls, she regretted putting them
out of work but she would give them several weeks' wages
to keep them going before they found other jobs. References
from so prestigious an establishment as the Maison Hortense
would almost certainly guarantee their re-employment, and
with the Season starting they would have no difficulty in
finding work.

There remained only the distressing duty of telling poor Theobald that she had decided irrevocably that she could not marry him, now or in the future. It was unlikely he would go on hoping she might change her mind if she implied she might well remain abroad indefinitely.

Theobald was hugely disappointed, although Charlotte's decision did not come entirely as a surprise. He had sensed her almost imperceptible withdrawal from him after those first few weeks following Madame's demise, when her manner had been so dependent and filled with gratitude. But once she had reopened the Maison and become immersed in its day to day management, she'd had less and less time for him. Even when she had spent an evening with him she had been almost too tired to converse. And never once that he could recall had Charlotte shown a willingness for any physical intimacy. If he held her hand during an emotional scene in an opera, she did not return the pressure and would withdraw her hand to her lap as soon as he released it.

Despite her emphatic declaration that she would never change her mind, he insisted upon telling her that should she do so, no matter how far in the future, he would be waiting; that under no circumstances would he marry anyone else.

Theobald was clearly so devastated by Charlotte's impending departure that occasionally during a sleepless night she found herself questioning whether she was out of her mind to refuse the life and devotion he was offering her. He didn't have Ket's good looks, his charm, his wonderful sense of humour, but he was kind, thoughtful and considerate, and there could be no doubt that he loved her faithfully and enduringly. If she couldn't marry the man she loved, why should she not accept this second best, this offer of a home, husband, security for the remainder of her life?

But by morning, Charlotte's resolve to travel abroad had returned in full force. She had no need to reiterate her decision to Theobald and, with a clear conscience, she set about closing down the Maison, writing references for the girls, selecting and packing both winter and summer garments for her travels. With utmost efficiency, Thomas Cook took care of her need for foreign currencies, renewed her passport and arranged for her to travel with a group of five other spinster ladies. She was soon in possession of her tickets for the boat and train, together with an itinerary of her journey to Spain and Greece and the names of the *pensiones* where she would be staying.

With three weeks to go before her departure, Charlotte's anxieties gave way to a heady excitement. There was no changing her mind now and she had even written in her halting Italian to Luisa to inform the Villa dell'Alba house-keeper of her impending visit. She would, of course, have to revert to the name of Mrs Conniston whilst at the villa, but that would not be too difficult. If Verity had a photograph to spare she might take one of the children to show Luisa – especially a likeness of little Florence, whose actual birth Luisa had witnessed. According to Verity, the little girl still resembled Guy but her hair had darkened quite a bit and the blue of her eyes had deepened.

With time now on her hands, Charlotte realized she must part with Daybreak, take him to Kneepwood and pay the fare-well visit she had promised Verity before she went abroad.

With Ket away and Sir Bertram so ill, I'm sorely in need of your company to cheer me, Verity had written, *even if it is only for a few days. Please, please come and visit, Charlotte . . .*

Knowing that this would be the last opportunity to see her dearest friend for a very long time, Charlotte wrote to say that she would come as soon as she could. She decided not to send a telegram advising Verity of the exact time of her arrival so that she could give her a surprise.

In a few days' time she would travel down in the train to Kneepwood Halt, Daybreak beside her in the little hamper she had purchased for the purpose. There she would hire the pony and trap from the landlord of the King's Head tavern to take her up to the house. With a sigh of satisfaction Charlotte considered her journey, imagining the look on Verity's and

251

the children's faces when Grainger announced her unexpected arrival at Kneepwood Court.

'I say, old chap, you couldn't have arrived at a more opportune moment!' Guy's voice was deepened by emotion as he placed an arm affectionately around his half-brother's shoulders. 'I don't suppose Grainger told you, did he? I'm afraid Father is pretty ill – had another stroke, you see.'

Ket sat down in one of the big leather-covered library chairs and regarded Guy's anxious face with concern. 'Anything at all I can do,' he said, 'you've only to say, Guy.'

Guy poured them each a whisky and soda and sat down opposite Ket. 'It happened pretty suddenly the day before yesterday,' he said. 'I sent you a telegram but I don't imagine you received it.'

'I was on my way home by then,' Ket said. 'Must have had a premonition, as I hadn't intended to come back so soon, but I broke my wrist, you see, falling down a mountain!' He grinned at the look of concern on Guy's face. 'No great harm done, but it curtailed my activities – couldn't even ride a horse, that sort of thing, so I decided to pack up and come home. Is Father . . . is he going to get better?'

Guy shook his head. 'The doctor says he might linger on another day at most. I suppose we shouldn't be too upset. Father was pretty badly affected after the last stroke, but this one . . . well, Freeman said if he does recover he will remain in a vegetative state for as long as he survives.'

Ket took a long drink from his glass and then gave a deep sigh. 'It is a bit of a shock, but I suppose in the circumstances we should be hoping the poor old fellow doesn't recover. You know, Guy, Father was always reasonably decent to me compared with the way he treated you. Of course, Matthew was the one he doted on, but he treated me fairly and although he didn't approve of it, he did always finance my travelling. But between you and me, we were never very close – not the way some fathers are with their sons. I've seen you, for example, with those girls of yours and they'll as soon run to you with their ups and downs as to their mother or Nanny.

252

Can't imagine one of us running to father for a hug and bit of comforting advice! Still, I'm sorry his life has to end like this. He never really recovered from poor old Matthew's death, did he?'

'Well, it's good to have you here, old chap!' Guy said warmly. 'No matter what the reason. Verity will be overjoyed to see you. She'll be agog to show you our handsome young son and heir. Did she write and tell you we're calling him Christopher after you?'

Ket nodded. 'Yes, she did! Wonderful thing to happen after all that time, eh?' Ket laughed. 'And what of that pretty little god-daughter of mine – Florence, isn't it? I've brought her a doll from Turkey. Looked a bit like her I thought!'

Verity came hurrying into the room and, seeing Ket, ran to kiss him warmly on both cheeks. 'Guy and I were only saying yesterday how much we wished you were here!' she said, sitting down on a footstool near him. 'Guy has brought you up to date with the news, I imagine?'

'Well, not all of it,' Ket replied, smiling. 'For instance, what news is there of my other sister-in-law? Is Monica still suffering from melancholy?'

Verity glanced briefly at the door, her expression one of anxiety lest Monica should walk in. 'As a matter of fact, she has taken on a new lease of life ever since Father had his first stroke!' Verity replied quietly. 'Although we had a professional nurse to take care of him, as soon as he was a little better, Monica suddenly dismissed the woman and took on the nursing duties herself. Father seemed to react very favourably to the change as he hated the trained nurse, who was actually very nice. The staff have all complained in roundabout ways that poor Monica is too dictatorial and I suppose she does keep them on their toes most of the day – and sometimes at night.' She gave a brief smile before continuing. 'The dower house was closed when Monica came here to nurse your father, and the children have moved in here with ours. Fortunately our new nanny didn't object to the addition to the nursery numbers as Miss Armstrong looks after the older girls and Nanny has sole charge of

Florence and little Christopher, who is really quite ador-
able and—'

'Verity, I suggest you send Grainger to find Nanny and ask
her to bring the children down to see their Uncle Ket,' Guy
interrupted with a smile. 'It will save hours of you "ooohing"
and "aaaahing" about them and let Ket see them for himself.
You don't mind, old fellow?'

'Far from it!' Ket said. 'I think I look forward to the
welcome I get from the children even more than I do
your own!'

'And what news of Charlotte?' he asked whilst they
awaited the arrival of Nanny with the children, all of whom
would have to be washed, brushed and put into their best
clothes before going downstairs to see their uncle. 'Is she
still running that dressmaking shop in London?' His voice
deepened as he added bitterly: 'I suppose she packed that in
when she married her solicitor fellow!'

Verity looked down at her hands clasped uneasily in her
lap. When Charlotte had written telling her of her plans
to travel, she had also confessed that she'd told Theobald
Samuels she would never marry him. But perhaps it was sensible to leave Ket under the misapprehension that Charlotte
was now beyond his reach. She understood only too well that
even if Charlotte found the courage to do the impossible and
confess to Ket that she had not only lain with another man –
his own brother – but borne his child, she could be no less
than disgraced in Ket's eyes.

Momentarily, Verity was overcome by the enormity of the
sacrifice Charlotte had made – for her and Guy! she thought
bitterly. And the reason for that sacrifice had been for nothing
with the baby a girl. Now, to compound their folly, not only
had Matthew died leaving the inheritance virtually in Guy's
hands, but she herself had produced a son. Her delight in
her new infant would always be tinged with enormous guilt,
Verity thought, knowing as she did that Charlotte's chances
of happiness had been ruined because of her willingness to
have a baby for them. Sometimes she had even found herself
wondering if Charlotte's life might not have been happier

had she, Verity, never intervened and removed her from the Maison Hortense. At such times, Guy would remind her that alone in the world, Charlotte had been on the brink of total poverty and once, but for Madame Hortense's intervention, might have died of starvation.

'I suppose her Mr Samuels is ideal husband material!' Ket said into the silence that had befallen. 'Steady income, reliable, dependable – in fact a thoroughly worthy fellow!' Quite the opposite of himself! he thought bitterly. No wonder Charlotte had turned him down.

'Charlotte wrote some little while ago, saying she was leasing the premises and would be going abroad,' Verity said vaguely. 'She mentioned returning to Italy to visit the places where we stayed.'

Ket was staring into his whisky glass as he said: 'Is this a belated honeymoon? You never wrote and told me you had been to Charlotte's wedding. When . . .'

Mercifully, Nanny's arrival with the baby and the children saved Verity a reply to Ket's question. The older girls ran to kiss and hug their uncle, only the two-year-old Florence remained clinging to Nanny's voluminous skirt.

'Florence, this is your godfather!' Guy prompted. 'Won't you spare a kiss for him?'

Ket shook his head as he smiled at the little girl. 'She's just shy, aren't you, Florence?' he said. 'You'll give your godfather a welcome home kiss soon enough when you see the special present I've brought for you.'

Immediately the other children clamoured for the gifts they knew he would have found for them, for he never returned from his travels without exciting foreign presents for everyone. Despite Sir Bertram's impending demise, it was as always the happiest of family occasions when Ket arrived home and one of the rare times when Nanny did not try to restrain the noisy exuberance of her charges. She, too, was not immune to Ket's charms as he found time to compliment her upon the children's appearances.

Ket was about to summon a footman to collect the packages in his valise when, without even knocking on the door,

Grainger came hurrying into the room. He went straight to Guy and as the children fell silent, he said in a low voice: 'It's Sir Bertram, Mr Guy. Mrs Matthew has sent Hanworth for the doctor. Mrs Matthew thinks it won't be long now, sir, before . . . before . . .' His voice broke with emotion for he had now been thirty years in Sir Bertram's service; had in fact known him longer than anyone in the room. His master's imminent passing was also a reminder of his own mortality. Quickly pulling himself together he added: 'Mrs Matthew thought you and Mr Ket and Madam might want to hurry, Mr Guy. She said the master has had another stroke.'

Charlotte was on the point of leaving the Maison Hortense to travel down to Kneepwood when a letter from Verity arrived, the black-bordered envelope indicating that there had been a death in the family. Anxiously, Charlotte perused the content.

> *Dearest Charlotte,* Verity had written, *Sir Bertram passed away this morning and his funeral is to take place at the end of the week. You will understand, therefore, why your proposed visit is not very propitious at this moment. The house is in a state of mourning such as you will recall when poor Matthew and Bertie died – curtains drawn, mirrors draped, messages of condolence arriving hourly.*
>
> *Poor old Grainger was, I think, truly devoted to his master so perhaps it's as well he has been kept so busy dealing with callers. It isn't easy to say if Monica's outward show of grief is genuine or not but she keeps to her room and won't even join us for meals downstairs. Perhaps it is uncharitable of me to suggest that because she so clearly enjoyed nursing her patient and ordering everyone about, she now misses her position of authority. In any event, I am kept inordinately busy myself, arranging matters for the funeral. Everyone seems to require a decision*

from me. It is quite exhausting. If I am upstairs I am
wanted downstairs and if I am down, I am needed up!
Much as I miss Mama and Papa I am thankful they have
returned home and are not party to this disruption.

I trust it will not incommode you to postpone your
visit until after the funeral, although I do realize this
will leave little time before you embark for the continent.
How excited you must be, dearest. I almost envy you.

The letter contained, by design, no mention of Ket's presence at Kneepwood. Verity feared that had she done so she might not see her friend again before she left England – and for how long? If Charlotte enjoyed her travels as greatly as she imagined, their separation could be for months – if not years.

Although momentarily disappointed, Charlotte decided to pass the time by going to the Printed Books Department of the British Museum. It had been built only a few years ago in the interior quadrangle of the museum; and with the vast number of books available to be perused in the reading room, Charlotte had no doubt she would find accounts of authors' travels in various countries, not least those areas less well known and frequented by tourists. However, before she had paid even the first of the visits she had planned, she received a lengthy telegram from Guy.

> *Verity has had a nasty fall and now has concussion.*
> *Miss Armstrong away visiting her sick mother and*
> *Nanny unable to cope with so many children and*
> *baby. Monica will not leave her room. Can you come*
> *at once? If so, please notify by telegram and will meet*
> *your train. Father's funeral day after tomorrow so no*
> *time to interview agency governesses. Your help sorely*
> *needed. Yours in grateful anticipation, Guy.*

By tea time that same day, Charlotte had arrived at Kneepwood station with Daybreak on a lead grasped firmly in one hand and her portmanteau in the other. She was relieved to see Gregory waiting with the brougham.

'It's a sad day, Miss,' Gregory said as he helped her into the coach and lifted the dog up beside her. 'What with Madam so poorly and Mrs Matthew still not herself and the funeral and all tomorrow. They'll all be right glad to see you, Miss, especially poor Nanny who doesn't know whichaway to turn with all them kiddies running around and no one to hush them.'

Despite the gravity of the situation, Charlotte smiled. 'I think death is beyond the comprehension of the very young, Gregory,' she said. 'Perhaps it is best if they don't grieve too much for their grandfather. This little dog I have brought down for them will be a useful distraction, I hope. How is Mr Guy?'

'Worried sick for Madam, Cook says, but the better for having Mr Ket alongside him. He—'

'*Mr Ket?*' The question was out before Charlotte could prevent it. 'Did you say Mr Ket was back home?'

'Why, yes, Miss. He got back same day as the master passed away, God rest his soul.'

But why, why, why hadn't Verity warned her? Charlotte thought, wondering if there were some way by which she could turn round and go back to London, yet knowing there was not. Guy was depending upon her. He, of course, might not know how desperately difficult it was going to be for her to be living in the same house as Ket. Yes, she would spend the greater part of her time in the nursery wing looking after the children, but inevitably she would be expected to take her meals downstairs, besides which there would be nothing to stop Ket coming to find her – if he had not yet found some other female to console him.

As Gregory now drove the horses at a smart trot through Kneepwood village, Charlotte cuddled Madame's little dog closer to her. She leant back against the seat cushions, her eyes unseeing of the familiar landscape. All she could envisage was the imminent meeting with Ket. Would he hold out his hand? Kiss her cheek? Welcome her in that slow husky voice? Smile from those dark-lashed, brilliant, teasing eyes. *I can't face it*, she thought. *I can't face him.*

258

Everyone will see the way I look at him and know at once that I love him.

But now they were travelling at walking pace up the long drive leading to Kneepwood Court. The rhododendrons and azaleas were in full bloom and a mass of tulips filled the flower beds bordering the terrace. The wild cherry tree was bursting with white blossom and bunches of mauve flowers hung from the wisteria covering the front of the house. The beauty of the spring garden cheered Charlotte's heart until she caught sight of the black beribboned wreath on the big oak door. Her breath caught in her throat and her heart pounded so fiercely she felt it might explode in her chest. Every other thought left her but that within a few minutes she might see Ket, the man she loved, the man she had not expected to see again until that love had finally died and she could face him with a quiet heart.

Twenty-one

May 1891

At breakfast that morning Guy had told Ket he was sending Charlotte a telegram asking her to come and cope with the household.

'Who knows how long it will be before my poor darling Verity is well enough to take charge once more. Mrs Barker is an excellent housekeeper but one can hardly ask her to be responsible for the children. Dolly, the nursemaid, is far too young and poor Nanny can't manage all the children's lessons as well as Florence and Christopher. You know, don't you Ket, that we now look after Matthew's offspring since the poor fellow died and Monica went into a decline.'

'Sounds like you've been having quite a time of it, old chap!' Ket said, patting his brother affectionately on the back. 'All the same, why Charlotte? I thought she'd married that solicitor fellow and was going abroad?'

Guy shook his head. 'You're out of date. That betrothal fell through, although it is true Charlotte is going abroad. Verity knows far more about it than I do. I just hope to goodness she hasn't left the country yet. She's first class with those children. Strange, really, as I don't believe she's all that fond of infants.' Guy cut himself off short, remembering how firmly he and Verity had agreed that nothing must ever be said that could lead anyone to suppose little Florence was Charlotte's child and that she had virtually disowned her.

'Surely you could get hold of a governess elsewhere?' Ket was saying.

'I believe Verity was trying to get hold of a temporary replacement for Miss Armstrong but hadn't yet found anyone

260

suitable when the accident happened,' Guy answered. With a sigh, he rose from the table. 'I have to go down to the church now to meet the vicar about tomorrow's formalities. He seems to think the villagers will turn out in force and the church will be full. About forty or so neighbours are expected to attend. Surprising really, I didn't think that number really cared too much about Father.'

'Want to be seen to be doing their duty, I expect!' Ket said with a grin. But no sooner had Guy departed than the smile was replaced by a look of abject misery. If he hadn't been obliged to remain for his father's funeral, he might have found some means of escape – of going far away where he wouldn't have to see Charlotte again. He had not forgotten a single detail of their last meeting – his pleas to her to change her mind about marrying the lawyer fellow; to admit that she loved him. But she had made it perfectly clear she wasn't interested in marriage to a penniless adventurer, not that she had used those words but he had taken her meaning. The fact that she didn't love him after all had hurt him beyond measure, and beyond forgetting. At least Guy's mention of her pending arrival enabled him to prepare for their encounter, and he could steel himself to greet her with a show of indifference – or polite friendliness might be more appropriate.

Deliberately, Ket did not go to meet Charlotte at the station, nor was he even in the front hall when Grainger opened the door to her. Instead, he absented himself by the easy ploy of going to the schoolroom to entertain the children. Thrilled as always by his presence, they were soon busy enacting a short play Ket invented for them based on the story of *Snow White and the Seven Dwarfs*, a fairy tale they all knew well. Kate, the eldest, was to be Snow White; Monica's eldest daughter, the wicked stepmother, and the rest of the children were the dwarfs. He himself would be the narrator, he told them as they crowded round him, little Florence with her arms round his neck, her adoration of this uncle no less than his particular fondness for his godchild. There was something about her which had a special appeal – an expression in her blue eyes;

a tiny lilt in her voice, a mannerism he could not identify but, whatever it was, she was his favourite – although he never let the others know it.

It was Nanny who first saw Charlotte when she arrived. She was on her way to the kitchen to see about the children's high tea. Recognizing Charlotte from the visit with the baby to London, she greeted her with pleasure. Things were in a bad way, she muttered, shaking her head so vigorously her cap was nearly dislodged. What with Sir Bertram's passing and now Madam so poorly and herself needing three pairs of hands, she'd been right glad when the master had told her Miss Wyndham would be arriving to help with the children.

If she were not too tired from her journey, she insisted, Charlotte should relieve Master Ket who was up in the nursery looking after the eight children, poor man, with only Dolly to help.

'Never mind, Nanny, I'm here now and I promise I won't leave until we're sure Madam is well again,' Charlotte replied. 'I'll relieve Mr Ket presently but first I must see your mistress.'

She entered Verity's room and, in reply to her questions, the resident nurse informed her that although there had been occasional moments when her patient had appeared to recognize her husband, she remained in an unconscious state. The doctor, however, seemed very hopeful of an eventual complete recovery. Having bent to kiss Verity's pale cheek, and noted her inert form, Charlotte realized there was nothing she could do in the sickroom. Taking some comfort from the nurse's reassurances, she decided she could no longer delay going up to the schoolroom to assist Ket as Nanny had requested.

As she opened the door she was briefly aware of Ket looking up from the nursery fender where he was seated. The next moment the children were crowding around her with joyful cries of welcome. Only Florence didn't leave her place on Ket's lap, although she did smile at Charlotte and appeared pleased to see her.

Ket stood up, putting Florence back on her feet and

announced to the children that, now Aunt Charlotte had arrived to look after them, it was time for him to go. But there were such cries of protest that he didn't have the heart to do so. Neither would they allow Charlotte to leave. So it happened that the meeting she and Ket had both dreaded was made easier by the children's demands that they should proceed with the play. Charlotte promised to think of a song the seven dwarfs might sing and Ket promised to produce a few pieces of suitable scenery if by the start of the following week the children had practised their parts well enough for the play to be performed downstairs for the staff.

'And Father and Mother, too!' Verity's children clamoured.

'If Mama is well enough!' Charlotte promised. 'It would certainly be a lovely get-well surprise for her.'

The customary practice of changing for dinner was negated by Guy in view of the formalities that would be required on the morrow. As Monica ate in her room, Guy, Ket and Charlotte were the only diners that evening, Ket and Charlotte having little to say to one another and leaving most of the conversation to Guy. Bowed down as he was by the coming funeral, he talked of little else, especially of his own and Ket's parts in it as pall-bearers. Charlotte was needed to receive the mourners after the service, Guy told her, and he would be grateful if she would see Cook and Mrs Barker after dinner to ensure that the catering was adequate, both in quality and quantity, for the number of guests expected.

'I'm so enormously grateful to you for coming so quickly, Charlotte, my dear,' he said as they rose from the dining table to go through to the drawing room for coffee. 'If it had been possible, I would have postponed Father's funeral but Verity's accident happened too much at the last minute for me to do so. Thank heaven Dr Freeman says that now she has started to regain her senses, her subsequent recovery should be quite rapid. But she will have to have a long convalescence. That's why I am glad you two are both here. She enjoys your company, Ket, and you'll be able to keep her amused, I know. As for you, Charlotte, I know

I don't have to tell you how much she will love having you here again.'

Charlotte looked down at her hands – a habit she had quickly acquired in order to avoid meeting Ket's eyes, which she sensed were frequently on her. 'It really is fortunate you are here, Ket,' she said. 'As Guy has just pointed out, you'll be able to keep Verity company which I shall not have much time to do with all those children to mind. But don't look so concerned, Guy, I shall enjoy the task, especially as I may not see them again for quite some time. I leave for the continent in two weeks' time, you see!' she added with a brief glance at Ket.

'And for how long, if I may be permitted to enquire?' Ket asked in a hard, stilted voice.

Charlotte felt the colour rise in her cheeks. 'I can't say exactly. It depends how agreeable I find my travels – and my companions.'

Ket's voice sharpened. 'You're not going alone then?'

'No, I will be going with a party of five. I think it should be quite jolly.'

Six ladies? Six gentlemen? Or three of each? Would she be unchaperoned? The questions burned on Ket's lips but he was too proud to enquire. Charlotte must not know the effect her words were having. She was clearly quite indifferent to his feelings, and was addressing him as if he were no more than a fellow guest at Guy's table.

He stood up abruptly and, excusing himself on the grounds that he needed to check that his valet had made ready his funeral attire for the following day, he bade Guy and Charlotte a quick goodnight, adding a slight bow in Charlotte's direction.

'Splendid chap, Ket!' Guy said as the door closed behind his brother. 'I've sometimes thought, Charlotte, how lucky I am that my darling Verity chose me rather than dear old Ket for a husband. Of course, he's quite a bit younger but I can see exactly why females of all ages adore him. I'm surprised you never succumbed to his charms, my dear.'

Charlotte hastily put down her coffee cup which was rattling quite audibly in its saucer as she strove for calm.

'Of course I agree with you, Guy, Ket's a real charmer, but whether he would make a responsible husband or not is quite another matter. I'm sure Verity has never regretted her choice. It's plain to see she worships the ground you tread on,' she added with a smile.

Guy's face softened. 'And I worship her. Do you know, Charlotte, when she fell down those stairs and Grainger called me from the library and I saw her lying there, I thought she might be dead. I thought if that was so, I too wished to be dead. Does that shock you, Charlotte?'

'No, I understand. I think I've always known – as long as I've known you both – that you are truly lovers, that you love one another completely. Perhaps that's why I have never married – because if I can't have what you and Verity have, then I don't want anything less.'

Guy frowned as he reached over and patted her hand. 'Neither Verity nor I like to think of you alone in this world,' he said. 'Perhaps you will yet meet the man who can make you happy. But if not, we both want you to know that we will always be here for you – as if we were your real family. You do know that, don't you, my dear?'

Charlotte nodded, too close to tears to speak. Although Verity had indeed become like a sister to her and Guy like a brother, she still could not tell him now that she had already met the one and only man she had ever wished to marry; that he was upstairs, in this house, perhaps even still a little in love with her. Verity understood and accepted the guilt, but Guy was unaware that the night she had spent with him trying to conceive his child had put her forever beyond Ket's reach.

As she bade Guy goodnight and went up to bed, she decided that no one living could ever regret as deeply as she did that it was she herself who had persuaded Verity to let her have Guy's baby, thus bringing about the hopeless situation she was now in.

It was now two weeks since his sons had buried Sir Bertram Conniston. The will had been read and Guy had inherited the estate and, with certain provisos, such monetary funds as

265

were in the bank. Matthew's horses and stables had been sold after his death, raising sufficient money to pay all his debts. At that time, Sir Bertram had bought an annuity for Monica and the children which would keep them in moderate comfort in the future. Ket, Sir Bertram had willed, was to have a small allowance to enable him to continue his explorations of the world or, if he were to find a rich wife, to marry.

Verity lay on the chaise longue in the morning room, with Charlotte seated beside her. She had completely recovered from her fall except for the severe loss of weight that had come about whilst she'd remained unconscious. Now the doctor had ordered plenty of good food and rest. Charlotte had continued to take on all her responsibilities with the exception of the employment of a temporary governess – something Verity insisted upon doing herself. The woman was now installed in the nursery quarters and seemed satisfactory in every respect.

'It means you can spend your last few days with me, dearest,' Verity had said. 'I shall miss you so dreadfully!'

'I am going to miss you,' Charlotte said now as she watched the dust motes drifting in a shaft of sunlight pouring through the windows. 'I shall write to you as often as I can, I promise. And I shall send the children lots and lots of postcards.'

It was Charlotte's last day at Kneepwood and Verity suggested they might take a short walk round the garden together. Charlotte's heart was heavy as they crossed the terrace leading to the rose garden, their arms entwined.

'Aren't you just a little sad at leaving us, dearest?' Verity enquired. 'Although I do understand you must be quite excited about your forthcoming travels.'

It was better that Verity should not know how desperately sad she was, Charlotte thought bitterly. As for feeling excitement at the thought of travelling with five as yet unknown companions, she had wondered since her return to Kneepwood how she could ever have conceived such a plan. Kneepwood had come to seem like her own home, and Verity, Guy and the children like her own family. Only the strained relationship between herself and Ket marred what could have been the happiest time of her life now that Verity was making the rapid recovery Dr Freeman had predicted. Guy appeared ten years younger since her recovery and the knowledge that the estate was now and for the rest of his life in his safe keeping. Moreover, he now had the dearest of little sons to follow in his footsteps.

The six-month-old child was enchanting, Charlotte thought as Verity stopped for a moment to admire the sweep of emerald green of the newly cut croquet lawn. But then so were all the Conniston children. It was strange, she reflected, that she had never felt any ties to the little girl she had borne. Even stranger that Ket of all people should find it impossible not to show that he favoured his godchild above the others. Perhaps Florence was beginning to look a little like herself, she thought anxiously, although the child still had Guy's blue-grey eyes.

'Come, dearest, it's time we went in to tea!' Verity said, turning back towards the garden door. 'I think we have had Dr Freeman's prescribed ten-minute perambulation!' She laughed as she spoke but the laughter gave way to a sigh as they entered the house. 'It's so lovely to know that summer will soon be here, and I could be so happy if you—'

'Hush, don't say it or I shall become tearful,' Charlotte interrupted.

Removing her coat and bonnet, Verity once more linked her arm through Charlotte's. 'You're quite right, of course!' she said. 'Come, dearest, let's go and see if Ket has returned from his ride. He will cheer us for certain, won't he?'

Despite the fact that he had thoroughly enjoyed his ride along bridleways leading to the northern boundary of the estate, Ket was far from cheerful as he noted the emerging signs of summer. The leaves of the beech trees were lime green; bluebells carpeted the woods; half-grown lambs gambolled in the meadows and a hundred songbirds drowned the soft beat of his horse's hooves in the damp earth. There was no country in the world Ket knew of which was more beautiful than England in May.

Perhaps with Charlotte leaving the following day, he

thought as he rode into the stable yard, he might himself stay longer at Kneepwood, although he was only too well aware how painfully he would miss her. Despite the fact that they seldom spoke at any length, that she avoided his company whenever possible, he could still see her, hear her voice, know that she slept under the same roof. Her departure would mean the final ending to his hopes and dreams of a future shared with her. Perhaps after all, it would be better for him to go away – far away, where there would be no immediate memories of her.

As he went into the house, one of the parlourmaids followed him into the drawing room to ask if he would like the fire lit, for it could become quite chilly once the sun went down. Grainger would be in with the tea as soon as the mistress and Miss Wyndham came in from their walk, she told him as, obedient to his nod, she put a match to the paper in the grate. Like all the Kneepwood servants she idolized Ket and now, seeing him with his long legs stretched out before him and his dark hair curling untidily over his forehead, she thought him even more handsome than the famous actor Sir Henry Irving dressed as Hamlet, Prince of Denmark, a picture postcard of whom had pride of place on the mantelpiece in her attic bedroom.

As she left the room. she stood back to allow Grainger to pass her. He went to stand in front of Ket's chair, holding out a small silver platter on which lay a calling card.

'Excuse me, Sir, but two ladies have called and asked to see you. I told them the family was in mourning and that Thursday was not a day for calling but . . . well, Sir, perhaps you know what the American people are like!' Ket smiled, seeing the pained look on the old butler's face. He leant forward and took the card from the tray.

'Hammel!' he exclaimed, reading the name aloud. 'Euphemia Hammel! Can't say I've the faintest idea who . . . Wait a minute, Grainger, I do know who this is – a Mrs Hammel I met when I was in America. Lived in an enormous great house near the Copleys – invited us all to dinner.' He grinned at the butler. 'She threatened to visit Kneepwood if she was ever in the south of England. Well, don't keep her waiting, Grainger. Show her in – and the other American who I seem to recall was her companion – Ashley, Oscar – no, Austin, I think.'

Grainger's look of disapproval remained in place as, on entering the drawing room, the large bulk that was Euphemia Hammel dressed quite extravagantly in a richly embroidered lime green costume with voluminous leg-of-mutton sleeves, pushed past him and flung her arms around Ket as he stood up to greet her. Her companion, more soberly dressed in a black tailor-made suit stood quietly listening as her employer explained their presence.

'We were in our carriage passing through Crowborough on our way to Tunbridge Wells,' she said in her loud Southern drawl. 'And would you believe it, Mr Conniston honey, Frances here pointed out the name on the signpost – Kneepwood. "Why that's where that delightful young Englishman lived," Frances reminded me. "The one who was the guest of the Copleys." I just knew we had to turn around and come visiting. And then Frances recalled we'd met your sister-in-law, Mrs Conniston and her friend in Italy – and I dare say you heard how they rescued us up a mountain near Florence – and I said to Frances, we just can't pass by so near where those two lovely English ladies live and not call in and thank them again, isn't that right, Frances? Now you must tell me, did Mrs Conniston give birth to that baby safely? We worried about her being up in the hills so near her time, didn't we, Frances?'

Suppressing a smile, Ket assured them that Verity had safely produced a lovely little girl. 'My sister-in-law and her friend, Miss Wyndham, will be here shortly so you will be able to meet them again,' he said, managing at last to seat his visitors in chairs opposite him. Before Mrs Hammel could break into a further monologue, he assured them they were both very welcome and must stay to tea.

'And dear Mrs Conniston's baby?' Mrs Hammel gushed. 'Why, it must be almost two years old by now, isn't that what we worked out on our way here, Frances?' Not waiting

269

or wanting a reply, she continued to regale Ket with reminiscences both of their meetings with him at the Copleys' and their adventures in Italy, monopolizing the conversation until the door opened and Verity and Charlotte came into the room. At once, she rose to her feet, not without some difficulty because of her bulk, and enveloped Charlotte in a totally unorthodox embrace.

'My dear Mrs Conniston!' she effused. 'This is just so wonderful. I've been telling your brother-in-law, dear Mr Conniston here, how we came to be passing nearby to Kneepwood village and just had to come calling. You are looking so well and pretty, my dear, is she not, Frances? You remember my companion, don't you?' She turned to Verity who was standing stone still, her expression horrified. But there was no stopping Mrs Hammel. 'Why Miss Wyndham, how well you look, too, my dear. Frances and I were only saying how fortunate we were to have you and Mrs Conniston rescue us that dreadful day our coach overturned.'

Ignoring the arrival of Grainger and the parlourmaid with the tea, she continued talking, putting her arm through Charlotte's. 'Shall we have the pleasure of meeting your husband, Mrs Conniston? And Frances and I would both just love to see your baby, dear!' she added, still looking at Charlotte. 'We often talked about you lovely English people and Frances was certain you'd have a little boy, dear, because she remembered you telling her that was what your husband wanted, but I guessed it would be a girl. If she resembles you, dear, she'll be very pretty!'

Neither Verity nor Charlotte could speak so great was their shock, but as Charlotte edged away from Mrs Hammel's grasp, Ket, totally silenced until now, found his voice. 'You were quite right, Mrs Hammel. The baby, a little girl, is called Florence – and you are also right in thinking her pretty, which indeed she is.' He turned to look directly at Charlotte as he added: 'I hadn't thought of it until you raised the subject, Mrs Hammel, but you are right in this respect also, she does bear quite a strong resemblance to her mother, although I had not been aware of it before.'

The shock of their exposure, following on from the previous stressful weeks, was Charlotte's undoing. Tears filled her eyes and before she could find her handkerchief, flowed slowly down her cheeks. As she turned and ran from the room, she heard Ket's voice saying: 'My father died quite recently, ladies, and with the funeral only a few days ago, I'm afraid my sister-in-law is a little over-emotional.' With the faintest smile about his lips he turned to Verity and said: 'If you will serve tea to these good people, Miss Wyndham, I'll go and see if Mrs Conniston is recovering.'

Still speechless but aware she must now play the part Ket had allotted her, Verity stepped forward and enquired how her guests liked their tea.

Meanwhile Charlotte, unable to stop the tears, had hurried into the sanctuary of the library. The room had been closed since Sir Bertram's death, but a fire was kept burning to ensure that his many shelves of books did not suffer from the damp. Throwing herself down on the hearthrug, Charlotte buried her head in her arms and felt the soft, cool leather of a chair against her hot cheek. She did not lift her head as the door opened and someone came into the room. She guessed it was Ket and she dreaded hearing his voice accusing her of deceit; of duplicity; of trickery; of lying. No matter how well-intentioned her motives had been, she was still guilty of all four.

'Charlotte!' Ket's voice was harsh as he repeated her name a second time. 'Charlotte, look at me! Florence is your child, isn't she? She is the reason you and Verity stayed so long in Italy – so the pair of you could swap identities. But why, Charlotte? Why? And who is the father of your child? I want the truth, so don't go telling me any more of your lies!'

Charlotte turned now to look up at his uncompromising expression, her eyes filled with bitterness as she murmured: 'We were so careful to keep our secret, Verity and I. No one was ever to know.'

Suddenly, Ket pulled her roughly to her feet and stood staring down at her, his eyes stormy. '*Who is he?*' he repeated fiercely, his hands gripping her arms. 'Is he that lawyer friend of yours who was supposed to marry you?' He paused only momentarily whilst another thought struck him. 'Does Guy know Verity has been covering up your indiscretions? Does he know Florence is your illegitimate child?'

He got no further with his angry tirade as, stung beyond endurance by Ket's accusations, Charlotte broke in. 'You don't understand, Ket. It was for Verity and Guy that I conceived the baby. We hoped it would be a boy so that your father would choose Guy rather than Matthew to inherit Kneepwood . . .'

The tears drying rapidly on her cheeks, she decided that since Ket had demanded the truth, she might as well enlighten him to all the facts. He couldn't think any worse of her than he did now. She drew away from him and walked across the room to the window before turning to face him, her arms folded across her body as if to protect herself from Ket's scornful eyes.

'If you want the whole truth, please hear me out,' she said as Ket took a stride towards her. 'You don't know what went on when you were on your travels abroad. Matthew was heavily in debt. He kept borrowing from the estate account which Guy badly needed to run Kneepwood. Guy couldn't refuse Matthew's demands because Sir Bertram always insisted they must be met. Your father didn't seem to realize that if he willed Kneepwood to Matthew it wouldn't be long before the estate was bankrupt.'

Ket's expression remained inscrutable as he said coldly: 'I fail to see what this has to do with you, Charlotte.'

'Be patient and you will, I hope, understand,' Charlotte replied, aware that Ket could not be any more appalled by her revelations than he was now. 'Your father always threatened Guy that if he couldn't beget at least one son to pass on the family name, then he would leave Kneepwood to Matthew and Bertie to follow into the next generation. You were in India when Verity miscarried . . . it was sometime in January or February three years ago. You were engaged to Naomi Copley. Dr Freeman told Verity she should not have any more babies and she was heartbroken. I love her dearly

272

and she has been so very good to me, I couldn't bear to see her so unhappy . . .'

Ket had moved a step nearer to her, his expression now thoughtful as he prompted her to continue. 'So you offered to have a baby for her, the pair of you hoping it would be a boy . . . But the father, Charlotte. You still haven't told me who was the father.'

Charlotte swallowed nervously, her voice almost a whisper as she said: 'It was Guy – not Theobald Samuels as you seemed to think. Guy is Florence's father. Perhaps God wanted to punish the three of us for trying to deceive everyone. Whatever the reason, I gave birth to a girl – not the son Guy wanted, needed. So you see, Ket, you have every right to despise me. The only thing I ask is that you don't let this confession affect your fondness for Florence. She clearly adores you and—'

She got no further before Ket reached her side and silenced her by gently covering her lips with his hand. 'Ssh, Charlotte, don't say any more. We have wasted so much time! If only you could have told me the truth after I returned from America. I think it was then I first realized I was hopelessly in love with you. Why couldn't you have told me? Trusted me?'

Charlotte returned his gaze, hers despairing. 'You must know the answer to that. Yes, when you returned from America you told me you loved me, but by that time it was too late! I had conceived your brother's child. What would you have thought if I'd confessed I had lain with Guy? I loved you, Ket, with all my heart. I couldn't bear to know you no longer cared for me; that you despised me.'

Ket gripped her arms. 'Then you do love me, Charlotte? That talk of you marrying Samuels? Was that a lie, too?'

Charlotte nodded, her expression hopeless. 'You say you're glad the truth has come out but how would you have felt, Ket, if when you proposed to me I had said "Yes, I do love you but I can't marry you because I have lain with your brother and given birth to his child"? What would you have replied?'

Ket drew a deep breath. His hold of her arms tightened as

273

he pulled her gently towards him, so close now that she was almost touching him. 'I would have wanted to know why you had done such a thing,' he said slowly. 'I suppose I would have wondered if you'd fallen in love with Guy, although I would have found it hard to believe either of you would have betrayed Verity, loving her as you both do.'

'And would you have despised me any the less had I told you the true reason – that Verity and Guy desperately needed a son to save Kneepwood? Not that any of it matters now. It's all too late and what we did cannot be undone.'

'Despise you? Charlotte, how could I possibly do so when all you intended was to sacrifice your future for their happiness! I love you, Charlotte. I have loved you for three long years. In real life, hearts don't break as the poets would have us believe but were it possible, mine was close to breaking when I thought you were going to marry someone else. It came even nearer to doing so when you made it so clear that you didn't love me and preferred to go travelling abroad on your own. Charlotte, don't you yet realize that I love you – with all my heart?'

'Then you can forgive me?' Charlotte asked incredulously, her heart beating so fiercely she feared she might stop breathing.

'Forgive you!' Ket repeated. 'Oh, Charlotte, my darling, precious love. What have I to forgive? The past is past and should be forgotten. It is our future that matters. When we're married, we will go travelling together, if that is what you would like.'

Charlotte's eyes were bright now, not with tears but with happiness. 'I love you, Ket. I will always love you. But can we really put the past behind us? Forget it happened? There is . . .' She paused briefly before saying softly. 'There is Florence.'

Ket gazed down at her with the hint of a smile in his eyes.

'Are you talking of my godchild? Am I not right in thinking that she is Verity's and Guy's third daughter? Sister to Kate, Lottie and little Christopher? I see no reason why she

274

shouldn't stay here at Kneepwood with her sisters and brother when we go travelling. After all, she will be perfectly safe, with her mother and father.'

Once again, tears filled Charlotte's eyes, but this time they were tears of happiness. As Ket bent to kiss her, she knew that never again would they be tears of sorrow or regret.

Epilogue

May 1892

One year later, Mr and Mrs Ket Conniston returned with their baby son from their travels in the Far East. For the remainder of the summer they planned to stay at Kneepwood Court where Verity's nanny would take care of the infant, who was to be christened in a month's time. They had left their *ayah* in Bombay where they had embarked on a liner to bring them home. Consequently, Charlotte had had to care for the baby herself and it was with some relief that she had handed little Harry over to Nanny whilst she and Ket changed out of their travelling clothes.

'Do you and Ket really want to take your baby with you to Mexico, Charlotte?' Guy asked as the four of them went into the garden to take tea in the shade of the big beech tree.

'He will require far more attention than he does now, dearest,' Verity added. 'He'll be a year old by the time you leave us . . . Crawling, if not walking, I expect – or at least trying to!'

Ket took Charlotte's hand in his and entwined his fingers with hers. 'What do you think, my darling? If Guy and Verity are willing, I suppose we could leave him at Kneepwood with Nanny.'

Charlotte turned to Verity. 'Would it really be all right if we did so? Somehow I don't think Harry would miss us.'

Verity clapped her hands. 'We'd love to keep him here, wouldn't we, Guy? You can tell that nanny I engaged for you that you don't need her after all. To be honest, she didn't sound very anxious to sail the Atlantic when I interviewed her. She'll probably be glad of the let out!'

They all laughed. Then Ket turned back to Charlotte. 'You're sure you won't miss the little rascal too much? He's a very demanding little fellow.'

'And so are you, my love!' Charlotte said. 'It will certainly make travelling a great deal easier for us.' Nor was that the only reason, she thought. Harry had been a honeymoon baby, so now it would be lovely to be alone with Ket, who was the most wonderful companion. Perhaps the day would come when they both wished to settle down with a houseful of children, but for the present, to see the world with Ket was as near to heaven as was possible.

When, shortly after Sir Bertram's funeral, Monica had inexplicably announced she was going to take the veil and dedicate the rest of her life to prayer in the Convent of the Holy Cross, Guy had decided to give the dower house to Ket and Charlotte as a wedding present.

'Not that the pair of you look like spending a great deal of time in it,' he'd said then, aware that Ket had planned an extended honeymoon in the Far East. Now, they were to spend only three months back in England after which they were off on another sojourn, this time to Mexico.

Verity gave a brief sideways glance at her friend who was looking very pretty, she thought, in a pale cream high-necked blouse and green, moiré silk skirt. 'You look nearer seventeen than twenty-seven, dearest,' she said, smiling.

Charlotte glanced at Ket who was grinning broadly as he tightened his hold on her hand. 'That's because married life suits her so well, eh, sweetheart?'

Seeing Charlotte's blushes, Verity tactfully changed the subject. 'I expect you're both wondering where the children have got to. When I received your telegram, I did tell them that you would be arriving this afternoon and they were really excited, but they had planned a picnic down by the river and begged me to allow them to postpone their welcome until their return. I did suggest that perhaps Florence might want to stay behind to . . . to welcome her much-loved godfather but . . . well, she seemed so anxious to go with the others that I didn't have the heart to keep her here.'

277

Ket's eyes were questioning as he gazed into Charlotte's. He felt the slight pressure of her fingers and, recognising their message, he turned back to Verity, his voice confident as he said: 'The last thing either of us would want, Verity, is for young Florence to be separated from her brother and sisters. We'll see them all later, won't we?'

For a moment, no one spoke until suddenly Guy stood up, saying: 'I'm going to ask Grainger to bring up a bottle of champagne so we can drink a toast to your safe return home.' Then, smiling, he added: 'Verity and I have really missed you both – not that I imagine either of you two lovebirds will have missed us, or will do so when you sail off to Mexico!'

Ket's voice was husky as he looked down once more at his wife. 'I don't suppose we will – not now we have each other!' he said, and was rewarded by Charlotte's loving smile.

As he turned to talk to Verity, Charlotte found herself wondering suddenly where the last ten years had gone. Could it really be so long since that night of her end-of-the-Season ball when she had found her father in his study and learned that her carefree life must change forever? She had not been really happy again until her wedding day. Even then, she reflected, she was not entirely free of misgivings. Would Ket really not mind that he wasn't the first man to possess her? Would the love he professed to have as they exchanged vows in Kneepwood church turn sour when later that night he held her in his arms?

Such concerns vanished forever when, at long last, he claimed her for his own. So great was the intensity of her love for him, so long denied, that she had responded with a passion that more than matched his own.

Ten years! she thought once more. It had in one way been a lifetime, yet such was her happiness now, she knew that her life had only just begun.

278